San Francisco Boxing

Friday, May 14, 1948

Thirty-Eight Rounds of Dynamite

Sponsored by the *San Francisco Inquirer* / Burnell Sanders, Promoter

MAIN EVENTS

(What this mystery is about)

COLD-BLOODED MURDER ALWAYS A LOCAL FAVORITE	VS.	TRAGIC ACCIDENT COULD SURPRISE
STEADFAST LOYALTY RELIABLE CAMPAIGNER	VS.	CLEVER DECEPTION SNEAKY, DANGEROUS
BRILLIANT CAREER UNTARNISHED RECORD ON THE LINE	VS.	MISGUIDED NOTION ONE-PUNCH KNOCKOUT POWER
MARITAL BONDS FORMIDABLE, HARD TO SHAKE	VS.	ILLICIT AFFAIR STRONG IN THE CLINCHES
THE TRUTH ELUSIVE	VS.	A GOOD STORY NEVER GET IN ITS WAY

FIGHTERS

(People this mystery is about)

BILLY NICHOLS "MR. BOXING" RUNYON OF THE WEST COAST	VS.	DET. FRANCIS O'CONNOR IRISH HOMICIDE DICK, UNDEFEATED
HACK ESCALANTE HARD-LUCK HEAVYWEIGHT	VS.	GIG LIARDI SHOULD HAVE DUCKED
IDA NICHOLS "MR. BOXING" BALL & CHAIN	VS.	CLAIRE ESCALANTE COULD HOLD THE KEY
BURNEY SANDERS LITTLE MAN, BIG IDEAS	VS.	EDDIE RYAN PONIES PRINCE SEEKING OFFICE
SID CONTE CHRYSLER-HAWKING FIGHT PILOT	VS.	JIMMY RYAN DANDY GAMBLING KINGPIN

A BURIED BODY. A BUSTED ROSARY. A LOST TURTLE. A LOCKED STRONGBOX. WILLIAM RANDOLPH HEARST. THE WILD BULL OF THE PAMPAS. JACK DEMPSEY. THE ROARING ALL-NIGHT CIRCUIT. LABOR UNIONS. HOTEL ROOM TRYSTS. AND A HEAVYWEIGHT TITLE FIGHT.

BOOKS BY EDDIE MULLER

NON-FICTION

Dark City Dames:
The Wicked Women of Film Noir

Dark City:
The Lost World of Film Noir

Grindhouse:
The Forbidden World of Adults Only Cinema

The Art of Noir:
Posters and Graphics from the Classic Film Noir Era

FICTION

The Distance

Shadow Boxer

UGLYTOWN

EDDIE

MULLER

THE

DISTANCE

UGLYTOWN PRESENTS A NOVEL BY EDDIE MULLER
"THE DISTANCE" FEATURING BILLY NICHOLS
INTRODUCTION BY LEONARD GARDNER

PUBLISHED BY UGLYTOWN LOS ANGELES 2004

Originally published in hardcover by Scribner

Library of Congress Cataloging-in-Publication data on file.

Find out more of the mystery: UglyTown.com/TheDistance

Printed in the United States of America

10 9 8 7 6 5 4 3 2 1

INTRODUCTION

For eighty years or so San Francisco was a leading boxing center, carried on a momentum generated in the early days of the gloved era, shortly before and after the turn of the century, by a number of legendary men: San Francisco's own home-grown world heavyweight champion, the great innovator Gentleman Jim Corbett, and Joe Choynski, Peter Jackson, Bob Fitzsimmons, Jim Jeffries, Jack Johnson, Stanley Ketchell, Joe Gans, Battling Nelson and others who gained lasting fame in epic battles around the bay. While boxing was illegal in many parts of the country, here a tradition was forged that occupied the consciousness of much of the local population. New generations of fighters arrived, promotions were frequent and news coverage extensive. From the 1940s through the 1970s San Francisco was the only city in the country with two daily boxing columnists, the *Chronicle*'s Jack Fiske and the *Examiner*'s Eddie Muller, both now legendary figures themselves. Muller, a local from the old Butchertown district, began his column "Shadow Boxing" in the 1930s and turned out six pieces a week for close to fifty years. Along the way he fathered the author of *The Distance*.

I grew up reading Muller's column and hearing talk of the ring from my father, a raconteur whose focus was on the fighters of the past. His accounts conveyed an unmistakable sense that there was a mystique to boxing that set it apart from every other sport or endeavor. That sense of mystique had to have been imparted to the younger Eddie Muller, growing up as he did. With his father he hung around the historic Newman-Herman Gym, a living museum of irreplaceable atmosphere, the beating heart of the mystique. As a twelve year-old he took boxing lessons from California Joe Lynch, a former contender from the thirties, a fixture at the gym conspicuous for his bow ties and resplendent handlebar mustache. Muller shared the company of his father's close friends, former lightweight contender Ray Lunny, referee Jack Downey, fight manager Joe Herman, and the great Willie Ritchie, at that time Chief Inspector for the California Athletic Commission. Ritchie, a stylist of the Joe Gans school, had won the world lightweight championship in 1912. And naturally there were newspaper friends. From *The Distance* it seems Muller had the run of the *Examiner* while his father phoned his contacts around the country and wrote his stories. The newspaper scenes in the novel are the work of a gifted observer. The gyms, the newspaper, the arenas, the scenes of downtown life in the forties—all have a persuasive vitality. Although Muller was not yet born at the time the novel takes place, much of the scene was still thriving during his early years, and the memories of some of the best of witnesses were at his disposal. The world he portrays has an accuracy of detail that is a pleasure to encounter. How many, anymore, would remember the *Redhead Sporting Weekly* with its boxing programs, or Honolulu fight manager Sad Sam Ichinose? Kindly trainer Johnny Carnation—Johnny Vidal—who was never seen without a fresh carnation in his buttonhole, turns up. Joe Herman is there, and Billy Newman, his partner in the gym, and trainer Vic Grupico, appearing under their own names, which seems appropriate, as they were landmarks as much as the locations where they could be found.

Authenticity, memory and nostalgia strengthen the weave and appeal of Muller's story. That it is an imagined story seems certain, yet it grows from characters who could well have been on the scene in the forties, notably the heavyweight, Hack Escalante, a combination of shyness and toughness, insecurity and courage, and his wife Claire, and the boxing columnist, Billy Nichols, the narrator, with whom Muller has a natural empathy. Nichols' voice is reminiscent of forties' noir narrators, but it is also the voice of a sportswriter. Muller works the angles of the noir genre but is too cagey to walk straight in. He bends the conventions of the mystery, using the structure while going his own way, constructing a noir plot while staying true to his father's world.

Much of that world is gone now. The times of the boxing columns are over, and without them the Bay Area ring scene has gone into eclipse. The rare local fight card can come and go with hardly a word of newsprint, ignored in favor of sports packaged for the mainstream. Essential hangouts like the Ringside bar are no more. Newman's Gym closed forever, its wise old proprietors passed on. A tradition seems to have passed as well, leaving for the nostalgists a sense that the town has lost some of its color and drama. Eddie Muller is clearly a nostalgist. *The Distance*, and his books on film noir, reveal him to be a writer whose heart is elsewhere—back in the forties. *The Distance* pays homage not so much to a genre as to an era and a way of life, and it refreshes the genre in the process.

Leonard Gardner
2004

for my father

THE DISTANCE

AUTHOR'S NOTE

The postwar San Francisco environment and its thriving newspaper business and boxing fraternity are the backdrop for this novel. Accordingly, real people and entities sometime saunter and sneak through these pages. The storyline and its characters, however, are utterly fictional. And while boxing, like any sport, indeed features the occasional person of dubious motivation, the actions and motives of all the characters in this novel, and the characters themselves—including central characters such as Billy Nichols and Hack Escalante—are entirely the work of the author's imagination.

I probably hit him too many times. You can knock a fellow out sometimes and then bring him around with another punch. I've seen it happen more than once.

—Jack Dempsey, on his fight with Gene Tunney

1

Something was seriously wrong. I tipped to that as soon as the door to Gig Liardi's flat cracked opened. Gig's fighter, Hack Escalante, peered through the gap, eyes rimmed red and puffy. When he saw who it was, he stepped back and let me in. Hack had been crying, and still hadn't managed to pull himself together.

"Where's Gig?" I asked. Loud enough, but a little shaky.

Hack turned away and pointed. My gut went into free-fall when I saw the blood smeared across his knuckles. Whenever I wrote about Hack's hands, I called them *paws* or *mitts*. Bunched into fifteen-inch fists, they'd cracked the bones of half a dozen opponents. From ringside I'd heard Johnny Hubbard's rib snap when Hack nailed him with a short hook above the liver.

Hack was pointing to the floor. Gig was lying between the chesterfield and the coffee table. He wasn't down there looking for dropped change.

"I think he's dead," Hack said.

I knelt and shook Gig's shoulder. I'd stared into my father's lifeless face, lying on the wet pavement, seconds after he'd died. Gig's eyes had the same dry, absent look.

"What the hell happened?" I pulled back from the body, arms at my sides, fighting the shakes that were coming on strong. Gig had phoned not more than thirty minutes before, begging me to drop by. Had something big to run past me. Probably another spiel on how he wanted to make Hack with Joe Louis, bring the fight to San Francisco, and pull the biggest gate in California history. His voice was practically ringing in my ear.

"I hit him." Hack gazed at his mitts again, like he couldn't believe they belonged to him.

The blinds were open. It was dark. Across the alley, I could see right into another flat that was all lit up. Some woman ambled down a narrow hallway, past the bright kitchen. I stepped around Hack and yanked the blinds shut.

"Jesus Christ Almighty, why'd you hit him?"

"I don't know. We were talkin' about the New York trip and he started in about a dream he had: he's holding up this big belt with jewels all over it and he's saying that I'd won the title, and then I said, 'How come you're holding the belt if I won the fight?'"

Hack started gulping for air and gasping out little yips and chokes. "And—an—an—that set him off and he starts tellin' me that I wouldn't have nothin' if it wasn't for him and that no—nobody's gonna cut him outta the picture—not Jacobs, not nobody."

"That's it?"

His face twisted up. I knew there was more.

"Claire—he started talking about Claire. He called her, he called her, he called—"

Hack put fists up in front of his face, like he was taking a flurry. All of a sudden he's down on his knees, gripping the legs of my trousers.

"He hit his head when he fell back. On the table. It was so quick! What am I gonna do? They'll put me in jail. Take me away from my family! I got babies!"

Hack tried to pull Gig up. "Guys get up when I hit 'em harder than that. Why can't he get back up? Get up! Get up!" Gig's head just dangled.

When Hack was sixteen his father, Mario, threw him out of the house. He didn't want a boxer for a son. Hack met Gig Liardi at the Young Men's Institute on Oak Street. I was there—1934. Liardi circled the big raw kid like a snake, then sidled up and swallowed him whole. Gig was a spent lightweight contender with a chip on his shoulder. A chip the size of Alcatraz. Beautiful right cross with nothing behind it. Couldn't bust a grape. But he knew prizefighting and was fishing for a kid he could bring along. Hack had lived with him for three years in this dank North Beach flat, in a room just down the hall. That was before Hack met and married Claire McKenna, before she wedged herself between them and changed everything.

"I'm scared," Hack cried into Gig's dead chest. "I'm scared." He kept repeating it over and over.

"Hack, get up. C'mon."

"I never wanted to hurt nobody. Never. Why'd this hafta happen?"

"Where'd he hit his head?"

Hack turned loose of Gig, stood up, staggered, and pointed to the edge of the coffee table. There was a slight crack, and some wood splinters. Looking closer I thought I could see a bit of blood and some hair. I took the display handkerchief from my suit pocket and wiped off the edge of the table.

"Move his head," I told Hack.

Hack cradled Gig's head in his massive hands and lifted it to the side. The gentle maneuver knotted up my stomach. This boy should never have been a fighter. Now he was a killer.

There was no blood that I could see on the floor. Gig had fallen on his side and his head had lodged awkwardly between the floor and the chesterfield. Any blood had stayed in his mouth. Must have been some kind of internal hemorrhage, or maybe his neck snapped. Didn't matter. Hack hit Gig. Gig died. That's the way one story ended and that's the way a whole other one began.

"How'd you get here, Hack?"

"Drove." He snuffed his nose and brushed the back of his hand across his face.

My heart was hammering. I looked around the room, stalling while I thought about what would happen to Hack now. The kid's life had barely started, and in seconds here it was in the dumper. I tried to act calm. I was, after all, the Answer Man. The guy they always called in a pinch. *Billy will know what to do.* What I did was wad my handkerchief so Gig's blood was buried deep in the folds. Then I retraced the few steps I'd taken since entering the place, swabbing my prints from the doorknob, the tabletop . . .

"Anybody know you're here?" I asked.

Hack turned his watery eyes my way, as though seeing me for the first time. He shook his head.

"No. Nobody."

"Not even your wife?" I wiped off the floor beside Gig's head, where I'd set my hand while crouching down. I rubbed the damp palm print into a smudge.

"I don't know," the kid muttered. "No, I don't think so."

It was my job to know everything about everybody in the fight fraternity, and what I knew about Gig Liardi was that he wouldn't be missed. Not to say that he deserved this. Nobody deserved this.

"What are you doing?" Hack asked, a note of dim hope in his voice.

"Doing you a favor," I huffed. Under my breath, so he couldn't hear, I added, "Returning a favor. A big one."

★

We drove from North Beach out to the far western reaches of Golden Gate Park. When we hadn't seen lights on the road for fifteen minutes, we got out. I carried Gig's suitcase, which I'd had Hack stuff with a bunch of Gig's traveling clothes. I wrapped the handkerchief around the grip. Hack had the shovel. Gloves were pointless for him. None of Gig's could possibly fit.

The fog was so thick you couldn't see the moon and the only sound was Hack's grunting and the incessant scrape of metal in the earth.

He wouldn't let me dig. He was the muscle, after all. I was just a sportswriter, albeit *Mr. Boxing*. I was supposed to be the watchdog. In my pocket, I nervously juggled the rosary beads I always carried with me. With nothing better than a half-assed shovel he grabbed out of Gig's basement, Hack dug the hole in about forty minutes. To a normal person, this would have a been a brutally exhausting ordeal. To Hack, it was like training. Don't think, just run. Don't think, just hurt the bag. Don't think, just dig.

In the time it took to excavate Gig's final resting place, I had plenty of chances to turn back, play it straight, do the law-abiding thing. Put myself, once again, at a safe remove. I knew why I was doing it. Hell, covering up for the naïve fighter was more premeditated than the sudden punch that accidentally ended Gig's life. Hack, for his part, didn't have a clue as to why his fate was so important to me, or why I'd shown an extra interest in his career, ever since he was a raw amateur.

I wondered if the truth would ever come out between us.

Hack went back to the car and hauled Gig out of the trunk. He was partially wrapped in a greasy blanket taken from his basement. With Gig slung over his shoulder, Hack trudged back into the thickets.

You're different, the world is different, after you bury those close to you. I'd felt the change when I stepped away from my father's grave, then my mother's, ten years later. It's bad enough when you inter them legit. For a few minutes, it seems the world is going to come apart, split down the middle. Then the hardness seeps in, to cover the dread.

My insides shook when a shovelful of dirt smacked Gig's face. I could only imagine what Hack was feeling, obliterating the guy who brought him all this way, who taught him how to deal it out.

But it was too late now. We'd decided there was no choice. Hack kept on shoveling.

Then, like that, Gig was gone.

It was almost one in the morning. I had Hack drop me on Taraval, so I could catch an "L" car. It wasn't smart to have him drive me home; somebody might see us together. When I looked at Hack's face in the glare of passing headlights, I couldn't imagine what was going through *his* mind. He was a simple guy, but I'd always felt there was something different about him. Something innocent and sad. He had all the tools to be a great fighter, the power, the stamina, the courage—but I could never believe it when I saw him climb in a ring. He didn't belong in this world.

"You don't know anything, Hack. Don't say a word about this to anybody, all right?"

He turned to me, his face caked with dried sweat and dirt. He nodded.

"Gig was working for that roofing company, right? They'll report him missing. When they go to his place, they'll find his suitcase and some clothes gone, and figure he left suddenly on a trip. Then they'll come to me, ask me what I know, and I'll handle it from there. Remember, you don't know anything. Anybody asks any questions, you just say 'I don't know,' and act like it's all a big surprise to you."

We sat quietly for a minute.

"How come you're doing this?" Hack finally asked. "You could have just walked out, or called the cops or something."

"Never mind. 'Why' doesn't really matter now, does it? Try not to think about it."

The headlight of a streetcar was approaching, making its long climb up the avenues from the beach. I got out to catch it, leaving Hack staring into space.

He'd never been stopped in any professional fight, never been off his feet. But slumped behind the wheel of his car, he didn't look like a guy ready to go the distance.

SECTION S FRIDAY, MAY 14, 1948 CCCC*

AN AMERICAN PAPER FOR THE AMERICAN PEOPLE

MONARCH OF THE DAILIES

San Francisco Inquirer Sports

REG US PAT OFF

Through THE ROPES

By BILLY NICHOLS

Tonight's tussle at Winterland will answer a lot of questions about walloping welterweight Young Corbett IV. Opponents have been dodging the hard-socking southpaw for months, ever since his pasting of Miguel Lada. Eddie Marino is as tough as they come, however, so this won't be a walkover for Corbett. . . .

2

The throng pushed into the building beneath buzzing red neon that glowed through the gauze of fog: *Winterland*. A wave of raucous, cackling voices, above which boomed the foghorn bleats of program and concession hawkers.

In the lobby, I surveyed the swarming mob. The old colored guy over by the door, bald, sporting a black coat too long for his tiny body, that'd be Deacon Jones. Everybody's got a glad hand for the Deacon. You'd never know it to look at him—he didn't tip a hundred pounds on the scale—but in his day he was the toughest man in town. Used to fight in bars. Story goes that one time a big white guy, better than two hundred pounds, came in a bar and wanted to rub the Deacon's head for luck. This guy was so big the Deacon had to jump on his chest to fight him. Grabbed the guy's ears and banged him with his head. Boom—knockout.

"Hey, Mr. Nichols, how are you tonight?"

"Good, Deacon. How 'bout yourself?"

"Holdin' steady. Always ready," and the Deacon struck his pugilistic pose.

I made my way into the arena, acknowledging the greetings of my loyal following. The boys of the fraternity flowed by, each offering a gesture of welcome. I waved or nodded or gave a touch on the arm. Even the newcomers recognized Billy Nichols from the caricature that accompanied my daily column, "Through the Ropes." The fedora, thin rakish mustache, rimless specs. Clark Gable, my wife insisted. Maybe

William Powell, hold the glamour. Ex-pugs, glad I remembered them, cherishing the write-ups I'd doled them years ago, would leap up to clasp my hand and clear the crowded aisle so *Mr. Boxing* could pass through to ringside. Whenever I started believing my own PR, the fight crowd felt like my flock.

"Hey, Bill. How's tricks?" Georgie Payne, a kid from the old neighborhood, clasped my hand in a vise grip. He'd grown into a good-looking Joe, black hair and devilish smile. Ran a beer distributorship and was working hard to get in bed with local boxing promoters. Back when, Georgie was cock of the walk in Butchertown. As a fifteen-year-old delivery boy he bragged about all the lush tail he cadged off housewives twice his age. Made me jealous as hell. Now Georgie was just one of the flock.

"Georgie, you're looking good. Keep it up."

"You know me," he said, smiling. It made me feel for any woman who was the target of that razor-sharp leer.

Looked like a full house tonight. The place was packed with old-timers. Plenty of them remembered when this sporting palace, on the corner of Post and Steiner, was called Dreamland Rink, commonly known as "The Barn." The cavernous, ramshackle structure hosted two decades of Friday night fight cards, mostly four-rounders staged under police supervision.

Professional fighting had been outlawed in California in 1914. A last gasp by the well-heeled to bury the Wild West. Four-round, "no decision" bouts replaced the grueling twenty-round spectacles that had been the specialty of local promoter Sunny Jim Coffroth. The lawmakers believed that exhibitions—with no winners or losers—would chase out the gamblers. But the newspapers played their part in keeping the action alive: the "ND" that had meant "No Decision" came to mean "Newspaper Decision." With sports scribes as arbiters, the wagering went on unabated.

By 1925, enough sportsmen were ingrained in the political fabric to influence repeal of the boxing prohibition. Politicos like San Francisco mayor Jim Rolph—another Sunny Jim—didn't waste time and tax money trying to regulate human nature. Rolph liked his town wide open. Businessmen of all stripes appreciated that attitude. Ira Zellerbach, scion of one of San Francisco's most loaded families, celebrated the rip-roaring times by reconstructing Dreamland Rink, turning "The Barn" into a 9,600-seat deco auditorium dedicated to sports and the arts. Two artists of note, Bud Taylor, the "Terre Haute Terror," and Santiago Zorilla, the "San Blas Indian," had been the headlined performers at New Dreamland's opening night, October 29, 1928.

Now, twenty years and a new ice-skating rink later, a mist of smoke hung over another full house in the rechristened Winterland. Heading down the aisle, I bumped into Jimmy Ryan, the town's top bookmaker. *Resplendent* didn't quite do Jimmy justice. Cut loose from the counting room, he was working it to the nines: spats, blousy pleated trousers, double-breasted charcoal jacket with a sharp pinstripe, natty bow tie, and a straw boater crowning his always perfectly lacquered blond hair. At one time or another, every stiff in this joint owed him money.

"Who do you like in the main event?" asked Jimmy. "You didn't make a pick in the paper."

"Corbett."

"Not worried about the layoff?"

"Nah. Marino's hand's still bum."

"Go the distance?"

"I figure."

"Okay, then. I'm glad you didn't give that out in the column. We pulled a lot of late money on Marino." Jimmy had a high, reedy voice he never liked to raise above the level of a child's lullaby. Guys had died from reading him wrong. He didn't do the dirty work himself, of course. Bodyguards lurked nearby, ready to fetch a bet or crush a welsher's windpipe.

"How's your brother?" I asked. "I haven't seen much of him lately." Jimmy's brother, Eddie, ran Golden State Racetrack. He was personally responsible for getting horse racing legalized in California.

"Fuck my brother."

He said it in the same lilting tone, a smile on his fair, narrow face. The Ryans were two guys you didn't want to get stuck between.

I made my way to ringside. Burney Sanders, a former trainer who was now an up-and-coming promoter, was talking to Toby Irwin, the referee. This was some pair; you couldn't ask for two guys with bigger cast-iron balls. I'd known Burney since he was a feisty hawk-faced kid named Burnell Theopolous, a squawking, belligerent frontliner who'd helped create the newspaper drivers' local. Burney was a rough street kid who wanted only two things in life: to fight, and to trade his mixed-up Greek/Gallic blood for dago red. But he was born to be a hustler, not a boxer. Told me he picked his new name from a display in a hardware store window. Too bad the place wasn't featuring buzz saws that week.

Toby Irwin was a pip. He ran the show here, had a not-so-secret slice of the promotion. He was as straight as Lombard Street.

"How's things, Burney? Anything going with the Bucket

of Blood?" The Bucket was a venerable old fight club, National Hall by its right name, that had fallen on hard times. Sanders wanted to become a player by reopening the Bucket, but hadn't found too many investors. Last I'd heard he was doing the money dance with local promoter Lou Thomas. They weren't exactly Lunt and Fontaine.

"I can't get Thomas off his ass," Burney said. "But I'll pull it off, you'll see. Nobody thinks I can do it, but it's gonna happen. Mark my words."

"How'd you make out down in Reseda?"

"Even before it was over I knew we were gonna get jobbed." Sanders went from carping to keening in a heartbeat. Everything was a personal affront to Burney. "We've always had shit luck down South," he went on. "But I figured if we broke even, I could handle the train ride back. Naturally, they give this kid from Riverside the decision over Jesse and Jesse gets hot. He goes up to the ref and starts bitching, before I can even get his gloves off. I'm yelling at him to grow up, but, you know, I'm pissed off, too. The ref didn't even have a say in the scoring, anyway. But before I can do anything—are you ready for this—the ref hauls off and belts Jesse."

That one got the cigar out of my mouth, leaving an incredulous "o" in the bottom of my face. "The *ref*?"

"Yeah, clipped him right on the chin. Jesse actually goes to one knee. Gets all glassy eyed. This son-of-a-bitch ref turns and climbs out the ropes, like nothing happened."

"I oughta try that sometime." Irwin laughed.

"I told Dewey to help Jesse and went downstairs to find the guy from the commission—"

"You didn't go after the ref?"

"He just dropped our toughest kid! The only commission guy there was that fat prick, the one from Pomona—Bremner, Breckner, whatever his name is."

There was a tug at my sleeve, and then a hand pumping mine in a vigorous shake.

"Good to see ya, Billy. Good to see you." Matt Calo, once a solid local lightweight, a bit before my time.

"I ever tell you the story of how this bastard jobbed me for over a year?" he asked, pointing at Irwin. "I was fighting here one time, when it was the Rink, a four-rounder when I was just starting out. They put me in against Gig Liardi. Great fight, they were throwing money from the rafters and everything. I won three out of four rounds, easy. No doubt about it. But Irwin here calls it a draw. That way they could bring us back every other week. Irwin was always the ref. I musta fought six draws with Liardi one year."

"Those were draws, straight down the line," said Irwin, waving Calo away.

"Every time I beat him!" Calo swiveled his head, scanning the faces around him. He found a familiar one a couple of rows back. "Jack! How many times I beat Gig Liardi?"

"Twice, three times, I don't know. How many times you fight?"

"Six times in 1929, my friend." Calo held up his fingers as testimony.

"Counting when the two of you sat on the floor?" Jack's ample padding shook with fits of laughter, followed by hacking coughs. Oh, Christ. This was Calo's cue to launch his trademark story, recounting his last fight with Liardi, back when it was Dreamland. A hydraulic ring, ballyhooed as a modern marvel, had been installed by Ira Zellerbach as a special attraction. Fighters climbed into the ring on a lower level and then the entire thing would be slowly hoisted into view. The marvel had a few technical problems. Sometimes it set crookedly, so boxers battled on a slope. When Liardi fought Calo the last time, the ring went haywire in the last round and lowered itself out of sight.

I knew the story well. I'd featured it several times in my column. Calo had given me the nugget, and I'd polished it into legend. Matt loved my version, had it down pat. My words had become his memory.

"When we realized nobody could see us," said Calo, "we just sat down and waited. When the ring went back up, Gig and me acted like we'd beaten the hell out of each other and everybody'd missed all the excitement."

"How'd it end up?" asked Burney, the perfect foil.

"What else—a draw!"

Nice delivery, Matt. Sorry I didn't bust up laughing like everybody else.

"Where is Gig, anyway?" asked Burney. "I usually see him by now. He's been pushing me so hard to help train Hack that he's driving me fruit."

"I'll fight him again right now," Calo barked, sparring the air. "Where is he?"

"Somebody said they saw him yesterday headed for the train station," I said. "Had a grip packed, too."

"I woulda thought he'd tell me if he was leaving town all of a sudden," said Burney.

"If you ask me, he can stay wherever he is," muttered Irwin, just loud enough to be heard.

That was it, the first lie on a path of deceit that would take me to the darkest place I'd ever been. It was so easy: I told a story, and it seemed as good as the truth. Better, maybe.

The circuit would continue to hum, with or without Gig Liardi.

★

I passed up a couple of invitations to Charlie Schwartz's Waffle Inn, on Ellis Street, where the boys always congregated for the boisterous postmortem after a Friday night card. Instead, I grabbed a lift from Gil Rayburn, my brother-in-law, and two guys from the circulation department going in for the night shift.

The usual bullshit was swirling around the car when Gil leaned over conspiratorially: "Saw you talking to Georgie Payne on the way in," he said.

I didn't say anything, since I couldn't figure why the hell Gil would have noticed that five-second exchange in the Winterland mob scene.

"Watch out for him."

"For Payne? What's he to me? Just another guy from the old neighborhood."

"Keep an eye on him, that's all." Gil cut the air with his hand, signaling that he was dropping the subject. He bounced across the Hyde Street car tracks and headed downtown.

Back at the office I wrote my full story for the morning edition. I used long rolls of teletype paper, with carbons, so I didn't have to change sheets in the typewriter. The editor got one copy, the other one got dumped in the bottom drawer of a four-drawer metal filing cabinet, where dozens of single-sheet stories were loosely jumbled.

Tonight's copy was brief but good. I always challenged myself to toss something new in, some little wrinkle. A kid on the undercard tonight, fighting his first pro bout, vomited all over his corner at the final bell. On top of that, he lost.

> Young McGuire came to fight and he saved nothing for later. In a losing effort he

> still earned roars from fans who knew that he'd left everything he had in the ring.

I brushed week-old envelopes and notes into the top drawer of the desk, ready to call it a night. But then I found myself turning back to the Royal, and tersely pounding out the words that had been running around in my head for the past two days.

> We hear through the grapevine that Gig Liardi has headed to the Southland to scope out the action, and see if there's any Ocean Park leather-pushers who might be a test for his heavy banger, Hack Escalante. Let's hope that Gig, one of the cleverest lightweights to ever come out of North Beach, has a good trip, and that he and Hack are in the money soon.

I tore the brief add off the roll and called for a boy to run the pages over to the copy editor.

It was already well past midnight. I had to wait about forty minutes to get a lift home from Tony Bernal, a typesetter pal. I got back to the house a little after two o'clock. The place was out in Forest Hills, the last rolling terrain on this side of town before the land sloped straight to the ocean. It was the Fog Belt, and tonight it was cinched tight. The moon looked like a streetlight that had floated away. I thanked Bernal and trudged up the thirty-six brick steps. The house was a tall, Moorish affair, with lots of little balconies and Spanish tile roofs. I'd definitely come up in the world since my days in blue-collar Butchertown, on the other side of the city.

Creeping into the entryway, I groped toward the banister. I didn't want to wake Ida. When I got to the bedroom doorway, though, she was sitting up in bed, the lamp glowing, her head a halo of blond pin curls. The newspaper was spread out in her lap.

"What are you still doing up?" I took off my hat and overcoat.

"Did you go out after the fights?"

"Nope, just went back to the office and wrote my story."

"But you said you'd be home earlier tonight."

"I had to wait for a ride. What did you do?"

"Nothing. Stayed home. Waited. Listened to the radio."

"How come you didn't do something with your sisters? You should have gone to a movie."

Ida abruptly folded the paper and tossed the mess to the floor.

"That would look nice. Going out alone with my sisters, when everybody knows I'm married. What would they think?"

"They'd think I was working."

"Or something."

"Jesus Christ! You think anybody cares? People know what I do for a living. They expect me to be at the fights, for chrissakes."

"A married woman shouldn't ever have to go out alone."

"Then invite somebody over if you don't want to go out."

"Oh, I should entertain here, is that it?"

"Sure, if you don't want to be by yourself."

"And when do I get entertained? When one of your big-shot friends wants to take you and the missus out? Make sure you give him a nice mention in the column?"

"What the hell is the matter with you? Can't I do my job

without having to listen to a bunch of shit about how you had nothing to do all night?"

"You think that's what this is about?"

"Oh, shit. Not the guessing thing. We're not gonna do the guessing thing at two-thirty in the morning, are we?"

"Why do you think I'm upset?"

She folded her arms across her chest; this one might go the full ten. I stepped out of my trousers and into the closet, searching for a hanger.

"Because I said I'd be home earlier tonight." My voice was swallowed up in the cramped closet.

"But you weren't. Can't you see how that makes me feel?"

"I told you—I had to go to the fights, then I had to write my story, then I had to wait for a ride."

"Is that an excuse? You had to wait for somebody to give you a ride? You could drive a car, you know. I understand there's no law against it. Everybody's doing it, even big shots. Or do the real big shots just wait for people to drive them around?"

I hung my jacket over the trousers and counted to myself.

"Does it make you feel good that all those guys are so eager to give you a ride? Does it? Well, how do you think I feel? Do you think I like it? I never heard of such a thing, a wife driving her husband every place they go. It's humiliating. Doesn't it bother you at all? What do you tell people when they ask about it? Do you tell them she's better than a nigger slave?"

I considered putting the suit on again and going back to the office. No ride, though, so that wasn't really an option. I silently approached the bed and got in, turning my back to Ida and waiting for her to run out of steam and switch off the light.

★

I was dreaming when a voice woke me up. Ida had moved beside me, her head pressed against my shoulder.

"Do you know why I wanted you to come home early tonight?"

I made a noise in my throat.

"There is something we can do, so I won't be lonely when you're not around."

"What's that?"

"Don't you think it's about time?"

"For what?"

"You know, we've been married five years. I want to have a baby. And now's a good time, you know. It's my time."

"Right now?"

"Are you going someplace?"

She pushed herself against me, curling her legs up onto the thick weave of my longjohns. I reached out toward the nightstand, probing about. As quietly as I could, I slipped in my false teeth. I was twenty-two when all the real ones were knocked out in a car accident on Market Street.

A rainy day in 1932, definitely the wrong place at the wrong time. Johnny McLish is slowing down to drop me off when another car makes a big sweeping turn across Market, right in front of two streetcars. They bash the side of Johnny's sedan so hard I'm tossed out the door. My mouth hits first, and what it hits is the curb. All I see is my hands in the stream of cold gutter water and blood and teeth rushing away in the current. Just white flashes after that, and me screaming. Johnny tells me later that the guys in the other car backed up two or three times to get loose while everyone was yelling and pointing. There was a cop standing right in the middle of the sidewalk, Johnny said, and he didn't make a move. He just stared, watching me spit teeth in the gutter. A woman called for an ambulance. The other car was making a delivery to a speakeasy, and the cop was covering them.

The telephone rang, shattering the quiet. Ida let out a gasp.

"Don't answer it," she said. "It has to be bad news at this time of the night." She had already started to cry. "It's one of my sisters. Oh, my God, my mother must have died."

I padded across the room and answered the phone.

"Mr. Nichols?"

"Yes?"

"I'm scared. What's going to happen?"

It was Hack. I rubbed my head and picked my words carefully.

"Don't worry, it'll be okay. I'm taking care of it."

"What am I going to do? I'm afraid I'll say something."

"Just relax, it won't be a problem."

"What we did, it wasn't right."

Everything was quiet for several moments. He needed an answer.

"Who is it? What's the matter?" Ida.

"Nothing. It's just some work stuff." Then, into the phone, I said, "It's done. It'll work out. Trust me."

3

Nothing matched the excitement of the composing room, not even the expectant clamor of a prizefight crowd. I'd always thought of it as the boiler room of a ship, the world's biggest ship, ever since I was a kid and first learned that Old Man Hearst liked to call the *Inquirer* the Flagship of the Hearst Empire.

The noise of the composing room was decisive, totally distinct from the fitful confusion that swirled through the various departments out on the floor. That was a jumble of eagerness, stress, and uncertainty. But once you walked into the composing room, uncertainty was stamped flat by the relentless linotype machines. Desperation was magically transformed into news as the hot hard slugs of metal were slapped into place.

I liked to walk an unofficial proofreading beat, to soak up the power of the news going to print. The metal flying into chases. Casting machines turning out plates for the presses. The world laid out, waiting to be painted with the proof of black ink. Sometimes the proof was barely dry before the sheets were bundled and tossed into the truck and the Flagship sailed into the streets, its cargo of the tragic and the uproarious—condensed and manageable—unloaded on every corner.

My old man got me my start, as an office boy. Vincent Nicholovich was a pressman. He worked back-breaker shifts, sweat streaking the ink smears on his face and hands, cotton balls shoved in his ears to muffle the roar of the machines.

I'd swing through the plant, just to say hi, before grabbing a bite at Breen's or the Kentucky Barrel House on Third. Ham on a hot biscuit, or coffee and a sugar doughnut, slipped to me quick by the counterman, keep your dime, kid. I was fourteen.

Every night I'd wait for my father so I could ride the streetcar home with him. It didn't matter if I had to wait hours. You couldn't be bored when you were right in the middle of the most important place in town. Those early morning hours, when the city was asleep, were the best times my father and I spent together, even if we couldn't hear each other over the presses. My father was tortured by back problems, but he seemed straighter and stronger whenever the paper ran. It was victory, watching the bundles carried out for street corner sales before dawn. San Francisco had seven newspapers vying for the public's loyalty, the *Call and Post*, the *Bulletin*, the *Illustrated Daily Herald*, the *Daily News*, the *Journal*, the *Chronicle* and the Monarch of the Dailies, Flagship of the Hearst Empire, the *Inquirer*. My paper.

When I got back to the sports department there was a stocky guy in a well-traveled Mackinaw standing by my desk. He clutched a cane in his left hand, made of mahogany or cherrywood or some rich exotic thing. On closer inspection, it had an ornate metal dragon's head for a handle, made of polished bronze. He was nudging stuff around the desktop, as though his free hand was doing it independently and he merely happened to glance down.

Up close, the Irish practically oozed from him. A square ruddy face starting to go florid, and a cropped bristle of white hair. He was maybe forty-five, and they'd been rough-and-tumble years.

"Ah, Mr. Nichols. Francis O'Connor. Detective with the SFPD. Might you have a few minutes you could spare?"

"A few. What's on your mind?"

"Now, that's a helluva nice item," he said, pointing to an autographed photo of Gene Tunney mired in the paper tumult. "I'm looking into the whereabouts of a local gentleman. Tomaso Gigliardi. Know him?"

"Sure. Gig Liardi. Dropped the Tomaso way back. Like fighters do."

"What do you mean? Can I sit here?"

"Go ahead. Lots of fighters change their names. Take Willie Ritchie. His right name is Gerhardt Steffen. Jewish fighters all want Irish names."

"No fooling. Such as?"

"Mushy Callahan's a Jew."

"Hell you say. Mushy's Irish as my Aunt Bridget."

"Right name's Morris Scheer. Oakland Jimmy Duffy . . . Hymie Gold. Jackie Fields . . . That'd be Jacob Finkelstein."

"How do you like that . . . anyways . . . seems Liardi hasn't been seen for a week or so. Fella from his work, a roofing company, told us that he'd not been in for several days. When I was reading your column the other day—which, I might add, is a ritual more important than Communion—it said you'd heard something about his maybe being in L.A. If you know more, it would surely help us out." He studied a scrap of paper he'd pulled from his pocket. "A Mr. Rancatore at A-1 Roofing wants to find out where his foreman is."

"Wish I could help. L.A. is all I heard."

"Where'd you hear that, if you recall?"

"Somebody mentioned it in passing. Just making conversation, you know."

"Can't remember who? Or where you might have been?"

"On the phone. Part of the daily mill."

"No more detail? Any notes?"

I slid open a desk drawer and let him take a good long look at the tangle of clippings, notebooks, promo sheets, photos, pencils, pens, letters, magazines—months of grist.

"Filing isn't my strong suit, Officer O'Connor."

"Detective. But call me Francis, if you please."

He sat back in the chair and propped the walking stick straight up between his legs, folding his hands across the top. A finger stroked the dragon's head that curved out from the handle. A long tongue flicked from between its bared fangs.

"Can you remember exactly how it was mentioned? That might help trigger something."

"It was quick, a few words. I was talking to somebody about local fighters who might pull some good purses outside of here and Hack Escalante's name came up and whoever it was said they'd heard that Gig was scouting down South, trying to put something together. It was fast, just like 'I heard Gig's down here prowling,' or something like that."

"Now, don't think that I'm trying to suggest that I have any idea how a professional sportswriter of your caliber does his job, but isn't it usual practice to attribute a name to such information?"

"In the course of a day I'll talk to maybe thirty or forty people. Sometimes I'm looking to get specific info on something I know I'm going to write. A lot of times it's just chat, you know, circulating, stirring it up. At the end of the day, if the deadline's coming and I need to fill out the column, I'll pop an item in there that I remember from the day. That's what happened."

O'Connor reached into an inside breast pocket and withdrew a folded piece of newspaper, unwrapping it deftly with one hand. My column. He scanned the bottom. "So that would be 'the grapevine' you refer to here? Just the stuff that floats around and then you snatch something and jot it down?"

"Exactly. That's a good way of putting it."

"I apologize if I seemed a little thorny there. I should have known that you hear so much in the ramble it'd be hard to put a name to every last remark."

"That's okay."

"Would you mind terribly letting me know, just the same, if you hear anything more about Liardi? If somebody you're talking to—"

"I'll get all the details. Not to worry. If I'd known it was important . . ."

"Do you know Liardi well?"

"Well enough."

"It seems he didn't have any family around here. What can you tell me about him? Wasn't he a pretty fair fighter years ago?"

"Fought Tony Canzoneri for the lightweight crown. Grew up in North Beach. His father ran a barbershop, maybe the numbers, too. Seems he always had a chip on his shoulder, always playing the angles and holding grudges. Smart guy, in a cunning kind of way. I guess that's why he thought he'd be a good manager. In the ring, he was fast, really fast, and he liked embarrassing guys with—what did I always call it? His *guile*."

I had to chuckle, thinking back. "Gig hated it whenever we called him *clever* in print. He told me once—" and suddenly I was impersonating Gig: his throaty whine and the index finger jabbing at the air. "Clever means you never get hit too bad, but you never knock nobody out. You can keep clever. Clever is the guy they use to test the next champ."

Christ, I must have heard him say it a hundred times. And he was right.

"What about his fighter, Escalante? Is he Liardi's only boy?"

"That's right."

"Isn't that a little odd? Don't managers usually have a whole stable?"

"Well, Gig wasn't exactly a fight manager in the class of a Dewey Thomas or a Johnny Flaherty. He wanted one kid, a puncher, that he could work with. A big kid. Somebody who could knock people out."

"I get the picture. Why do you say he wasn't exactly a fight manager?"

"He never learned to make the contacts or play the game. Always on the outside, looking in. A loner. That's not a good thing to be when you're trying to score good purses."

"You said *wasn't*, though. That he *wasn't* a fight manager in other guys' class." O'Connor smiled. A little laugh bubbled from him. "Some confidential inside info you're holding out on? Has he quit?"

"Did I say that? Sorry. No. He's still in the dodge. Though strictly between you and me, he's not cut out for it."

"Neither was I. Christ Almighty, I loved boxing when I was a kid. I was a newsie, you know. I sold the *Call* down by the cable car turnaround at the Ferry Building. And you had to fight, you know. Protect your territory. I thought I was another Packy McFarland until I broke three knuckles on this hand mixing it up with some guinea kid who was trying to poach some of my regulars. But for bad hands you might have been writing about me!"

He stabbed his cane down on the floor and rubbed the burr on his head.

"Those were the days for the papers, right? Jesus, Mary, and Joseph, it was fierce. If somebody tried to move in on your prime selling spot, the beef had to get settled. Over at the SP depot the station cop always told us to take the fight behind the MJB Coffee building."

"I remember," I said. "A lot of my pals were bootjacks."

"The workers leaned out the windows to watch the fights, remember? That whole alley smelled like roasting coffee, just wafting through there thick as could be. I can smell it now."

I took the cue to lead him further down Memory Lane, away from his Missing Person's case.

"When I was a boy there was a priest at our parish, St. Elizabeth's, named Father Petri," I reminisced. "He'd been a CYO boxing champion. And he used to give lessons to all the neighborhood kids after school. But the monsignor over there, Brennan, he didn't think this fit with the church's image. One day he interrupted one of Father Petri's lessons and he said, 'Jesus told us to turn the other cheek.' And Father Petri, not missing a beat, said, 'Jesus didn't sell papers for a living.'"

O'Connor slammed the cane down again and shook his head side to side. He tightly pursed his lips, as if he couldn't allow a laugh for fear it would blow out the entire third floor.

"Remember Dago Louie?" I asked.

O'Connor's howl turned every head in the department.

The *Chronicle* had a circulation boss named Dago Louie, who, in a legendary attempt to ruin the credibility of the rival *Journal*, walked into its composing room late one night and overturned all the forms for the morning edition. Such inspired tactics got the Dago shot and killed in the basement of the *Chron* some years later.

"Let the Dago in here," my dad would holler as the papers rolled, even though no one heard him. "Let him try it here!" I suddenly saw my father and me, riding a car home, the lights of Oakland shining across the bay. My father's hands were permanently stained from press work. Even fierce scrubbing couldn't bring them clean again, and his grimy work clothes were blotched with ink, like patches of black blood.

"Nobody ever got pinched for doing the Dago, either." O'Connor laughed. A big hollow rumble in his throat. "Goddamn if selling papers wasn't a serious fucking business."

"Safer to be a cop, huh?"

"Ah, unlike the ring, we get to introduce foreign objects legally," he cracked. He pulled open his overcoat and jacket to reveal the butt of a revolver holstered next to his heart.

He stood up, barely leaning on the stick. It looked to be more for show than support. "That's one hell of a cane," I noted. "Where'd you come by it?"

"I used to be with Jack Manion's Chinatown Squad," he began, and I knew I was getting a well-honed tale. "You'll remember that we settled a lot of hash in the twenties trying to clean the tongs out of Chinatown. I got my rather unique walk courtesy of a highbinder with bad aim. Had me dead to rights in the hallway of a hotel on Stockton Street, but hit me only once. In my hip. I fell down three flights of stairs and was thankful for it. We figured he was hired by a tong running some of the Pai Gow and Fan Tan we were busting up. Crazy to shoot a cop. They probably sliced him into the soup for bringing down the wrath of the fucking Irish. I got this later"—he twirled the walking stick—"from some mates on the squad. They told me it belonged to the boss tong." He winked. "And I choose to believe them."

"Well, at least you've earned safer duty now."

"Oh, we still get our share of shit in homicide, believe me."

I tried stacking papers and tidying things for a few long seconds.

"Why would homicide be involved in this Liardi thing?"

O'Connor gave me his deluxe smile, just brimming with that Irish brand of fuck-the-world-and-I-don't-care merriment.

"No damn reason 'tall. Just an excuse to come shoot the shit with you. I've read your column every day for years. This mighta been my only chance at a private audience. Been a pleasure. We should do it again sometime."

In lieu of a handshake he tapped his stick on the side of my desk twice, turned, and weaved his unique walk through the maze of desks.

4

"I've never had to wait in a line in my life," Ida whispered. There was a heavy fog on Francisco Street. We were still a good ten yards from the entrance to Lucca's, smack in the middle of a huddled queue of eager diners. "Don't you know somebody?" she asked. She pulled that card after a full ten-minute wait.

Whenever Ida saw fit to leave her safe domestic confines, dipping an unsullied toe into the real world, she was quick to trade on my renown. I'm not tooting my own horn. San Francisco was a real fight town, and scrapping was an art form. Unions had battled for their lives and won. The workers who controlled the streets wore the bluest of collars. And I was sitting in a prime spot on the heap, treated with a deference I found wholly undeserved.

I could never shake the feeling that I was getting away with something. That the juice that flowed to me as a newspaperman was squeezed from some big confidence game. Ida, though—she was drunk on the juice. She had no idea how it all worked, and she didn't care. My wife only knew that she was entitled. A joint like Lucca's, that was torture for her. It was the most popular eatery in North Beach, but much of its charm was in the democratic seating philosophy: let the mayor wait his turn alongside the welder and meter reader.

The line stretched down to Powell and rounded the corner, as it had since the day Pierino Gavello, the Piedmontese owner, first put out the ALL YOU CAN EAT FOR FIFTY CENTS sign years earlier. Gavello served up a princely feast on his

Florentine crockery: hefty platters of antipasti and ravioli, bottomless tureens of minestrone, wine flasks shaped like horses or doves bestowed on those who tied on the biggest feedbag, after-dinner petit fours, which, if unfinished, were boxed in pink cardboard and tied with string, compliments of the house.

This sort of deluxe atmosphere once made Ida girlishly giddy. For many locals, Lucca's was part of the courtship ritual. It had been for us. But five years into our marriage, Ida's giggles were spent.

She'd dolled herself up, of course, as she did for any public appearance. A blue pillbox tilted primly on her blond waves and the fog's brace flushed her cheeks a shade darker than her rouge. Impatient sighs puffed white through her expertly applied lipstick. Her glare was locked on the unruly Italian brood ahead of us, particularly their caterwauling little kid. He'd inherited his shiny dress shoes from an elder brother, I gathered, and the tight fit was killing him. Winsome, whiny kids were a cinch to spark Ida's maternal fuse.

My wife doted on other couples' children. She'd fawn, or gently scold them for mussing up their hair, or lecture them for wearing their jacket wrong. Often she prompted nasty exchanges with mothers who told her to mind her own business. It was all for my benefit, I knew that. When she'd stare down her nose at another woman and launch into an *If that was my child sermon*, it was really aimed at me.

Sometimes I felt sorry for Ida, I really did. As a grade-A social climber, she thought hooking me was trading up. What she didn't know, until it was too late, was that kids never figured in my plan. Sure, there was talk about cashing me in, but she couldn't bring herself to do it. She was paralyzed by the possibility of trading down.

"Billy Nichols, right?"

I turned to find Claire Escalante smiling broadly. Hack was behind her, nervous and uncomfortable. Nothing new. Ida took a gander at the tall, gregarious redhead and stiffened at once.

"Baby, didn't you see Mr. Nichols? Hack, c'mere." Most guys never quit soft-soaping me. Hack, he had to take a none-too-subtle elbow from his wife before sticking out his mitt.

"I wanted to say thanks for all the nice things you wrote about Hack. He gets so excited. He saves them all, you know." Claire beamed.

I made introductions. Ida squeezed up closer to me.

"Where you folks headed?" I asked.

"Right here!" said Claire.

Ida gave my arm a warning squeeze.

"The line must be around the block by now," I said, craning my neck to see.

"Yeah?" sighed Hack—his first audible word. He stepped back to scope the crowd.

Claire stood her ground.

"You know, I've never been here," she said. "Everybody at the office raves about it, but we've never been. But we thought it'd be nice to get out of the house, away from the kids for a while." She groped for Hack's arm, but he was still hanging back, absently surveying the crowd. She motioned for him to come to her side and whispered to me, "This whole thing with Gig. It's all kinda spooky. It's getting to him. Something good's gotta happen or he's gonna go crazy. Him and me both."

After more than three weeks, Gig's "disappearance" was now a full-fledged mystery. Liardi's name floated through the gyms and saloons like lingering smoke from a fire that had been doused. But I'd seen nothing more of Detective Francis O'Connor.

The maître d' appeared. We were now the head of the line.

"How many?"

"Four!" Claire said.

"Hon, what do you want to have?" Claire asked Hack. His menu was still closed. She opened it.

"What are you getting?" He shut the leather folder.

"Make up your own mind," she said mildly, opening the menu again. Hack stared at the vast pages, scanning them. Then his gaze popped to Ida. "What's good here?" he asked.

"I always have the sweetbreads," Ida told him, her menu clapping with an air of finality. "I love them. And they're especially good here."

Hack nodded, pondering the suggestion. Claire put a hand on her husband's shoulder. "I don't think you'll want those," she said. She raised her eyes to Ida and said, "Do you know what they are?"

"Huh?" Hack grunted. "Yeah, sweetbreads, sure."

Claire ignored her husband. "You know where they come from and you still want to eat them?"

"They are a delicacy," said Ida, defensive.

"But what are they?" Claire pressed, grinning slightly.

Hack started searching for the waiter, embarrassed.

"Some things—if you like 'em, you like 'em." I laughed. "No matter what they are."

"That's right," Ida said. Beneath the table she patted my knee.

An antsy waiter, at the limit of his professional composure, delivered the bread and antipasti and flipped to a blank order page. Hack's interminable inspection of the menu continued while the rest of us ordered. He finally settled on spaghetti and meatballs, but Claire vetoed it. "C'mon, I cook that all the time, have something different," she demanded.

"What do you suggest?" Hack asked the waiter.

The waiter, keeping tabs on other tables, tapped his pencil on the Daily Special clipped to the top of Hack's menu. "This—excellent," he said.

"Sounds good," Hack said quickly, sealing the deal before Claire could interfere. "I'll have that."

"Sweetbreads, okay." The waiter swept up the menus and vanished.

Claire's fair face flushed almost crimson. Hack fell back into tense silence while Claire issued herself a ration of house chianti. Hack was no game player, I knew that. He hadn't ordered sweetbreads to show up his wife.

He simply couldn't read, is how I figured it. Saved all my write-ups even though he couldn't read. Everything I thought I knew about him, and I never knew that. What else was I going to find out?

"What about this deal with Gig?" I said, cutting into my veal. "I'm assuming you haven't heard anything." I was only saying what would be expected in that situation, but Hack reacted like I'd jabbed a fork into his hand.

"Oh, you've hit a sore spot there," Claire said. "It might have been best not to mention that bum."

"Who's Gig?" Ida asked.

"Hack's manager," I explained.

"*Former* manager," Claire said. She looked at me. "Wherever Gig is, he's out of the picture now. It's time for Hack to get a better guy in his corner."

"Well, I'm sure there'll be lots of pilots around town who'd take Hack on, but, you know, it's an awkward spot. They wouldn't want to be accused of poaching another guy's fighter."

"Forget about Gig," Claire said, like she was nailing him in a box. She put her hand on top of Hack's. "Good riddance to bad rubbish, is what I say."

I tried to read Hack's eyes, but he wouldn't look at me. Either his wife had been dishing bitterness toward Liardi for a long while—or she was flashing big hints that she knew where Gig was at this very moment.

"You mentioned something about an office." Ida turned to Claire, deftly changing the subject. "Is that someplace you work?"

"Yeah, Dr. Kaiser, Four-fifty Sutter. You know, the Med-Dent Building."

"What are you, a nurse?"

"I wish. A receptionist. How about you? Anything?"

Ida smirked and glanced toward me. "He takes care of that."

"Kids?"

"Not yet," said Ida.

"One of these days," I lied.

"Jesus, no day job, no kids to take care of. Wanna switch places?" Claire turned to Hack and said, "Just kidding, hon." He grinned gamefully through a mouthful of whatever sweetbreads were.

"Look who's here," he said, chin jutting toward the door, thankful for the distraction.

Jimmy Ryan blew into the joint, helming a party of six. My guess was the bookmaker had spent nine or ten seconds on line. Two and two added up to Gavello being into Ryan for a pile of pennies. Every eye in the joint was drawn to the pack of rollers as the maître d' quickly arranged a booth for them. I made the out-of-towner in the brand-new homburg and cashmere topcoat as a charter member of the Sicilian Benevolence Society. The rest of the party carried weight—torpedoes all the way, two per player. Gavello'd better slaughter another cow.

When Jimmy saw me he sauntered over. Straitjackets couldn't have restrained Ida and Claire from some fast primping. Ryan's associate hung back. Introductions must not have suited him.

"How do you guys rate?" Jimmy said. "Two dolls like these, slumming with a couple of rubes."

Ida was chilly, but Claire offered her left hand across the table. When Jimmy reached for it, she turned it palm down, deftly knocking him down a peg or two. He appreciatively pantomimed a courtly kiss of her hand.

"Jimmy's a kidder," I said, mostly for Ida's benefit.

"He'd better be." Claire smiled. "My husband could kill him without breaking a sweat."

Jimmy raised an eyebrow and gave Claire a lengthy appraisal. "Jimmy Ryan," he said, flashing his rakish grin at Claire, then Ida. He nudged Hack on the arm and gestured toward his wife: "I'll bet she keeps you in line, huh, Hack?"

"Pretty much." Hack tried to laugh convincingly. No sale.

"What gives with Liardi, anyway?" Ryan asked. "Still no word?"

"Nothing," I said, with my best *go figure* shrug. Hack aped it immediately.

"Billy fixing you up with a fresh pilot, Hack? Ought to go with Dewey, he's the best."

Jimmy motioned for his colleague to come over. The guy

shot his cuffs, adjusted his tie, played with his ring—all in the ten steps it took to reach our table. A climber, probably connected by blood, not savvy.

"Meet Paul Ingrassio, friend of mine from Chicago. Paulie, shake hands with Billy Nichols—*Mr. Boxing*." He had to be the brother of Frank "The Immune" Ingrassio, late of Nitti's Windy City crew. Paulie's brother wasn't immune to a dime stretch at Leavenworth.

"Billy here has picked the winner of every heavyweight title fight since 1934," Jimmy bragged to Paulie. "Which includes Braddock over Baer, the one *nobody* called."

Ingrassio showed teeth. "You must know somebody," he laughed.

"Paulie, don't insult the man. Bill's strictly on the level."

"What brings you to town, Paul?" I asked.

"Personal business."

That was Jimmy's cue to start a graceful exit. Showy adieus all around, reeling in the charmless mob scout. He left us with an invitation: "My new club's opening next month, up on Polk. Make sure you all stop by. See ya round, Bill."

Claire sipped her wine and watched Jimmy rhumba back to his table. Was she sizing him up, weighing the balance of smarm versus charm?

"That's some operator," was her conclusion.

Ida was less generous: "That guy's nothing but a cheap hoodlum."

Claire feigned shock. "Really? He didn't seem cheap to me."

Time for dessert. Ida passed on the spumoni ice cream everyone else ordered.

"I'll have the special," she said.

"Special?" A perplexed smile from the waiter.

"You know, the one that's not on the menu."

Claire nudged her husband under the table. Our first time at Lucca's I told Ida about special off-the-menu desserts that you could only get if you knew to ask. That was right up her alley. She'd positively glowed when the waiter presented her with a glistening mound of fresh orange sherbet, served in its own hollowed-out peel. There weren't any others in sight.

"Not on the menu, I don't know," our waiter said. "We got ice cream, though. Spumoni, very good."

"Tell the chef I'll have one of his special orange sherbets," Ida snapped.

The waiter trailed exasperation behind him. On his return he placed three dishes of spumoni down. "Sorry, no special dessert like you say. You want spumoni, I'll bring you."

"No, nothing," Ida muttered.

I pushed my ice cream toward her, but she jerked her head no. "Get some of those little candy cakes you like, have 'em wrap up a box," I suggested.

"I don't want them," Ida said, touching her hair. "This place has really gone downhill."

At the parking lot, Ida started to drive away before I could get in. I banged on the window until she braked abruptly.

"What'rya doing?" I hollered, yanking open the door.

"Don't you dare yell at me." She looked around to see if anyone was watching. "I should let you walk home. What was the idea of letting those people eat with us? I thought you were taking *me* out."

"I didn't want to be rude," I said, sliding into the shotgun seat.

"But it's just fine to be rude to me. You should have told

that bitch to get her own place in line. *'Four!'* she says, like we're all best friends. If you need to associate with that low-class element in your job, that's one thing. But don't expect me go along with you if you're going to mix with such, such *crumbs*."

SECTION S TUESDAY, JUNE 25, 1948 CCCC*

AN AMERICAN PAPER FOR THE AMERICAN PEOPLE

MONARCH OF THE DAILIES

San Francisco Inquirer Sports

REG US PAT OFF

Through THE ROPES

By BILLY NICHOLS

It was an escape worthy of Houdini. I'm talking about Hack Escalante's split decision win over rugged Carmel Whitten on Saturday night at the Civic. This third tilt between local heavies wasn't quite the barnburner one and all had anticipated, considering that their previous seminar was a ring war second to none.

In the early going, Whitten worried Escalante with a heavy jab, like Maggie nags Jiggs with the rolling pin. Hack countered with body work that kept the affair in balance. But only a late rally in the final cantos pulled this one out for the local lad.

Chalk up his erratic showing to the predicament he's endured the past month—the vanishing act pulled by his manager, Gig Liardi, followed by the adoption of an acting pilot, local bon vivant Sid Conte.

Smilin' Sid claims he's stepped into the breach only on an interim basis, and he won't fuss should Gig bounce back to the Bay Area. We'll have to wait and see about that. . . .

5

The crisp linen of Sid Conte's custard-colored suit flapped and crackled in the wind like the plastic pennants that hung around his used car lot. He threw out a hand in greeting. Heavy rings and lacquered fingernails reflected every glint of sunlight.

Conte was situated at Van Ness and Eddy. He competed with his mentor, Horse Trader Ned Ballati, whose more high-toned lots were up a few blocks. Sid played up the protégé routine, having learned the ropes from the Horse Trader years ago. But he loved the bare-knuckled hustle that was the essence of life on Auto Row even more. All that professor-pupil shit be damned—Conte's Klassic Kar Korral went head-to-head with Horse Trader Ned.

But after a few years those bright pennants snapping in the wind and late-day sun spotlighting his once-owned fleet didn't satisfy him anymore. He decided it would be better for his image, and his business, to strut through Bimbo's 365 or Shanty Malone's as a fight manager, not a used car salesman. Sid was no stranger to the circuit; he made it to almost every big card, some slinky tart in tow, his huge smile shining in the lights from the third-row ringside. He'd been hit up so often by stiffs flogging ad space in ring weeklies like *Referee* and *Redhead* that he should have been permanently comped. He had an obsession with the fight game, but no talent for it beyond an innate ruthlessness. He lit up like a Christmas tree when blood spattered the canvas or ink on paper closed a sale.

"Hey, Bill, glad you made it by. Great to see you." Conte manipulated my hand. "Got a neat little bit of business for your column, like I said on the phone." Conte glanced around me, but all he saw was sidewalk. "Where's the camera guy?" He flashed me the full set. His nickname, Smilin' Sid, was on the level. That smile, bursting out of a swarthy face tanned even darker, was a thing of scary ferocity. Choppers so dazzling white he must have applied a fresh coat of high-gloss enamel every night.

"He's coming from another assignment. He'll be here."

"Great, great. I mean, your story, your style, are all it needs, Bill—but the picture, the picture will really make it unique. Really put it over."

Conte blew more smoke, building me up, as he guided me through rows of secondhand Fords and Buicks to the far side of the lot. There, hunched over the left front fender of a Pontiac Super Streamliner, was Hack. He was using a soft chamois cloth to polish the Pontiac.

"Hack, look who's here."

The boxer raised his thick torso with a grunt and turned to face us. "Hello, Mr. Nichols. Nice to see you," Hack said. We shook hands. "In the market for a car?"

"He's looking for a story, kid." Conte cut him short. "And we got a good one right here. Get you some ink."

The armpits of Hack's flannel shirt were damp. I'd figured this was all an amateur publicity gaff. But there was a line of gleaming autos stretched out behind the Pontiac. Holy Christ, it was legit. Conte had a potential heavyweight contender buffing used cars.

"Here you go! Over here!" yelled Conte as the photographer entered the lot, bags of equipment dangling. The lensman, a young guy named Seymour Snaer, sauntered toward us, tossing away the stub of a cigarette and trailing smoke. He sported stingy cheaters and kept pushing lank black hair back from his forehead. Snaer skeptically eyed Conte and Hack. The chamois flicked against the fender.

"How's it going, Seymour?" I said.

"Afternoon, Bill. What's the setup?"

"New training method," Conte answered, pulling at Seymour's sleeve and leading him toward the hood of the Streamliner. "Hack, really get some rubbing going there. Bring up that good shine." Conte crouched down, directing Seymour, who tolerated him with a bemused grin. "If you can get in for a close-up, you can get the nice reflection right there, see him twice. See his face in that shine? Classy, huh? This is okay light, you think? We can use one of the other cars if you want."

Seymour loaded his camera, second nature. "That's what we got? This guy waxing up a car?"

It was me he asked, but Conte sniffed the trace of disdain, and turned up the volume: "A while back Hack complained that his muscles were sore and stiff after a workout at the gym—even after a rubdown," Conte recited. "As you know, Hack works out down at Newman's Gym, about eight blocks from here."

Like I didn't know Newman's.

Sid had scripted this patter in advance; it sounded like a vocal press release and he pitched it like he would a once-driven DeSoto.

"I consulted with some fitness experts. It seems that Hack's problem was that he was stopping too fast after working out—he needed to cool down gradual, not just stop so sudden. The rubdowns weren't helping him get loose. Guess what? I realized one day that the motion of polishing a car, that soothing back-and-forth action, might be just the ticket to help Hack taper off after a good workout. What do you know? I was right! It smoothed out all the stiffness in his arms and shoulders."

Conte ignored Seymour's snorts. He smiled, though, once he heard the sounds of the camera coming to life.

"Hack, show 'em how you do it. Straight across the panels, circular motion on the top and fenders, right?"

The three of us watched Hack work the rag over the car's surface, the muscles of his arms and back bulging and stretching beneath his shirt. Seymour dropped to one knee for a better angle, but didn't shoot. "You gotta look like you enjoy it," he said to Hack, whose face was a rictus of concentration.

"He loves it!" Conte stepped in behind Hack, gripping his broad shoulders, imitating a masseur, flashing the broad row of teeth. "No more stiffness, no more aches. Say cheese, Hack!"

Click. *Wind.* Click. *Wind.* Click. *Wind.*

A quick glance between fighter and manager, both showing wide grins. Hack's huge hand rubbing the chamois over the hood. Behind him, Conte's hand pointing out a missed spot. A calculating glint in Conte's eyes. Seymour bought the program in spite of himself. Pros know a keeper when they shoot it.

"Seymour, let's do a couple of Sid here by himself," I proposed, after he'd blown a whole roll, including some where he made Hack strip down to his T-shirt in the chill wind. "I'd like to have some in the file, just in case," I said to Conte. "How about over there by the sign."

Conte's eyes didn't miss a side-view mirror all the way across the lot.

I turned back to Hack, who had put on a jacket. I wanted

to ask him why he'd thrown in with a potzer like Conte, but I knew better. I'd tried to get Dewey Thomas to take him on, but he wasn't biting.

"How you holding up, Hack?"

He leaned back against the Pontiac. "Not so good. I'm all screwed up. You mean you ain't?"

"What are you telling me?"

"The cops came around. Had a bunch of questions about Gig."

I looked over at Conte, his fluorescent Florsheims on a bumper, ivories displayed for Seymour's lens.

"Did you stick to the story? What did you say to them?"

"I said I never saw Gig since we left the gym together that day."

"Did they ask anything else?"

"Did they? Jesus, what didn't they ask? I thought that guy was gonna invite himself for dinner. Like a fucking gabby barber. Kept talking and talking."

"Cop's name O'Connor?"

"Right. Irish all the way. With the mick accent."

I looked down the long row of shining cars. If I pressed Hack, he'd only sweat in front of Sid and raise suspicions. I needed to get him alone and find out what he'd told O'Connor. I changed the subject.

"You don't have to do this, you know. You're a fighter, not some slave."

"You know about something better?" Hack pivoted and started polishing the roof, shocked at his own tone of voice.

"Dump this cheap shit cocksucker and go with somebody who knows what he's doing."

"Liardi. Conte. What's the fucking difference? I ain't a comer no more, I'm a goer. Sid's a big gasbag, but he don't cheat me. My problem is I can't do nothing else." He puffed on the side mirror and rubbed it clean. "Way I look at it, I'm lucky a guy can make a dollar hittin' people. Claire, she wants me to do another Navy hitch."

"Why?"

"Regular paycheck. I wouldn't be that far away from home."

"You gotta tell me something, Hack, and it's gotta be the truth. Did you tell Claire what happened?"

"What? Whatd'ya mean?" He looked away. "You mean the thing?"

"Yeah, goddammit—*the thing*. Did you tell her?"

"No, I didn't. I never did. I swear to God."

"It sure sounded like she knew something that night at Lucca's."

"She never had no use for Gig. You know, that whole thing in New York that time. She never thought he did right by me."

"So what did you tell her?"

"I told you, nothin'."

"She never asked you what happened to him, or where he might have gone?"

"Gig disappeared. Nobody's seen him." The canned response.

He hadn't looked at me once. He tugged and twisted the chamois in his huge hands.

"I gotta get away for a while," he said. "Just get a change of scenery. Maybe that'd help."

Conte ushered me toward the front of the lot. "Did you get all that stuff before?" he asked, resting a hand on my shoulder. "I noticed you didn't write nothing down."

"Oh, I got it all right." I pulled out a cigar and tried to light it, but the wind wouldn't cooperate. Conte flipped open his own silver lighter, thick as a hip flask, but the wind whipped it, too. I shrugged and stuck the stogie back in my pocket.

"Don't you ever write stuff down?" he asked.

"Nah. Grantland Rice, Red Smith, me . . . none of us write anything down."

"And you know what? You're better than all of 'em. Really, I mean it. The best. I cut it out. I cut out all your stuff."

I spit a stray piece of tobacco from my lip. Conte understood it: cut the bullshit. He just shifted gears.

"Thanks for coming by, Bill. Hack needs a tumble, you know, keep his name out there."

"Can't hurt your business, either."

"Hey," Smilin' Sid beamed, "it's best when everybody gets well, am I right?"

6

Fuzzy Reasnor, the sports editor, stood over my desk. He surveyed the jumble of wires and clippings from around the country, the stacks of envelopes with cribbed scrawls on them, the mound of cigar ashes and butts in the big leather-covered ashtray shaped like a boxing glove. He also gave the fisheye to his boxing columnist, who stared across the vast expanse of the third floor while a blank roll waited in the typewriter, innocent of copy.

"These could stand a little explanation," Reasnor began. He shook a handful of still-damp prints at me. I winced at the frozen poses of Sid Conte and Hack Escalante.

"Nope. Can't do it, Fuzz." I pushed my chair back. "Just kill the whole thing." I stood up and pretended to look for something in another heap of detritus atop the filing cabinet.

"Come again?"

"It's the shits. Worthless. We should never have sent Seymour out there. My fault. I shoulda had a better take on it before we wasted his time."

"Billy," Reasnor said, "you *can't* waste Seymour's time. Seymour makes a living shooting chicks in swimsuits staging crab races at the wharf. So what's with"—he flipped through the pictures—"a guy polishing a car while this other knucklehead stands around?"

"Never mind. I won't write it. It's humiliating."

"It's a silly goddamn photograph." He set the pictures on

the only clear spot on my desk and rapped a knuckle on them. "But it's not worth a bucket of whale shit without some inches under it."

"I'm not gonna do it. Tell that new kid to write it, he'll enjoy that. I cover boxing, not . . . this bullshit." I slapped the pictures off the desk and slumped back into the chair.

"I'm gonna do you a favor and pick those up. By the time I set them back on your desk, my highbrow friend, you will have reminded yourself that nobody is ever *that* good. We're holding a space for this thing. A three-column hole. Needs about four column inches of text. Knock out some of your deathless prose so we can get tomorrow's paper out."

My editor bent over and retrieved the pile of photos.

"If I worried about what was humiliating," he said, flinging the prints back on my desk, "I'd be in the goddamn nuthouse."

Fuzzy left me to stew, which I continued to do, trying to burn Conte's oiliness out of my system. I went through the late mail. In with the usual barrage was a ritzy, gilt-edged invitation from Jimmy Ryan:

You are cordially invited to get lucky
At the grand opening of the city's
Newest saloon and nightspot
THE DAILY DOUBLE

I had to laugh at the name Jimmy picked, the cheeky mix of hooch and horseplaying. It was a cinch to piss off his brother, Eddie, who tried to downplay any connection with his bookmaking sibling. Although Jimmy was strictly independent when he started his first handbooks years ago, he was sensing the Sicilian squeeze. San Francisco, way out on the edge of the nation, had always been proud that its vice was homegrown. Now more and more scouts for the outfit, like Paul Ingrassio, were sizing up the action. Soon Jimmy would have to cut deals.

Eddie Ryan had dutifully greased the political machine for years until he scored his jackpot: legal horse racing in California. He built from scratch and operated the state's two biggest tracks. All that schmoozing and deal-making suited him; he was now a buttoned-down businessman. One with political aspirations. Last thing Eddie needed was a mobbed-up brother to remind people that under all the philanthropy he was a scheming little mick picking the public's pocket. When you got down to it, the difference between the Ryan boys was only a matter of style. Jimmy read Eddie as a puffed-up, double-talking hypocrite. Eddie thought Jimmy was flashy, no-class gutter trash. They tended to ignore their common ground: both made out like bandits, raking in the chips, the squandered proceeds of other people's legit labor.

Finally I manhandled Conte's car-lot claptrap into shape, with all the relish of a bum extracting lunch from a trashcan. Then I beat it out of there to the Embarcadero, to catch a ferry across the bay. Big fight card that night at the Oakland Auditorium. Earl Turner and Sheik Rangel, good East Bay middleweights, were headlining. The boat made good time. I bummed a ride to the Ringside Café on Franklin. I'd mingle for a few hours before the first prelim.

The Ringside was known to the fraternity as "The Poor Man's Stork Club." It was co-owned by Harold Algernon Broom, right name Andrea Carnaga, and Lucky Jimmy Dundee—Rinaldo Annunzio on his license. Broom picked up his moniker early, sweeping out the gym that Johnny Rohan had behind his coal and feed company at Fifth and Washington. Broom grew into Oakland's top trainer and ticket hawker, affecting the elegant *Algernon* in the process. Broom, standing alone, just wouldn't do.

Dundee had been a boxer. He bagged it one day in 1924 while training for a fight in Portland. He'd split his last four bouts on decisions and had clearly lost his edge. When a mean and hungry kid walked into the gym and said he wanted to fight, Dundee stripped all his gear off and turned it over. "*I* knew when to quit," he'd declare proudly from then on if some pug tried to run a hard-luck story past him.

I was sipping straight bourbon at the bar, finishing the Macanudo I'd started on the ferry over, cutting up touches with Burney Sanders, Irish Johnny Smith, Speed Reilly, all the usual guys who flowed around every show, either side of the bay. Your typical fight night seminar—until Detective Francis O'Connor sidled through the crowd.

O'Connor smiled broadly when he saw me and thwacked his cane against the leg of my stool. He was off-duty, happy to report, joining some pals for boys-night-out. I made introductions to everybody within earshot, selling O'Connor like the greatest cop to ever pin on a badge.

He declined my offer of a cigar. I told Broom to get him an Irish whiskey.

"Scotch, if you wouldn't mind," O'Connor said. He winked. "Long as we keep it from the congregation."

"So what the fuck happened to Gig?" Burney said. Like he was challenging O'Connor to live up to my big intro.

"Odd thing about that." O'Connor nodded at Burney, measuring the feisty promoter as Broom set up his scotch. "We learned he was starting a new enterprise, getting out of the roofing job and into his own housepainting company. He was taking on a partner, guy name of Grazziani. Anybody heard of him?"

Shrugs all around, myself included.

"Doesn't it seem curious to you," he went on, "that a fellow would skip out on a brand-new business just as he's trying to get it off the ground?"

I tried to resemble a guy pondering all the possibilities. Burney cut right in:

"I'd chase the money. Maybe Gig got hold of a bunch of cash up front and went Dixie with it."

"Ah, now you're thinking like a cop."

Burney looked insulted.

"But that's the moment where it gets really strange," O'Connor continued.

I gnawed on what was left of my cigar.

"It was the partner, Grazziani, who was minding all the dough. In a separate business account. They'd pooled the start-up money. Grazziani showed me the deposit book. They'd each ponied up seven-fifty. You'll appreciate the name of the concern"—he rapped at the stool again and clipped my ankle—"Knockout Painting. I thought that was kind of charming."

"What's all this mean, Francis? Where are you going with this?" I rocked on my heels and stuck my hands in my pockets so he couldn't see them rattle.

"Foul play, of course." He said it with gusto, playing to the balcony.

"You're kidding," I said. "Who'd want to kill Gig?"

Burney did a cartoon spit-take with his drink. O'Connor missed it.

"Damn!" O'Connor laughed. "I was hoping you'd tell me.

From what I understand, our Mr. Liardi was a bit of a prick. Had he any known enemies?"

"Francis," I said, "this is boxing. You get to beat up your enemies. You don't have to kill 'em."

"And besides," Burney said, "we're all pricks."

"Or known enemies," I added.

O'Connor rolled one of his throaty laughs around and slowly savored a sip of his scotch. He was prepared to wait out the flippant stuff.

"A fine turn of phrase, Billy," he continued, dabbing at his lips. "And a no doubt apt observation," he said, nodding toward Burney. "Although I'm sure that neither is entirely true. Not with all the gambling that accompanies this fine sport. Was Liardi involved in any of that?"

"No way," Sanders said.

"Gig may have been a prick," I said, "but he was a clean prick."

"Now, there's an enviable epitaph," O'Connor said, reaching across us to set his drink on the bar. He gazed grimly at me, with all the mirth drained from his face. "I think about him now in the past tense, too. Our man is dead, I'm certain of it."

My own slipup echoed in my ears. I shook my head and ground out the cigar on the floor. It seemed to take several minutes.

"How about Liardi's heavyweight, this Escalante?" O'Connor inquired at large. "How'd those two get along?"

"Like father and son," I assured him.

"Most fathers and sons are at each other's throats. The Escalante boy seemed nervous as a whore in church when I talked to him. I went out to his house for the interview and he was nearly climbing up the walls."

"Hack gets the willies when you look at him sideways," Burney volunteered. "That don't mean nothing. Take my word."

"He and Gig were close," I added. "This has got to be hard for Hack."

"Not so close he didn't go right out and get a new manager," O'Connor countered.

"He's got himself a used car salesman, is what he's got," Burney said.

"Yeah, he should have gone with Dewey," offered Broom, finally jumping in. To Broom, a suspicion of murder was nothing; switching managers, that was dead serious.

"This is a cutthroat business, Francis," I said. "The clock's running on a fighter like Hack. He's gotta make hay while the sun shines."

"You said it," Burney declared. He hoisted his highball, apparently toasting struggling pugs everywhere.

Broom, wary of the gloomy cloud gathering over his bar, yanked the conversation back to shoptalk: "You went down to Los Angeles when Conte took Hack to fight at the Hollywood Legion, right?" he asked Sanders.

"Yeah, yeah, I was on that trip. He did the Legion, what about it?"

"Well, Hack said he paid his own way—the train, the hotel, food. Then after the trip Conte hits him with a tab for three bills in expenses."

"I never heard that," I said, grateful to get off Liardi.

"I'm just saying what I hear," Broom said with a shrug. "That's what some people were telling me."

"Hack say it himself?" Burney asked.

"Yeah, right. And I shot dice with the Holy Ghost right after."

O'Connor seemed merrily amused by the back-and-forth. He cocked his head at Broom and asked me, "What's he mean by that?"

"Hack don't kick," Burney informed him. "Whether he's getting his beating in the ring or out, Hack takes it like a man. Pitching a beef, that don't sound like him."

O'Connor tugged at my sleeve and drew me away from the bar. We propped ourselves up against the phone booth in back. The luminous clock face above us showed forty minutes till jump-off. The regulars were packed in all around, jabbering to beat the band. Charlie Rustican was the fossil inside the booth, no doubt barking to his bookie, trying to get late action. O'Connor dipped inside his coat, as if he was going for his piece. Out came an envelope. He offered it to me confidentially.

"I shouldn't be doing this," he whispered.

Bare-bones address, handprinted letters:

BILLY NICHOLS
INQUIRER

No return address, no stamp. Never posted. I turned it over. It was sealed.

"What's this?"

"An item found in Mr. Liardi's residence. Thought there might be some significance to it."

I flipped it a couple of times, front to back, while I ran my options.

"What's it say?" I ventured.

"Now, how would I know that? The item is sealed." He played it blank. He'd had a lot of practice at this stuff. I had to restrain my stomach from bipping like a simon-pure in his first pro bout. I decided to take an interest in some old fight pictures on the wall.

"It's got your name on it," O'Connor pointed out. As if a cop nosing for murder leads respected privacy. Say he found the letter open, read it, and had a reason for passing it on. Just to see how I'd react.

I was in a corner. And I don't do well with my back to the ropes.

I tucked the envelope in my coat pocket.

"Thanks," I said, like you would to the postman.

For a second he eyed me the way he probably sized up some dinge dope dealer. That lasted a few heartbeats.

"You'll let me know, won't you, if there's anything of interest in there?"

I patted the pocket where I'd put the letter.

"Like a suicide note? You bet."

"That may be evidence," the cop warned.

I grinned. This was a strenuous workout.

"Don't get too excited, Francis. Characters are sending me stuff all the time. That's how I get my items. Most of it doesn't amount to much."

"Of course. I recall. That grapevine we talked about," O'Connor said, nodding. "You explained to me how it works."

Then he mixed me up, like a righty switching to southpaw in the middle of a round.

"I want to get in on that grapevine," O'Connor said, his merry old self easing back to the surface. "I'm going to tell you something and I'd be grateful indeed if you'd drop it in your column, the way you explained it to me. Would that be suitable?"

"I decide what goes in my column."

"Of course, of course, but this is the goods—I guarantee you'll want to run it."

"Why not tell me what it is?" This guy had a way of wearing you down.

"I've located a witness who recalls she saw two individuals put a large object in a car outside Liardi's flat, then drive off. She's good on the date—the twelfth of last month. The last day anyone encountered Mr. Liardi. Alive."

I forced myself to stare into O'Connor's ruddy face. His eyes gleamed happily.

"Is this a reliable witness? I don't like to go off half-cocked."

O'Connor cut loose with a single short burst of laughter, then whipped off his hat and rubbed his head vigorously.

"Jesus Christ, I hope you'll excuse me—but since when do newspapers give a flying fuck about a witness's reliability? I thought I was doing you a favor, that I was handing you a juicy one for your daily, setting up a real live murder mystery amidst the local fight crowd. Jesus, you'd have people reading your column before they can even take a piss in the morning. How can you pass that up?"

"Is it true?"

"Let's just say it's something you snatched out of the air—from a reliable source, of course."

At a quarter to midnight the ferry churned through rough waters, heading back to the city. A hardy contingent of fight fans congregated on the forward deck, tight clusters of hats and overcoats, tobacco smoke and steaming breath yanked away on the wind. The bay was bracing these sated boys for the trudge home, to sleeping families or empty rooms. Flasks went hand-to-hand, fortification for either destination.

Beyond them jutted the sliver of land that was my town. Lights glistened in the swells and valleys from Butchertown to Twin Peaks, from Nob Hill to North Beach. Land's End—west beyond the Gate was endless ocean. It seemed that the seven-mile stretch of city, floating between the black dome of sky and the blacker bay below, was hanging on to the edge of the world.

We steamed past one of the huge towers of the Bay Bridge. The massive roadway drifted above for a few seconds, cutting the moonlight. Then we reemerged, halfway home. Alone against a starboard railing, I watched the red neon Port of San Francisco sign rise and dip with the rhythm of the waves. I'd moved away from the boys: six bouts, twenty-nine rounds, twelve pages of notes, and several dozen schmoozes had to start boiling down to ten column inches.

But the brewing wouldn't be smooth tonight. Every second I'd been aware of the envelope in my pocket. It wasn't until we crossed under the bridge, back into my hometown's gravitational pull, that I decided to play O'Connor's gambit. Beneath a glowing deck lamp I opened the envelope and removed two thin pages. It was stationery copped from the Hotel Rex in Manhattan, a memento of our aborted Eastern campaign of more than two years ago.

Before I even started reading I sensed the knotted-up anger in the way Gig's cribbed scrawl bit into the paper. The barely contained scratchings brought Gig back, strong. A shiver shot through me and I bristled, as if he were right on the deck, in the circuit, as always.

Dear Mr. Boxing,

I been trying to figure out how we came out of New York without two nickels to rub together. A lot of it is your fault. I spent months building Hack up about a break in NYC getting him on the way to big money. I would repeat over and over what you told me from the Bosnich fight on. Nothing new to you. People believe everything you tell them. Your big buildup had both Hack and me beliefing we could get Jacobs to bite on a decent deal.

So what happened? How come we come back to town with our tails between our legs while stiffs like Beshore and Lesnevich get walkovers that put them in line for a shot? I'll tell you why. You are not the big man they all think you are. You didn't carry weight with Big Mike or none of the boys back there. You may be King Shit on Market Street but outside SF you don't turn the tip.

How did you get the juice in the first place? Who did you ever fight? How do you have any fucking idea what it takes to get in there and go the distance? How come you make out better than any of us and you never took one punch? How come I scrape like a bastard more than twenty years and I got nothing to show? Answer that if you know so goddam much.

No windup, no sign-off. He'd punched himself out.

I considered giving it a burial at sea. Instead I refolded it and slipped it back into the envelope. I ran the facts, to cool the burning at the back of my neck. The bobbing of the ferry in the choppy waves flipped my stomach. There was a vital fact that would cut through the emotion. I searched for it, the way a fighter did, so he could stand clear and ready at the opening bell.

No postage, Gig. That was the main thing. You left your fight in the gym. Worked yourself into a righteous rage, but couldn't carry it to center-ring. We call that a forfeit.

I scanned the deck for the roughest fucker aboard. Over on the port side, knocking back nips from a short dog, was Buddy Doyle, a once-feisty lightweight who'd earned a rep for fighting dirty. He felt the rules didn't apply against coloreds. Thumbed Sam Barber in a clinch and nearly popped his eye out. Buddy was a Mission boy whose juiced-up old man was facedown in a saloon the night Mrs. Doyle hanged herself. About the time Buddy made his first impression on a police blotter—aggravated assault, age fifteen—I was getting kicked out of Cogswell Polytechnic for a lesser offense: delivering a graphic oral report about the night I sneaked into the Bucket of Blood for a Friday night fight card. I got a lecture that there was "no future in fighting." Little did they know.

"How's it going, Buddy?"

He straightened right up, waving off the last swallow of Jim Beam being proferred by Sam Rinaldi, a sofa salesman who owned a piece of Buddy in his prime.

"Good, Mr. Nichols. Real good. How you doin'?"

"Can't kick."

Six years earlier I'd battered these words onto a blank roll in the Royal:

> No one present will ever forget the sight of Doyle, claret streaming from the widening gash, gallantly rallying as the last seconds ticked away. A right knocked Lemos into a vulnerable spot, and the left hook that Doyle followed with brought the crowd to its feet in a thunderous roar. Lemos was down, and out, with two ticks to go. Doyle triumphed on pure guts.

The copy boy ran it to lino. The words became hot metal.

The ink coursed through tubes from the vats to the plates. The proof flowed black. Presses pounded. Sheets were bundled and tied. Buddy Doyle's validation was loaded and delivered.

I'd give short odds that the clip was in his wallet. Right now. Always.

"Buddy, you ever think what would have happened if you hadn't walked into Dewey's club that day, spoiling for a fight?" I asked him. I took out my last cigar and bit off the end.

A crooked smile split Buddy's pink, wind-whipped face. "I'd prolly be in the joint, fightin' for nothin'." He laughed, and everybody joined in.

As far as guys like Doyle were concerned, a one-day starring role in the sports section beat a benediction from the pope, hands down. As long as he had that clip in his billfold, he may as well have had the city seal tattooed on his ass. He was *legit*.

Doyle flashed a lighter from his pocket and cupped the flame for me. Rinaldi moved in to block the wind.

"You need a lift?" Buddy asked.

"Just to the office. Thanks."

Nobody said life was fair, Gig.

7

Childish hands stroked the turtle's carapace, testing the smooth ridges on the hard shell. Small fingers then curled into a pudgy fist and punched the shell, hard as a three-year-old could muster.

"Marie, what'd I tell you? Don't hit the turtle," Hack told his daughter.

"Why don't he come out?" Marie asked. Her head tilted sideways, peering into the hole where the reptile had retreated.

"He can't come out. It's where he lives."

I'd taken a taxi out to Hack's place in the avenues. My own invite. It was a bright Saturday, surprisingly free of fog. The whole Escalante family was home. They lived in a two-story stucco job on Thirty-sixth Avenue: fenced-in backyard, garage, partial ocean view from the back bedrooms. You could watch the tidal waves of fog roll in every afternoon. Used to be nothing but sand dunes that far west. Now developers couldn't build tract homes fast enough. Pretty soon people would be living cheek by jowl all the way to the ocean. On their joint income, Hack and Claire were precariously poised at the doorstep to middle class. But I wouldn't have wanted to juggle the numbers come bill-paying time.

Earlier that day Hack had gone to a pet store. He wanted something to surprise the kids. Tony, five years old, Hack's eldest, looked quizzically from the turtle to his father. "Why'd you get a turtle, Dad?"

"You been bugging your mother and me for a pet. A turtle is a pet."

"You're going to stay for lunch, aren't you?" Claire asked. Adult talk again. She was fixing the food while she kept one eye on the youngest kid, thrashing around in his playpen in the corner. Setting the table in the dining nook, she had to step gingerly around tarps and painting supplies that cluttered the room.

"I don't want to impose," I said. "I need to get to the office soon, and—"

"You came all the way out here, don't turn right around and go back. Have something to eat with us. Excuse the mess. Gig was supposed to get us a deal on this paint job—buddies of his. 'They'll do right by you,' he tells us. Well, they show up three weeks ago at eleven in the morning, dump all this stuff. They're gone before lunchtime because I'm at the store with the checkbook and they won't start without the deposit. Haven't seen them since. And they didn't hear anything about a special deal. So we don't know what to do."

She set out plates while she talked. Like a blackjack dealer, her hands were large, the fingers long and tapered. Freshly painted nails, bright red. The hair wasn't a salon job, but it swept around her face in the right places.

I looked away from her, out the window. "You've got quite a plantation out there."

"Thanks. Planted all that myself. I always wanted a garden, more than anything."

"Looks like you've got the green thumb."

An apron stretched tight across her full chest, and when she walked over to the pantry it was impossible not to admire the tall, strong length of her. Claire was no frail. If she and Hack went toe-to-toe, I might handicap it even.

"Thanks," she called from the kitchen. "How 'bout a beer?"

"Don't mind if I do."

I walked back into the living room to look at Hack and the kids. Claire brought the beer a moment later, and we both stood, watching.

"It's not a dumb pet," Hack assured Tony, displaying the turtle. "It's so slow you can't lose it. You feed it people left-overs. And it lives forever."

"Is that what the guy at the store told you?" asked Claire.

"That sounded pretty good to me. Last thing I want is some puppy or kitten that's gonna get sick and die on you or get lost or hit by a car or something."

"What does a turtle do?" Tony asked. The kid had his father's features, but his mother's big green eyes and contrary nature.

Marie punched the turtle's shell again. Hack lowered it into the sanctuary of a cardboard box.

"It can live in the garden."

Claire issued a mock warning: "It better not eat my flowers."

"How do you play with it?" Marie asked. She kicked the box.

"We'll think of something," Hack assured them.

Out of the box, the turtle crawled around the floor some while we chewed cold-cut sandwiches and sipped reheated soup. The kids got down there with it, squealing. Tony pushed it around like a toy car until Claire told him to knock it off and let the thing get around on its own.

"I understand Hack's thinking of signing on for another Navy hitch," I said to Claire.

"Done deal," Hack said, wiping his mouth. "They took me

already, no questions asked." He and Claire traded a quick look, or so it seemed.

"If it's not my business, tell me, but why do that? You've got this new house, the kids, a lovely wife—who makes good minestrone."

"I gotta do something besides fight," Hack said, as though that explained everything. He stared out the window.

"It was my idea," Claire admitted. "I think it's for the best."

"Why's that?"

"There's no future in boxing. You probably know better than most. Maybe there's a healthy career in writing about it. Not in the real thing," she said. "Hack puts in his time, he'll be able to draw a pension. He can learn a trade. We've got three kids to think about."

"Then it's money?"

"Yeah, it's money," sighed Hack. He tossed down his napkin. On the dodge, he picked it right back up and wadded it in his hand. "It'll work out good. I'll probably be stationed in Alameda mostly, so it's not like I'm going to Okinawa or someplace."

"Were you in the service?" she asked, trying to divert my line of questioning.

"I wasn't called," I said, not bothering to deliniate the list of physical shortcomings—flat feet, brittle bones, nearsightedness—that ranked an otherwise hale thirty-one-year-old as a 4-F reject. Thanks be to God—and Hearst.

"You could have enlisted," she said, raising an eyebrow but not looking at me. I knew she was only trying to rile me, get me to stop drilling Hack. "I did serve," I replied instead. "People need the newspaper, just like they need gas and water and electricity."

Claire put her hand on her husband's arm. "Hon, you want some more soup?" she asked. They traded a look that didn't have anything to do with lunch.

This whole deal smelled. She had to know about Gig, I figured. Hack would never confess to me that he'd told her, but I could see for myself. *She knew.* The Navy re-up was a ruse: she wanted to hide him, get him out of circulation where he couldn't hang himself with a slip of the tongue.

The kids went on playing with the turtle, crawling around our legs under the table. I checked out Claire, then Hack. He might have been a stallion in the ring, but he was strictly a gelding in the domestic arena. She had ten times his stones, not to mention smarts. There was no way he could lie down next to her and not own up to what he'd done.

Hack dissected a leaf of lettuce from his sandwich. He set the small pieces of turtle food on the floor. "See if he likes this," he told the kids.

Claire was watching me, delicately picking at the crust of her bread.

"You don't think it's a good idea?" she asked. "His going back in the Navy?"

"It's not my business. If it makes sense to you . . ."

Another glance between them.

I excused myself to use the bathroom.

I rinsed my face and tried to get my thoughts straight. *So what if she knew?* Claire would never draw heat on her husband. But did she know *I* was in on it? Did he spill that, too? Had to. What else were those sidelong glances about? She's checking to see how I'm holding up, if there's any chance I'll sell him out down the road. She was a savvy dame, you had to give her that. Just what I needed—another sparring partner.

I opened a drawer by the sink, looking for a brush or comb. Claire's girl stuff was jumbled inside. Lipstick, mascara, eyelash curler, nail clippers, compacts—and a half-empty box of rubbers. I got a quick flash of her and Hack together, her body naked and damp. I slid the drawer shut and went back out, hair drooping over my forehead.

Mrs. Escalante was clearing plates from the table.

"Get enough to eat?" she asked.

"Yeah, thanks. That hit the spot."

"Let's talk out back," Hack called from the kitchen door.

I sat next to him on a stairway facing the lush garden. All kinds of flowers bloomed everywhere. I didn't know plants by name. They all looked different, they all looked beautiful. Alongside the steps, a terrace of tall stalks and delicate lavender bells nodded in a gentle ocean breeze.

"I can't remember what it used to be like, to wake up without all kinds of shit running around in your head," Hack began. "You know what I mean? I hate it. I can't stand that feeling. I know nobody liked Gig too much. But he was my friend. The first person ever gave a damn about me. Better'n my family, no contest. Him and me, together fifteen years. Shit. *Fifteen years*."

I smoothed out my pants leg, looked again at the garden, compared it with the bald brown lawn on the other side of the fence. There was no slick way to get to it, so I just waded in.

"That Irish cop come out to see you again?"

"No. Why?"

"He found a witness. She saw two guys put something in a car outside Gig's that night."

"Oh, Jesus. Oh, Jesus." Hack huddled up, wrapping his

huge arms around his knees. If he could have pulled his head inside himself, like that turtle, he would have.

"Don't panic. If he really had something, we'd know. O'Connor was awful careful about what he said. He didn't even say 'guys,' he said *individuals*. This broad might not be clear on *what* she saw. She sure as hell never said she saw a *man* being put in the car."

"How come you know all this?"

"The cop told it to me."

"But *why*?"

"He's promoting that I write it up in my column."

This was a tough play for Hack to figure. For half a minute he just made noises with his heavy breaths. This was too close for comfort.

"It's a story," I explained. "People like to give me stories."

"What the hell am I supposed to do now?"

"Remember when you asked how come I helped you out that night?"

Hack looked at me, his eyes going moist.

"I figured you deserved a chance. It wasn't hard to see what would have happened to Claire, to the kids, if I just walked away, or called the cops."

"I know, I know . . ."

"Hack, if you crack now, I go down with you. You've got to tough it out. It'll get easier, believe me. Just concentrate on what you do, keep busy. The rest will take care of itself."

He stood up, paced around. "I wish I could run," he finally said. "When I lived out the Ingleside I used to get up when it was still dark and nobody was awake and I'd walk past all the closed-up shops on Geneva and go up into that big hill.

Just running, all alone. That's what I wish I could do now. Just run. Like a dog."

"So run. Go run on the beach."

"You don't get it," he said, dropping his head. "I ain't got the words, not like you. Me, I got no way out."

"Shake it off."

He plopped back down on the steps. I clapped him on the back, like we were pals.

"*You* didn't kill him," he croaked. He stared right up into the high sun, like it might burn the pictures out of his head. No go. After a few seconds, he clamped his eyes shut.

Honest to God, I don't know why I did help Hack get rid of Gig that night. If I'd taken a hard left, walked out that door, or dialed up the cops, my whole life would have been different. *Tough spot, kid. I know a good lawyer might get you manslaughter, reduced to five.* Sometimes what you do, there's no explanation for. You go through life shaking your head at all the stupid things people do, convinced you're smarter. Then in a minute, just like that, you're chest-deep in the same shit as everybody else.

I could hear Claire starting to wash dishes through the kitchen window. I switched gears, pronto.

"I heard Sid's dinging you for expenses."

"Shit. What is there you don't know?"

"So it's true?"

"He said he'd make it up to me. Once we got some bigger purses."

"Claire know?"

I got the gelding's glare. Christ, he had a domestic bout coming up that would make his fight with Whitten look like high tea.

"What the hell good is Sid Conte as a manager?" I asked. "You could do better."

"I think he's in a spot."

"What spot?"

"In the hole."

"Gambling?"

He nodded, then rubbed his face.

"How deep? I never read Sid as a chronic."

"Twice I've been working at the car lot. Muscle, shows up to lean on him."

"No shit. Sid ask you to lean back?"

"I said I would the first time. I didn't know what was going on. But they took off, anyway."

"Know what I think? Sid's getting one helluva deal out of you. He gets an earner, a workhorse, and a bodyguard, all in one."

"I ain't much of a bodyguard, I know that."

"You kidding? There's nobod—"

"Second time those guys showed up, I sidelined it."

"How come?"

"I made 'em from that night at Lucca's. Jimmy Ryan's boys."

"You'll never be a reporter, Hack."

"Huh?"

"That should have been your lead. How far down the hole you think Sid is?"

"You think he'd tell me?"

The kids banged on the back door.

"Daddy, can we take the turtle out?" Hack's little girl called from inside.

We stood up. Hack opened the door and the kids practically knocked each other down getting out. Tony carried the turtle while Marie grappled for it. They headed down a narrow stone path, searching for the perfect place to put it.

"I wish you wouldn't write those things about Gig in the paper," Hack said, quietly.

"Whatd'ya mean?"

"You know, all that 'Where is he?' and 'What's the story?' stuff. I don't like that. It scares me."

"So don't read it."

"I always read your column."

She reads it to you, I thought.

"Trust me, Hack, it'd be worse if I didn't put that stuff in. How would it look if I just ignored Gig completely?"

"I went over there."

"What?"

"I went over to the place. Just to look. To make sure."

"Jesus fucking Christ Almighty—what is the matter with you! You can't do that!"

"Watch the language." He nodded toward the kids. "It was all right. You can't see nothing different. We'll be okay."

"What are you gonna do next—put a fucking cross on it?"

Hack pinched a flower off its stem and twirled it between his fingers. In the window above us, I saw the drapes quickly pulled together.

8

Half past two. I bagged the cab and opted for a streetcar back downtown. I needed time to myself, letting the pulse return to normal. Hard to stay on balance, fast as stuff was coming. While I waited at the car stop, a procession of partiers drove by, the sun drawing them to Ocean Beach like honey lures ants. These latecomers wouldn't even get a good burn started before the fog rolled in.

The "L" was packed with giddy beachgoers, headed home for a rinse. As the car rumbled the steady grade toward West Portal, guys roasted red stood in the sand-flecked aisle, lavishing attention on seated nubiles. Some of the young lovelies let their beach robes slide teasingly open, revealing burnished thighs. They smelled of salt and coconut oil and they shook their hair dry and they laughed nonstop, even if nothing was funny. It was bright and hot at Ocean Beach, and that was enough. The clubs would be thick with sun-drunk revelers tonight.

Some of the group's hilarity was probably at my expense. I was wedged into a window seat, cloaked in suit, tie, overcoat, hat—the daily uniform. I even had the long johns underneath. I wasn't much older than most of this carefree bunch, but I felt like Granddad in the middle of a pack of squealing kids.

It was Gig who took my mind off the beach party. I'd read his letter more than once since the other night, and it brought back the New York fiasco, fresh and frustrating. I'd been trying to figure how Gig could lay the dismal finish on me. I ignored the chirping little blonde in the next seat and walked it around again.

By 1946 Gig had developed Hack into a solid local draw. Good heavyweights were scarce by then, and Hack, at twenty-eight, had knocked guys out at a steady clip and pulled solid gates. He started out a raw banger, short on defense. There was always the chance he'd get clocked before he could starch a guy. Just what crowds loved, and what the fight game lived off. After he stopped Oscar Fiducia on a TKO, a first for that tough cookie, Hack had the look of a top-tier earner. But the real dough was in New York.

I was going back to cover the second Louis-Conn fight and I'd pulled the few strings I had there to get Gig and his charge an audience with the Pope. That would be Mike Jacobs, a canny hustler who'd worked his way from the arcades at Coney Island to management of all the concessions at Tammany Hall. His outfit, the Twentieth Century Sporting Club, ruled the roost in New York. It controlled not only Madison Square Garden, the Mecca of prizefighting, but all the other important New York fight clubs: the Hippodrome, Dyckman Oval, St. Nick's. As for the mantle *Mr. Boxing*, Gig was savvy on that score: it was just a catchy moniker the paper hung on me—Mike Jacobs was the McCoy.

Hack had never been out of the Bay Area, so he hit Manhattan like a wide-eyed kid at Christmas, anticipating the biggest present of his life. But the Big Apple brought him up short, and Mike Jacobs was no Santa Claus. The meeting went south before it even started. Jacobs made us dangle for almost an hour, and Gig went in steaming. After some perfunctory small talk, I got the bum's rush: even though Dan Parker of the *Evening-Journal* greased the skids for me,

Jacobs didn't feature writers being privy to his business, especially ones he didn't know personally. When I got the boot, Gig and Hack looked like they'd had their tongues cut out. Which wasn't far from the truth.

Near as I could piece together, Jacobs dealt them typical big-league stuff. He'd take a healthy slice of Hack's first purses in the Garden. If Hack showed well in a couple of contests, he'd become the property of the Twentieth Century Sporting Club. Liardi could handle Hack and draw a cut, but he'd have no vote on money or matchmaking. Jacobs held all the cards.

"It was strictly take-it-or-leave-it—so I left it," Gig told me later over highballs at Dempsey's. His face was still flushed and his eyes burned and darted, like a rabid dog.

"And that was it?" I felt brutal for poor Hack, thinking about the buildup he'd probably given his wife.

"Pretty much. Except for the part at the end where I called him a miserable no-good cocksucking kike chiseler."

He wasn't joking, I learned in short order. Parker got back to me, toot sweet and pissed off. He'd vouched for me and I'd vouched for Gig and Gig spit in Jacobs's face. Any prayer Hack may have had to get over in New York, or anywhere back East, had gone down in flames.

Gig was never the same after that. More than two years he stewed, trying to figure how the big break slipped away. Meanwhile, Hack's meter kept running. I don't know when Liardi wrote the letter to me. But in his final version of the story, he'd cast himself as the only straight-talking, stand-up guy in the dodge, a guy who wouldn't bend over for anybody. Me—*I* was the weak link. Hooked up just enough to get the door open, but not enough to bust it in. After all the sweat and blood he'd put into the fight racket, Liardi couldn't admit that he'd blown his chance by shooting off his mouth.

If he'd learned from that little Eastern escapade how to bite his tongue, maybe he'd still be alive.

I got off at West Portal station to call Ida and say I needed to go to the office for a few hours. Before I made the call I ran into Frank Bennett, a desk cop at downtown headquarters who'd just moved his family into a nice place on Ulloa, up the hill. Bennett was a huge fight fan. Whenever I ate at Joe's, on the corner right across from the station, Bennett would badge whoever was next to me at the counter, chasing him off. "Official police business," he'd say, then sit down to shoot the shit. I'd drop ducats on him and he'd keep me posted on the latest, most vinegary vice action.

When I made the call home, there was no answer. Ida must have gone to visit one of her sisters, or out shopping. If she came home spent, maybe I'd catch a break and not have to suffer her wrath for not planning a Saturday night out.

I hopped an "M" headed down. At the office I managed an hour of light housekeeping, barely making a dent in the desk mess. Johnny Smiley called and begged me to drop by Newman's for a look at a welterweight he'd just brought to town. When I got there, Moose Taussig, who used to own the gym with Paddy Ryan, was holding court. Moose had sold out to Bill Newman, but was back in town for a visit. He regaled the boys with stories of his retirement paradise in Hawaii. He oversold the lush life; it was clear he missed the circuit.

Moose led an entourage to the Round Table lounge up the street. We commandeered the window table and slung shit fast and furious, bringing Moose up to speed on local doings. The Liardi thing got a sarcastic bellow out of him: "I'll bet they're really beating the bushes to turn *him* up."

It was the balmiest evening anybody remembered. The fog had decided to take a night off. Young women glided by in sundresses, even when there was no more sun to be had. They waited for their dates under awnings or on corners, glowing with anticipation.

Just before six I remembered some shirts I had at the Waterway around the corner. I scooted in just as Sammy was locking up. Ida couldn't figure why I took my shirts all the way downtown to be laundered. Sammy was a Butchertown boy, like me. He'd sunk everything into this cleaning business. What else was there to know?

Headed back to Market, I popped in at the Ringside Smoke Shop to re-up on my Jamaicans. That ended up as thirty minutes of gab with Charlie Chastain and Jack Reed, who happened by. They were headed for steaks at Tiny's, a twenty-four-hour spot on Powell, but I begged off. Had to get home for dinner, I told them.

By the time I climbed aboard a westbound "M," it was half past seven.

The house was pitch dark when I got home, except for the green glass banker's lamp glowing on the foyer desk. Alone on the desktop was a single piece of paper set squarely in the small pool of light.

I'm leaving.

It was written in big curlicue letters. Same as the handwriting on the girlish notes Ida would slip me when I'd leave her parents' house after dinner. Those said *You're the best* and

I can't wait and *I love you.* I tried to figure out what I'd done this time to get her hackles up. She was probably just commiserating with one of the coven of sisters. She'd be back late, wound up, ready to unload a fresh ration.

I checked the garage. No car.

I went through the house, still wearing the overcoat, turning on lights. Things were a little too tidy. Upstairs in the bedroom I checked the closet. The suitcases were gone. The normally cramped space seemed thinned out.

Wandering through rooms, I inventoried all the showy stuff she'd filled the house with. The ornate gold-leaf picture frames, the frippy Louis XIV–style chairs and end tables, the elaborately carved casework furniture with beveled glass cabinets. None of it meant a damn thing to me, but I couldn't see her leaving it all behind. Who was she without it?

She'd be back.

I walked down the hill to Joe's for dinner. I skimmed a couple of the other dailies and tried to puzzle out what I'd done wrong this time, what prompted this new level of drama. I figured she'd be waiting with the answer when I got home, so I ordered rice pudding for dessert and went two refills on the coffee.

The house was still empty at ten. It started to sink in. I pondered the note again while I matched a fresh cigar. The clincher hit me, and I went straight to the dining room, to check the china—no way she'd vamoose without that. Even when we weren't entertaining I'd see her sometimes open the sideboard and lift out some piece of the set. She'd trace her finger along the rose and turquoise deco pattern, threaded with gilded accents. Sometimes she'd count all the pieces: salad plates, soup bowls, tureen, water pitcher, coffee cups, saucers, the heavy silver service in its soft brown wool wrap. The complete spread, enough for twelve place settings. When she'd registered at Gump's she'd hoped desperately for eight.

It was all there. I picked the small envelope off the top plate and flipped it open. It was worn from years of handling. There had never been a dinner at this table where Ida didn't make the guests open this little envelope. She'd point her chin at them as they oohed and ahhed. The card inside had embossed gold lettering:

With sincere best wishes
For a long, happy marriage
W. R. Hearst

I'd already been ushered into the comfortable confines of the Hearst empire when I first set eyes on eighteen-year-old Ida Lindstrom. She may have only been a kid, but she knew a catch when she saw one. So did her three sisters. I was from the old neighborhood, but had more dough and savvy than most. I could run my patter from Nob Hill to Niggertown, gesturing with uncalloused hands. I wasn't the typical son of a butcher or bricklayer. To an impressionable girl, I held the promise of something more than just security. They cooed that I looked like Gable, so it followed that whoever landed me was Carole Lombard.

Most people would have suspected that a thirty-five-year-old bachelor was queer. But Ida and her sisters never asked why I was still available. They were too busy vying for my attention. The Lindstrom sisters competed for everything. Not like boys, of course. Boys threw down their shit and went at it, then dusted off and moved on. Girls had more elaborate rituals: scheming and subterfuge. But Ida held an advantage, and she knew it. She was the prettiest of the brood. And she was diligent at maintaining the edge. She trained hard for courtship, always working on that one extra move—a flower in the hair, a fresh blush of rouge, a provocatively rolled-down stocking—that would earn her the decision. She'd go the distance to beat the competition.

It must have worked. I fell for it.

The phone rang. I grabbed it up, certain that an answer waited on the other end, embarrassed that I'd wasted time working myself up.

"Hello?" I tried to balance between frazzled and forgiving.

"Well?" It wasn't Ida. It was one of her sisters.

"Well, what? Who is this?"

"I guess nothing's perfect." She was gloating, not even trying to hide it. "Or nobody," she added. That was probably meant for her sister, a bilious bit of sibling rivalry. I still couldn't figure out which one was on the line. They were interchangeable.

"Do you know where she is?"

I sighed and thought about hanging up.

"Has she called you yet?"

"Which one are you?" I asked, just to buy time.

"This is Mary." The one married to Gil Rayburn.

"What is it you want, Mary?"

"Settle a bet for me, Bill. Phyllis thinks you know what's going on, but I got a feeling you don't have a clue. Who's right?"

"Is Gil there? Put Gil on the phone."

"Who's right? Me or Phyl?"

I didn't say anything. The note was still on the desk, under the lamp, untouched.

"You don't get it, do you?" she asked.

I pushed the note with my finger across the leather desk blotter. While I waited her out, I thought about my mother. Dead seven years. She'd gone to seed after my father died, but she hung on more than ten years while we took care of each other. She said she'd tough it out only until I got married. She almost made it. I wondered if I was now completely alone.

"Ida is pregnant, you idiot. Almost seven months. Couldn't you even tell? Some marriage you've got there, Mr. Man-About-Town."

I made a noise in my throat.

"Paula drove up with her to Reno. They're going someplace where they'll take care of her. This all news to you?"

I crumpled the note. Before I could hang up the phone, Mary's tinny voice said, "You had no idea, right? Am I right?"

The heavy black receiver slid from my hand and rattled back into the cradle.

Blind, I bolted upright. Somewhere in the dark, the phone was ringing. I threw off the clammy bedclothes and lurched to my feet. A dozen rings. More. I made no move for the phone.

Had to be Ida. That two-timing bitch. Or one of the shrew sisters. Maybe helpless Hack. Or that sneaky son of a bitch O'Connor. Any of them. All of them. Trying to ruin me. Trying to break into my house.

My eyes adjusted. This didn't feel like home anymore. Floral wallpaper, velvet cushions, quilted bedspreads. I recognized it all. But none of it registered as part of my life.

The ringing finally stopped. At the telephone table, the last jangle still throbbed in my ears. I'd left the strand of rosary beads there: my mother's. I'd been carrying them for years. For her. I picked them up. I couldn't recite a rosary on a bet. As if it mattered. Some people thought that church stuff gave them an edge, but my card said we're all on our own, just slugging it out. Even odds, or worse.

Sitting on the rug, back against the wall, I looked at the crumpled linens on the bed. I ran the beads and cross and fragile silver chain through my fingers. The cross was cool, its edges worn smooth. My mother used to give it to me to hold when I was scared.

Almost seven months pregnant.

It was just over two months since we buried Gig. That next night, when I got home late from Winterland—Ida wanted to do it, even after we'd had a hell of a dust-up. Woke me up, begging for that baby. She'd been doing that more often during those weeks, it occurred to me.

Now I was wise to the setup. Ida was already knocked up by then. She tried to coax me into fucking her to cover up the pregnancy. So she could later claim that it was mine. Not possible. I was always too careful. She used to cry when I broke the mood, when I stopped fooling around to put on a rubber. Pretty soon there wasn't any point to it. We stopped going through the motions altogether when it became clear that I wasn't interested in having a child.

Whoever got her pregnant must have put it to her right in this bed, one night while I was working. Maybe lots of nights.

My body broiled, like the rug and wall were on fire. If I could just make it to the light, just a few more hours, everything would be all right. Back in the circuit.

Hail Mary, full of grace, one on top of the other, I stacked prayers. *The Lord is with thee* clacking them end to end like I was building a wall *Blessed art thou amongst women* not thinking, just mouthing the magic words over and over, trying to fill all the cracks with mortar *And blessed is the fruit of thy womb, Jesus.*

The chain burst apart in my hands. I threw the rosary beads across the room.

Still before dawn, the street lamps burning, I sat in the breakfast nook, dressed for work, swallowing oatmeal. I left the pot and bowl in the sink, but then did a pivot. I put on a grease-speckled apron, soaped and rinsed the pot and bowl, and set them on the counter to dry.

At daybreak I boarded an inbound "L." Suit sharply pressed, shoes buffed to a gleam, tie knotted tight as a pea, I was as slick and colorful as a nine-ball nestled in a fresh rack. On the back of an envelope I listed all the calls I had to make that day. Work was what mattered. Nobody had to know my wife left me. It wouldn't even occur to them.

As the sun rose over the downtown buildings, I navigated the Market Street bustle, into the buzz of the newsroom. I hammered the phone hard, tapping East Coast contacts. A cacophony of voices, gab, and gossip came across the blower. I scrawled copious notes, propped up sloppy quotes, and banged out punchy copy. By afternoon I had managed to get lost in the circuit, ricocheting in the clattering mix.

It paid to maintain two separate lives.

The circuit was my real home. No question. Moving south of the Slot, hiking Kearny to North Beach, jumping a cable car over Russian Hill, doubling back to the International Settlement. For me it was like going from kitchen to bedroom to bath. News streamed through pool halls, newsstands, saloons, gymnasiums, hash houses, nightclubs. You overheard it stepping off a street corner. Shouted from a cruising Buick, it darted down a one-way alley only to drift back into the current somewhere downriver. A rumor, tossed across the bar at the Spur Club like a message in a bottle, washed up over dinner at John's Grill not an hour later.

Every day my job was to rise to the bait, follow the leads, see the patterns, and keep the minutes. I'd never been more grateful to have it.

SECTION S FRIDAY, JULY 2, 1948 CCCC*

AN AMERICAN PAPER FOR THE AMERICAN PEOPLE

MONARCH OF THE DAILIES

San Francisco Inquirer Sports

REG US PAT OFF

Through THE ROPES

By BILLY NICHOLS

Local launderers must be doing land-office business today. Pugs and politicos alike are pulling out the formal wear and giving it a good pressing, so they'll look presentable for Sunday's opening of the Daily Double, local sportsman Jimmy Ryan's posh new club on Polk. We hear The Gent has gone all out to make his place the crown jewel of San Francisco nightlife.

"I'm proud to open my doors on the Fourth of July," Ryan told us, "so we can celebrate independence and free enterprise in proper style."

A hot rumor

Gig Liardi, recently missing from the local action, may be in New York. Word filtered in the other day that he passed through Grossinger's Gym, asking the whereabouts of former champ Tony Canzoneri. He battled Canzo, you'll remember, for the lightweight crown back in the days. We burned up the wires trying to track him down, but my East Coast sources came up empty. Come home, Gig. All is forgiven. . . .

9

The Daily Double. Spelled out in electric blue neon script, it floated over a mural of tumbling dice, galloping racehorses, leggy chorines, and swingin' jazzmen. The tableau was rendered in heroic WPA salt-of-the-earth style. Jimmy Ryan had few equals when it came to nose-thumbing moxie.

A blast of be-bop blew over me as I swung into the grand opening of Ryan's new club. The joint was jammed and jumping. I surrendered my invite to Pete Donovan, a fading light-heavy working the door, and surveyed Jimmy's dream-come-true. The project had been under wraps for months. Tonight it busted out in high style. The town hadn't seen such reckless ritz since well before the war.

Everything was done up in a high-toned Chinoise. Black lacquer tables and chairs, trimmed in glistening red. Barmaids slinked the theme along, their lush shapes filling out satin China-doll brocade gowns. Jimmy was looking to shanghai the atmosphere of old Barbary Coast pleasure palaces.

Drinkers held noisy sway in the front third of the club. Diners were ushered to posh, dimly lit booths in the rear. Dandies and their dates spun around a dance floor in the middle. A five-piece band wailed away to the right, with a white-suited finger-popping Louis Jordan sound-alike fronting the show.

Enveloping the interior were huge murals, male and female athletes sketched at the sinewy apex of their sporting endeavors. Had to be Howard Brodie's work. Brodie was a popular local artist who was the beneficiary of constant bidding wars by the *Inquirer* and *Chronicle*. Neither paper offered him the canvas Jimmy did: buttery rich walls twenty feet high, bathed in Louvre-like light. For the swells, the sports theme may have clashed with the fine china—I saw it as Ryan's nod to what paid the freight.

I elbowed past the local luminaries and came up for air at the bar. Four mixologists plied the duckboards, swirling, shaking, and pouring nonstop. The bar was made of heavy glass blocks, through which ribbons of red neon cast a lurid and alluring glow. Reflected in the silver mirror, five tiers high, was the most comprehensive catalog of booze I'd ever seen. No call would go unserved in Jimmy's joint.

One of the barticians pegged me and comped a rock and rye, which I nursed while soaking up the play. The Daily Double was so ripe it was leaking juice. I could have killed an hour playing connect-the-dots with the operators in attendance. A Who's Who of local How-to. Old money down from Pacific Heights, the generals rubbing shoulders for one night with the grunts who actually ran the machine. Union honchos from the building trades and service locals. A wary group from DA Brown's office, including Pat's chief assistant, Tom Lynch. They'd be camera shy, for sure. Supervisors Chester McPhee, Dan Gallagher, P. J. McMurray—toasting Jimmy, one more mick made good. Judge Herman Van Der Zee, stiffly appraising the proceedings, careful not to get any on himself. Competing scribes from various rags worked the crowd, photographers in tow. I saw Seymour, dangling his bulky camera like a blackjack, his eyes mining the crowd with devious intent. Mixing and matching, scouting for something nice and embarrassing. They saw him coming: bastions of morality jockied to avoid being frozen in a flash-pop with any players of ill-repute.

Ryan had even invited—I assumed—his rival for the town's drop, Bones Remmer. That took stones. Remmer, who tipped the scales at close to three hundred, respected Ryan enough to put in an appearance. When Jimmy started crafting his handbooks into a real operation, Bones didn't go Chicago on him. West Coast guys had a more live-and-let-live approach to vice. Bones let Jimmy have his play, and he turned his sights on the State Line action growing around Tahoe and Reno. Some of Remmer's cannoli-eating pals installed him as gaming manager of the Cal-Neva Lodge and Casino, a mountain retreat for gambling grannies and rusticating racketeers. Bones looked flush. His local take was nickel and dime compared to the Cal-Neva skim.

I had to smile, pondering my position in the scheme of things. Boxing threaded through it all. It pulled its players—fighters, trainers, managers, matchmakers, promoters, boosters—from the same sweaty pool as the unions. Gambling floated the whole thing. Prize money was pocket change. It was the nonstop flow of discretionary cash that drew the grifters and gangsters to the sport. The spoils got funneled into legit enterprises. Political patronage and well-funded lobbies kept elected do-gooders in check. I helped sell the spectacle to the uptowners, with a tease, a taste, a little dangerous slumming. There was something wholly satisfying about folding the cream together with the grease and stirring well.

This evening, Jimmy was a four-star chef, cooking up a heartily corrupt soufflé.

I circulated toward the rear, looking for our host. He was gliding through the crowd, natty as ever in a tuxedo pressed razor sharp. He beelined to a prime booth. With good reason. There sat the hefty hub from which all spokes emanated:

Artie Samish. He had both hands deep into trucking, labor, liquor—and all the graft that filled the cracks between them. Samish was the guy who called shots at the capital. A "lobbyist" in political parlance. He could get it done, or undone. His office was downtown in the Kohl Building, just three well-trod blocks from the DA. He was the man who taught Mickey Cohen the finer points of power brokering, polishing a strong-arm thug into a kingpin. Cohen didn't undo his trousers without consulting his mentor.

Around Samish, Jimmy ditched the attitude and got deferential. It was only right: without Samish's pull, San Francisco could be less than hospitable to a left-handed entrepreneur like Jimmy Ryan.

"Eddie's gonna love this."

Behind me, the unmistakable raspy cackle of Burney Sanders. His starched cuffs stuck too far out of the tuxedo sleeves. Rental.

"Oh, yeah," I said. "Jimmy's stealing his thunder."

We shook—Burney limply offering his left. He clutched something tall and blue in the right.

"What the hell is that?"

"Some daffy shit. House special, the guy told me. Tastes like coconut and aftershave. How do you figure a dirty mick like Jimmy pitching all this hoity-toity crap? Look at him over there, greasing Samish. Where does he get off?"

"The penthouse. Christ, Burney—you sound jealous."

Sanders scanned the undulating crowd, wiping a bubble of blue froth off his lip. "Well, Bill, I'm here to report that Jimmy ain't the only guy bringing back the glory days. It's a go with the Bucket of Blood."

"That's great. Good for you." I saluted him with the dregs of my drink. "How'd you finally scrape up the scratch?"

Burney shook the chimney glass, swirled the contents, cast a jaundiced eye on it. He turned to a woman at the bar, a big peacock feather sprouting from her hat. He set the rest of the drink in front of her, ignoring the glare of the dame's date.

"Here. My compliments.

"Can't tell you that right now," Burney said, turning my way. "It's kinda on the QT."

"It's what? Who the hell you talking to? You don't hold out on me. Who's staking you?"

"No can do. My guy don't want the pub. It could look bad. He's what you'd call a silent partner. He wants to keep it that way. The good news is, I hired a solid crew for the renovation. Some good union Joes, giving me a break. I figure we'll be able to show in four months. I'm gonna keep it like it was, just class it up. I'll be the promoter and the matchmaker—plus I'll own the fucking building. The hat trick. Put that in your pipe and smoke it."

Out of the pack edged Sid Conte, the custard suit broad and billowy. He must have owned twenty of them. The choppers flashed by reflex when he saw us. That didn't take a bite out of the anxiety that clung to him.

"Hey, Sid. Good to see you," I lied. My hand stayed out there, dangling off the end of my arm.

"Sorry, Bill." Conte twitched his arm nervously. The smile throttled back to an uneasy grin. In the wash of red light from the bar, both Burney and I could see the white tape wrapped thickly around the fingers of Conte's right hand. Three digits braced by splints. Only the pinkie wiggled free, its lonely chunk of gold reflecting a bloody glint.

"Somebody slam the bedroom window on that?" Burney drawled, deadpan.

"Funny. A blue-hair caught it in the door of an Oldsmobile. My fault. I knew she was just putting me through the paces. I can tell buyers from browsers. I shoulda told her to drift. I was too nice. Ah, my own fault."

Conte's jumpy eyes searched the crowd. On the lookout for that two-hundred-and-fifty-pound blue-haired bone-breaker right now. If Hack hadn't tipped me to Conte's being deep into Ryan's debt book, I might have bought the little old lady story.

"I hear Hack's off into the wild blue yonder," Burney said. He was so quick to ride people, Burney sometimes mixed *himself* up.

"Wild blue yonders would be the Air Force," I corrected. "You mean more like 'Anchors Aweigh.' "

"Whatever. Where's that leave you, Sid?" Burney nudged.

"Up Shit's Creek. They'll probably only want him to do charity shows. That's money for them, not me. The timing is fucked. I was ready to roll. Burnett's a slugfish. Hack could take the state belt from him easy."

"You're not going to drop him, are you?" I asked.

"Nah. But I don't know how long I can wait."

"Get him some good exhibitions while he's in," Burney advised. "Then yank him out in six months, and I'll see what I can do about headlining him and Burnett. Get a state title fight up here, in the city."

"Thomas'll want some of that," I said. Lou Thomas was coming on strong as the town's top promoter. He and upstart Burney fought tooth and nail for any bout that smelled like a big gate.

"Fuck Lou. I get National Hall going again, I'll be the man around here. You know what I'm going to call my outfit? The American Boxing Club. A-B-C. I'm gonna be bringing the fight game back around here. All the way back. Write it up."

Burney looked around, like he'd dropped something.

"Shit, we gotta toast to that. Sid—buy me a decent drink."

Schmoozing ate another hour. I paid my respects to Jimmy, but passed on his offer of another drink. My brain might misplace some of the evening's dope if I got looped. When Johnny Tarantino told me he was headed out to cruise his nightly route, I tagged along. The tiny Tarantino was known as Jockey John. He'd been a top earner in the silks until a hard spill almost broke his back. Couldn't saddle up after that. Everybody figured him for a horse trainer, but he steered clear of the stables, like a heartbroken lover icing an old flame. "If I can't ride 'em, I can't look at 'em," he said. The best was over for him, but he wouldn't break. He started training fighters instead, and was now a good cornerman. Wrapped hands better than anybody.

We left the Daily Double about eleven. Jockey John was delivering the next day's *Racing Form* to his drops around town. Eddie Ryan fixed him up with the job, a way to stay connected to the tracks. Even as it approached midnight, the weather held clear and mild. The ga-ga bars and restuarants closed and the street ramble trickled to a scattered few. The town seemed small, like a miniature village inside one of those peeping-hole Easter eggs.

Not once did Jockey John ask me why all of a sudden—after knowing him five years—I was riding shotgun on his route. He may have sensed I wasn't quite right, he may have thought I had some problems at home—but it just didn't matter. We were hooked up in the circuit. You didn't throw a wrench in when it was arcing nicely. I remembered when

Chicky Hannifin, face all pink and maudlin, came to the Waffle Inn one night bursting with some big personal problem. He flopped down at a table, but before he could say a word, Jockey John wrapped an arm around him and said: "Don't do it, Chick. Don't drop your drawers. That's all we'll remember when you're dead."

We turned off Taylor onto Ellis. Ed Barrows and Mickey Leary were stepping from beneath the entry awning to a second-story pool hall. Barrows, dapper and dignified, could have passed for a preacher: actually he was a track cashier and billiard hustler. Leary was a mutuel clerk at Golden State, and freelanced a handicap chart for the *Call-Bulletin*. Leary customarily sported spit-shined cap-toed shoes and a straw boater. He hailed from back East and claimed to have given Runyon the idea for "The Lemon Drop Kid."

Jockey John eased the car curbside and slapped a *Form* on each of them. "How'd you do tonight?" he asked Barrows, nodding at the cue case.

"Kept it small," Barrows said, smiling. "I like to come back here."

"Where'd you get those cuff links?" Jockey John baited Leary. Everybody knew the answer. Leary had apprised us all, whenever possible.

"Compliments of my good friend Mickey Rooney," he replied, straight-faced.

"No shit?" mocked Jockey John.

"He's twice your size too, you little dago dwarf." Leary smiled.

We drove on. Above us, behind windows cracked open to catch any balmy breeze, citizens plumped their pillows. Down on the streets, you could almost sense a slender trail of Jimmy Ryan's blue neon, threading through town, still crackling quietly. In various back rooms, the day's take was being tallied. Menus, and odds, updated for the morning boards. Back at the plant, the presses rumbled with the dawn edition.

The city nodded off. The circuit kept on humming.

10

Nichols col for 7/9

Hack Escalante is fighting for Uncle Sam now. The local heavy has pulled another hitch with the Navy. He spent a year of the Big Fuss at sea, combing the coast for Japs. Remember the good old days, when all we feared coming ashore was contraband Canadian Club?

Hack hoped to be stationed locally, but the brass just shipped him to San Diego.

There are plenty of naysayers around town who will crow when they read this news. These are the boys who hooted that Hack looked used-up in his June fight against Carmel Whitten, before he rallied late to cop a split decision.

Lieutenant Colonel Emmett Bishop, a naval doctor and ardent ring fan, has taken an interest in Escalante's welfare. He told me the other day that after watching Hack's go-round with Whitten, he couldn't figure why a young husky like the local lad appeared to tire so easily. "I'm recommending they give him a steady diet of vitamins," said Dr. Bishop. "We call them morale-builders. In his shape, at his age, he should have the stamina of a bull."

> So. Cal. fistic fans may get to see for themselves if the good doc's prescription pays off. There's talk of Hack being tapped to headline a veterans' charity show at San Diego's Memorial Auditorium within the next month.

I let it go at that. Doc Bishop was a windbag: he tinned my ear for almost thirty minutes on the phone. I shit-canned all his psychiatric mumbo jumbo.

"I don't think there's anything physically wrong with him," Bishop had said. "It's all in his mind. Tell him he's tired, he'll be tired. Tell him he looks like hell, he'll look like hell. We'll fill him with horse pills and tell him he's getting healthier and stronger—then see what happens."

I didn't share my diagnosis with this crackpot headshrinker: guilt was devouring the poor kid like cancer. Just the same, I leapt at the chance for an official, albeit bogus, alibi to help explain away Hack's morose behavior.

I had a copy boy run the sheet to Fuzzy, then sifted the morning mail. Amid the usual flak was yet another letter from Ida. They arrived once or twice a week now, addressed only:

BILLY NICHOLS, INQUIRER, S.F.

She never sent them to the house. I took it as her recognition that this was my real address.

I tapped the blunt end of my Soft Black Extra Smooth 722 on the envelope. I already knew what was inside. The same routine, over and over. She'd go on about the Nevada heat, what she'd had to eat that day, or some funny thing she'd seen on her way to the post, and what lowlifes all the cowpokes were up there. Like she was keeping a vacation journal. Then she'd lob in a grenade, smooth as you please: "The doctor says I'm doing fine and it might be any day now."

Lately, the letters had gotten stranger, pleading for me to write, to visit. All coated with a syrup of *Sweeties* and *Honeys* and breathy scribblings about how we could set everything right if only I'd come to see her.

This morning's letter I left sealed. I'd gotten tired of copy-editing all of Ida's spelling and grammatical gaffes.

The phone rang.

"Nichols." My hard-ass voice.

"Billy . . . Francis O'Connor." The brogue that ought to have been soothing.

It was almost a month since he braced me at the Ringside. I figured his "witness" had fallen down. If there'd ever been one.

"What can I do for you?"

"You never ran that teaser I provided, about our absent impresario, Mr. Gig Liardi."

"A judgment call. It seemed flimsy. Nothing personal."

"Oh, agreed. Still, it's a shame you weren't tempted. Might have had yourself a *scoop*."

Reflexively, I flipped over Ida's envelope, exposing a clean field. The fat pencil was poised in my hand. It felt like part of me was floating away, watching some other guy at my desk going through the motions.

"How's that?" I heard myself say.

As O'Connor talked, my fingers pushed the pencil rapidly over the back of the envelope. The clear field filled in quickly; someone was taking the notes that could bury *Mr. Boxing*.

★

O'Connor's call yielded four terse grafs. I beckoned over the boy and handed him the new sheet. The kid was about fifteen, skinny and blasé. Nothing like the tail-wagging brown-noser I once was. The penciled scrawl across the top of the sheet read: "New lede."

I felt empty, cored out, as though I'd filed my own obit.

Nothing left to do, no place else to go. I walked my usual composing room beat. Soaking it up, like I was walking the last mile. Hot metal was still flying into chases, but it was a slow news day. The Tokyo war tribunal had finally come in with a guilty verdict on Tojo and his henchmen. It only took two years. An Eastern seaboard dock strike threatened to spread to all coasts. Shipowners saw Reds everywhere. Some things never change. Patio furniture was on sale at Weinstein's. Macy's was pitching fly-front ladies slacks, whatever they were, $8.95 a pair.

I skipped the headline stories. You pick those up from office chatter and the radio. The filler, the incidentals used to plaster over little gaps between the articles and the ads, that's what always caught my eye.

WOMAN KILLS SELF
IN L.A. HOTEL LEAP

Los Angeles—July 10 (INS)—Mrs. Marie M. Samuels, 48, today ended her life with a leap from the fourth-story window of a downtown hotel. Several telegrams addressed to her son by a former marriage, Vernon K. Perkingson of San Francisco, were found in her room. None of these had been sent. Police reported the woman had separated from her current husband, Paul Samuels, two weeks earlier. Police reports noted the woman had first slashed her wrists with a razor before jumping to her death.

I gave a nod to Mike, quickest typesetter on staff. Been in the boiler room more than twenty years, since they built every word by hand. He could feed a chase with his eyes closed. Neat trick when you're doing it backward. I'd been slipping him tickets for years. He knew my old man, remembered when I was nothing but a yapping pup.

"We got your column set," Mike said. "Barney nearly shat when he proofed it. Ain't that something—whatd'ya think happened?"

"We'll see where it goes."

"Could be a helluva story in there. You gonna follow up?"

"You bet."

Along the assembling table, I scanned the filler items. This was how the common folk made it into the paper—little eight-point tragedies, plugging holes in the vast sails of the Hearst flagship.

TRAIN BEHEADS TODDLER

Mother Cooks Dinner Nearby
While Child Dies

> Edward Taliaferro, 5, son of Mr. and Mrs. James Taliaferro of Fresno, was decapitated by a northbound Santa Cruz to San Francisco excursion train yesterday. The child had been playing on the right of way while his mother prepared the family dinner in a trailer parked on the highway alongside the tracks. The train crew, unaware of the accident, did not stop.

I walked from the composing room to the imposition tables inside the foundry. Mike's previous form was already having proofs pulled from it. A press-checker and proofreader gave the page thumbs-up. A couple of new molders, guys I didn't know, hurriedly rinsed ink residue from the form, prepping it for the soft paper flong. The hydraulic press would then stamp a matrix—an imprint of the full page.

I picked a spent matrix from the trash, one from which stereoplates had already been made. The top of the page was dominated by a three-column halftone shot of a guy sprawled dying in an Ellis Street gutter. The photo was credited to a fortunate amateur, on the scene when a cop shot the unlucky crook. The guy was trying to lift twenty bucks from the till of the Edison Hotel. Would he live? I'd keep on wondering: without the sensational Weegee-style photo, there'd never be a follow-up.

Lower on the page, next to the big appliance ads, two more squibs:

MOTHER HELD, KILLED BABY

Following her confession that she had killed her baby daughter "so that no one would know I had it," Miss Nora Hernandez, 27, was held to answer to the Alameda County Superior Court yesterday on a charge of manslaughter. She made her admission in pleading guilty to the manslaughter charge before Police Judge A. W. Bruner in San Leandro.

THROAT SLASH FATAL

Los Angeles—July 10 (INS)—His throat slashed ear to ear with a razor, the body of Demetrius Mahas, 45, a cook, was found last night in front of his apartment.

"How 'bout this weather, huh?" said a foundry worker as he shuffled past me, carrying the fresh hard-baked matrix to the casting department. There it would be curved onto a cylinder beside the concave, with molten metal poured between them to form a plate for the presses. A previous chase, made up by Mike only minutes earlier, was being lugged back to the composing room, its brief mission accomplished. It would await the next edition or else be broken apart for reuse—the display type rearranged into other heads, other splats of daily drama. I dropped the matrix back into the trash and headed out through the pressroom.

All my life, this was the safest place in the world. When you worked for the paper, you were immune to the onslaught, above the brutal judgments meted out in hot metal to poor, luckless slobs. It was in the cavernous pressroom that my father staked his claim in this town. Thanks to him, my career began there, too.

"Billy Nichols" was born one night in 1928. I came on shift and saw Jack Lewis's desk completely clean. Lewis was the daily boxing guy.

"Let me see you over here," Jake Galloway, the editor, yelled.

My face got hot. I'd deferred to Jack Lewis in every way. Never passed a smart remark about him. But I'd finally worn him down. For two years I'd made it to every fight card, playing chin music with the managers, promoters, and matchmakers. A "good luck" and a "great fight" for every boxer. Soon Galloway had me cover fights Lewis couldn't. I'd glad-hand like Herbert Hoover at ringside, swapping news and stories. Found I could go entire conversations without taking the cigar out of my mouth.

Now water rings and cigarette burns on the desktop were the only trace of the Jack Lewis decade at the Monarch of the Dailies.

"Said he got a bid from a sheet in St. Louis. That would be his old hometown," Galloway reported skeptically. "So as to be near his mother. Apparently she's on her last legs."

"That's rough," I said. "I hope it all works out for him."

"Rough? It's a load of shit, is what it is. Nobody quits this paper to go be a candy-striper. Don't kid yourself. You outhustled his ass." Galloway glared. "You gave him a beating and he never even took a swing at you. You turned him into a full-time juicehead. Not that it took much work."

I stared down at the painted swirls on my new tie, feeling a flush climb higher up my cheeks.

"So you'll take his desk, if that's suitable. Meanwhile, let's talk about your name."

"What about it?"

"Nobody's going to read anything by a kid named Nicholovich. What is that, Russky? Czech? Drop it—or the micks and wops'll never trust you. Lewis's real name was Levitz, you know—a Jew. You gotta make it clean, none of this Old Country shit. Whole new ball game over here. The paper, the movies, they've gotta be above it all. Use your real name and they'll say, 'He must be related to that fucking bohunk butcher, poisoned my cousin with some bad meat.'"

I laughed. "Same with fighters," I recited, like a wise old sage of the ring. "Willie Ritchie's real name was Gerhardt Steffen. Jews, they all want Irish names."

"Let's just shorten yours. Billy Nichols. It's punchy. Jangles. Like money in your pocket. That's really good. That's what it is, starting tomorrow. Now go give me six good column inches worthy of the name."

Hoists fed giant reels of paper to the presses. Rotary pumps delivered rivers of ink from supply vats to the presses' receivers. *All clear* was sounded and the cylinders revolved. Early sheets read fresh and clear, no adjustment needed. As the presses gathered speed, the roar grew louder.

The predatory eagle, the newspaper's logo, spread its talons above the masthead. A banner furled around its wings, inscribed *An American Paper for the American People.*

Between the proud bird and the box touting RACE RESULTS was the tiny union "bug." You'd never notice it unless you were looking. To hear my father tell it, that bug was the most important thing we printed every day.

My father wasn't at his station when I ambled into the plant that day in '28. I was playing cool, but I couldn't wait to tell the old man his kid would be getting a byline. I meandered beneath towering machinery. The skeleton crew didn't pay me any mind. No use in shouting. My voice couldn't squeak past the thunder of the presses.

I figured I'd drift over to Breen's and see if my promotion rated a free beer. Moving through the back bay, I dropped down off the dock and headed for the rear exit gate. Then I noticed a cluster of guys huddled in the shadows. Among them, my father's posture: hands pressed into his lower back, bending like a bow. You could practically *hear* the pain.

This wasn't a normal smoke break, I realized as I got closer. Between the wind and the rumbling presses I couldn't hear too clearly. But I picked it up enough to stop me in my tracks.

"I say we wait. See if these guys can really organize. Fact is, they got broke before."

"Why risk it at all? They need us more than we need them."

"No! Don't you get it?" My father's voice. "We're lucky that we got a decent union. When I came on I had nothing. Played it straight with the local and it did right by me. Without the shop I'd still be scrounging odd jobs."

"But what's the good right now? Nothing. We can only lose. We get behind these guys, the boss starts screaming that we're Red. Next day they're marching scabs in here with a police escort. I got a family—you do, too. You can afford to take that risk?"

"You get it all right," my father said, poking another worker in the chest. "You just don't have any guts. This is all about your family, and mine, and his and his and his. It's about everybody getting a fair shake. Not just today—always."

"You heard what they're thinking about?" someone else's angry voice cut in. "Boxes—metal boxes on the corner to hold the papers. People put the money in, pull out a paper. No more stand agents, no more newsboys. Then why not machines that load paper to the press? Machines that stack 'em in the truck? A machine that *drives* the fucking truck—they'll do it soon as they figure out how."

"See—same point. That's why we have to join. This stuff happens fast. You need to face a simple truth: workers won't ever get their hands on the money. That's why we have to take control of the work!"

"We'll talk to them," my father said. "There's a Sunday meeting at the longshoremen's hall. I want to let them know they can count on us. I want us all agreed. Think about it."

The discussion ended. Glowing cigarettes moved my way. The announcement of my big promotion would keep. I didn't need resentful stares from the pressmen as I crowed about my desk job. I hid while they shuffled past.

★

Back on the line, my father wiped the last of the ink residue from a blanket.

"You ready?" he asked.

"I got the job." I'd removed my new, crisp fedora. Dad didn't view it as a wise expenditure.

"You're going to be a reporter?" He eyed me closely.

"Yeah," I mumbled. "They're giving me Jack Lewis's job."

Expressionless, he wiped his hands, then tossed the cloth into a big bin.

"What about Lewis?" He motioned for me to walk with him.

I shrugged. "Don't know. Quit, they said. His name was Levitz, you know."

My father went into the washroom. I didn't follow. Minutes later, he went to his locker and put on his coat and hat.

"You get a contract?" he asked.

"Not yet. Already wrote my first story, though. It'll be in tomorrow."

I decided not to mention the name change yet.

"Get it in writing," my father said, draping his arm around me. "Get everything in writing. Salary, work schedule, days off, everything. Let me look it over. Put your hat on."

We walked out the back. He paused to bellow at some cronies, still clutching me around the neck. "Hey—do it right! You're printing my son's stuff!"

It was either a baptism or a confirmation. Now here I was, twenty years later, on the same spot. I'd built a kingdom for myself in this building, where I lived at a safe remove. But the siege was on the way. One more wrong move and I'd be down there with the peasants.

I craned my neck to read an item on the back of the News section as the papers flew off the end of the run. The words shimmered as sheet after sheet was whisked away and replaced. They got slapped and stacked and folded, propelled into their one-day life span.

BOY, 15, HANGS HIMSELF

Student's Body Found by
His Sister

The nude body of Russell E. Jones, an El Cerrito High School freshman, was found hanging yesterday in the basement of his family home at 5434 Alameda Avenue, Richmond. The youth's father, Robert C. Jones, said Russell had gone downstairs Tuesday morning. His family did not search for him until yesterday. When they found the basement door locked, a sister, Rhoda, crawled in through a window and found the body.

The parents said the youth had been moody. Police, who found no note, said the boy had stuck pins in his chest before tying his feet together and then hanging himself.

Nasty business, living. The kid just needed an escape route. Something to point the way above the shit and the fear. A job writing about it, for instance.

I squeezed through the bustle at the rear truck bays, hungry for air. I waved off shouted *How are ya's* and walked up Market to Powell. Thought about heading up Leavenworth to the gym. Couldn't face it. Ducked into States for a light lunch. Left an egg salad sandwich untouched. By the time I paid the bill, the *Inquirer* driver was off the truck and trading the morning paper for the two-star edition.

I opened one to Sports, searching out my column. I felt like a three- year-old: if I closed and opened my eyes, it'd all be gone. No dice. It was there, as always, in black and white.

SECTION S SATURDAY, JULY 10, 1948 CCCC*

AN AMERICAN PAPER FOR THE AMERICAN PEOPLE — MONARCH OF THE DAILIES

San Francisco Inquirer Sports

REG US PAT OFF

Through THE ROPES

By BILLY NICHOLS

The mystery of Gig Liardi's whereabouts is over. Wish we had better news. Local police confirmed today that the body of the one-time lightweight contender was discovered yesterday in a remote area of Golden Gate Park.

According to homicide detective Francis O'Connor, the grisly discovery was made by a photography hobbyist and his model. Liardi's body had been partially dug up, probably by feral dogs that roam the far end of the park, near Ocean Beach.

Detective O'Connor is requesting anyone with information that may shed light on this shocking crime to come forward. "This won't go unpunished," O'Connor vowed.

We certainly hope not. To say we are stunned would be understatement. Gig was a fixture on the ring scene for more than twenty years. He gave champ Tony Canzoneri all he could handle in a challenge for the crown back in 1933. We always considered him one of the cleverest of mittmen. More recently he enjoyed success piloting the career of popular local heavyweight Hack Escalante.

On the subject of Escalante—he's doing his fighting for Uncle Sam now. The local heavyweight has hitched up with the Navy and

Mashing the paper into a jumble, I tucked it under my arm and considered taking a streetcar home. Call in sick the rest of the day. I leaned against the window of the Owl Drug Store and watched people pass for about ten minutes. Tourists lined up to ride a cable car over the hills to Aquatic Park or North Beach. My vision had the clarity of a condemned man at the gallows, listening to the creak of the trapdoor, waiting for the hood.

I dropped the paper in an ashcan and headed back to the office to finish out my shift. When they wanted to find me, that's where I'd be.

Playing out the string.

11

Eventually, I had to go back to the house. Lying on the bed, still in street clothes, I read a letter from an old pal, Johnny Rogers. He was on the road, writing from Cleveland. They'd hired him to help prop up a porcelain-jawed middleweight on his maiden crusade.

Shortly before eight o'clock the phone started. There was nothing good on the other end, so I let it ring itself out. The house was big and quiet and cold. I was paying the mortgage on a giant hotel room. I pondered relacing the shoes and heading down the hill to Joe's for dinner.

The damn phone started in again. This time I answered. Another momentous decision, but who knew?

"Is this Billy Nichols?" A woman's voice. But not one of the sisters. Thank Christ.

"Yeah."

"Hello, Billy. It's Claire Escalante."

"Is something wrong with Hack? He okay?"

"You never know, going by what you read in the papers. But I guess he's a damn sight better off than Gig."

"Yeah. That's a shame. It's a damn shame."

"Am I interrupting something?" She had some steady nerves.

"Ah, no. Well—dinner. I was just, we were about to go out."

"I called to get your feeling on the, well, the situation."

"Right. From what standpoint, in particular?"

"This doesn't look too good for Hack."

"How's that?"

"O'Connor's a real bull. He scared Hack half to death with his questions before. I'm afraid to think what happens now."

"You think O'Connor likes Hack as a suspect?"

"Don't you?"

"What I think is that if this cop does his job, he'll find a whole lot of guys pissed off enough to kill Gig. Hack might be pretty far down the list."

"Yeah, you might be right. It's just that . . ."

"Do you know where Hack was that night? When Gig went missing?"

"What's this—now you with the third degree?"

"If Hack's got an alibi, how is there a problem? You know where he was?"

Clicks and buzzes on the line. She was thinking it over.

"I know exactly where he was," Claire finally said.

"Which would be—where?"

"With me. Of course."

"Right. Well, there you go. No worries."

"Uh-huh." She wasn't done. "About that other thing you wrote. What that doctor said?"

"Was there a problem with it?"

"How come you never talk to a guy's wife when you do your stories? Why take the word of some quack? Bishop couldn't even hold a civilian job. He's supposed to understand my husband? Call *me* next time—I'll give you the real story."

"What story would that be?"

"One with more going on than you might realize."

"Meaning?"

"Meaning maybe you should get your facts straight about Hack. I could tell you some interesting things."

"What kind of things?"

"Never know—I might be a good interview."

"Why not come downtown tomorrow? You can tell me all about what it's like to be the wife of a prizefighter. Maybe I can work it into a special feature."

She laughed, sudden and strong. It took me back a little.

"You're serious?"

"Sure. There's a free lunch in it, at least."

She agreed. We set a place and time.

I entertained the notion that she was on the up-and-up. Maybe Hack hadn't told her about killing Gig. Maybe she was only protecting her meal ticket. None of it sat right. Something was up, and tomorrow at one o'clock, at the Clinton Cafeteria, I was going to find out what.

Our sparring conversation had sucked all the air out of the house. I could hardly breathe. So I strolled to Joe's and ordered a Bruno's Special and a glass of wine.

I hadn't even buttered my first hunk of sourdough when Frank Bennett sauntered in. Jesus, *he* had a wife and kids: how about going home to the family, Frank? He badged the old gal next to me, scooting her down a stool or two. Of course, he started right in:

"Howd'ya like this Liardi thing?"

"I'm not so good on facts," I said. "What do you hear? O'Connor chasing anything solid?"

"I'm not on top of it. But I'll listen up. Let you know if I hear anything hot. Maybe you can scoop the city desk. I gotta figure that'd be worth maybe *four* ringside seats."

He pulled a folded copy of the *Referee* from his inside topcoat pocket. He turned the pages until he came to this week's fight cards.

"Whod'ya like in this Ortega-Flores bout?"

12

She spruced up for our meeting, wearing a crisp white straw hat with a blue gardenia garnish, white gloves, and a snugly tailored dark blue dress accented by white polka dots. I'm sure I glanced a few too many times at the freckles splashed above her square-cut bodice. She struck me as the type who didn't mind the admiring double-takes. She wasn't just a dish. She was the blue-plate special. And she knew it.

Once we were seated we played around with chitchat for several minutes. I'd be lying if I said there was no blood rush, just being at the table with her. But a miniature cold shower came each time she asked about my *lovely* wife. After Claire's third query, I scotched the small talk, produced my notebook, and made like a real reporter.

"Hack can't read, can he?" You have to open strong.

She dusted bread crumbs off the table and stared at her iced tea before looking back at me.

"You get that from the night at Lucca's, or did you notice it before?"

"It hadn't occurred to me before then."

"Pretty sharp." Her look was more suspicious than admiring. Then she winced, at the memory of that night. "He does read—and write—a lot better than when we first met. Then he couldn't manage much more than his name. I've worked with him. We used to use your column for lessons. But in spots like that night at Lucca's, around people, he gets awful nervous. He's afraid they'll know."

She saw my pencil wasn't moving.

"Isn't this what they call 'human interest'?"

"I was just asking out of curiosity, not to embarrass anybody. If Hack can't read, that's nobody's business but your own."

"He isn't stupid."

I held palms up as Claire took a long pull of the tea, long enough to let her roll around how she wanted to get started. I expected her to just cut it loose right away, unravel that unspoken knot between us. But for what seemed like the hundredth time in the past few days, I was blindsided.

"Ralph—you knew that's Hack's real name? Ralph Gianotti? He was the baby, last of six kids. His dad had a feed and hardware store out the Ingleside. I never met the old man, but I've heard all the stories. Not nice ones. Mario, Mr. Gianotti, was strictly from the Old Country. Reputation as a real hard-nosed bastard. Ralph's mother was pregnant all the time. That way there'd always be kids to work the store. His sister, Marie, she was the only one went to school regularly. The old man wanted her good at math, so she could do his books. The boys were basically slaves. You get the picture. Mario had the proverbial iron fist. And he didn't spare the dago backhand.

"He once beat his wife when she suggested American names for the boys. They were getting picked on. Ralph's born name was Rafael. She had to go to the parish priest and beg him to tell Mario that it wasn't a sin to call Giuseppe 'Joe' or call Francesco 'Frank' . . ."

I was about to mention my own rehab'd name, but she wasn't about to be short-stopped.

"Anyway, Ralph was no good in school. He always fell behind, and once Mario saw how big and strong he was getting, he pulled him out and used him in the business.

Lugging stuff around, loading and unloading. If you ask me, Ralph's not . . . slow. He just never got a chance."

"Then how'd he end up getting into boxing? To be honest, he never struck me as the type."

"No kidding. I can't believe it myself sometimes. But if you have to know one thing about Ralph, it's that he's afraid. He once told me he was always afraid. All the time, of everything. He said that's why he did so lousy in school. Scared of the nuns, scared of other kids, scared they'd call him dumb, scared he'd be punished for being dumb. You name it—it scared him."

"Airplanes."

"That's another one! God, don't even start. How'd you know that?"

"On the train back from New York. We had a talk."

"That was one time Ralph was glad Gig was so cheap. The train was cheaper than a plane. He wouldn't have gone if he had to fly."

"Me neither. I'm like Hack that way. You'll never get me up there."

"Really? Oh, God, I'd love to fly away. Europe or someplace? Let's go."

She gazed through the front windows. The street ramble didn't seem to register. She was elsewhere, maybe some Paris café. I brought her back.

"Too bad about that New York trip," I said.

"Ralph cried two days straight when he came back." She picked up her glass and held it out in a mock toast. "To the late Gig Liardi—who couldn't find a payday if you shoved it up his ass."

All things being equal, it wasn't the most charitable statement. And it brought Gig to the table right when I was ready to cut him loose, at least for a while. Where would we go from there? Mercifully, our lunch arrived. Claire was the corned beef sandwich. I went for the brisket. She removed her gloves. A fresh application of the same scarlet nail polish from that Saturday at her house.

"So how'd Hack get into boxing if he was scared of everything?"

"You remember a fighter named Red Caits?"

"Sure. Light heavyweight from out the road. Hell of a left hook. Had a shot at the title."

"Ralph idolized him. Never saw him fight, he was just a kid. But Caits was from the neighborhood, and Ralph couldn't get over how this guy walked around—not a bully, but like he owned the street. Nobody could touch him. That's what Hack wanted more than anything, to have that kind of shell around him. That you-don't-mess-with-me thing."

"How old was he when he started boxing?"

"Fifteen. Sixteen, at the most. He'd take the streetcar to the Young Men's Institute on Oak Street. That's where he hooked up with Gig."

"I was there the day they met. I used to go there to check out the Golden Gloves prospects."

"So you *knew* him back then?"

"Not really. Just keeping tabs. Watch who's around, how they rate, who they tie up with. Hack may have been scared, but he had the one thing you look for. He never backed up. He was burly, so they put him in with Earl Booker. Booker was the middleweight champ of the Gloves. They didn't bother to tell Hack. Booker pasted him, but Hack never took a step back. You can teach everything else, but not that."

"You were there from the beginning. You've probably seen all his fights."

"Want to know the one that impressed me most?"

"I know—the second one against Carmel Whitten. That's what everybody says."

"No. This one's not even on his record. He ever tell you about the bout on Pier Seventeen?"

She leaned in, intrigued.

"Before he turned pro. We're talking 1934. He had to be a teenager. Labor organizers used to comb the gyms looking for mugs who could stand up to the imported muscle. Management, of course, was scouting the same talent, trying to buy 'em out. They'd use 'em as strikebreakers. You ever hear anything about this?"

"Not from Ralph."

"The first time I really saw your man fight was that day on Pier Seventeen. The stevedores were trying to keep a ship from loading. I got sent over from the paper because they were shorthanded. There were labor flare-ups all over town—too many to cover. So I ran down there from Third and Market, with a camera guy."

"I have *never* heard this—what happened?"

"The point guy for the goons was a big Norwegian bastard, name of Berquist or something similar. Big as Primo Carnera. Voice like a bullhorn. You could hear him from two blocks away. He was on the bumper of the lead truck, swinging a big club. He was crazy. I was off to the side—relatively safe—and I could hear the arguments about who was gonna take him on. The married guys, the guys with kids, they didn't want any part of this Berquist.

"Before you know it, there's this kid, right in front of the truck. I recognized him from the YMI, four or five months before. Hack—or Ralph, I guess, back then. He was gonna get his skull crushed. I couldn't stand to watch. That big goon's eyes lit up and he jumped down off the truck to get better purchase or whatever. He took a big swipe with that club and Hack stepped straight in—textbook form—right under it. He hit that big fucking Norwegian with about six body shots—*boom boom boom*—and Eric the Red kind of froze for a second. Like he couldn't believe it. Then Hack came up with a short right hand—couldn't have thrown it more than six inches. You could hear the guy's nose break. He just crushed it. Imagine you threw an egg against the wall. Stuff just slopped all down the front of him. Like you'd turned on a faucet, it's gushing out. And the big goon keels over face first.

"Forget it after that—all the dockers surged forward and started rocking the trucks and pulling out the drivers. It was unbelievable."

Claire's corned beef sandwich was hung up halfway to her mouth. She looked at me wide-eyed.

"Sorry," I said. "For the graphic description."

She set the sandwich back on the plate. I got a charge from telling her something about Hack she didn't know. I wanted to push the throttle, explain why that day stayed so vivid in my memory, as if it had been me in the middle. But how could I explain the paralyzing dread that went through me when I heard the Norwegian fucker's voice in that bullhorn? That's a story nobody knew, and never would. I switched gears.

"How did you and Hack meet?" I asked her.

"On the streetcar. We rode the same line. I'd seen him sitting there a few times, that grip full of gear in his lap.

He was big and kind of tough-looking, but underneath he was just a little boy. Like most men. He'd stare out the window, nervous, trying like hell to look as if he hadn't noticed me."

"And how did you know that?"

"Excuse *me*—he was the only guy in the car *not* looking. I sat next to him three times without him saying word one to me. I finally just started talking to him.

"He was amazed that I lived alone, I remember that. He didn't know anybody who lived by themselves. I was renting a studio apartment in North Beach. He couldn't even imagine a woman living like that. He lied about his age. Claimed he was twenty-two, but later I figured out that he had to be more like eighteen or nineteen."

"You were older."

"Still am." She grinned. "He was always headed over to Ryan's Gym when I'd see him on the car. I invited him to come by my apartment for dinner some night."

"Pretty forward."

"As I said—he was scared of everything. I had to take the initiative. But, Jesus, it must have taken three months for him to pick up on it. By this time he'd left home and was living with Gig. I think he told Gig he was going to a Jimmy Cagney movie over at the Casino or something."

"Why'd he have to lie?"

"Gig was overly protective, shall we say. Maybe he was worried that I'd take the fight out of his boy." The corners of her mouth crept back in a playfully wicked grin. Then she raised her big green eyes. "You men have some strange ideas, especially you guys mixed up in boxing."

"For example?"

"Poor Ralph was bouncing back and forth between me

and Gig. When he was with me, it was like he was breaking training. So Gig wasn't my biggest fan."

"The reason being . . . ?" I wasn't really that stupid. I just wanted to hear how she'd explain it.

"Let's just say that Gig taught Ralph all he needed to know about fighting. And I taught him everything else."

Holy hell—the kid never had a chance.

"Now I want to tell you about this reading thing. It's not a mental problem. A doctor I know said it might be a problem with how his eyes work. But we never had the money to pay for the tests that would prove it. Not to mention that for some reason he's afraid to. See, I want him to go to school, to take some classes. If he got badly hurt in a fight, so that he couldn't box anymore—he'd have trouble even filling out a job application.

"He's been under too much pressure," she went on. "That's why I wanted him to go back to the Navy. Give him a chance to get sorted out. He's a real brooder—he thinks and thinks and thinks. He might not say much, but never stops stewing over stuff. He'd be a better fighter too, I think, without all the pressure. He puts too much on himself. When I went back to work, he was furious. Threw a full-scale fit in the house, screaming that he could take care of his family without his wife having to work."

She noticed that my pencil hadn't budged. I'd set it on the notebook.

"Here's something you should write down—he's never hit me. I asked once why he never took a poke at me, what with all the times we've gone at it. Know what he said? It's because he knew he'd kill me. One good shot and I'd be dead."

"That must have scared you."

"It wasn't scary. It was actually sweet in a weird kind of way. He knows how strong he is. They talk about people who don't know their own strength. But Ralph knows he can't make a mistake."

It was the first opening she'd allowed since we sat down.

"And you don't think he's ever made a mistake?" I asked. It wasn't exactly hammering away at the opening, but the tentative jab seemed to land. She backpedaled for a spell. Drew out the ritual of putting her white gloves back on.

"I'm still standing," she finally said. "But if you mean could he have killed Gig—I told you—he was with me that night. Besides, my husband wouldn't think to bury a body out in Golden Gate Park. *His* brain doesn't exactly work that way."

She was quite the counter-puncher. I tried to adjust.

"All right, but how about you? We've only been talking all about Hack. What's your story?"

"Not much to it. Born in Tacoma, but I don't remember the place. My father moved us around a lot. One year we lived in Seattle. Then Portland. Lot of different parts of L.A., when he was trying to catch on at the studios. Mostly I remember him preaching every time that the next place would be the perfect place. The answer was just down the road. End-of-the-rainbow crap."

"What was his name? Your maiden name."

"McKenna. James Jerome McKenna and his wife, Francine. They had two daughters, Adele and me. He moved us—"

"What's your middle name?"

"Eleanor. Let me get on with this. He moved us here in the early thirties. He talked up all the opportunities, on account of the labor trouble. Good spot for a scab. Only he called it 'honest work for a free man not afraid of Commie gangs.'"

"I see. So did he get the steady work?"

"Some. But 'steady' wasn't the old man's strong suit."

"My father was the flip side of that coin."

"Union man?"

"Through and through. A pressman. They always had a solid shop. He was an organizer to boot."

"At the *Inquirer*?"

"Yeah. He got me my first job there. Copy boy."

"He still working? Or did he get a nice union pension?"

"He's dead."

"Sorry."

"How'd we start talking about me? Go on. You must have been in school when you moved here. Where'd you go?"

"Mission, the last two years. I graduated, though."

"More than you can say for me."

"Get out—where'd you go to college? Berkeley? Stanford?"

"Cogswell Polytechnic High. Far as I went. My claim to academic fame was getting suspended for giving an oral report about sneaking into the fights at the old Bucket of Blood. Too many gory details. As you might have noted earlier."

"You mean National Hall? Over on Sixteenth and Capp?"

"You know it?"

"Ralph had his first pro fight there. You really never went to college at all? I thought writers had to have the big pedigree."

"It's the knack more than the diploma. If I can't spell, my editor can. Where'd you get *your* degree?"

"Ha, ha—thanks for the boost. I had other fish to fry. I needed cash to get the hell out of the house."

"How's that?"

"The old man walked out. Packed some clean shirts and a big bourbon habit in his cardboard suitcase and vamoosed. No clue where he ended up. But when I walked the streets, I could never look at the soup lines. Walked right past every guy begging a nickel."

"Afraid you'd see your father panhandling?"

"Right. In which case I'd have popped him a good one."

"So how'd you make ends meet?"

"Name it. I've been working since I was sixteen. Milliner's assistant. Seamstress. Shopgirl for a jeweler on Market Street. Not Samuel's, the smaller one down the block. Pretty good job. The boss liked me and I learned a lot about stones. Later, of course, that all fell apart. But I got by. Doing whatever."

A forlorn thought, or memory, passed through her eyes. She tilted her chin toward me, casting it off: "Why do men fight?" she asked.

"To prove themselves," I said, without much hesitation.

She smiled. "That's just what I figured. To show they're good enough. That they're worth something even if they come from nothing. That's it, huh?"

"I've never met a rich fighter—at least none born that way."

"I'd have made a good fighter." She nodded. "But what's a poor girl to do? How do we prove ourselves? Marrying the right guy? Having kids? Keeping a neat house? A nice garden?"

"I figured you for the nursery business. That backyard is really something."

"That's so sweet of you to say." Claire reached her regloved hand across the table and touched my arm. She held on for a moment.

"It's mostly luck," she demurred. "And the ocean air helps

an awful lot. And I guess I am good at it. I really love that garden."

"What about your mom? She still around?"

"That's how I met Ralph—playing the dutiful daughter. I guess we both were doing our duty riding that streetcar."

"How's that?"

"I'd go every week from North Beach out to the Mission, to visit her. I'd bring pastries and magazines with me, trying to prove I was a good daughter. That's where I met Ralph. On the streetcar headed home."

"It's nice you'd visit her that way. You still do that?"

"That's funny," she said, but the smile was mirthless. "That's what Ralph told me, the first time I talked to him. 'It's nice that you go see your mother every week.' And I just started laughing. God, he turned beet red."

"I don't follow. What's so funny about it?"

"My mother was a fall-down drunk. Just like her ex. We'd make small talk till she got shit-faced. Sometimes she was knee-walking before I even got there. After dear old Dad took off, she had even better reasons to get smashed. And I was the only one with guts enough to come around. Adele bailed out and moved to Los Angeles. Leaving me to get blamed for everything. Complete bullshit. People sink or swim on their own. How was it my fault she picked a loser for a husband?"

"Do you still—"

"The last day, I went out there with my pink carton of pastries all tied up and a stack of newspapers and magazines—and there she was—dead on the floor. I called the meat wagon and waited. Read the paper and ate almost all the pastries before they got there. My folks were quitters, you see? And I'm not. It's a hard road, you know? You never know if you're doing the right thing. I try—we both try—but I still see people looking at us like we somehow don't belong in a nice neighborhood—"

She stopped when she noticed my pencil was still: "You're not taking many notes, I notice."

"You, uh . . . You threw me for a loop there. You seem to have a pretty . . . tough attitude about it. Dying, I mean. Your mother. Your father. Gig."

"Dying's easy. To go on living is tougher. It bothers me to see people throw their time away. You don't get that time back. So you can't quit. You gotta keep trying, no matter what."

"So how's it going so far?"

She settled back in her seat and gave me a long appraising look. Mulling whether I deserved an honest answer, I guessed.

"Everything I've got," she sighed, "is fit into that house. You've seen it. I'll be honest—this isn't how I figured it was gonna go. I wanted life to be like a train ride. You can't wait to see where you'll end up next. Well, it's nothing like that. I got three kids and I have to make do on what my husband earns taking a beating so that a crowd of juiced-up working stiffs can have something to cheer about."

I sat silently. Maybe I cleared my throat. It wasn't the first confession I'd heard in this line of work. It wouldn't be the last.

"Then I realized there's no percentage in sitting around moaning," she went on. "If you don't like where the train is going"—those big green eyes fixed on me—"you can always jump off and walk around. Maybe you'll learn something new."

My face heated up. I rubbed my napkin across my lips, to

have something to do. Her words percolated in my head. Was I brewing them into something she never intended?

When I glanced back, she was still staring straight at me. Then she picked up a spoon and rapped it against her water glass. The *ding* sounded like a ring bell. Her lips spread into a knowing smile and her eyes shone with a look I recognized, but couldn't name.

"I think it's probably time to go," she said.

13

We strolled Powell toward Union Square. Afternoon sun stayed warm beneath a stiffening breeze. Defying local custom, Claire hadn't brought a jacket or sweater. Confident gal. The smell of popcorn wafted from the Owl Drug Store and trailed us up the block.

"I wonder what you'll make of all this," she said, slipping on tortoiseshell cheaters extracted from her small white clutch. "I'm hoping Hack won't mind. Were you going to talk to him for this story? Maybe you've got second thoughts. Should I even mention it to him?"

"I got enough from you to write a book."

Two guys waved to me, coming out of Clancy's.

"I didn't see you write much down."

"Photographic memory. Comes in handy. I'll put it together, then see if I need to talk to Hack. Ralph. Whichever." Right there: the perfect cue for my yarn of how Hack got his name—another way I was connected to her husband. But before I could get out the lead, she stopped the presses:

"You might want to go over some things with him," she mused. "Get all our stories straight." She looked over: "Fact-checking—isn't that what it's called?"

She served up a little smile. Her lips matched the color of her nail polish.

"After all, how do you know I can be trusted?" She lowered her head to peer over the green lenses. "And you could have used some better facts for those items you ran about

Gig's supposed whereabouts. Won't those look a little funny now? What's O'Connor going to make of that?"

"He won't make anything of it," I shot back. My guard dropped a notch: "I was only trying to help," I said. Then I was compelled to nudge it further out there: "I think you know that."

Tension—palpable, legitimate, but not entirely unpleasant—coursed between us, buzzing across the swirl of bustling pedestrians. Mutual suspicion was binding Claire and me together. I didn't too much mind the rope burns. A cable car clanged through the intersection. Ga-gas hung off the sides, snapping souvenirs. Now Claire seemed to be looking straight through me.

"C'mon," she said abruptly. "Let me drop you someplace."

Her white-gloved hand reached toward me. The fingers curled an invitation.

"I'm only going back to the office." I nodded back the way we'd come.

"I'll drop you. Ride with me."

"Goddamn it!" she blurted as we turned onto Post Street.

There was a parking ticket on the windshield of her Buick coupe.

"I knew it was too good to be true when I saw it," she said. Before she could assess the damage I snatched it from her.

"My treat. I'll put it on my expense report."

She didn't argue, opening the passenger door for me.

"Okay. It's your damn fault anyway," she said. "For being such a good listener."

She got in and started the car. She teased the clutch, waiting for a break in the stream of cars.

"I'm taking you out of your way," I apologized. "Don't you work just up the street, on Sutter?"

"I'm playing hooky today. Called in sick. It's no bother."

While she watched the traffic, I stole an eyeful of her. She looked like six million bucks, and I wondered how much of the morning she'd spent primping for our date. She eased away from the curb and into the flow.

"You know Ralph thinks the world of you," she said, downshifting when the light at Stockton Street went red. "He saves all his clippings, but yours—*yours* he pastes in a book."

"Well, this'll be a fine addition to the scrapbook. I know just the guy to come out and take your picture. Seymour Sn—"

"I don't think so. You won't need a picture and all of that."

"Of course we will. Readers want to know what you look like."

"But you don't have pictures in your column. You have those funny little cartoons sometimes, but—"

"This wouldn't be for the column. We'd play it as a short feature. Don't tell me you're camera shy? You certainly got no reason to be."

"Thanks, but forget it. Really."

"You kidding? C'mon—people die to get their pictures in the paper."

"I mean it. No picture. If you have to have one, let's forget the whole thing."

The signal changed. She bobbled the clutch and the gears ground. She shot nervous glances in the rearview mirror.

"Sorry," she said, and the car lurched. We covered the blocks to Market in uneasy silence. I couldn't decipher the photo thing at all.

Where Post fed into Market, she asked, "I'm going right, right?" I glanced at my watch: only a few hours left in my workday. No column due tomorrow, and no other deadlines. Far up Market, the first tendrils of fog spilled out around Twin Peaks.

"If you're headed home, you could drop me at my place."

"Aren't you going back to work?"

"I'm done for the day."

A horn bleated behind us.

"Which way do I go?"

"Out Market, all the way. I'm the other side of Twin Peaks."

She managed the stick smoothly that time.

I hooked a thumb at the Loew's Warfield. The marquee spanned the sidewalk, all the way to the street. At night it blazed bright enough to light the block.

"You know the Loew's up here on the right?" I asked.

"Sure. I used to go there all the time."

"You know what's downstairs? It's where Jimmy Ryan runs his book. You met him that night at Lucca's—remember? He came over to our table. He's a bookmaker. As in gambling, not making books."

"You're not riding with Shirley Temple here, Mr. Nichols."

"Jimmy's brother, Eddie, he's the one who brought horse racing to the state. Runs Golden State, down the peninsula. Lots of horse rooms around, but Jimmy's the top operation. Pulls action from all over: the tracks, boxing, college football, Coast League baseball, even politics."

You'd have thought I said they were killing babies down there, to judge by the look on her face. She shook it off. "So they make book on elections?" It was a desultory query. She was distracted all of a sudden.

"Tell you a funny story: One time a street sweeper laid down twenty grand that Angelo Rossi wouldn't be reelected mayor. Rossi's guys griped when the story got around. They paid Jimmy a visit. Jimmy tells 'em, 'Don't blame me, blame Angie—he's got the highest-paid street sweepers in the country.' "

She manufactured a cheap chuckle, shy of the good guffaw I usually got with that one. Another furtive glance at the car mirror.

"Right up here is the Orpheum," I went on. "When I was a kid, Spider Roach fought an exhibition there with Benny Leonard, during the intermission of some hoity-toity play. Brought the house down."

I swiveled and peered through the back window. Cars behind. A streetcar gliding up on the left. Nothing out of the ordinary.

"The Whitcomb, across the street, is where the athletic commission used to hold its meetings. Up on the roof, in the restaurant. After the Quake it was the temporary City Hall. Nice view up there, all the way to the waterfront. At night you can look right down into the Agua Caliente miniature golf course, right across the street."

She braked for the light. I leaned over and pointed across her chest, to where I used to hang out with my buddies, sinking putts under the gas lamps and the neon.

"Well, it used to be there. I forgot—they tore out the course a few years back." I wasn't deterred. "Up the next block, of course, is a place you know—Civic Auditorium. Where Hack Escalante has earned many a paych—"

Claire stomped the gas and the car screeched forward into the crosswalk. She jerked the wheel to the right.

"Jesus Christ!" I slammed against the door.

The clutch revved for a split second, then caught. She wrenched the Buick forward—straight into oncoming traffic.

"Hold on!" she shouted.

Cars were hurtling head-on down Hyde. A yelp stuck in my throat. The transmission whined for me, shrill and high. She shifted again and the Buick was in the wide intersection, cutting across a wave of oncoming cars. Horns blared, the sound swelling as bumpers bore down on us. Coming on fast—two panicked faces atop the business end of a big Packard engine. I was in the death seat, paralyzed.

Then we were on the other side of Hyde—onto Grove Street—and my life could finally flash before my eyes. We went half a block in silence, waiting for the sirens. She stayed firm on the gas, still well over the limit. She eyed the rear-view.

"What the hell was that about?" My heart was in my throat, my voice pinched and reedy.

"We were being followed."

I turned to look. She veered sharply onto Larkin, doing neary thirty. I pitched against the door again.

"Who the hell—"

"I don't know. Maybe the cops." She tore off the sunglasses and flung them on the dash. "I had a feeling I was being watched."

"Since when?"

"For at least a week."

"No, I mean today—you had this feeling at the restaurant?"

"There was a guy across the street, the whole time we were there. Watching through the window."

While I assumed she was dreaming of Paris, she was scoping out this snoop. I should have paid less attention to her freckles.

"Was he still there when we left? Did he follow us to the car?"

"I'm not sure. I'm sorry. Forget it. I'm just jumpy."

"That's why you wanted me to ride with you?"

She didn't answer. Instead, she grabbed the shades again and slid them back on as we drove into the sun. At Hayes she turned left, headed back toward Market.

"Why would they want to follow me?" she muttered.

They aren't following *you*, I thought. But I kept my mouth shut. For once.

14

Claire was still jittery as she pulled up in front of my house. If we'd had a tail, she shook it. The streets out here were quiet. She cut the engine and all you could hear were birds twittering all around. She got out of the car, folded her arms across the roof, and openly ogled the ritzy digs. The real estate guy called it Moorish Moderne, with a Mediterranean color scheme. Whatever the hell that meant. Claire eyed the serpentine stairway of brick and painted tiles. The Spanish -style terra-cotta shingles jutting out over unexpected balconies and whatnot. Ida damn near wet herself when she first trained her sights on the place.

"I didn't know words paid *this* well," Claire said. I muttered a demurral in response.

"Can I ask a favor now? Trade you for the lift?" She walked around the car to the driveway. "I need to call my neighbor. She's watching the kids. I should have called from the restaurant, but we were blabbing away."

"Absolutely. Let's go in. Maybe I can talk you into one for the road. Smooth us both out after that Keystone Kops scene back there."

I sensed her taking stock of the place as we climbed the zigzag steps to the front door.

"Where's your wife this afternoon?" she asked, after hanging up the phone.

"Visiting her sister. One of her sisters. She's got a bunch of sisters. What can I get you to drink?"

"A short Scotch'll do."

In the dining room I decanted us a couple of fingers each. She took inventory, running a gloved hand along the big carved mahogany dinner table. Checked the fancy silver service on the sideboard. I hadn't noticed this stuff in months. She glanced at an orchid plant, now dried out and sickly. Behind those eyes, I could sense her adding machine at work, tabulating. She clinked glasses with me, then wandered into the living room, appraising. It was nothing much for a Snob Hill socialite, but Claire acted like she was touring the Taj Mahal.

"My goodness," she said from the other room. "Would you look at that."

She stood before the fireplace, admiring a painting over the mantel. A portrait of Mr. Boxing, presented to me at a testimonial dinner.

"Done by an ex-boxer," I explained. "Wasn't my idea to hang it there. It's a little much." While she evaluated Joe Lynch's brushwork, I studied the seams running up her nylons.

"Pretty good," she decided. "The likeness is pretty good."

My neck burned as she came closer. "Let me see," she said, and turned my chin so I had the portrait pose. "Not bad at all." She smiled. "But then you're sort of distinctive. The eyes. The glasses. The Errol Flynn mustache. That drawing in the paper doesn't do you justice."

"Here I always thought the 'stache made me look like William Powell."

"I like Flynn better."

I could feel the ropes across my back, turnbuckle pressed between the shoulder blades. I retreated to the sofa for a breather. But there was no timekeeper. She kept right on coming.

"Can't say I've met too many people like you, Billy. Not one, in fact." She sat beside me and set her drink on the coffee table. She used her palms to rub the dress over her thighs, trying to brush off the polka dots.

"How's that?" I asked.

"You worked a cozy deal for yourself. The riffraff you associate with, all of 'em banging it out with each other, going for the throat just to get by—you watch it all from ringside and write it up. And do better than all of them put together. Nice work, if you can get it."

Was she running me down or building me up? Tough call. I nursed Scotch and zipped the lip.

"You've done all right for flunking out of high school," she said. "You ought to be proud. All this, on account of putting words together." She waved a hand between me and the painting, squinting. "You know, something's a little off."

Her gaze fixed on my mouth. She reached over and touched my upper lip. "This is what's different. You've got a scar under your mustache."

"Don't." I grabbed her fingers.

She gave me those green eyes again, unblinking. Christ Almighty.

"Car accident," I explained, still clutching her hand. "That was one spot on Market Street I didn't point out."

"When did you say your wife was coming back?"

The knot in my throat was the size of a fist.

"Not anytime soon."

★

"Undo me," she said.

Deliberately, I drew the zipper down the back of her dress. The material spread open and her shoulders shrugged free. She pushed the blue folds and polka dots down over her hips. The dress dropped with a whisper to the bedroom floor. She turned to face me, the white gloves still on. Her breasts rose and fell beneath a sheer pink brassiere. I watched those freckles come closer.

I was sitting in the chair beside the telephone. The night before I'd been lying on the bed right there, lost and empty. Then she called. It seemed like a week ago at least.

She eased down her half slip, revealing a pink garter belt and lace pants. With her foot, she nudged the slip onto the jumbled dress. When she straddled me, her nylons made a soft rubbing sound against the twill of my trousers. Her arms rested across my shoulders.

"Take off my brassiere."

I pried the tiny hooks. Several thudding heartbeats later, it separated. My head dropped to her shoulder and I took a desperate breath, like a diver breaking the surface, in the hollow of her pulsing throat. A faint trace of perfume mingled with her own scent. Nothing had ever smelled that good. My hands roamed over her hips and back. Moans nuzzled against my forehead.

"Feel this," she whispered. Her hand guided mine down into damp silk.

I had a full view of the bedroom whenever I opened my eyes. The vanity—Ida used to focus on it like fighters concentrated on the speed bag. The closet door—tacked with liturgy she saved from various Masses. The preserved rectangle on the wallpaper—from which I'd removed the wedding portrait.

My fist clenched Claire's coppery hair. I jabbed into her harder.

"Ow!" she grunted, biting her lip. Her cheek was pressed into the sheets. She reached back and swatted my hand away. "We're fucking, not fighting," she gasped.

I stiffened, sensing the inevitable. I ground my teeth, the immense pressure surging in me.

"Wait, wait, wait!" she sputtered. She crumpled forward and I came out of her, already past the point of no return, spewing across her back. She laughed, and crooked her head to look at me, wide-eyed yet again. Her hand reached up and felt the stickiness in her hair.

"My God! You must have been saving that up for a while."

I hit the pillows, spent. The world drifted. When my eyes refocused she was tossing her hair back and taking a deep breath. She rolled over onto her back, eyes shut. One of her nylons was missing, the other bunched below the knee. Her body glistened with a sheen of sweat. She bent an arm and used the sheet to swab her back. At length, she saw me staring at her.

"Jesus, what's wrong with you? You don't look like you enjoyed that very much." She sat up, pushing the wad of soiled sheet aside. "I have right here some evidence to the contrary."

"What was that all about?" I asked, coming out of it. It sounded ruder than I meant. But consequences were looming all around us, practically taking shape in the darkening room.

"Well, I can't speak for you," she said, nonchalantly draping an arm across her breasts, "but as far as I'm concerned, I jumped off the train and took a walk around."

I crab-walked off the bed, found my pants, and hastily

pulled them up. Through the bedroom window you could see out to the ocean, past where Claire's garden grew, and Hack's kids waited for their mom to fix them dinner. The fog would soon be taking over, enveloping the neighborhood in a cool twilight haze.

When I turned back I saw Claire Escalante, naked, in the middle of my bedroom, stooping to pluck her blue and white polka-dot interview dress off the floor. She reclaimed her tossed-away purse and I watched as she stuffed one nylon stocking inside.

Beside the bed I rummaged through the sheets, untangling the other sheer stocking. Rubbed the seam with my thumb. I held it out to her.

"You don't want to forget this."

She managed a small taut grin as she accepted it. No laughs. No thanks.

Then she said: "We wouldn't want Ida to find out our little secret."

"Unless you meant to leave it."

She picked up a fistful of slip and showed me eyes filled with daggers. The temperature dropped rapidly.

"What does that mean exactly?" She stood ramrod straight, one arm defiantly akimbo. I couldn't hold a thought when I looked at her like that, so I shuffled the bedclothes around, pretending I was smoothing everything out. I could feel her watching me.

"I might as well tell you," I said. "Ida isn't visiting a sister. She's not coming back. Ever. She left me."

"Sorry to hear that." Something glinted wetly in her eyes.

"So in case you think this'll give you some leverage on me, you might think again." They were nasty lines. My guts were getting ready to send back lunch.

She stepped over and belted me, right across the kisser. Open-handed.

"What the *fuck* are you talking about? You see some sinister motive here?" she asked, a rough edge on her voice. "Is that the deal? You think I'm setting you up? Well, get this straight. This was something we *both* decided to do. Don't let your guilt fuck up your thinking. I had a nice eventful afternoon. I can tell you did, too. So don't go all Catholic schoolboy on me, and start making me out some kind of whore. Or that I'm running the okey-doke. Don't you dare do that to me."

She pressed a finger to her eyes, stanching tears. She fitted the brassiere back on, adjusted it, hooked it deftly.

"Sorry," I said, rubbing my jaw. Good thing she didn't make a fist. "I'm just not used to this."

"Used to what? Cheating on your wife—or keeping secrets?"

She shimmied the dress back on and turned her back to me, holding her hair up off her neck. I took the cue and zipped her. She flashed fiery eyes over her shoulder:

"Don't worry. With a little practice you could get better—at both."

Once we'd put ourselves back together, I offered to walk her down to the car.

"This isn't the junior prom," she said.

Through the living room curtains I watched as she navigated her high heels down the stairway, across the drive, into the Buick. She backed into the driveway to turn the car around, then swept onto Magellan and down the hill.

Across the street, at the corner where Magellan intersected

my block, a black sedan pulled from the curb a moment later. It swung a wide "U" in her direction and glided silently away.

I roamed the house. Policed an ashtray, then filled it up again. Drank a glass of red. Debated with myself. Had another. Heated a can of soup. Stared at it in the bowl, let it go cold. Sloppily paid some bills. Switched to bourbon. Methodically, painfully, I endured three hours that way, before finally surrendering and grabbing up the phone.

"Hello?" She sounded harried. It was a relief to hear her voice.

"Hey. Wanted to make sure you got home okay. No trouble? No one followed you?"

No response. Kids were in the background, raising a racket. Squealing, running footsteps. Holler. Thud. General child chaos. The reality on the other end of the line didn't have anything to do with me anymore.

"I'm okay." She might have been more convincing.

Dredging up words was like hauling heavy stone out of a quarry.

"I wanted to say again that I'm sorry."

"So there. You did. Forget it."

The little girl's voice cut in: "Is it Daddy? I wanna talk to him."

"Oh, shit." Gut-punched. By a fucking kid.

"This isn't a good time to talk," she said. "How 'bout if I call you later?"

"All right."

Half past eight, the phone finally rang.

"Billy? Francis O'Connor."

This bastard wasn't going to give me any breathing room. If I was anything like my old man, I'd have taken the offensive. Jumped right down his throat. Asked why he put that tail on me, what he was trying to prove. Tear him a new one, call his bluff.

But I wasn't my old man: "How are you?" I asked. "Anything new on the Liardi front?"

"I'm working up some theories. And your assistance would be invaluable—now that we *officially* have a murder on our hands."

"How's that?"

"You know everybody in the racket. The odds are pretty good you know whoever killed him."

"How the hell would I know who killed him?" Wild, like a fighter in trouble swinging desperately. *Regroup*, hold on to some control.

"Not what I meant," O'Connor said. "I'd be grateful if you'd help me build a list of likely lads. Possible suspects. It'll be great fun. Hell, I might even deputize you." He laughed. The prick really loved his job. This must have been what Abe Simon felt like when Louis toyed with him. Let the poor sap grope his way around Queer Street for thirteen rounds before lowering the boom.

"I don't know as I have much to offer. What do you have in mind?"

"Meet me tomorrow night, if the wife'll let you out. Over at Liardi's place. I'll give you the address if you don't have it. And bring that letter I gave you, if you please."

She never called. I didn't change the sheets. I couldn't sleep for the smell of her.

At 3 A.M. I was rooting around the floor, searching for my

mother's lost and busted rosary. Took almost half an hour to locate the damned thing.

I rummaged through the suits in my closet until I found the one with the small brown bag in the pocket. Inside was a silver chain I'd bought weeks ago from Blackie, the discount jeweler.

Sitting at my desk, in the small office I kept upstairs, I spent long minutes relinking the rosary.

15

I knocked at the door of Gig's flat, like the night the whole thing started. This time there was an official Police Department document tacked to the door, advising that the premises were off limits, and that trespassing was a punishable offense. The door cracked open, and Francis O'Connor's chunk of florid mug peered through the gap. He escorted me inside.

"It's as well you didn't get here ten minutes earlier," O'Connor said. He was draped in the rumpled mack, the cane gripped in his mitt. A green felt fedora fitted squarely on his bristled dome. "I had a minor difference of opinion with the landlord," he explained. "He's understandably eager to rent the premises, but I'm not quite ready to abandon it as a crime scene. He wanted reimbursement for his two months of lost rent." O'Connor chortled. "Christ, it's getting more difficult all the time to persuade people to behave in the interest of justice."

"Christ, it's dank in here," I groused. The flat was gloomy as a tomb, a floor lamp throwing dim wattage. Months of deathly stillness hung heavy in the confined space. O'Connor took a few gimpy steps to the window, shuttered by venetian blinds. He found the cord and gave it a vigorous tug. Slats clattered up, forming a tight bunch. He jerked and cinched. Electric light spilled in from the narrow gap between duplexes.

Across the way sat a woman, at a small two-seat dinette table. She faced us, a newspaper spread out before her. She was still dressed from work or else expecting someone. Maybe she knew she'd be seen, and wanted to look her best.

She glanced up. Again. A third time. Once more for good measure.

"Get the light switch, if you would," O'Connor asked. I was flummoxed, looking all around. "Usually by the front door," he said.

I flipped the switch, but it didn't do much. Two of the three bulbs in the ceiling fixture were dead. Dead bugs laid scattered in the frosted glass. At a glance, the surroundings were as I'd last seen them, although I avoided a close inspection. If I was going to play it smart, I didn't need reminders.

"What do you expect to find here after all this time?" I asked.

"Naturally, we've gone over what there is of this place. That didn't turn up much. We won't uncover *new* evidence. What's here could take on a different meaning, do you see, once we have identifiable suspects. I like it laid out here, instead of boxed up in an evidence room. Despite the economic hardship this presents for the landlord."

"Anything interesting so far?"

"What do you make of this?"

He held out a square book, making me walk to the window to take it from him. Fiddling with my glasses like I couldn't see, I moved to the floor lamp for more light. There, I carefully studied the item, with my back to the window.

It was a scrapbook: pebbled brown leather cover, bound with a length of rawhide. I opened it and was hit with everything I'd ever written about Gig Liardi. Dozens and dozens of pieces starring the erstwhile "Pride of North Beach." Yellowed extracts pasted neatly on the black pages. Going back all the way to '29. Dates painstakingly hand-lettered in white ink beside each clipping. After the splashy article—heralded with a six-column halftone—recounting Gig's losing effort against Tony Canzoneri, the clips began to shrink. In the latter half of the book the remaining squibs—some just tiny excerpts from the column—were loose among the sheets.

"Mr. Liardi appears to have preserved every word you wrote about him," O'Connor said.

I thought of the letter the cop had given me, the one Gig wrote but never mailed. I'd left it, intentionally, on my dresser.

At the back of the scrapbook, the pages fell open to a large manila envelope. I unfastened the clasp and out came a batch of glossy eight-by-tens—the Escalante wedding photos. Claire was a radiant, statuesque bride, while Hack shunned the lens in every shot, preferring to focus on her. Who could blame him? The camera loved her—*why would she dread a photo for the paper?* As I thumbed through the pictures, two smaller ones fluttered to the floor. Actually, it was one photo, cut in half. On one piece was Gig, beside the groom, clutching his arm and flashing what, on him, passed for a smile. On the other half, separated from the boys by a razor slice, was Claire. *What was that about?*

"I found it interesting that he didn't take the time to paste the last items in," O'Connor mused. He jabbed at the scrapbook with the metal tip of the cane. He got some mileage out of that prop. I set the two halves of the severed photo side-by-side on the coffee table. But I didn't look the subjects in the eyes.

"Gig was on the backside by then." I shut the book and set it down, gazing off down the hallway, toward the dark recesses of the flat, feigning interest in the shoe-box bedrooms and postage stamp–sized water closet. Keeping my face away from the woman in the window.

"What would be his reason for cutting that one up?" The cane tip pinned Claire's porcelain features.

I shrugged.

"How close was Liardi to Escalante?" O'Connor pressed.

"Fifteen years they'd been together."

"Did the woman come between them?" I glanced at the photo and saw the suggestion bluntly stated. It didn't figure, so I kept quiet. A more common occurrence these days.

He extended the cane again, prodding the scrapbook. "So where would we find the second volume? Where are your accounts of Mr. Liardi and his young contender? That's what has me confounded. Fifteen years, you mean to say, and he didn't save a word of it?"

I raised an eyebrow. "You're right. It doesn't figure."

"Take a guess where I found Volume One."

I acted out a search for neat hiding places. O'Connor was warming up, getting loose. I didn't want to play his games, but it was his call.

"Toilet reading, maybe? I've heard that about some of my efforts."

He let it pass: "It was under his mattress. That strike you as odd?"

"People squirrel things away for posterity," I responded. "My wife hides stuff in dresser drawers, under her clothes."

"Makes it difficult to show your trophies off to visitors, I'd think."

"Gig wasn't exactly the type to entertain."

"Was he the type who'd have a woman over?"

"I wouldn't know about that. You mean a girlfriend, or paid dates?"

"Either/or. Did you know of any girlfriend?"

"I never saw him out with anybody. As for *in*—who knows?"

"Would he have men up here, then?"

"Guys from the gym, you mean?"

"Or guys from Finocchio's. You ever get the notion our man putted from the rough?"

"Jesus. You thinking that some faggot pickup could have killed him?"

"Would you consider that a possibility—as far as you know?" O'Connor was handing me a choice red herring, gift-wrapped. I made sure not to grab for it too desperately.

"I never saw him with a woman, since you mention it." I cocked my head, like I was trying to tip this new concept into place. My eyes fell on the split photo, flashing on where O'Connor could be headed, turning onto a shadowy side street I hadn't even seen.

"Not many recollections of a life in this place," he commented, limping the few steps between rooms. "Nothing in the kitchen, no pictures, no books, no records. Appears to have been a lonely life."

"Could be. But this wasn't where he lived," I said.

"What are you saying?" O'Connor asked, crowding me. "Did he have another apartment?"

"Gig lived in the circuit. He just flopped here. Made coffee. Changed clothes. It's that way for a lot of guys in the racket."

"So you're telling me that he was hardly ever here."

I waved at the spartan surroundings: "What does it look like?"

"That being the case, it makes it all the more intriguing that he'd be killed here."

I flipped on the light in the lavatory and studied the checkerboard green and white tiles. Two framed pictures, mildew-stained and warped by steam, hung above the toilet: Gig in a posed gym shot from his own fighting days, the other with him raising Hack's hand after the first Whitten fight. I was punching out my story at ringside when that flashbulb popped.

"How can you be sure it happened here?" I finally asked. O'Connor had moved back by the window. I flipped off the light, stepped into the cramped corridor, and repeated the question.

"Liardi was a fighter," he answered. "Fighters, I would suppose, are similar to cops in certain ways. They recognize the smell of tension. Their antenna's always up, especially on the street. It would be a tough proposition to get the drop on a fighter in the 'circuit,' as you call it. Likewise a cop on his beat. Wouldn't you agree?"

"It's a fair assumption."

"But at home? With the guard down a bit? In the company of someone you know? You could get blindsided, don't you think?"

My head in the kitchenette, I groped around unsuccessfully again for a light switch.

"The oven's clean as a whistle," came O'Connor's voice. "He took all his meals out. Like you suggested."

"Still, isn't it a leap to assume he was killed here?" I stepped gingerly from the kitchen doorway. "Just because you—"

"There's also the matter of the witness I told you about. That would tend to bolster the theory somewhat."

I gestured toward the window without looking that way: "Is that your witness over there?"

"It is, in fact."

"All of a sudden I feel like *I'm* a suspect."

The cop cut loose a derisive snort. To my prickly ears it sounded convincing, reassuring.

"Sorry if I gave off that impression. It's something of an occupational hazard with me. My wife has asked on occasion if she should hire an attorney."

The relief was shallow and short-lived.

"Refresh me—when was the last time you saw Mr. Liardi?"

I looked at the photo halves and Gig's scrapbook on the table. O'Connor paced behind me, exactly where Hack and I had wrapped Gig in the blanket. Then we dragged the dead weight to the door.

The witness, the woman across the alley, turned a page and lifted her gaze toward us.

I had to stay cool, like Ray Robinson when LaMotta kept on pressing. "It was probably down at the Royal," I suggested. True enough; that was the last time I'd seen Gig alive. "I came in at the tail end of some dust-up he was having with Burney Sanders."

"Who's this Sanders? What the dispute was about? Remember the day?"

I pulled a sour face for his benefit. "You met him. At the Ringside in Oakland. Burney's a local promoter. Those two were always getting into it. About everything. Money, mostly."

"You don't think that encounter might be important?"

"If arguing with Gig is motive for murder"—I pulled my little address book from my inside coat pocket—"then here's your full list of suspects."

"Thanks all the same." He smiled. "I won't be needing

it." By then I'd learned that a smile, as practiced by Francis O'Connor, was a dangerous thing indeed. "Have a seat," he directed, gesturing to the chesterfield.

My wing tips rested right where Gig had died.

"Did you speak to Mr. Liardi on the twelfth of May? On the telephone?"

"Nothing stands out. That the day he went missing?" Fuck. I hadn't even considered phone records.

"That it is. His telephone bill listed a call to the *Inquirer* switchboard. My thought was perhaps he'd called you."

"Don't think so."

"Could be he was just canceling his delivery service."

"The son of a bitch," I said, playing out the gag. "That'd be reason enough to kill him."

O'Connor let out two quick bursts of laughter, then slid straight into a soliloquy: "I'll let you in on a little secret," he said. "One of those a cop should never reveal. Motive is overrated. It serves admirably in the movies, not so well in real life. Part of me agrees with what you're hinting at. The likelihood is that we won't identify our culprit by searching for motive among the deceased's disgruntled associates."

Back and forth he paced, an actor on the boards. For emphasis, stabs of the cane on the hardwood. The neighbors below would be banging back, retaliating before too long. The tutorial continued.

"A killing is rarely premeditated. It can happen in a heartbeat. A citizen loses control. And the victim, sadly, often has little connection to what we might charitably call a 'motive.' Only yesterday: a couple on Russian Hill come home to find their daughter dead. Broken neck. The front door was unlocked. The stricken parents screamed for a dragnet. They wanted the entire SFPD mobilized. My experience tells me to start close to home. In this case, the dead girl had a brother. I found him up at the playground, playing basketball.

"To make a short story even shorter," he went on, "this lad had his bicycle stolen earlier that day. Went home in a foul humor. Took some additional grief from his sister and so he knocked her down the stairs. Hauled her back up, swearing all the while that she was faking, trying to get him into trouble. That's all it requires most of the time. Motive? No. A fraction of a second when someone's out of control."

The account was legit. I'd seen the story on a chase in the composing room that morning. O'Connor was probably the unnamed source.

"What should I take away from that?"

"Whoever killed Mr. Liardi didn't need a reason—he merely had to be close to him. Like brother and sister. Like father and son."

O'Connor was good. He pulled that quote back from our encounter at the Ringside. I took two cigars from my breast pocket. Offered him one. No sale.

"Let me find you an ashtray," O'Connor said, "so we can preserve our little crime scene."

That had to be his idea of a joke. He'd already encouraged me to put my hands all over the place, including the scrapbook, which felt unnervingly like pertinent evidence. Now O'Connor was handling every drawer and cabinet in the kitchenette, noisily rummaging about. "Not so much as a coffee can," he said.

"Gig was a teetotaler. No booze, no smokes. Not even coffee."

"I'd noticed," O'Connor said. "Not a drop of Irish in the house. A man not to be trusted."

He supplied a stubby Mason jar.

"How closely acquainted are you with Hack Escalante?" he asked, handing over the ersatz ashtray. "That's not his right name, is it?"

I was getting the range on O'Connor. He had a trademark one-two: a zinger question, followed up quickly by a tamer one. Designed to see which you'd slip, how you'd counter. I realized that O'Connor couldn't have cared less about the small clues a crime scene may have contained. His forte was people. Poking them, prodding them, breaking them down. He could finesse a line of patter, but under that he was a brawler at heart.

"No, his right name is Gianotti," I answered casually. "Ralph Gianotti."

"A dago. That's what I thought. I couldn't figure 'Escalante.' We've got an Escalante in Vice, but he's a Portugee. Why'd Signore Gianotti become an Escalante?"

"I wouldn't know." I struck a match and flamed up the cheroot.

"What can you tell me about the man?"

I sketched a brief bio, the same one I'd pitched by rote into dozens of programs over the years. Nothing you could hang a hat on.

"What about his personal life? Anything juicy there?"

"Zero."

"Then I would have to presume it's entirely incidental you had lunch yesterday with his wife."

That one was telegraphed. I was ready. Slipped it and stepped right in.

"We met to talk about a possible story."

"A story about what, if I might ask?"

"She was upset over the piece I ran the other day on Hack. Seemed only right to smooth the waters."

"What did you discuss, specifically?"

"The trials and tribulations that confront a prizefighter's wife."

"And what's that like?"

"Probably like being the wife of a cop." I chewed the cigar, tired of eating O'Connor's jabs. I got brazen: out came my reporter's notebook. "Want to see my notes?"

"I'd appreciate that a great deal." He took the skinny, spiral-bound pad and riffled through the pages.

I'd spent the morning filling them up with a reconstruction of yesterday's luncheon chat, tossing in some judicious references to Gig and a couple of bullshit quotes I'd let O'Connor attribute to Claire.

Across the alley, the cop's prize witness fired up a kettle.

"Which one of us were you having followed?" I sneered, offering him a jab of my own.

Red ridges creased his pink forehead as he shot me a look. This was the hardest I'd seen him work, and it actually seemed to hurt.

"I didn't have you tailed. Neither of you."

"Of course not. How'd you know I had lunch with her?"

"I called the office looking for you, to arrange this meeting. Your editor consulted a to-do list found on your desk, and said it looked like you were having lunch with a 'C. Escalante.'"

"Fuzzy gave you that?"

"The police depend upon the cooperation of dutiful citizens like Mr. Reasnor. And yourself."

O'Connor parked himself in Gig's easy chair, resting the cane against the wall. "Is this everything she told you?" he asked, perusing pages of thickly scrawled notes. Cleaner than my usual cribbed, indecipherable shorthand.

"Everything? No. But it's the gist."

"Did she talk about Liardi?"

"Whatever's in there."

"She ask you for a favor of any sort?"

"How's that?"

"Here's how I'm piecing this together. I figure her husband for the crime. And into the bargain, the day after Liardi's body turns up, Escalante's wife is all over you. That has the look of a trail of circumstance to me."

"Aha. Where's a trail like that supposed to lead?"

"That's what I'll find out—with your help. Why'd she want to talk to you? Besides the 'story' idea?"

"Look, your intuition is right, to a degree at least. She's afraid her husband will be a suspect, and—"

"Did you ask her where her man was on the night Liardi disappeared?"

"Why would I? You must have that dope already—you questioned Hack, didn't you?"

"What I asked is, what did she tell *you*?"

"She said they were together."

"Where?"

"I didn't ask. I didn't bring my rubber hose. It was lunch, not an interrogation. But I assume she meant at home."

"That's not an alibi. Maybe they *were* together. But maybe they were together *here*."

I glanced into the adjoining flat. A witness making dinner, still stealing glimpses. "You mean *they* might be your two suspects? Putting something in a car? Look, all I can say is that Claire Escalante convinced me that her husband isn't capable of murder. She told me about their life together. What a child the big guy is, underneath it all."

"Umm. Why not promote that to the cops? Why not tell it to me? That's the thinking I don't follow."

I picked Gig's scrapbook off the table and tossed it in O'Connor's lap.

"Have another look. *I* write their life stories. Not the cops."

He set the relic aside, with more respect than I'd shown it. "Noted," he blandly intoned.

"How was the missus as a storyteller?" He waved my notebook, so the pages fanned.

"Not bad." My blood was up. "But not as good as me. When I write up that human-interest story, I'll have subscribers crying in their coffee."

O'Connor set the notebook on the armrest and covered it with his hand. *Go ahead, confiscate it.* Precisely what it was manufactured for.

"Let me try my hand at a story," he said, settling back into the chair. Daunting words from a self-assured Irishman. "I'll make it brief, but unsubtle enough that you can't miss the moral.

"Years ago I knew a young lady. We became acquainted when I worked in Chinatown. She, as it happened, was Japanese. A beautiful girl, named Grace Osaki. She'd grown up as an orphan and hadn't a soul in the world. Went to school, worked afternoons and evenings in a store on Pacific Avenue. It broke my heart to see her so abandoned. Then she met a fellow. Hiro Matsuoko. A graduate student at Cal, a kibei—perfect all the way around for her. They got married. She kindly invited me to the wedding. I couldn't have been happier for her. In fact, I was a little jealous of Matsuoko-san. This was 1939."

Here he spiced his tale with a hard gaze my way. He had me going. I had no idea where, but he had me going.

"A couple of years later Matsuoko came to see me. Informed me of his plans to divorce Grace. Added that he wanted *me* to marry her. The internment was coming, you see, and he needed to protect his wife. He knew they wouldn't come after her if she'd gotten married to a big white Irish cop who positively reeked of law."

"So? What happened?"

"Hiro Matsuoko died at Manzanar. Grace Osaki is still my wife."

He clapped his hands together and guffawed.

"The look on your face. Oh, clearly you had me yoked to some Colleen."

"All right—what's the moral that's so hard to miss?"

"Jesus, Mary, and Joseph—hold your horses. This is the fastest this story has ever been told."

"Is there any truth to it?"

"The gospel. In its entirety."

"The moral?"

"Not complicated, my friend. Human beings will do anything—*anything*—when they really love someone. Hiro Matsuoko gave up his wife because he loved her so much."

"He thought he'd be getting her back."

"Well, there's another lesson for you: you can never predict how things are going to turn out."

"Your wife must be indebted to you."

"Not really. In her culture, they take the opposite perspective. If you go out of your way to help someone, you're the one who's obligated. It's a responsibility you carry the remainder of your days."

I glanced at the floor. It shifted, like a silent quake had hit.

A surge of panic: could O'Connor hear Hack's teary pleading, too? For a second, I knew how an overmatched boxer felt, teetering over the void, out on his feet. I fought my way back, clawing for the here-and-now:

"So you're still together," I mustered.

"I'd do anything for Grace," O'Connor said, leaning forward. "And I'd bet Claire Escalante would do anything for Hack. *If* the love comes with obligation." He fondled my notebook, as though the keys to love and obligation might be engraved on its pages.

"You're assuming that she'd lie to cover for her husband."

"Oh, for the love of Christ—lying is a given. It's chump change, especially when the stakes get this high. There's no limit to what a wife might do to protect her man."

I knocked ash into the Mason jar and tried not to seem like I was pondering *that* too intently.

"Fact remains, if you want dope from me that'll tie up Escalante, you've heard all I've got to offer." I pointed my dwindling cigar at the notebook. O'Connor was drumming his fingers on it.

"If you don't figure Escalante for the crime," he said, "give me somewhere else to go, another avenue."

"Like what? A list of all the guys who couldn't stand Liardi? I told you. We'll be here all week."

"Understood. In that case, I'd be grateful for your notes relating to the several Liardi sightings mentioned in your column."

"I don't follow."

"Course you do. The coroner says Liardi's been dead at least two months. Three weeks ago you ran an item in your column promoting that he'd been spotted in New York. What's that all about?"

"It's called nosing around, trying to turn something up, like you suggested."

"Any sources bring Liardi up without your prompting?"

"I don't know. Why?"

"That should be pretty self-evident. An individual claims to have seen him when he's rotting under three feet of dirt? I wouldn't rule that man out as the killer. Or tied up with it somehow."

I squinted through the cloud of cigar smoke with which I'd cloaked myself.

O'Connor had more: "So let's have a look at those notes, shall we?" He stood, gathered in his cane and my notebook: "I'll take this one along as a down payment."

"I'll need those back at some point, to do my story." I tried to come off casual. "But you're welcome to them, if you can decipher my shorthand."

"It's surprisingly readable," he said, sliding the pad into his coat pocket. "Did you bring that letter I gave you?"

I rose and gave him my best *tsk*, with the rictus and a shake of the head.

"I've got to have that back," O'Connor said flatly. "I don't know what I was thinking, letting possible evidence out of my hands like that. I guess I wanted to do *you* a favor. What was in it, anyway?"

"Nothing earthshaking. Mainly Gig going over plans he'd had for taking Hack back East. Ancient history."

"Why would he never have sent it?"

"Wasn't worth the stamp."

O'Connor tugged the venetian blind cord. A witness eating, and still watching. The slats dropped, wiping her from view. I went into the kitchen, shook the ashes into the sink, and rinsed out the jar. O'Connor filled the door frame.

"I'm overdue for a libation," he announced. The deeper brogue indicating that he was my best pal again. "Buy you a quick one at Gino and Carlo?"

"Another time. I have to get home."

"Wife holding supper?"

"She's holding something." I squeezed past him into the entryway, checking my watch. "Word is I work too late as it is."

"All right, Dagwood. Listen, I'm going to level with you. I'm chagrined and disappointed. I thought you'd greet this with more enthusiasm. I'm out on a limb for you with that letter. And I thought you'd relish this adventure. That we'd have a hell of a time. I featured it as a serial in your column. You'd be ringside to the investigation and at the bell we both come out smelling like a pair of roses when I nail the killer. What am I not seeing?"

"You're asking me to put the heat on guys I know. All on the off chance one of 'em popped Gig. Who isn't widely missed. Can't you see that's a tough spot for me? It doesn't sit right."

"What doesn't sit right with me is your taking a pass on a red-hot story. Fight manager strangled, right in Mr. Boxing's own backyard? Why leave that to the city desk?"

"What do you mean *strangled*?"

"I mean strangled. They found ligature marks on his throat. Looks like somebody started choking our man and in the struggle he cracked his head. That's probably what killed him. But what precipitated the struggle—he was being strangled."

"And you think Escalante would have choked him? C'mon. If he was angry at him he'd have slugged him."

Hadn't I seen evidence of a punch on Gig's jaw? Blood on Hack's knuckles? Or was I just believing what Hack told me?

"He wouldn't have grabbed the guy by the throat," I declared. "No fighter would. Not in the heat of the moment."

The look on O'Connor's face told me that he'd been thinking along the same lines. I took some solace in realizing that we were both swimming in the same murky water. Leave it to O'Connor to darken things further:

"We're not certain he used his hands," the cop sighed. "The marks could have come from a tie or a scarf or some such thing. It appears Liardi was attacked from behind, and in the struggle, he might have fallen and cracked his head. Probably in this room. Probably on that table."

For a moment the only sound was the two of us breathing, uncomfortably, and the muted noises of a disinterested city.

"Maybe it wasn't in the heat of moment," O'Connor finally murmured. "Maybe it *was* premeditated. He choked him because he didn't want to hurt his hands—the tools of his trade."

I didn't say anything more.

16

Strangled? Strangled. *Strangled.*

Hack held out on me. Lying son of a bitch. Now he was a storyteller, too? It wasn't a flukey clip on the chin that dropped Gig for the final count. Liardi's boy had choked the life out of him. After that he played me for a chump. A deft maneuver. It was too late now to turn Hack over. I was in it with him, up to my eyebrows.

At my desk the next morning I ran it all again, scribbling notes. I replayed the whole go-round with O'Connor the way I brought back a finished fight. Every jab, hook, and head feint. Even sharper, now that it was me in the pit.

It didn't feel at all coincidental that O'Connor's only "witness" was watching us from the cheap seats. But if he saw me as a second suspect, why promote the notion that Hack and Claire had been there together, choking Gig the night of May 12? O'Connor was still groping to build a story, is how I figured it.

The scrapbook. In itself, it was innocuous. But O'Connor had a point—why wasn't there another one? One with Gig and Hack together? Hack was Liardi's ticket back to the big time, his chance at replacing lost glory. He would have kept a memoir, documenting all of that. Did Hack heist it for some reason? And why was Gig's book stuffed under a mattress? Who was he hiding it from?

God damn O'Connor—he'd pushed this shit deeper under my skin. There was another story here, tracking parallel to mine.

How realistic was that homo pitch? It could have served as a good blind, until I tipped to the cop fishing for fruit action between Gig and Hack. Admit it, Mr. Boxing—all you knew about Tomaso Gigliardi was what you fit in the paper. Could he have been a nance who longed to be something more than a mentor? How much did he really feel Hack owed him? Was that why he literally cut Claire out of that picture? Some kind of swishy voodoo?

I still wasn't buying it. But I couldn't shake it off.

And what about the tail on Claire and me that afternoon? Twenty years in the dodge had refined my take on people—O'Connor didn't lie when he claimed that tail wasn't his. He blew plenty of smoke that night, but on the surveillance score he was level.

What the hell was going on?

I called the naval station in San Diego. Claire had it right: fact-checking *was* in order. I'd also have to handle Hack differently in the future. Could be the lug wasn't quite as thick as he came off. But if I braced him, O'Connor style, to get the real story, he might disintegrate. Take me down with him. I'd have to shore him up before O'Connor got hold of him and squeezed harder the second time around. I'd be a booster, whisper little war chants in Hack's ear. Convince him he could go a few more rounds. Like I'd seen Gig do dozens of times.

After I'd been patched through three switchboards, they told me Hack was on patrol. I didn't leave a message. My trail was long enough.

The morning mail arrived. Postcards, the new *Ring*, wallets of assorted clippings from contacts East, another letter from

Ida. If she knew how jammed up I was, would she still try to wheedle her way back in? I let the letter rest.

As I digested the latest clips, an idea fell dead in my lap.

I rummaged through my files, going after items at least two weeks old. *Bingo*: Bill Corum's column, from the *New York Mirror*—a fond farewell to Whitey Epstein, cornerman supreme. Heart attack tolled his ten, aged fifty-eight.

Deeper in the desk detritus I dug, looking for a spent notebook. Scanned the scribbles to confirm chronology. Found a timely page and studied my pencil marks: halfway blunt and hurried. I rubbed down a sharp 722 on the back of my wife's latest plea. When the lead was shaped the way I wanted, I filled in a gap in the notebook:

Whitey Eps—Gig in NYC? seen at Grossingers/
askd about Canzo/hung awhile/blew

Shorthand backup for the last Gig item I had run, with Epstein now revealed as my source. If O'Connor wanted more, he could go shake Whitey down. Last report, he was working the corner at Forest Lawn.

The department's communal telephone directory was kept on a file cabinet next to the teletypes. They hammered away while I reviewed the listing of physicians, trying to remember the name of the quack Claire worked for. It popped: Kaiser, 450 Sutter.

She picked up on the second ring: "Dr. Kaiser's office."

I got caught short—why was a savvy dame like Claire somebody's phone jockey?

"It's Billy Nichols." I was going to say *You didn't call like you said you would*, but bit my tongue.

"How may I help you?" There was office noise behind her, voices nearby.

"I think our story needs more fleshing out."

"Uh-huh. All right, sir. And where is the pain, exactly?"

"I saw O'Connor last night. He brought up new things you should know."

"How uncomfortable is it?"

"Tolerable, for now. But O'Connor may want to operate. We need to talk. Right away."

"In that case we can fit you in tomorrow. Say at noon? We'll free up an hour. Do you know where our office is downtown?"

She was quicker on her feet than Willie Pep. And ten times more exciting.

"No place public. I think something's up."

"I'm sure it is." That one nearly skipped past me. She moved right on: "And what was the name again?"

It took me a few seconds to get back on her track: "The Temple Hotel. You know where that is?"

"That should be fine, sir. Thank you for calling."

She hung up.

I thought of the mutilated photo on Liardi's table, underneath O'Connor's cane. The splendor of her, a laugh on her lips, supreme confidence wrapped in a white lace gown. Dour Gig on the other side, holding on to Hack, his glare at the camera impossible to read.

Why'd you ring me, Gig, on May 12? What did you want to tell me, on the night you died?

Which side of that scissored picture was for me? Where the hell did I fit in?

17

The drapes billowed to reveal a bright and blustery San Francisco noon. To the left, Bush slanted downtown. People hustled in and out of apartment lobbies and storefronts. Men fingered their brims to secure their hats, women clutched their coats to keep their skirts from swelling. A few miles south, a freighter labored into its berth. Beyond the piers was Butchertown, where I was born. To the east, cars sped across the Bay Bridge. Ornate deco structures, erected for the '39 International Exposition, jutted up from Treasure Island. A cutter skimmed beneath the bridge, outbound to the Gate.

I drew the shades and dropped the room into darkness.

Room 412, Temple Hotel. It wasn't the address or the atmosphere. I'd picked it because of the desk man, Leo Most. He owed me. I'd fixed him up with this job after he'd drawn a ten-year bounce in Soledad. Manslaughter. Decked a gin-mill loudmouth who'd barked one too many times. The guy went down and cracked his cranium on the brass footrail. Ten and out, forever. The judge gave Leo a ten-year jolt, reasoning that as a one-time middleweight prospect his hands were "deadly weapons." Leo hung tough: he did a nickel clean and walked on good behavior.

Not unlike what might have happened to Hack, if I hadn't stuck in my two cents.

The Temple was an inoffensive hostelry for visiting fighters. Management turned a blind eye to the hot sheet trade, too. Leo kept me posted when the two enterprises overlapped.

Those indiscretions were never set in type, of course. It was part of my job to know the comings and the goings.

Now I was a coming and a going. I banked on Leo's gratitude knowing no bounds.

A laughing couple exited a room down the corridor, their banter muffled by the door. I picked up the suit coat draped over the chair and decided to hang it in the closet instead. I took the rosary out of my pocket. Sitting on the edge of the bed, I counted off the minutes on the beads that dangled through my fingers. It was an excruciating crawl. Too much time to think about what a fool I was. To realize I was risking everything I'd built, day after day, for more than twenty years. To consider the consequences of another bonehead move, another step off-balance.

Bead fifteen accompanied a quiet knock on the door.

"Sorry I'm late." She wore a pink and yellow floral-print skirt, starched white blouse, fuzzy pink sweater, open. She still had the shades on. A yellow scarf disguised the flames of hair. Not a bad idea to go incognito. She walked past me, letting her fingers graze my face.

"It's like a cave," she sighed. "Can't we have some light?"

Straight to the window. She whisked open the drapes. Day invaded the room, a shaft of sun burning the narrow bed. "Much better," she pronounced, "without the guilt and gloom. How'd you settle on this place?"

I stepped past her, taking in the fragrances of shampoo and perfume. I mouthed the Leo Most saga, pruned bare bones. Meanwhile, I scanned the building across the street, searching for a woman in a window, a witness fixing me with a suspicious stare. Spooked, that's what I was. On the street below, through grids of fire escape, innocent people rambled, unconcerned, oblivious.

The scarf undone, Claire flounced her hair, the cheaters still in place. "What did O'Connor say?" She slid her sweater off and dropped it on the chair.

"He thinks Hack killed Gig. I told him he was way off base." I left O'Connor's dark view of her unspoken for the moment. I wasn't ready to start talking about conspiracies and strangulation.

"That's supposed to be news? He's thought that all along, hasn't he?" The tails of her blouse unfurled from the waistband of the skirt. "That stuff in your column, though—it seemed to keep him off. Did he ask you about that?"

"That and other things. He wanted details about Liardi. More about Hack. Names of other possible suspects. Plus my notes."

"You give him anything good?" Her fingernails shone scarlet against the snow-white blouse as she undid buttons.

"He's got some offbeat theories of his own. For instance: Gig was queer on Hack."

She froze the blouse halfway undone. It was true. I talked too much.

"He isn't *serious*?" Eyebrows arched above the dark green lenses.

"I think he was just trying it out. See what my reaction was."

"Are you joining the party?" she asked, nodding at my fully dressed self. "Or will you be a spectator today?"

"O'Connor knows we met," I said. I slipped off the braces, pulled out the shirt. "But he claims that bird dog wasn't his. And I believe him."

"What makes you so sure?" She stepped out of the skirt.

A big fist reached out and slugged me. I couldn't slip it anymore. It nailed me everywhere at once—head, heart, gut.

Banged me illegally below the belt. It was the most powerful thing that could hit a man. A short right from the Brown Bomber could clean your clock. But it couldn't fill your head with words, then strangle them all in your throat. Or infect every minute of your day, or dominate your dreams, making you twist around all night. She didn't even have to do anything. She just stood there, half undressed. Her breasts and behind silhouetted by the open blouse, her face framed by those tawny waves. Behind the sunglasses lurked the promise of her flashing eyes—inviting me to worship at her church.

"I see you got yourself some boxer shorts, Mr. Boxing."

She kicked off her shoes and stepped over to me. I took a seat on the bed.

"O'Connor's suspicious," I breathed. "He thinks you're up to something."

She shook off the blouse and let it fall to the floor.

"What would that be?"

Protecting your husband, got stalled on its way out. The air was too hot and humid between us. There was no more room for words. She unhooked herself this time. Slowly. Her eyes were masked, but I could feel them staring down at me. The brassiere slid off, revealing her. I tasted those freckles again. I could have knelt and prayed all afternoon at the Communion rail.

"Here's something that's not on the menu," she said, sinking to her knees. "I bet you never had it served at home."

A minute later her head rose from my lap. Wet lips, glistening red, slid off me. I had two fists full of bedspread. "That's enough for now," she said. "The fans want *Mr. Boxing* to go the distance."

I had to see her eyes. I'd know at a glance if this was real.

I had to wipe away my doubts. Brusquely, I grabbed for her dark glasses.

"Hey!" One of the struts snagged in her hair. She shook it loose.

A muddy purple crescent rimmed her right eye.

"Sorry," I said. "I wanted to look at your eyes."

She sat back on her haunches. "I slipped and fell," she said, fingering the tender bruise. "Rounding up the kids. Tripped and banged it on a doorknob." She strove to get the familiar confidence back. It had to evict another tenant first. Someone sad, it seemed to me.

She picked the cheaters off the bed and folded them before flipping them onto the chair with her discarded clothes.

"Sorry," I said again. It felt like I'd broken something.

"Stop apologizing all the time, okay?"

"Sorry. Look, we don't have to do this."

She leaned forward and summoned a breathy chuckle: "Someone here begs to differ."

Communion at the Church of the Big Fist. Bless me, Father, I cannot resist.

"Did Hack do that to you?"

I stroked her bruise. We were back on the pillows, drained. Gulping air was all I'd manage for a while, after the most energetic quarter hour on my career record.

She turned her head to me: "What would make you think that?"

"I phoned down to San Diego yesterday, and they said he was out on patrol. I got worried that maybe—"

"You're a nervous wreck. What, he's going to patrol five hundred miles? He's still down south. And I told you before—he doesn't hit me. He *never* has."

My head sank into the pillows. I stared at the ceiling, thinking about where I was going next. I didn't want to get started.

"O'Connor said that Gig was strangled."

Her steady breathing turned hesitant. It's hard to hide a slight nervous reaction when you're lying naked next to somebody.

She mustered a blithe "So?"

Christ, if I wasn't in a spot. I couldn't tell her that her husband had lied to me about how Gig died, because I'd be admitting I was there. I'd be an accomplice. And if I called her a liar, and put her in there with Hack, waxing Gig . . . Well, if it turned out to be wrong she'd never speak to me again.

"So I just thought you should know," I sighed. Then I changed the subject: "You said Hack had a scrapbook. Was it his, or did he get it from Gig?"

"It was his. He'd paste the cutouts in himself. Why?"

"A scrapbook might be missing from Gig's place. O'Connor thinks it might be a lead. He mentioned it more than once."

She propped herself on an elbow and looked at me. Her breasts rolled against my ribs.

"What your problem is, is that you've got a big imagination. A bad thing for a reporter, I'd think." She glanced at her watch.

"Is our hour up, Doctor?" I murmured.

"We've got some time." She repositioned herself on top, the luxuriant length of her pressed against me—instantaneous delirium. "How'd you get to be a writer, anyway?" she asked. "Dropout and all. You read a lot as a kid?"

"Not a lot. Jack London. It was the newspaper business I loved, but I never thought writing would be my ticket in."

"When did you know?"

"September 14, 1923."

"That the day they hired you?"

"I was already at the paper. Copy boy. I ran drafts from the reporters to the editors and galleys to the composing room. But that was the day I first realized I wanted to be a writer. When Dempsey defended the title against Firpo. You know about that fight?"

"I know Jack Dempsey is the 'Manassa Mauler.' Does that count for anything?"

"You get points. And Luis Angel Firpo was the 'Wild Bull of the Pampas.' From Argentina. The fight was at the Polo Grounds, upper Manhattan. Crowd of eighty-eight thousand. Western Union telegraphed it round-by-round to papers nationwide. Jake Galloway, the sports editor, he knew I was a big boxing fan, so he let me have the job of running wire copy to the composer."

She propped her chin in a palm, grinning. Settling in for a tale.

"Way before the fight jumped off, staff from other departments were milling outside Sports. They wanted first crack at the feeds from back East. The wire, you need to know, lagged a few minutes behind the action. But I'll tell you—for me, the chugging of those teletypes was so goddamned exciting—it was almost as good as being at the fight. Even more real, somehow.

"So the feed from the first round comes through, and all the writers huddle around it. Everybody else is shouting, *Tell us what happened!* Making a big ruckus. The guys in Sports are howling and slapping themselves—"

"So? Tell us what happened!" She dug her elbow into me.

"Dempsey—the King of Kings—is knocked down right

at the opening bell. He roars back, sending the Wild Bull to the canvas *seven* times. Remember, all we got to see was crooked type on yellow paper, but everybody knew this was the wildest fight of all time. At the end of the round Dempsey gets knocked *through the ropes.*

"Suddenly, everything stops. The teletype falls silent. Galloway grabs the feed from one of the reporters and scans it. A big smile spreads across his face. *Billy!* he shouts. I run up and he hands me the sheet.

"'Go,' Galloway says.

"At first I stand there, reading the wire, all excited. The workers hanging on the gates of the Sports department are pleading for details. Screaming to know what's going on.

"'Go,' Galloway barks at me again."

I grabbed Claire's shoulders and pushed her off. She whooped. I flipped myself up and over her, straddling her stomach, looking down into her wide eyes. My arms free, I gave the rest of the story full flourish. Playing to the balcony. Pantomiming the punches. Chewing up the scenery.

"'The round's not over yet,' I tell Galloway. 'It would have said "End of round." But it doesn't say it here.' Galloway snatches back the sheet and checks it over. He shoves it back at me and lurches over to the teletype and starts hammering on it. All the reporters start pounding the machine. They're sweating and swearing up a storm.

"I turn to the crowd, brandishing my telegraph sheet like I'm Moses with the tablets. I launch into a blow-by-blow of the first round, pouring in details off the top of my head: the first flash knockdown of Dempsey, all the vicious uppercuts, roundhouse rights, dirty chopping ax blows. Dempsey knocked through the ropes, right onto ringside reporters.

"Then I shut up—mimicking the teletype.

"*'And the round ain't over yet,'* I teased them in a whisper. I stared into dozens of dumbstruck faces. I *had* 'em."

I clenched my fists.

"That was the moment. When I knew I wanted to be a writer."

"*Well?* Go on, for chrissakes!" Claire playfully hammered her fists on my chest. "How'd it end up!" Her hair fanned out on the pillow and her eyes caught a glint of the sunlight streaming through the window. It was warm on my skin. I felt the hammering of that fifteen-year-old kid's heart.

"The teletype starts chattering again," I went on. "Dempsey—keeps his crown. KO'd Firpo fifty-seven seconds into the second stanza.

"*'He tore out the cable!'* I shout. Everybody looks at me. 'When Dempsey tumbled through the ropes, he yanked out the telegraph wire! That's why we stopped getting the feed!'"

Claire laughed: "Quick thinking for a snot-nosed kid."

"I had no idea whether it was true or not. But the crowd laughed and whistled. They shook their heads, 'cause the idea of it was just so perfect. Too good a story, you couldn't ruin it. Two days later Galloway gives me my first assignment, covering a card at Dreamland because the regular guy called in sick. 'This ain't Dempsey and Firpo,' he told me. 'Just make sure you get the winners right.'"

"I can tell you love your job," Claire said. She gazed down at her belly, where my erection had rekindled. She drummed her fingers on it.

"Now I've got a story for you," she said. "Were you aware we've met before?"

"How's that?"

"Don't make me doubt your photographic memory. I'll

admit, it was a long time ago—1938—at Izzy Gomez's. Don't you remember?"

Pictures started coming back, but instead of calling them up I said: "Tell me the story."

"Gig dragged us there, Ralph and me. He was looking all around for you. We'd been to six different spots, hunting you down. He kept telling Ralph you were the guy who could make him in this town, boost him into an attraction—"

"I remember. It was pissing down rain that day and—"

"Shut up. This is *my* story now. It was pissing down rain that day. We looked like three mongrel dogs in off the street. And Gig made me wait over by myself while he reintroduced you and Ralph. You seemed pleased to see Ralph, pumping his hand like some long-lost pal. That lit Gig up. And then he sent Ralph back over, like a father with his kid. We sat there while Gig greased you. Ralph took out a little penknife and started carving our names in the table—"

"A time-honored ritual at Izzy's place."

"I kept looking over at you, wondering, *Who is this guy? How come these tough guys bend over for him?* Remember? There was a crowd of busted-up old-timers hanging around—"

"Powell Street Cowboys."

"—and I'm asking, *How's the fresh-faced kid rate?* I'm watching Gig, who I've only seen with a two-ton chip on his shoulder, and he's coming at you, his hat in his hand, like he's sniffing for a handout. Then you go over to the table where the old guys are, and the next thing I know, everybody's laughing and shouting—and you're standing there chewing a cigar like the cat that ate the canary. You remember this?"

"Without question."

"Remember me? Stuck over to the side, some young frail at the boys' club?"

"Absolutely."

"Liar. You didn't even look at me. Imagine my surprise when Gig comes back all jazzed up and tells us Ralph's got himself a new name. I started to give him grief, but Gig said don't fuck around, it's done. And I looked at you and thought, *This guy has the power to baptize people? Who the hell is* he?"

"Ralph's no kind of name for a boxer."

She laughed, then covered her face as the chuckling turned dry and humorless.

"What?"

"Poor Ralph." Her voice was muffled by her hands. "Gig looks down at him sitting there and says from now on his name is Hack Escalante." She took her hands away. Her eyes had welled with tears. "And Ralph looks at where he just carved 'Claire + Ralph 4-Ever' into the table. He gets this dopey, kept-after-school look on his face." She wiped at her eyes. "Oh, my God . . ."

She pushed her way up off the bed. The first thing she grabbed off the chair were the sunglasses, which she clumsily slid over her eyes.

I'd beared up under Hack's whining, and O'Connor's probing. But it was Claire's crying that told me things were bound to turn out bad. I said nothing as she hastily dressed, the anticipation and excitement of our tryst now replaced by this sudden awkwardness. She wrapped herself in her clothes like she was trying to bandage open wounds.

The last garment on was the yellow scarf, which she stretched tautly, then fanned out into a triangle. She draped her head with it and knotted it fiercely beneath her chin.

SECTION S MONDAY, AUGUST 2, 1948 CCCC*

AN AMERICAN PAPER FOR THE AMERICAN PEOPLE · MONARCH OF THE DAILIES

San Francisco Inquirer Sports

REG US PAT OFF

Through THE ROPES

By BILLY NICHOLS

For most of us in the ring dodge, fight night is when all the grunt work and great expectations collide head-on. Fighters, managers, and trainers all live for the moment when the endless sparring and roadwork pays off in victory. If not, it's back to the boards at Tough Luck U.

Fans spill into the night, satiated. They'll hold their own expert seminars on the action until the following week, when we do it all again. Rarely do we think twice about where the warrior goes after battle, often in search of consolation.

Heavyweight Hack Escalante is one of the lucky pugs. He returns home, win or lose, to his wife, Claire. She knows well the peculiar anguish of waiting in limbo while her husband puts it on the line to earn the daily bread. "I used to go watch Hack fight, when we were both younger," she revealed recently. "But I can't do it anymore."

Instead, the attractive and vivacious Mrs. Escalante spends fight night being a model mother for her three children: Anthony, five; Marie, three, and William, one year.

"The children don't know what their father does for a living," she says, "and I think we'll keep it that way for a while yet." Has she given any thought to when they'll explain it? "Oh, I'm sure it'll be the first time Tony comes home with a black eye," she laughs. . . .

18

Truth is, I'd never really planned to write that piece about the life of a fighter's wife. If O'Connor didn't believe that my meeting with Claire Escalante was strictly research, screw him. Potential stories get eighty-sixed all the time.

But in the days that followed our encounter in the Temple, as the number of unreturned calls to her home and office stacked up, I changed my mind about writing that piece. Even Fuzzy liked the idea. "She a looker?" he asked, ready to assign Seymour to the job. I lied in my usually convincing way, telling him that she was down south, visiting her husband for a week.

"I'll just do it as a column," I told Fuzzy. "I got squat for Monday, let's run it then."

I worked that piece for all it was worth, determined to flush Claire out. I'd give the public a stirring testimonial to her courage, faith, and devotion, and keep the irony for myself. She wouldn't be able to resist.

Newman's Gym was wall-to-wall Filipinos. They packed the pews of the gallery, tighter than sardines, all sporting snap brims and topcoats and stolid rapture on their faces. In the presence of their idols, Orientals were devotees, not fans.

Dado Marino was the object of their reverence. The Hawaii-based cutie was training for a title bout versus Manuel Ortiz, for the flyweight crown. Dado dominated the main ring, all 112 pounds of him, buzzing circles around his sparring partner, flicking peppery jabs. More of a wasp than a fly.

Marino's first name was originally Salvador. His pilot, the shrewd, irascible Sad Sam Ichinose, pasted "Dado" over his boy's moniker to coat-tail him to such Filipino favorites as Speedy Dado and Little Dado. Speedy was huge in the thirties. Pulled a thirty-five-hundred-dollar gate one night at crackerbox National Hall. Filipinos were literally hanging from the rafters to watch their little man box.

By 1940, Speedy's fistic filibuster was played out and he was stone- cold broke. A new model Dado got brought along to attract fresh Filipino action.

Slouching against one of the gym's square columns, I scrutinized the latest Dado as I kibitzed with Joe Herman. Joe was now a partner in the place with Bill Newman, finally securing himself part of a permanent address after thirty years humping it up and down the coast. Herman's right name was Anton Scherer. He started scrapping as an Angeleno newsboy, aged twelve. Too much of a hustler to stick with the solitary regimen of training, Herman opted for managing in the twenties. Piloted a land yacht back then, picked up on the cheap, which he used to haul his whole stable, sometimes ten guys at a time, to venues like Marysville or Petaluma, or some county fair in the sticks. He'd furnish a promoter with the entire card. If one of his boys got sick and couldn't go, Joe would suit up in his stead. It was in his blood, but thick.

"Surprised me with that column today," Herman said. "I figured you musta been stumped for something to write about."

"Change of pace," I said. "Clean out the pipes."

"It was good. Got me going there when she says, 'Dying's easy. Living's tough. Don't throw your time away. You don't get it back. Never quit. Keep trying, no matter what.' Shit, I could use her in the corner."

Behind us, the regulars composed gymnasium music: the step-slide-scrape of solo sparring, the rapid beat of a jump rope slapping the warped and worn wood, the leathery thwack of heavy bags taking punishment, the incessant takata-takata-takata rhythmically tattooed on the speed bags. General huffing and grunting and bull-like exhalations pushed noisily past crumpled cartilage.

Across the fetid confines a familiar custard-colored figure approached. Sid Conte beelined when he spotted me in the mix. His crispness had wilted; he seemed soiled. Herman paid him no mind, gave not an ounce of respect. Sid rated zilch with the old school. It almost made you feel for him, until you caught a snootful of Sid's aroma: Aqua Velva splashed over copious sweat.

Sid pressed up so close I could've checked his teeth for cavities. "Can I get a minute from you, Billy?" His breath smelled like he'd fed a roll of Sen-Sen to a sour stomach. Herman floated Conte the fisheye, encouraging Sid to drift.

Conte tugged my sleeve awkwardly with his left hand. The right one still featured gauze, adhesive tape, and metal splints. He pulled me over to another column, backed me up under the no smoking sign. It hung there for laughs. A fog bank of cigarette and cigar smoke hovered near the ceiling, thick as cotton around the lights.

"Nice piece on Hack in the paper today," Sid said, distracted.

"You mustn't have read it too closely. It was about his wife, not him."

"Well, you know. Same diff. Keeping his name out there. Appreciate it, really. Hey, I can talk to you on the level, right?"

I looked at his shirt collar, stained and soggy, and matched a cheroot to parry the odoriferous assault. "I need to know I can talk to you in confidence," he nattered on. "And confidentially."

He should have known this was an insult. I didn't dignify it.

"I'm all ears, Sid."

"I'm jammed up right now. Something touchy has come up." Priming himself to touch me for a C-note. To keep Jimmy's hitters from snapping his pinkie, too, I figured.

"The cops braced me about Gig," Conte said. "They're acting like I'm a suspect." Blood fed the splotches on his cheeks.

I popped the cigar out of my face and studied Sid. His eyes were pinwheeling in his head. "Where'd they get that idea?" I asked.

"How the hell would I know? They picked me up yesterday at the lot and they take me over to Telegraph Hill. In a black-and-white, can you picture it? Like some low-life crook!" He notched his voice down to a hoarse, harsh whisper. "I should file a complaint on the bastards—parading me in and out of a squad car. In public."

Ordinarily, I'd have enjoyed pondering whether a used car pitchman could have his reputation sullied. The notion didn't take today: "Let's hear what happened, Sid."

"I was hoping maybe you knew somebody, somebody downtown who could get this crazy Paddy off my ass."

"Slow it down, Sid. If you're looking for help—first tell me the story."

"Two uniform bulls haul me over to Telegraph Hill, muscle me into this apartment, then leave and lock the door. I'm there dangling, no explanation."

"You didn't know where you were?"

"Not the first fucking clue. Until I get bored and pick up an old scrapbook on a table. It's full of clips about Liardi, all your write-ups. I about shit my pants—I'm cooling my heels in Gig's place."

"You figured that how? Because of the scrapbook?"

"Nobody's told me nothing. There's a detective wants to ask me some questions, they said. Didn't Gig live on Telegraph Hill?"

I decided to go for a cagey play, keeping the hole card hidden: "Yeah. On Green. Up from Stockton. Across from friends of mine—they live next door in an upstairs flat."

Sid's eyes spun faster, desperate to move the tumblers into place.

"I saw her. Uphill side? She was in the kitchen the whole time I was there."

"This Paddy you mentioned—he really put the screws to you?"

"Once he showed up. Had to be twenty minutes before he lets himself in. Asked me was the place like I remembered it? Starts right in sweating me. How'd I know Liardi? Business or social? Jealous of him? Any grudge? How long did I have eyes for his fighter? All this kind of shit. He was fixing me for a fall."

"Who's the cop?"

"Name's O'Connor. I couldn't get over this guy. Measuring me for a noose. Paddy fuck."

"Where'd you leave it with him?"

"He wants to know where I was on May 12."

"So how's the alibi?"

"Shit! How do I know *where* the hell I was! Out, around—who the hell remembers where they were six months ago? Do *you* know where you were May 12?"

I shrugged. "He's got nothing solid. If he did, he'd be playing by the book."

"You think?" Sid wanted to believe. I represented reassurance. What a joke.

"He's trying to scare something up is all. See who flinches when he says *Boo*."

"But that could still fuck me up, if he comes hard. With Hack, with my business. I gotta get this bull offa me."

"So get somebody to stand up for you on the date."

"Now you're talking. You're always around—you're everyplace. You tell this cop you saw me on the twelfth and I'll be golden."

"Sid, I can't alibi you—"

We were cheek by jowl, his mustache tickling my ear: "I'll fix you up with a car—top of the line."

"Sid—I don't drive."

"Your wife can pick one out. Whatever she wants."

"Easy, Sid. You're coming on a little too guilty."

That put him back on his heels. Herman had sauntered over, lured by the tension Conte oozed. He eyed me over Sid's shoulder.

"Whatd'ya hear from Hack?" I blared, my voice at public volume. Conte tipped, and spotted Herman loitering nearby. He backed off. Sid was beat, all in.

"I could have told you this Navy deal would be a bust," he said. "But that wife of his, she gives the marching orders."

"How's that?"

"I called the base this morning and they say he's in the infirmary—"

"What—he's sick? An accident?"

For a split second I was filled with guilty hope. Maybe Hack was *dead*. How about that—risked my ass to save him and then I get a boner at the thought of him in a pine box. It was the quickest, dirtiest solution for everything that ailed me. The rational part of me—what was left of it—swiftly boxed that dark shit into a corner. But it had been loose out there, prancing center-ring, long enough to feel the hot lights.

"Don't worry, he's not gonna die or nothing," Conte went on. "But get this—the goofy prick draws KP duty for the first time ever. And he somehow manages to put a potato peeler right through the back of his knee. I can't even figure out how he did it. How dumb can one guy be?"

Herman, eavesdropping, couldn't resist: "What's your excuse?" he cracked, pointing at Conte's splinted digits.

"Hack's a mope. He's just unlucky," I said. "Remember at the Civic when the microphone came down and hit him in the head?"

"Never saw that much blood in a ring," Herman shot back, "and the fight hadn't even started. Gig had to shell out to get him fixed." Herman turned to Conte: "He had liquid plastic shot into Hack's eyebrows, you know that? To stop him from cutting so easy."

Conte shook out his right leg, like he was feeling his fighter's pain. "I don't really know how bad it is yet. I mean, if he cut something important in there, it could be a long time before he can get back in a ring."

Herman looked down at his own leg. "How the hell do you stab your own self in the back of the knee?"

"If he ends up with some kind of wobbly pin," Conte went on, "we're out of business. I need a break in the worst way, Billy. You gotta think about what I said. *Please.* And don't go advertising this around. Give me—give *us*—a break."

Conte slunk away. He and Joe Herman took to each

other like a snake and a mongoose. Sid lingered about twenty feet away to watch Dado rain a flurry on his fourth sacrificial sparring mate of the session. I measured the deflated car salesman: medium build, dark hair, trimmed mustache. Give him a hat and glasses . . .

"Joe," I said, nodding in Conte's direction, "you think me and Sid have anything in common?"

"Such as what?"

"I mean, from here—could we kinda look alike?"

19

Leaving the gym, I hoofed it to Market and caught an outbound car. I was heading out to the Mission to see if Burney Sanders was making headway with his infusion of cash into the Bucket of Blood.

I've done some of my best work on streetcars. Rumbling through the corridors of the city, inspiration crisscrossing everywhere. Unhappy couple beefing in the front seat of a parked Nash. A beat cop darting under an awning, then taking the stairs two at a time. A guy crumpled on the curb, head sagging into his hands. Local color spilling into every intersection, across every lunch counter, down every hotel hallway. Trapped behind the windows, bottled up in bedrooms, ready to blow.

I'd observed these vignettes all my life, inside the safety of the glass. Killing time, wondering which incidents were harmless and which were hurtling down a one-way street, careering brakeless toward the big dead end. Now here I sat, rattling down that steep grade myself. Groping around for the cord that would let me off on an avenue of escape.

Across the aisle, a guy was reading my column, absorbing my canonization of Claire Escalante. I could see the involuntary bobbing of the Adam's apple and the satisfied smile as he read the final line, shamelessly cribbed from John Milton:

They also fight, who only stand and wait.

He pressed the folded paper on the woman sitting beside

him, no doubt his wife. He jabbed a finger at the column and implored her to read. Wonder if he'd have been as effusive if I'd laid out the truth. That the loyal wife was screwing the guy who wrote the column, while the punch-drunk pugilist was hiding out from a murder rap. Instead, I'd fabricated a glorious, perfumed ruse, stripped of thorns. It wasn't a lie, I rationalized. It just wasn't the whole truth. All you had to do was exert some selective editing and assemble the remaining facts in a particular order.

The woman finished the column and turned to her companion. Emotion swam in her eyes and her lips trembled in a tight smile.

That's when I knew my only hope of salvation would come in the form of a story. So, naturally, I starting concocting one. Fact or fiction? Tough call. But here's how it went:

Sid and Hack were bound up, exactly how I couldn't see yet.

Yes, that's the way it had all begun. They'd been connected awhile, well before they waxed Gig. Sid was on the premises that night, no question. He hid when I showed up, knowing I'd never stick my neck out for *him*. But he was there all right, sweating in one of the dark back rooms, ear to the door.

First, he and Hack overheard Gig's call to me. They flashed each other a look when Gig told me to hurry over 'cause he had big news to spill. Gig was puffed up and defiant—calling Sid's bluff on something.

Like what? What card was Gig holding?

Forget the particulars. Gig was set to deal Sid a losing hand. That's when Conte snapped—in a heartbeat, as O'Connor theorized. Between Gig's summons and my arrival, everybody's life turned upside-down. Instead of hightailing it out of there, the boys pull me into the picture. Hack opens the door, leading me front row, center. He and Conte could have gone to ground until the coast was clear. But no: they make me the guest of honor. Only possible explanation—I was of use to them.

Now, Hack, he's no deep thinker. This ballsy an enterprise presented sufficient complications and consequences to paralyze his brain. Like I'd said to Sid and Joe Herman, Hack was a mope, an unlucky stiff resigned to life booting him relentlessly in the ass. He had a crucial role to play, one he'd manage only if he could follow a simple script: hook me with a sob story, that's what he had to do. Bring out my good shepherd instincts. After all, for twenty years I'd been defending my flock against every variety of critic—blowhard legislators, holier-than-thou church groups, crusading women's leagues, ass-backward editorialists, and, of course, the vagaries of Fate. Over the distance I'd compiled a record of defense as good as Jake Erlich's or Jerry Geisler's.

It's called hubris. Look it up if you don't savvy.

Maybe I got played. But Hack's chain is likewise getting yanked. Conte's just the guy to do it. For starters, boxers don't choke anybody. A pug blows his top—he swings. The way Hack said he did. Makes sense, you can buy it. I'm the proof. But clotheslining a guy? Strictly for gangsters and chickenshits. A coward's way of dealing with somebody you can't take head-on. Surprise them from behind, never have a face-off. That's where O'Connor scored another point: he talked about a "blindside," how Gig's guard was down. He'd let somebody get behind him.

I fit the basic description from O'Connor's witness. That's why he staged the floor show at Gig's flat for the audience of one. But I'd only been in the joint a minute on May 12 before I dropped the blinds. No time for that broad to cadge an eyeful.

But Sid—she must have got a good gander at him. And as Joe Herman grudgingly admitted, me and Sid could pass for brothers, from twenty feet away.

It would have been Sid's idea to rope me in that night. He was a gambling man, no stranger to the high-risk, low-percentage play. In his tightest spot, he wagered from the gut: I wouldn't let the husky drop, I'd come up with some way out. And once I bit, Sid knew he'd be tapped into juice that would boost his chances tenfold. Come to think of it, not much of a longshot—what did they have to lose?

Sid bet the farm. He had Hack saddle up and ride me, right to the wire, sobbing and shaking and begging for his life. Hack went to the whiphand like Eddie Arcaro.

It all meant that Sid strangled Gig. He had something on Hack to seal the kid's lips. Another reason Hack was spooked whenever I was near. He was doubly guilty: about Gig, and about giving me the okey-doke. When O'Connor starts breathing down Conte's neck, Sid reaches for his hole card: he becomes the helpless innocent, wanting me to manufacture him an alibi. Put us both together, someplace else, that night. Solder up the circuit, so to say.

By the time I strolled into National Hall to survey Burney Sanders's reconstruction job, I had Sid's custard-colored suits traded in for prison stripes. He might even take the pipe, if I could pry him loose from me and Hack.

Burney's work crew hammered and sawed and smoothed mud with practiced efficiency. Their efforts boomed and echoed through the hall. All around, calloused hands had deftly labored to rebuild the structure: bracing support beams, shoring up joists under weak spots in the floor, replacing crumbling lath and plaster with clean new gypsum boards. Quite an impressive display. It'd be hard to remember this place as the old sweatbox Bucket of Blood.

Like my father would have said: when you want to build something—a sporting venue, say, or a good, tight story—use only craft-certified union professionals.

"Can I help you with something?" A woman's voice, right behind me, trying to sound accommodating, but clearly harried. A feminine note within all the construction clatter was certainly unexpected, and when I turned around and got a gander at the sharp girlish features and blond bob, her presence seemed even more incongruous. An unlatched briefcase brimming with paperwork was clutched to her chest like a shield, an impression made all the more vivid by the scripted VW monogrammed into the leather flap.

"Who are you?" I chuckled.

"You first—*I* belong here." A spark of defiance in her wide eyes was at odds with the pointed delicacy of her nose and chin. Her mouth featured an amused curl of the lip.

"Billy Nichols. I'm looking for Burney Sanders." Her demeanor didn't invite a handshake.

"You have an appointment?"

That caused me to laugh some more, which made her legs set in a guarded stance. An excuse for a brief admiring glance.

"So Burney has a secretary now?" I waved toward the refurbished surroundings. "Did you come with the package?"

"I've been with Mr. Sanders more than two years." She caught the lift in my eyebrow and coolly added, "As a personal assistant."

"How'd I manage to miss you?"

"You must not be very observant."

That's when Burney blew in, an afternoon edition tucked under his arm. "What'd I tell you, huh?" He beamed. "Can you believe how great this place is gonna be? Lookit that—whole new mezzanine level, with VIP boxes, and a whole row of offices behind that side over there. Plenty of room for concessions front and back. Brand-new dressing rooms downstairs. Unbelievable. You're gonna think you died and went to heaven!"

The secretary stared at the floor, embarrassed that her boss was pitching the hell out of me and paying her no mind.

"I gotta say, Burney, I'm impressed. All this, and a doll of a secretary to boot."

She shot me an edgy look I couldn't quite read. My unsubtle prod shook Burney out of his spiel. "I guess you two met, huh?"

"Not officially," I said.

"Did you get that stuff notarized, like I told you?" Burney curtly asked her, nodding at the briefcase.

"Yes, I did." Her cheeks flushed.

Sanders tugged more papers from inside his jacket and handed them to her. She deftly flipped open the briefcase flap, stuck them in with the others, and snapped the latches shut while Burney turned his attention back to me. She'd been dismissed.

"How 'bout this place?" Sanders chimed. "Didn't think I had it in me, did you?"

"I wouldn't say that, Burney. What I didn't think you had in—"

He whisked the newspaper from his armpit and slapped it with his other hand.

"That was some piece you had in today." He grinned. "I

don't know how you come up with this stuff. Beautiful, just beautiful. You must have had fun with that. She sure sounds like a great gal. Hack is one lucky stiff to have a lady like that looking after him."

Burney's secretary appraised me again, but this time it wasn't a sprightly challenge in her eyes. She was looking for something, but I'll be damned if I knew what it was.

"Virginia Wagner," she stated, and gave me a shake that ended with an extra bit of firmness.

"*Virginia*," Sanders scoffed. "What, you're around this big shot for five minutes and suddenly Ginny ain't good enough?" He said it with a smile, but it didn't come out nice.

She attached a hook-on strap to the heavy briefcase, slipped it over her shoulder, and shot Burney a drop-dead glance. "Look who's talking," she said, with more than a little icing. She turned on her heel and strode out the doors to the bright street.

"That split-tail's looking to get shitcanned," Burney sighed.

"How come I've never seen her around before?"

"She won't have nothing to do with boxing. I use her for other stuff."

I waited for his words to drift back to him. Shortly, he hit me with the paper.

"Strictly business," he said. "Strictly business."

20

I rang off the day's phone work and tagged a "30" to the latest column. Excavating the paper piles, I uncovered the most recent letter from the AWOL ball and chain. Reno postmark. Still holed up at the ranch for unwed mothers and inconvenienced harlots. On the back of the envelope I'd scrawled notes: *Waterman in hospital / heart attack / veterans / Dick Brubaker angle 26 1 more month / $1,850 net stockton Dalima beat McCusher / Jurich 10–8 over Romero.*

I unfolded the perfumed pages. Without fail, I ended up reading all of Ida's missives. A twisted compulsion. I marveled at her uncanny ability to submerge the truth under a fragrant tide of fantasy. She never mentioned how she cheated on me, never apologized, never asked forgiveness. Cuckolding me, having a baby by some other guy, all that was referred to only as "this thing." As in, "Let's decide this thing never happened." She played it immaculate, like no dick had been involved. Virgin Mary carrying the Christ-child. And I was supposed to play her sorry-ass Joseph?

> *"Dearest":*
>
> *I suppose I can guess why you have not written but I am praying with all my heart that you will call or write and say that you are willing to try again. This has not been an easy time for me. The baby came early and it was very scary for a while. He is okey they say, but I am so lonely here. It is not right for a mother and child to be made to suffer so.*

If only you could see the baby. Vincent is the most adorable thing in the world. He is such a towhead and he has the sweetest face. You will love him so much the minute you see him. He can sock a little bit to as he has given me a couple of good ones. You will have to get him some boxing gloves and show him how to use them. That can wait a while as now he would put them in his own mouth instead of somebody else's.

I read your collums in the paper as it always makes me feel a little closer to you. It was very good but I was serprised to read in there about that Escalante woman. I had to check to make sure you still wrote in the sports section. That's enough of that! You be a good boy and stay away from those dames—especialy those redheads!

Can't you see that I have never stopped loving you? I know we can still work something out. In my heart I know we can. George won't be a problem. He does not even visit any more. There will be no trouble that way if you know what I mean.

Please "dear" let me know your intentions—what do you want to do? It is such a dirty rotten shame things had to go like this and I am sick at heart over it. I am so low and it should not be this way at all. We should be a family. You know what they say—love is what makes the world go around and I know that it is true because I have nothing but love for you and little Vincent to.

Please "sweetheart" write or call and tell me that you still love me and that we can work this out. I can not belief that we are finished. All my love and kisses as I love you "dearest."

Your Ida

P.S. Please exuse my mistakes as it is so hot here I

sometimes do not think my best, and I do not want to copy this over to make it perfect. I know you will understand.

xoxoxoxox

I was making my reflexive proofreader's corrections when I got brought up short: *George won't be a problem . . .*

This was a new wrinkle. I hadn't yet risen to the bait, so I guessed she was trying a different tack: the first mention ever of the prick responsible, her solitary reference to a mortal male's participation. George. Who the hell was *George*?

I called a Reno operator and got a number for the Hall of Records. When I got through I told the girl I was Dick Brubaker of the *San Francisco Inquirer*, fact-checking a birth announcement: one Ida Nichols was the mother, I said, and we needed to confirm her child's date of birth.

The clerk didn't balk, but I still made up a story: "Ida, see, she's the sister of one of our sportswriters and we wanted to surprise him by running a little item under his next column. He'll get a kick out of it. One for the scrapbook, you know." Serving up the BS to a civil servant who couldn't have cared less. She grunted, put the phone down, and came back a couple of minutes later with the date.

"Thanks. Can I check the spelling of the father's name while I have you on the line?"

"That would be Nichols. N-I-C-H-O-L-S. William Vincent Nichols."

I didn't know who she thought was going to buy all this. Try to pull a fast one, she'd be in for a surprise. This son of a bitch *George* would have to be reminded of his parental responsibilities. Once I found out who he was.

It didn't take long to review my options. The watch said 4:45 P.M. when I picked up the phone again.

On the second ring: "Dr. Kaiser's office."

"I need to see you, right away."

There was a pause, a long one. I hoped she was waiting for someone to drift out of earshot. "I can't. I'm sorry, it's not a good idea. I have to go home."

"Then I'm coming by tonight, after dinner. There's something we have to talk about."

She began to protest but I hung up.

Claire scoped out the potted plant in my hand as soon as she opened the door. I wish I could report that her face brightened.

"Is that for me?" she deadpanned.

Some kind of azalea, bought and wrapped earlier at Podesta Baldocchi. The pink petals reminded me of the dress she wore to the Temple Hotel that day. I'd really picked it because "azalea" put me in mind of Tony Zale, the middleweight boss. Even though his real name was Zalenski.

"Yeah," I stammered, "the guy told me you could plant them outside. I got it for your garden." I was a rube, standing at her stoop in the half-light that spilled out from inside her home. She hadn't left the porch light on for me.

She gave up a stiff grin. The kids were making kid noises elsewhere in the house. Back down the walkway, the taxi that delivered me idled at the curb, its low engine rumble the only sound in the neighborhood.

"You shouldn't give me flowers," Claire said. But she took it, cradling the basket in its bright foil wrapper. She searched for a place to set it, as if it scalded her fingers.

"I was hoping we could talk for a few minutes," I said, taking off my hat as a none-too-subtle signal.

"Come in, then," she said, empty of enthusiasm.

I gave the cabbie a down-low wave, cutting him loose.

The kids were posing as angels as we entered the dining room. Tony and Marie, displaying perfect bogus etiquette in their chairs, hands folded, lips pressed tight to stanch the giggles. A quick glance at the baby in the high chair—with pieces of dinner splattered on, around, and behind him—and Claire caught on to their game: target practice at the table.

She didn't reintroduce me to her kids. Cautious, maybe sensible. They might remember me to their father. Instead, she shooed them out, telling them to play upstairs, and to be quiet about it. Then she gave the baby's face a gentle wipe-down.

"Want something to drink?" she asked, dabbing a wet cloth over the kid's cheeks and mouth.

"You'll join me?"

"I could use a beer," she said. She scooped stray food from the high- chair tray into her waiting palm, then onto one of the kids' plates. Neither had eaten much. "What a waste," she sighed, collecting dishes and utensils. She nodded toward the gurgling baby: "Would you bring him into the kitchen? I gotta do these dishes. I don't mean to be rude. It's a thing with me. Gotta do the dishes right after dinner, or I'll leave 'em. Sorry."

"So you want me to carry him in there, or . . ."

"Bring the whole chair." She set the last plate on the stack and left.

The baby twisted his head every which way, trying to get a look at me standing behind him. He thrashed and kicked and keened like an animal. I put my hat back on to free up both hands and hoisted the high chair. Claire's older kids charged down the hallway upstairs, their footsteps thudding on the ceiling. The baby forced his head all the way back, staring up at me with big saucer eyes as I carted him into the next room. I stopped just inside the kitchen. Claire was scraping food from the plates into the garbage, a stain-spotted apron over her housedress.

I could have been Dad, getting home late, still in my overcoat and hat. *How was your day, hon?* Three kids, steady paycheck, firm grip on the rungs of the ladder. No wife of mine would have to work. As she bent to fetch a box of soap from beneath the sink, I wondered, *Could I be Dad?* I let the notion settle a moment. It nudged against the fear and the pain.

She set the soap on the tile drainboard and turned to me, blowing a stray lock of hair off her forehead. "Set him by the table. Have a seat yourself—I'll get us that beer."

A small built-in booth, enameled apple green to match the counter tiles, anchored one side of the kitchen. I installed the baby between that and the sink and sat, dropping my hat on the facing bench. Claire's heels click-clacked on the green and white linoleum squares. While she pushed things around in the icebox, I studied the flowing seams on the backs of her nylons. Then the baby yowled and Claire turned around holding a Schlitz.

"I want to thank you for the article," she finally said. She took a glass from the cupboard and opened the bottle with a church key bolted under the counter. Her cheeks flushed; she was embarrassed, it seemed, by my glowing testimonial.

"Not exactly the big spread I was promoting. Without a photo, I couldn't play it up so much," I said. "Big picture, big spread. That's how it works."

She poured several mouthfuls of beer into the glass and handed me the rest of the bottle. "I don't think you have any idea how much what you write means to people," she said, not meeting my eyes.

"How's that?"

"I never stop working my ass off, having to prove to the world that I'm a good wife and mother and—bang bang bang—you put it down in black and white and there it is: the proof. Nobody can argue it now." She stared at her baby's face, then stepped over to smooth his hair. "It meant a lot to me, Billy. More than you could ever know, probably."

She sighted me for the first time in several minutes: "Even if it was just an alibi." She saluted and took a swig. "Thanks anyway."

"We should have used your wedding picture," I said around the lump in my throat. "You looked sensational."

She set the beer glass on the drainboard and ran water in the sink, waiting for steam to rise, tugging on a pair of yellow rubber gloves to protect her perfect red nails.

Finally, over her shoulder: "Where'd you see my wedding pictures?"

"At Gig's. In his scrapbook."

"No kidding. That's a surprise."

"You were cut out of one of the shots. What do you think that was about?"

Her shoulders knotted. I'd seen that body language in plenty of locker rooms. Tight, nervous. The baby started whining again, threatening a full fit. Without turning, Claire said: "There's a box of animal crackers on the table—give him one."

I fished out a shortbread camel and leaned across the table to the high chair. The kid clutched my whole hand and eagerly started gnawing. When I looked back at Claire, she'd slackened, realizing how she'd tensed up.

"You were saying?" I prompted.

"How do I know why Gig did the things he did?" she said, staring out the window over the sink, absently sponging a plate. "Meanwhile, why'd you come all the way out here? Not just to give me a plant, I hope. To talk, you said. What about?"

We'd sparred enough. It was time for me to start mixing it up. Risky, but I didn't have too many options left.

"I think Sid Conte may have killed Gig."

She turned just far enough for me to read her profile, which was seriously bewildered: "What are you talking about?"

"Let's drop the cat-and-mouse," I snapped. "We both know me and Hack are in this way over our heads. You know what happened, but you might not know it all. Like the fact that Gig was strangled."

She kept her back to me. Deliberately, she went on soaping and rinsing dishes and setting them in a rack on the drainboard.

I laid it all out—my rough draft for the night of May 12. The kitchen shrank to the dimensions of a confessional. The air became close and heavy and still. The baby kept on staring at me with his mother's big eyes, gumming the pasty remnants of the cookie. The riskiest sacrifice of my life wouldn't even be a vague memory to this kid. The words poured, like I was pounding the Royal.

Halfway through my pitch, right at the point where I had Sid coming up on Gig, slipping off his loud silk tie, Claire started crying.

She tossed the sponge to the tiles and whirled, propping herself against the counter. Big tears. The kid swiveled to watch his mother, worry in his eyes and wet crumbs all over his chin. Claire snapped off the rubber gloves, inside-out, and pitched them aside. Black rivulets of mascara trickled down her cheeks, nearing the curve of her throat.

She came to me like a licked fighter retreating to the corner. She slumped to her knees beside the table.

I never expected this. Not from Claire. She was too tough. But now she looked up at me, her flooded green eyes spilling tears. My chest was sealed tight, like cement had been poured down my throat.

"It's not right," she gasped. "Stop doing this."

"It makes sense. O'Connor gave Conte the third degree. Says he fits the description from a witness next door."

She put her hands on my leg and dug in for all she was worth. "I said *Stop!* You don't even understand what you're doing. You're making up a story. Is that what you did with me? You just made up whatever sounded right, whatever you thought people wanted to hear?"

"This story could very easily be true. It explains what happened. It makes sense. Listen to me—"

"No! You listen to *me*. Go back to your job and stop all this. Get out now. If you want to make something up, make it up so that none of this ever happened, okay? You never went to Gig's that night—we were never together. That's the story you need to write now."

"It all happened. We can't pretend it didn't."

"*You* can! You have to!"

She stood abruptly, instinct alerting her that the older offspring were about to tumble in, drawn by the commotion. "It's all right," she called to them. "Mommy's okay. She just heard some bad news." Claire unhooked the swinging door and let it close off the kitchen. Pitched into the corner, her figure sagged with defeat.

Slowly, awkwardly, I moved behind her. It was all I could do not to pull her into my arms. The kids probably had ears to the door. I pressed my face against their mother's hair.

"None of this should have happened," she moaned. "It all ought to have been different."

I jockeyed her out of the corner and gently turned her around. Her eyes wouldn't meet mine. She buried her face in my chest to muffle the shuddering sobs.

It all *should* have been different. She had that right. Claire was supposed to have ridden *my* streetcar line, not Hack's. Then everything would have been different. Everything.

"You should have walked away when you had the chance," she murmured. "You don't belong in this mess. I'm sorry. I'm so sorry. Forgive me. Oh, God, forgive me. Why did you have to do it? Why'd you get yourself involved?"

Maybe this was what I'd wanted all along. To confess the *why*.

"I'll tell you, if you really want to know." I stepped back, affording breathing room but still clutching her arms. "Remember when I told you that story at lunch, how Hack knocked out that strikebreaker? Remember that?"

She wriggled out of my clinch and rubbed her hands over her soiled cheeks and nodded.

"For what it's worth, I want to tell you something. Something I've never told anybody else. If you'll listen. Because I need you to listen. Will you?"

She untied the frayed apron cord. "Another story," she sighed, using the wadded-up apron to wipe the streaks from her face. "Is *this* one true?"

"I wish it wasn't. But it is."

And I told her the story. My story.

★

It was our regular alleyway shortcut, and we'd almost reached Market Street when my father froze. I took a few more steps, oblivious, until I felt his tug on my arm. My father yanked me back the way we'd come. That's when I saw the two men, jumping from a parked car. Like wild dogs breaking from a cage.

One of them threw me to the ground. When I looked back, the taller thug was beating my father on the knees and shoulders with what looked like a table leg. I couldn't scream. I couldn't do anything. The other guy loomed over me, pulling me up. He slapped me across the face, knocking my hat into a puddle. He stared right into my eyes. Something he saw made him laugh. He shoved me into the wall so hard all the breath shot out of me. I went down.

My dad was on his knees. He wasn't going to take a count.

"You gonna keep your mouth shut, right?" one of the guys yelled.

"You want closed shops, this is what you get," the other one said. "Pass the word." They kicked him in the chest and then the face and my dad crumpled backward to the pavement.

I climbed up, plotting the best maneuver. A sharp kidney punch would stagger the tall guy. A jab or two, with a following right cross, might stun the other one. If the tall one went down, uppercuts would finish him before he could get back to his feet. They'd have to be short punches, all right on the mark.

"Who else is talking about a union? Give some names!" the tall goon hollered. He slammed my father in the hip with the table leg. I heard two cracks. "Give!" the guy barked. It made him crazier to see my father still trying to get up.

Now, I told myself. The hitter closest to me was wide open for a left hook. I could get in three or four good body shots before he knew what hit him.

"Fuck you, you cocksucking goon," I heard my old man say, the words thick and wet from the blood filling his mouth.

The guy swung the table leg with both hands and hit my dad square on the side of the head.

As they went past me, one of the dogs said, "You just stay there like a good boy."

"He died."

I was slumped in the booth, staring at the speckled Formica tabletop. The baby gave me the fish-eye, reaching out and flexing his fists open and closed. Claire kneeled nearby, back on her haunches.

"When did that happen? How old were you?"

"I was sixteen."

"Go home," she said suddenly. "Or go get drunk. Forget all this. It'll make you crazy."

"I owed your husband something, see? He paid that debt for me. And look how I repaid him."

"What do you mean, he paid the debt? You mean the guy he beat up on the dock was the guy who killed your father?"

"I don't know. It was years later. I'm not sure."

"You just want to *think* it was."

"That's right. That's exactly right. Hack did the thing I couldn't do."

"Listen to me, Billy," she said, putting a hand on my arm. "We've all got something we're trying to live down. Ralph, you, me—we're not perfect. Believe me, I'm so far from the woman you described in that story it's not even funny. But you—you're out of the muck, you're on top. And you need to stay there. Believe me, you've done enough. Don't try to do any more."

She shifted, allowing me to slip my arms under hers in an awkward embrace. She held me to her. I took a deep, difficult breath and my head filled with the smell of her.

"If you're going further into this mess on my account," she whispered, "don't—I'm not worth the trouble. Believe me."

The kitchen door creaked open and over her shoulder I could see the two children peering in at us. I wondered how many times they'd seen their mother like this, consoling their father after a brutal night at the office.

"Claire, I—"

"Don't. Don't say any more. You have to stay away from me now. You don't understand what you're dealing with, and I'm not going to explain. We don't have a choice. Forgive me, if you can. But leave me alone."

She showed me to the front door.

"My hat," I slurred, in a daze, not firing on all cylinders.

She retrieved the lid from the kitchen.

"It wasn't your fault," she said, handing me the fedora. "What happened to your father—don't keep on blaming yourself."

"I'm sorry," I mumbled. For what, I wasn't sure. But I felt sorry as hell. About everything.

"You're not half as sorry as me," she said. "How come you're sorry? For not going crazy and getting killed by those goons? Look what you ended up making of yourself. Your old man would be so proud. You've proven yourself. Don't you dare screw it up now."

I held her by the crook of her arm and kissed her. I didn't give a fuck if the kids were watching. She finally broke it off. I would have sold what was left of my soul for one of her laughs right then, but she was fresh out.

"What about you?" I asked. "Before, you were saying that there was something I didn't understand, something you didn't want to talk about."

"Thanks again for the story. I'm serious. It means everything to me. When the kids learn to read, I'm going to make them recite it every night before they go to bed. Instead of saying their prayers."

"Claire, what's going on? What aren't you telling me?"

"You know, I cleaned out the newsstand the other day. Mailed a bunch of clippings to Ralph. He'll be beside himself. He's already your biggest fan—this might put him over the edge."

"Claire . . ."

"Thanks for giving me something to live up to. And thanks for the azalea," she said. "I'll plant it out back."

She closed her front door. That left me on the street, wondering where I was and how in the hell I was going to get back to what I once called home.

21

Throbbing feet propped on a cleared corner of the cluttered desk, I dealt with the morning mail. After leaving Claire's the night before, I'd walked all the way home, up Taraval, untempted by the "L" cars hauling light loads of lonesome night owls. The hike broke in a new pair of Roblee brogues, but my dogs paid the price. They barked all night and were still whimpering the next day.

My trek proved again how compact my city was—tract homes built on the wind-whipped dunes were but a steady trudge from hilly, wooded enclaves. A ghetto kid with a good arm could heave a rock through an uptown picture window without leaving his stoop. You could amble from Skid Row to Snob Hill without soiling a clean shirt.

Once more, the city itself was where I'd turned for solace. Floating through its streets, isolated, was less treacherous than navigating women's deep water.

Claire had thrown me for a loop. Her dismissal, still fresh, felt as much like a benediction as a rejection. I couldn't figure that out, any more than I could reconcile the woman I'd made love to with the mother who seemed to have suddenly lost her humor and savvy and passion.

I chalked it up to guilt, of course. I chalked most things up to guilt. Claire'd gotten off her train, making a detour from the grind. But she caught sight of herself in the mirror—or more likely, in her kids' eyes. She panicked and decided it was all a mistake. Not difficult to understand, but hard as hell for me to stomach. Each glance at the phone made me think of calling. Every fleeting flash of a woman fired that little kick to my heart, the hope that it might be her, convinced our detour was the right route after all.

An envelope with a San Diego postmark brought me up straight in the chair. I figured it for a thank-you, gushing about Claire's piece in the paper.

I tore off the end and read the typewritten message inside. The words were dark, the ink hammered onto the page by a heavy hand.

> I got a visit from the cop. He thinks I am mixed up in it. I told him I was with my wife that night. She will back me up. He ask a lot of questions about you. Also Sid. What does this guy have? I did not say nothing. I swear. Cant you do something about this guy? He scares me.

Hack was upping the ante on his stupidity, writing that and posting it. Shit, for all I knew, he had to recruit somebody to help him with his spelling. A goddamn letter like this could put us away if O'Connor ever got hold of it. When I felt the paper and gave it an up-close inspection, my dread doubled. It was typed on a sheet that once had a carbon backing, like what I used when I wrote a story. It meant there was another copy, one I'd never be able to account for. Was Hack chump enough to save it for some reason? Drop it in the trash, or leave it lying out? Christ, he'd pounded the keys so hard he probably embedded it on the typewriter roll. Another loose end for me to worry about.

Still, it could have been worse—he could have been writing to advise me that I was a dead man. That he planned to kill me the first chance he got, because he'd found out about me and Claire. That was probably the worst horse in the race, and I hoped like hell it wasn't going to show.

Chicky Hannifin spotted me pushing through the doors of the Hearst Building and offered to give me a lift into North Beach. As he cruised his Nash onto Kearny, he socked me in the arm and pointed to the newsstand on the corner.

"Hey, lookit you—the big star!"

My mug, replete with jutting stogie, smiled out from placards wired to the racks. *Mr. Boxing is Billy Nichols—Inquirer Sports!* Latest street promotion from our marketing boys.

"Old Man Hearst must like you!" Chicky chortled. I let him think he was squiring a wheel; the truth was that every scribbler in Sports would sooner or later get his snout on the racks.

I wondered if my old man *would* have been proud, like Claire said.

Hearst despised trade unions after all, especially those that presumed to challenge his imperial publishing policies. Back in '34, though traveling in Europe at the time, Hearst played a major role in quashing the city's general strike. Rolling inland from the waterfront, triggered by the longshoremen, the walk-out spread to all the local trades and brought the city to a standstill. For the West Coast, it was an unprecedented display of labor's clout.

John F. Neylan, a former reporter at the Hearst-owned *Bulletin*, who became the Old Man's attorney and right-hand man, went to the mayor with Hearst's cabled command to break the strike. Neylan established a compound at the Palace Hotel and brought the five big sheets into Hearst's fold, securing a united front against the workers. The other papers' owners may have hated Hearst's guts, but when the grunts threatened to lift an extra buck from their pockets, they all fell in behind Hearst's high horse. Suddenly they pitched the newspaper business as a profession, not a trade—a bastion of independence, not of collective bargaining. It was also a preemptive salvo aimed at the fledgling Newspaper Guild, which wanted to unionize writers, not just production laborers.

I cut out Hearst's splenetic editorial and tucked it under my desk blotter:

> There are many thousands of honest, upright, God-fearing, hard-working union men now part of the so-called general strike. The total of these against the handful of communistic radicals, who have gotten them into this mess, is so overwhelming as to make us wonder how they have permitted themselves to be led from wise leadership into this revolt against their very selves. . . .

While the owners moaned or orated, Hearst encouraged them to kick in for strikebreakers. Take the high ground, but keep the low road covered. All kinds of beatings, mayhem all over the city, as management and labor slugged it out. My old man was a casualty—even if only I knew it. And I never said a word. I was just a kid, but I was being groomed for a spot in the empire. I wonder if I'd have sacrificed that spot if I knew then what I'd learn later.

"You ever meet Hearst himself?" asked Chicky. "Big-ticket guy like you, I figure maybe you got an invite down to the castle, am I right?"

"No, Chick, I've never made it to the ranch."

Hannifin punched the horn when a three-wheel motorbike cut him off to make a left onto California. He didn't miss a beat: "But you met him, huh? The Old Man."

"Not exactly." I looked over and saw the eagerness on Chicky's face. He was waiting for a story, a good one pulled out of the ether. A colorful thread in the tapestry, a glittering tile in the mosaic. That's the way I paid my freight. What was I supposed to do—*stiff him?*

"I can't say I met Hearst—but I did save his life."

"You did what? That's gonna take some explaining!"

"Back when I was still an office boy—1926. Yeah, that'd be right. It was about a quarter to two on a Thursday morning, that I know. The final was put to bed. The cards were coming out for the poker games. Bill Mason was on the city desk. With that same cigar plugged in his face. They lasted him a whole shift because he'd never light up. Just chewed on them. He's talking on the phone and calls me over.

"'How much you got on you?' he asks. I had a buck, maybe a buck and a half. Mason says: 'Guy just called, said he's the chief's secretary.' Chief as in Hearst. 'Says the Old Man is in Suite 315 over at the Palace. They want sandwiches and milk sent over, but they can't let anybody know he's in town. Get the food, go up the back elevator on the alley side of the hotel. Knock four times on 315.' "

"Why all the mystery?" Chicky inquires.

"Hearst was always doing stuff like that. Sneaking in to check on his papers, or smuggling Marion Davies around with him. Who knows why? But there I am, it's the dead of night. All the regular spots are closed. I know this little one-arm joint in an alley off Third, stuck between two hocks. I'd go there some nights for coffee and a roll, waiting for my dad to get off work. They're open and I tell Dutch, the counterman, 'I got a big order. Eight of the deluxe. Make that four cheese and four ham. A little bit of mustard on each. Put two bottles of milk in with 'em.'

"Dutch gives me grief. He says, 'Sounds like a party. I can put lettuce on them special if you want.' Damage came to eighty-seven cents. I remember that exactly. Seven each for the sandwiches, rest for the milk.

"I grab the bags and hustle down Annie Street to the Palace. A guard sees me waiting for the elevator. He looks me over, doesn't say anything. I'm out of breath and the top of the bags are all crumpled and wet by the time I knock on 315. The door opens a crack and a hand comes out and snatches the grub.

"'Thank you, young man,' a voice says. Then the door slams shut."

Chicky was dejected: "That's it? That's your meeting with Hearst?"

"Chick, I'm not done yet. Hold on. Later that night I'm riding the car home with my dad and I'm depressed. I can't believe I've been stiffed by the Chief. I mean, fresh sandwiches at two-thirty in the A.M., the money outta my own pocket—I was pissed! Worse yet, my old man thought I was being played for a sap. I told him the whole story, all excited, and after about ten minutes he turns to me and says, 'It was a prank, William. It was not Mr. Hearst. Someone was just playing a joke at your expense.' I was crushed. I'd never been that humiliated."

"Was it a joke?" Chicky wanted to know.

"You'll have to get used to it if you want to stay in this business," my father said finally, staring off toward the front of the streetcar.

I looked out the greasy window. The scattered lights of Oakland across the bay came and went in the gaps between the slaughterhouses. We didn't speak for maybe a dozen blocks.

"What are you talking about?" I said testily, to hide my hurt feelings.

"Don't tell yourself it's anything more than another job, William. I've seen the way you look at those editors ordering everybody around, and the big-shot politicians riding up in their cars from City Hall. They like to play with people like us. They can afford it, they got the money. They don't have to work for a living. For fun some people dance or sail boats or go to the fights. The bosses, they get their fun by pulling strings, by controlling everything. That's their kind of fun. Don't be impressed by your Mr. Hearst—while decent men beg for food, he builds himself a castle. You don't want to fall for his game. Even if you think you know the rules, you'll never win."

My father dropped his hand on my leg and gripped it. I studied the thick fingers, dyed gray by oceans of ink.

"They were playing a joke on you," he repeated, squeezing harder.

"So what was the deal? Was it a joke or not?" Chicky lit another Chesterfield, waiting for the Go where Columbus crossed Broadway.

"There was a call to our house the next morning. Me and my father were still asleep. It was Tom Connor, from payroll, who cut me my weekly check. 'We heard everything turned out all right,' he said. I didn't know what he meant at first.

"Then Connor says, 'The Chief's secretary, Mr. Willecomb, left an envelope this morning. There's a note that says, *"Please give this to the young man who saved Mr. Hearst's life."* There's a ten-dollar bill in there.' "

"Shit, ten bucks!" Chicky exclaimed. "You made out okay."

"I told Connor that the sandwiches cost twenty-five cents apiece. They reimbursed me that, and the milk money, in addition to Hearst's heavy tip."

"Christ, some operator you were. But what's this stuff about saving the Old Man's life?"

"Blowing smoke. Toying with an impressionable kid."

"What'd you do with the loot?"

"New shirt, new tie. Got a Dobbs, too, nice one with a black band."

"How'd your father take it?"

"How's that?"

"Your old man. That one-upped him pretty good. What did he say?"

"Nothing. I never talked to him about it."

22

I stood Chicky to dinner at Green Valley. We ran into Joe Flaherty and Viggio Marretti and had a nice supper. Vig told about his cousin Auggie having to spend the rest of his life in a wheelchair on account of getting shot in the spine trying to break up a robbery at a bar out in the Ingleside. We all agreed that the city wasn't what it used to be. Back before the war was a different story. You felt safe.

It could have been worse for Auggie, I submitted, offering some balm to Vig's bitterness. If he'd gotten killed, then none of the kids in the family would get to hear his stories. The one about how he met his wife, Magaña, on a boat from Australia. How he got to Australia in the first place—coming back drunk to the wrong ship in a Mediterranean port. The famous night at Coliseum Bowl, back when he was fighting. The ring announcer accidentally poked him in the eye during the introductions and Auggie, swinging on instinct, knocked the emcee cold.

We adjourned to Capp's to hoist one in Auggie's honor. Joe Herman showed up, an Englishman in tow, Nigel Sewell-Rutter or some such. The Brit claimed to be an advance man for some European promoters. We filled him up with local lore and let him buy the steam beer for more than two hours. Flaherty finally advised Mr. Sewell-Rutter that "if you took all the really good British boxers that have ever fought and laid them end-to-end—I wouldn't be surprised." Chicky delivered the coup de grâce, reminding our guest of how Brit judges jobbed Willie Ritchie—a local favorite—out of the lightweight crown when he fought Freddie Welsh in London. Should Sewell-Rutter's promoters wish to bring Welsh to San Francisco, Chicky offered to personally kick his limey arse. With a good meal and a half-dozen cocktails under his belt, Chicky was ready to go. It didn't matter a bit that the bum call in question happened thirty-three years earlier.

I navigated while Chicky grappled with the Nash. We got to my house around a quarter past eleven. I must have had half a heat on myself. It didn't even register, for instance, that the lights were on. And I only noticed the luggage when I tripped over it walking into the bedroom.

Ida was standing by the bed, changing a baby's diaper.

For a second, it seemed like she was going to run to me. But she finished pinning the diaper, lifted the baby up, and carried him over with her. She kissed me on the cheek.

"Isn't he beautiful? Didn't I tell you?"

She was doing her best to act natural. The eyes gave it away: hope, anger, anticipation, defiance—and that was only the stuff swimming around on the surface.

"Have you gone crazy?" I croaked.

"Crazy? Of course not. Why would you say that?"

"What are you doing here?"

"I told you I was coming back. You knew that this was what I wanted."

"It isn't right. I need more time. I need more time to think about things."

"About what?"

"About what?" I lurched away from her. I couldn't even take off my overcoat. It would have made the scene feel too familiar. Like business as usual. "About whether I *wanted* you to come back!" I shouted.

Ida clutched the baby even more tightly to her chest, so tight I thought she might smother it. She walked to the bed, slumped onto it, and started crying. Ida was skilled with the tears when she wanted to be, in a class with Stanwyck or Crawford. But this wasn't like any tantrum I'd seen before. Everything in her turned to tears, and they couldn't get out of her fast enough. The waterworks went on for three, maybe four minutes.

Still stunned, I looked around the room. She'd already rehung the wedding pictures and the framed religious clippings.

"Why wouldn't you want me to come back?" she sobbed.

This was no dream; dreams seemed more real.

"You left me! For chrissakes—you hatched this little bastard with some other guy!"

"Only because you wouldn't have our baby with me. Didn't you read my letters? Don't you understand—I love *you*."

Ida was a resilient piece of work. I knew she'd been rehearsing those lines for months, training, over and over in front of the mirror, like shadow boxing. Testing inflections, tone, pitch—all for that critical moment when it was do-or-die.

It clipped me like a short right hand you see coming when you're turned flat-footed. Nothing you can do except brace yourself and hope.

"This is all pretty sudden," I stammered.

"Sudden? I've been writing and calling for months. I've been begging you to tell me something. To let me know what you wanted to do."

"And what did you hear me say?"

"I know you were angry. I can understand that."

"What did you hear me say?"

"I know this might seem complicated, with a baby and all, but—"

"What did I say!"

"You didn't say anything!" she hollered. "*Nothing!* That's what you said! What you didn't say! Nothing's not something—what was I supposed to think!"

I stared at her, center-ring. "Who's George?" I asked stonily.

Ida laid the baby down in a portable crib next to her old side of the bed. It cried when she turned away, but she ignored it. She came at me.

"You actually think I'm crazy? Is that the truth?"

"Who's this George? Huh? Let's start with that."

"He's no one. That's not the point. We're still married, aren't we? You're the one listed on that birth certificate as—"

"Who is George?" I clenched her arm. Something hard and nasty was growing in my throat, burning high up on my cheeks. She winced and I bent the arm sharply down, making her twist in pain. "Tell me who you fucked right here in this bed! The one you screwed so you could bring his kid into my house. Tell me—who is he?"

"He's nobody! Don't you get it!" she shrieked. The little bastard wailed, too.

I twisted her arm so hard I thought it was going to pop right out of the socket.

"George Payne," she cried.

My old pal Georgie. Ladykiller from the old neighborhood. Big swordsman, servicing housewives like he was pumping gas.

I shoved her down. Ida banged off the footboard and onto the floor. The room tilted. Not all the alcohol had burned off. Rage siphoned bile up into my throat. Georgie Payne fucked my wife. Now his spawn was in my house. The kid thrashed around in the crib, wailing. The drapes were open, and the scattered lights of the neighborhood glittered beyond French doors that opened onto a small balcony.

"This is our child," Ida said, climbing to her feet between me and the crib. "I consider this boy *our* child."

"Really? What's George have to say about that? Let's call him and find out." I stamped over to the phone and grabbed it from the cradle, feeling the heft, brandishing it. "What's the fucker's number? You have to remember—all the times you dialed it from here. What's his fucking number!"

"I don't care about George! George doesn't matter!"

"You're completely fucking crazy."

"Am I? Am I? Why is that? Because I only want what everybody else in the world gets to have? Because all I want is what's natural for every woman and man? Is that why you say I'm crazy? Because I want a child I can love and raise and watch grow up? That's what makes me crazy? You're the one that's crazy—you're the one that's made himself into this completely different person who can't have a normal life like anybody else. You're the one that's crazy—you'd rather act like some character out of one of your newspaper stories! Always getting everybody to charge your batteries, strutting around all eight-million, ten-million—*Mr. Boxing*!"

"Don't even start," I sighed, a tide of nausea making me suddenly weary. "I've heard it too many times."

"Well, I'm sick of it, too. From now on, I'm going to have what I want. I deserve a life, too!"

"Go get one. Who's stopping you?" I yanked the bedroom door wide open and waved a hand. "Let's see how you like it out there," I said. "Let's see how far you get on your own. Let's see how far Georgie Payne's juice takes you. Oh, I forgot—that's why you're back. Ol' Georgie must be tapped out already."

"This is my home," Ida said. "This is where we are going to live now."

"Don't be too sure."

I was the one who went through the doorway and down the stairs. Ida followed. She leaned over the banister.

"Where are you going?"

"Why should you care? You've got your life, remember?"

"Is there somebody else?"

The fire and defiance vanished when she said it. Just like that she'd exposed her most vulnerable spot—the fear that she might run second to some other woman. She'd dropped her guard, left herself wide open, begging to be hit. I wanted to throw that knockout punch. I could feel it, could feel the words coming out, splitting the space between us with a rush of finality. I could feel the massive hurt of it, caving her in, crushing her.

But instead it was me who felt the crush. Because there wasn't somebody else.

Somebody else had made that perfectly clear.

SECTION S FRIDAY, AUGUST 6, 1948 CCCC*

AN AMERICAN PAPER FOR THE AMERICAN PEOPLE — MONARCH OF THE DAILIES

San Francisco Inquirer Sports

REG US PAT OFF

Through THE ROPES

By BILLY NICHOLS

Our weekly wind-up of odds and ends jumps off today with the odd. Word reaches us that happy-go-lucky gamester Dummy Mahan is about to undergo some rather exotic therapy to cure his lifelong hearing malady. As fistic fans know, Dummy has been deaf and dumb since birth. It never stopped the tough middleweight scrapper from becoming a ring favorite.

His manager, Gus Averill, thinks he can help Dummy regain his hearing by taking him on a plane trip. Paris? London? No such luck for Dummy. They're just circling the Bay Area. But the view is guaranteed to be unique—ten thousand feet up and getting closer every second.

"He's going to jump—with a parachute, of course," Averill explained with a laugh. "I heard about a guy in Europe who got back his hearing after a fall, so I figured it could work for Dummy."

I wouldn't want to see Jimmy Ryan's odds on this stunt paying off, but I will say this: if it does do the trick, I want to be there for Dummy's next fight, when he can finally hear the cheers of all those fans who've applauded his whirlwind style for so many years.

After champ Chester Carter disposes of Gus Lesnevich later this week, ring fans everywhere will all be wondering who Jim Norris and his IBC cronies will trot out next for the Jacksonville Jewel. Joe Louis's "bum of the month" club doesn't look so sorry now, does it? This is no knock on Chet, who gives as much value to the division as a beefed-up light-heavy can. . . .

A few ducats are still to be had for the annual James J. Corbett Dinner this Wednesday, honoring one of our favorite fellows, the legendary Tim McGrath. . . .

23

The wide stone stairway of SS Peter & Paul Church, one of the Lord's most majestic San Francisco addresses, was filled with fighters. Stained-glass apostles, basking in the sun, presided over the gathering. Every local pug had been drawn to the Catholic heart of North Beach, along with every stable manager, matchmaker, promoter, trainer, ticket hawker, two-buck wagerer, and hanger-on.

I brushed past Vern Bybee, who was swapping stories with Ray Lunny. They performed before a cluster of tin-ears. Mock reenactment of their battles at the Civic. They'd wanted to assassinate each other in the ring. Now they acted like altar boys, sharing dirty jokes before entering the sacristy. They squared off and somebody popped a picture.

It was all fairly festive, considering. The fraternity renewed acquaintances and sunshine eased the aches and pains as the updates, personal and professional, circulated. Old stories drew the same guffaws for the hundredth time.

Dummy would have loved it, too. Unfortunately, he was inside, pieced together in a closed casket, waiting for the gang to pay its last respects.

This crowd was different from the one that turned out for Frankie Campbell. Same cast, same venue, but that day crept by under skies as gray as freshly poured concrete. Nobody cut up touches or laughed to let off steam. It was row after row of bowed heads, above fists clenched together so hard the knuckles looked fit to burst. Frankie was a North Beach hero, who'd beaten guys from L.A. and New York. He had the shimmer of a potential champ. But in a rough tussle at old Recreation Park, Max Baer had hemorrhaged his brain. Campbell got tangled in the ropes in a corner and couldn't take a knee. Ref Toby Irwin had never liked Frankie, and he let Baer uncork a few free shots, just for the hell of it. So much for Frankie's potential.

No one felt like fighting for some time after that. The city fathers even pondered a ban on boxing, while Baer, instead of Irwin, stood trial for manslaughter. A few months passed and the circuit started clicking again. Baer was issued an acquittal. Business went back to normal.

Dummy, he was another kind of story. If Campbell was the leading man, Mahan was the comic relief. Hellbent-for-leather in the ring, Dummy was a far better boxer than he let on. His handicap relegated him to undercards; a sideshow, a brawling oddity. Champs were guys like Frankie. Guys like Dummy, they were made to be used. And Dummy let himself be used, thoroughly and often. That's why everybody liked him.

He and Frankie were equals now.

Burney Sanders buttonholed me as I headed inside the church. I was in no mood for chat, but there was never any stopping Burney.

"Hey, Bill—how's the wife?"

"She's fine," I told him, as flatly as I'd ever responded to anything. She and the kid had taken over the master bedroom. I was set up in the old maid's quarters, downstairs. When I was home. Happy family. Domestic bliss.

"Got some major news for you," Sanders went on, "but it's gotta stay under the hat for a few days. I've got a state title fight lined up. Here, probably at the Civic. Or else Oakland, if I can't work a deal with Thomas."

"Heavyweight?" Purvis Burnett held the California heavy crown. A smart but uninspiring fighter with little gate appeal, and no following nationally.

"Right. Burnett and Escalante. End of the month. Sid's game, and I already cleared it so Hack gets leave to fight."

"You think those two can fill the Civic?"

"Local white boy up against a spade from down South? It's a natural. Plus, we got two whole months to build it. It'll sell out easy. Then I'll use that to pump up the grand opening of the new Bucket of Blood. I got a good thing rolling here."

I congratulated Burney halfheartedly and moved on, crossing through the bright portal into the immensity of the church. Scattered souls moved in and out of the transepts, holding flames to votive candles, murmuring prayers, fingering rosaries. I walked down a side aisle, beneath stations of the cross, stopping at a confessional. A plaque on the door gave the priest's name: Father Petri.

I slipped inside. The panel slid open.

"Bless me, Father, I have sinned," I began, dredging up the protocol from way back.

"How long since your last confession?"

"Longer than you'd want to know."

"What is it that brings you here today?"

"Things have happened." I had wondered what would surface first. "I . . . took something. Something that wasn't mine. That belonged to someone else."

"Then you have stolen?"

"In a manner of speaking. I suppose so."

"What did you do exactly? Do you regret your action now?"

The wooden underpinnings of the booth creaked as I fidgeted. I could hear the boys outside, shuffling into pews.

"Let me ask you something, Father. Change the subject for a moment. Why do you think Dummy died?"

"A tragic accident, I heard."

"One way to put it. He jumped out of a plane because his handler told him it would cure his deafness. Well, it did. The chute didn't open. That's *how* he died. But I mean *why?* Why do you suppose that happened?"

"I'm not sure I understand your question."

"I'm asking why you think it happened."

"There is a reason, rest assured. The Lord works—"

"—in mysterious ways? So I've heard, but I don't know. I can't believe that Dummy died as part of some divine plan, Father. He died because he was a dupe. He could be talked into anything."

"In any event, his soul is at peace now."

"How do you know that? I don't reckon he was saying his prayers as he fell. I'll bet all he was thinking about was what an idiot he was for going along with such a harebrained publicity stunt."

"What does this have to do with your own situation? You said that you had sinned, that you had taken something that was not yours."

"I did. But hold on. Wait a minute. Explain this to me—almost every fighter I know prays before he climbs into the ring. But they go ahead and get knocked out anyway. Aren't their prayers as good as the other guy's? Soldiers pray to God in the foxhole, too, just before they die. Don't they?"

For a moment all I heard was the rustling of his cassock on the other side of the screen.

"Not all prayers can be answered," he finally declared. "But the Lord rewards those who demonstrate their faith in Him. Eventually."

"So you've just got to believe hard enough, is that it? If Frankie Campbell believed hard enough, if he'd demonstrated better, he wouldn't have got his brains beaten out?"

"The Lord's hand has a purpose we cannot expect to understand. We must simply believe. If we cannot always comprehend the *why*—there is a reason for that, as well."

"Could be He just doesn't care."

"Your anger . . . where does it come from?"

"It's because you can't win. You try to do the right thing. You play by the rules, but the rules get bent. Every day. They get bought and paid for. You want to believe in something bigger, but the world is the same all-around shitty place, day after day. What the hell can prayers do? I say the mumbo jumbo and try to convince myself it'll make a difference somehow, in some way. But it never does. It's just every man for himself out there. Always has been. Always will be."

"That is not so. Faith can make a difference. Life isn't about winning and losing. That's what you don't see. It's about acceptance, belief in the power of something greater. A greater good."

"How's that? If you pray hard enough you get special dispensation? You get to cut in line for the big payoff?"

The priest heaved a long, exasperated sigh.

C'mon, Father. Don't quit now. Show me you can go the distance.

"If you no longer believe," he countered, "why do you want absolution?" He'd dropped some of the hushed haughtiness.

"Because I don't think I'm a bad man, Father. I am *not* a bad man."

"What took place for you to feel you need the Lord's forgiveness?"

Well, that was the question, wasn't it? How do you

total the sum of your sins, if you can even them all out? I'd allowed my father to be killed, but maybe I'd done him proud in the long run. I'd covered up a murder, lied to the law, yet spared a young man and his family. I'd coveted that man's wife—but can you help falling in love?

"I'm not sure, Father. I'm not exactly sure what I've done."

"Make your peace with the Lord, and you'll be forgiven."

"I'd like to believe that. I honestly would."

"Believe that you must prove yourself to be accepted into everlasting light. Boxers know this. Each one must believe that the struggle will be worth the effort in the end. Pain, even failure, is part of the training. That's what the commandments tell us, don't you see? Our life here requires dedication and discipline."

That was more like the Father Petri I remembered from St. Elizabeth's, the one who taught boxing after school and had been the CYO heavyweight champion five years running. The one who'd knelt and prayed over the prostrate kid he'd cold-cocked.

"If you have stolen, you have violated one of the commandments, and that cannot be dismissed lightly. A mortal sin is a violation of God's trust in you."

"What's my penance?"

"The answer lies in prayer."

"The world's not a good place, Father. I don't know if praying is going to be enough."

"The condition of the world is not the fault of God. The fault is ours, for failing Him. He does not offer us protection, least of all from ourselves. All He asks is that we believe. That we believe in His sacrifice, and a power beyond ourselves."

"I'm trying, Father. Against all odds, I'm trying."

"Do you renounce all of your worldly sins and beg forgiveness of the Lord, our Father?"

"I do." What the hell, I thought. It couldn't hurt.

"Say ten Hail Marys and ten Our Fathers," he instructed. "But what you say is right—prayer is not enough. You will have to examine your life and question your actions. Then you must demonstrate your faith through an act of contrition."

I sneaked into a pew next to Burney Sanders. He wore the glazed expression of a guy waiting for his wife to finish shopping.

If I was supposed to take Ida back as my act of contrition, some kind of balance needed to be struck.

"Burney, think you could do me a favor?" I whispered. "Strictly on the cuff. I figure you might know somebody who knows somebody."

He perked right up: "What's the pitch?"

"Fellow name of George Payne. Works for a local beer distributor. He needs to find employment someplace else. Someplace far away. And he'll need a little push in that direction."

"No reason that can't be done."

"I'll make sure you get big play on the fight. We'll do it up right."

Burney couldn't contain a hard laugh. Its echo boomed through the church as the monsignor ascended the pulpit. Sanders looked momentarily sheepish, then flashed me a smile.

"We got a deal, Bill," he said, shaking my hand.

24

From the stack of mail on the foyer desk I plucked out a small envelope addressed to Ida. Irrationally, I suspected a clandestine communiqué from Payne. It was from Ida's sister Paula, and had already been opened. Tucked inside was a snapshot, with the year, 1918, scratched in pen along the top. The young Lindstrom girls, dressed as nurses, surgical masks knotted tight. White uniforms stood out against a dark day and shadowy front porch. A sign propped in front of them read skidoo you flu in childish lettering. On the back of the picture Paula had written:

> *Ida—remember this? Thirty years, can you believe it? We made it through the flu, the crash, and the war and they haven't found anything to stop us yet. Say hello to Bill. We're so happy everything's back to normal.*
>
> *Love,*
> *Paula*

I inspected the picture more closely, searching for my wife's eyes between the bright white of the hat and the mask.

I took the photo into the bedroom. "Cute picture," I commented. Ida, in a robe, poked her head out of the closet. She'd been looking for a space to hang a dress. The closet was already jammed and thick with the chemical odor of mothballs. She'd stuffed it with new garments brought back from Nevada. Several dresses were draped over the rails of the crib, where her baby slept.

When she saw me with the picture, she immediately snatched it from my hand, slinging the dress over her arm.

"I've got to save that one," she said. "It's priceless."

Ida accorded tremendous value to her personal mementoes. Grainy family portraits; books she'd never read; brittle newspapers stacked in a laundry hamper; restaurant menus; decades' worth of ephemera tenderly wrapped in tissue, forgotten but not gone.

She added the flu photo to a bulging cache of similar treasures in an overstuffed dresser drawer, safe beneath dozens of pairs of undergarments. The drawer issued a labored complaint when she urged it shut with her hip.

"You going to go to the dinner tonight?" I asked. "It's at the Village. We can ride with Jack."

"Do you *want* me to go?" This is how it began. Every time.

"Only if you want to. You always say it's the same old faces, the same old stories. And that's what it'll be, so . . ."

"So you don't want me to go."

"I didn't say that."

"That's quite all right. If you want to go by yourself, charge your batteries, you go right ahead."

"Is that what you think I said?"

"That's what it sounded like to me."

"Well, maybe you should listen to what I'm saying, instead of what you want to hear."

"I heard you fine. What you were saying is that I'd probably be bored, and you'd be happier if I stayed home."

"That is *not* what I said."

"No, but it's what you meant."

"You obviously don't know what I meant."

"Then you *admit* you meant something else besides what you said."

I wrenched my jacket off and hurled it into a chair. A button popped off when I yanked at the cuff. Change from my pockets rained on the dresser. I counted to ten. Then I did it again, swallowing, pulling in air.

"I'm presenting one of the awards," I told the dresser top. "That means I'm up at the head table. I gotta let Art know if I need one seat or two. Simple as that. Yes or no?"

"This is awful short notice," Ida sighed, touching her hair. "It's going to be too late to get a beauty parlor appointment. I'll have to call Paula and see if she'll come do me. And sit with the baby."

My own closet was a musty jumble, the floor strewn with worn wing tips, the shelves stacked with blocked, unused fedoras. Acquaintances were always giving me hats, thinking the lid was my trademark. Like Confucius said: Gifts of hats will make your presents felt. I picked a clean, dark suit from the wardrobe warehouse and stepped back into the dressing room between the bed and bath.

At least it was designed to be a dressing room. Ida had years ago upgraded it into a prayer room. Facing the back wall was a prayer bench, complete with an altar. The kneeler was upholstered in red velvet, worn down from devotion or daydreaming. Take your pick. A table was arrayed with odes to faith clipped from newspapers and magazines, and there were votive candles in red glass. A plaster bust of Christ, adorned forlornly with His crown of thorns, hung beside the door leading to the water closet. It was festooned with fragile and decaying fronds, dispensed over the years at Palm

Sunday Masses. They'd been tacked to the wallpaper, whose fleur-de-lis pattern would have suited one of Sally Stanford's whorehouses.

Within this little chamber of supplication I faced the full-length mirror on the back side of the bedroom door.

"It's my privilege this evening to introduce our guest of honor at the annual James J. Corbett Dinner," I intoned while suiting up. "Tim McGrath may be the most colorful figure in local boxing lore—at least among those of us who didn't earn our reputations pushing leather. This gentleman has seen it all. From being a second to Corbett in his legendary barge fight against the great Joe Choynski, through his glory days patrolling the boulevards with his great pal Spider Kelly—"

Sharp pounding on the other side of the door. My reflection wobbled.

"Who are you talking to in there!" Ida shouted.

"Nobody! Chrissakes, you scared me half to death. I'm only practicing what I have to say tonight."

"Paula and Mary are downstairs. You might come out and say hello at least."

The sisters were in a huddle around a playpen, watching their respective offspring crawl and climb and tumble. Paula and Mary noticed me, standing in the archway. The cooing stopped and their faces tightened.

Ida waved me in. She hoisted up her baby boy. "Say hello to Daddy, Vincent. Can you say, 'Hi, Daddy'?"

The women cast their eyes down, then stole glances at each other. This coven, especially that bitch Mary, should be grateful for chivalry. It's what kept me from slapping them, one by one, across each smirking face.

I sauntered over. "Paula. Mary." I stroked the baby's hair

and chucked its chin and emitted an amusing gurgling noise. The kid coughed a little and managed a gummy grin. Ida positively glowed. She flashed a world-beating smile at her siblings.

Seems she had the leg up on them once again. She finally got her baby—and still had the hook in her big-shot husband. Through sheer force of will, Ida was pulling off a world-class rewrite. It put to shame what I'd tried to accomplish reconfiguring the circumstances of Gig Liardi's death. My wife blithely buried the truth and made life conform to her fantasies. All she had to do was *act*. The Nevada episode never happened. Everything was in its proper place. She'd get away with it—assuming I went along.

For my part, I recognized it as a pact, a negotiation. This wasn't my life. A drafted doughboy in the trench, a swab in his fo'c'sle, a slugfish in the ring—are those their *lives*? It's just duty, service. As for me, my life was elsewhere. At the office, out in the circuit. This was nothing but a puff piece, the filler, the human-interest angle.

"I think he's got his father's eyes," said Mary, flashing me a nasty smile.

I showed teeth right back, wondering if the little bastard's father would still have eyes after Burney's boys were done with him.

Two spectral figures waltzed to and fro, battling vaguely in the half-bubble of the Philco screen. Chester Carter was defending the NBA heavyweight crown against Gus Lesnevich; it was every bit as exciting as me balancing a checkbook. The round mercifully ended, the picture fading to an advertisement for Rheingold beer.

"This is pitiful," said Joe Herman, on the blower. I was

back in the archway of the living room, the phone cord stretching from the foyer desk. Herman was calling from the Spur Club, crammed in a phone booth, watching the fight on a set above the bar. "Carter doesn't have the same pop since he killed Jerrone," he said.

Red Jerrone had died last February, allegedly from cerebral complications sustained in a set-to with Carter. My sources noted that Jerrone was damaged goods *before* he swapped blows with the Jacksonville Jewel, who didn't typically trade in haymakers.

But Carter was a skillful boxer; he'd outfinessed both Ezzard Charles and Jersey Joe Walcott for the vacant title, following Joe Louis's retirement. The public was cool toward his coronation. Louis still reigned. He'd been undisputed champ more than eleven years, and fans were spoiled by his clean demolitions, his surgical savagery. Carter, unlike Louis, couldn't pack an arena with the promise of thunder and lightning erupting from his fists.

The jingly commercial spiel over, Round Seven began. Carter stalked his prey methodically. Lesnevich seemed gassed.

"I talked to Hurley today," I mentioned to Herman. "He told me the gate for this would barely top sixty grand. Can you imagine? For a title fight?"

"I can't get used to this," Herman muttered.

"To what? Not seeing Louis in there?"

"This television thing. It ain't the same watching a fight this way. It ain't right. You're supposed to go out, you gotta go to a club. This catches on, we'll all be in trouble. Guy like Burney, he'll take a bath at National Hall—all the dough he's sunk in there. Your customers'll stay home to watch some fight back East."

"I know what you mean. Gives me a bad feeling. It's a whole new racket, different guys in charge. A lot of money is gonna get wrapped up in it. Advertisers, sponsors. It's gonna change everything."

"Hold it—did I just see Gus throw a punch? I hear Norris is friendly with the wrong people. What's your take?"

Jim Norris was boxing's latest kingpin. He was heir to a Midwest grain fortune, but hopped off the straight and narrow early on, preferring to breed thoroughbreds in Kentucky and purchase pieces of promising heavyweights. He liked to gamble big, and had a weakness for slumming not uncommon among the gentry's black sheep. Norris wedged himself into the heavyweight picture after a stroke retired Mike Jacobs to his Jersey rose garden. Norris formed the International Boxing Club and mesmerized Louis with all kinds of promises.

Poor Joe was getting pummeled pounds and pennies: alimony and back taxes, a killer combination. The champ saw the virtues of a steady payoff that didn't require undue extension of his chin. Norris's setup was a complex scheme to which I wasn't yet altogether savvy. But the outlines were ugly. Louis, trying to get out from under an uncle (Sam) and three ex-wives, had stabbed Jacobs, his Svengali, in the back. It was enough to make you feel sorry for Mike. Almost.

"Hurley says Carbo and Palermo practically live in Norris's pants," I said. "It doesn't look good. Those mob goons will louse him up."

"Hang on, here we go—Carter is coming on now, you see it? Nice combination."

"Gus is gonna go."

"You know, this television thing . . . It's like you got just one gigantic hall. That means one outfit will be taking the tickets, so to say, no matter where the fight is, am I right? Oh shit, good right hand—"

"And figuring how these outfits shell out big loot up front for their shows, they'll want more and more say-so. Next thing you know, these stations will have their own fighters on the payroll, hand-picked, and then—*there he goes*. Say good night, Gus."

"It ain't like it used to be, that's what we're saying, Billy."

"Hey, what is?"

"My point. I went into that Fantasia, the one on Powell? Coffee and a danish. Guess how much."

"Two bits at least."

"Thirty! Can you believe it? And no refill."

"Remember the Merry-Go-Round on O'Farrell, over by there? Had the desserts on a conveyor belt, going around the counter?"

"The best. No extra charge if you wanted the à la mode on your pie. Right? All the dessert you wanted, no extra charge, wasn't that the deal?"

"Absolutely."

"Bill, I gotta pee. I'll call you back."

The phone rang ten minutes later. I figured Joe was done splashing the stones. I'd moved to my study upstairs, working at a small rolltop the paper donated to me when they reappointed our offices with metal furniture. I was jotting a note to Jack Hurley, fishing for more dope on Norris and his cronies.

"I can't get it," Ida yelled from down the hall. "I've got the baby in the tub. You better answer it, Dad."

Marching to the bedroom, I answered the phone.

"Hello, Billy. How are you?"

My heart skipped. I didn't—couldn't—say a word.

"Don't tell me you don't recognize my voice."

"You know I do," I said throatily. She already had the whole picture, from my stammered delivery. Claire was that sharp.

We paused, measuring the distance between us.

"I'm guessing that your wife is back."

"Yeah, yeah, that's right."

"Well, best of luck. We're both gonna need it."

Her voice was thick around the edges. She'd had a couple. Maybe more.

"Tell me what's going on," I said.

"Bad things. Things you ought to know. I . . . never should have lied to you in the first place."

"How's that? I don't follow."

She hesitated. The silence gained weight. It grew heavier with each second that passed in a fog-bound house by the ocean, the kids tucked away, their mom getting loaded at the kitchen table where I'd spilled my guts.

"It's not what you think, Billy. None of it. But you're a nice guy, see? One of the good ones. The fortunate few. Maybe that's part of the problem. You're giving everybody a break. Stop it. Don't. Oh, *shit*. I don't know what I'm gonna do. I'm in big trouble."

"What kind? Tell me," I implored in a desperate whisper.

"Every kind. For starters—I'm pregnant."

"You're, uh . . . you are? Huh. Why are you, uh . . ."

"We both know who the father is."

I set myself down heavily in the chair and looked at my shoes.

Ida walked in, cradling the baby in a terry-cloth towel: "Did you get the—"

I slashed at the air, shutting her up. There was only static on the line for a few long seconds.

"Don't worry," Claire said. "I won't make a big scene."

"Uh-huh, uh-huh," I agreed, nodding my head for Ida's benefit. "What are you gonna do?" I asked, watching as Ida gently set her baby in its crib.

"Well, I sure as hell can't keep it. Four kids? There's just no way. And I gotta do something before I'm showing. Jesus, I can't believe this."

"Uh-huh, I see. That's, uh . . . too bad. Really a shame."

"I'm embarrassed as hell about this, but I gotta ask you for some money. I heard about a doctor who's supposed to be safe, but I don't have that kind of cash sitting around."

"Uh-huh, sure, sure . . . whatever you say."

"I know, I know. She's in the room. How do you like that? For once Mr. Boxing can't talk."

"I wish I could. I really wish I could."

"Well, I'd appreciate it, if you can send it to me right away."

"I could drop it off. How much?"

Ida looked over. Her radar was finely tuned to the greenback wavelength.

"Can you spare a couple hundred?" Claire asked, miserable humiliation in her voice. "And please, I'm serious—don't be gallant and come hammering on my front door. Nothing good can come of it. I wish it was all different, but there's no way . . ."

"I'll get it. It'll work out. Don't worry."

"Yeah, I've tried that," she said. "It doesn't work. It's worse than you can imagine—and you've got one hell of an imagination."

"I'm not clear on the whole story," I improvised. "Maybe we can meet—"

"No! That's how we made our first mistake, Billy. Just stay away. I'm in the corner, pal. On the ropes. And I don't see too many ways out. But I'm not going without a fight. I'm going to prove who I *really* am in this whole fucked-up thing."

"Let me help," I said, too urgently. Ida looked over, concerned.

"If I pull this off, you won't have a thing to worry about. Tough it out with the wife and keep your nose clean. You're better off. Believe me. And forgive me. I'm not proud of all this."

"All what?"

A choked-off gasp, a click, then nothing.

"Who was that?" Ida asked, turning from the crib.

My head jerked up. "How's that? Oh, it was . . . just another fighter."

"They're always looking for a favor, aren't they," Ida sniffed.

25

"What can I do you for, Bill?"

Jimmy Ryan gestured to his mixologist, a subtle rotation of the wrist. A little move, yet loaded with authority. Imperious almost. Seconds later, a fresh fizzing libation appeared on the plank beside Jimmy's lazily propped elbow.

"Whatever you're having, Jimmy."

"Tonic and bitters, buddy. I quit drinking."

"Rock and rye," I told the bartician.

It was early, not even six. My workday had ended hours ago, but Ryan and his Daily Double were just gearing up. Busboys dressed tables, smoothing starched linens. Waitresses sauntered in sporadically, twittering like schoolgirls. Within a half hour, painted, pinned, and poured into their silks, they'd radiate an exotic allure.

A splinter of the fraternity had hoofed it to Jimmy's cool oasis from the humid confines of the Royal Athletic Club, down on Turk. I'd exited the roisterous confab to snag Jimmy alone.

"That Carter fight last week was sure a dog," Ryan said. "Billy, you look beat. Something eating you?"

"Lot of things piling up. I need to talk to you—off the record."

Ryan sipped his virgin beverage and waited. When streamlined Jimmy double-clutched into his idling gear, a stillness came over him that could give pause to the uninitiated. I gave it the gas and skimmed past the frostiness.

"How well you know Sid Conte?" I began.

Jimmy set down his tonic: "Personally or professionally?"

"Either way."

"Not at all, personally. Otherwise . . . He's a player. He likes the action."

"Betting man, is he?"

"Much as the next guy."

"Sake of argument, let's assume the next guy is a chronic. We on the same page?"

Jimmy sipped again, pinkie extended. He swirled an ice cube, inhaled it, cracked it with his molars. When Jimmy was finished with you, he let you know. No response? Go ahead on, with caution.

"I know Sid's in the hole," I continued. "Makes no difference to me. My question is if he's ever touted to you how he plans to climb out. Grand designs, big schemes—that kind of thing."

"This sort of talk is vague," Jimmy said, grinning. "Even for me, this is vague."

"Okay, try it like this. I figure Sid's under a lot of pressure. On deadline. I know the feeling. In that situation you might say things. Stuff you wouldn't say under normal circumstances. It's different when you're trying to get out from under . . . I figure he's cried on your shoulder once or twice. Am I right?"

"I don't feature the general direction we're headed," said Jimmy. "If you got something specific in mind . . ."

"Gig Liardi," I said, and Jimmy tensed up right on cue.

The barkeep flipped a switch and the ribbon of red neon swirling beneath the glass bar crackled to life. Jimmy's white suit flushed pink.

"You're not in the picture. Nobody's saying that," I went

on. "But if you've got anything that puts Conte with Liardi, I'd like to know."

"Are the cops thinking that Sid killed Liardi?" Jimmy whispered. He leaned closer. The hook was in him, nice and snug.

"Go ask. I'm just sniffing around to see what puts Sid and Gig together."

"Well, that'd have to be Hack, right?"

"For sure. But what if there's something else we don't know about? A previous connection, so to say."

"Won't the cops dig that up?"

"Their methods of persuasion are limited. I know you and Sid have gotten close the last few months. You can talk to him. And he might tell you things he wouldn't tell anybody else."

"What's your angle?" Jimmy gave me the cocked eyebrow.

"You know me, Jimmy. Working a story—that's all."

Ryan fidgeted. Hooks can do that to you. He slid his drained glass across the bar and gave himself the once-over in the mirror.

"If I find out something, I'll be in touch," he said.

Ryan slithered past me. At the far end of the bar he paused to review a booze receipt handed to him. The delivery guy was my brother-in-law, Gil Rayburn. Mary Lindstrom's no-doubt-beleaguered husband. Coworker of a certain George Payne. Gil flashed me the "hold on" sign, and hustled over after Jimmy had signed off on the shipment.

"What's the good word, Gil?"

"Guess you heard about Georgie." No idle chatter for Gil. He was on the clock.

I played it dumb: "Payne? What about him?"

Gil gave me a look that slashed through the smoke screen.

He was clued in on the latest. We were, after all, hitched to sisters.

"Way I heard it, two guys beat the shit out of Georgie. Then they drive him all the way to fucking Solvang. Dump him out on the side of the road. Plus, they keep his wallet, and his pants."

"Jesus. Why Solvang? They must have wanted soup. That's the split pea capital of the world, you know."

Gil didn't crack a smile. He should have been happy for his associate. Payne should have been happy, too. Relieved, at least. The goons hadn't gotten carried away, as goons often did.

"Georgie called work," Gil continued. "Collect. Had one of the crew bring his shit down to him."

"Humiliating. What was it all about?"

Again, the glare from Gil. I played it like Jimmy—blank as a fresh piece of foolscap.

"We're replacing him," Gil said. "He's in L.A. now. We'll get him a spot at one of our plants down there."

"Just like ol' Georgie to land on his feet. Good for him." I toasted the worthless fuck with a sip of Old Hypocrite.

"I tried to tell you about him," Gil muttered. "A long time ago."

I hoisted my glass in another empty salute: "Give my very best to your lovely wife," I proclaimed, then walked back to rejoin the boisterous boys.

"Grab a chair, Billy," hollered Moe Connelly. "You're right on time—we need ya. Ike was trying to tell Hutch the Swansy Hollow story. Butchering it all to hell. Tell the story—tell it right."

"Christ, Ike. Haven't you got that one memorized yet?" I said, dropping into the chair that Irish Johnny Smith pulled over.

"This was back in '40," I started. "Down in Los Angeles. Armstrong and Garcia, for the middleweight title—"

"Helluva fight," barked Joe Atkinson. "In the fourth round Garcia was—"

"Joe, shut up! Billy's telling the story!"

"—and Willie Ritchie, state athletic commissioner—as you all know—Ritchie had just picked a new inspector for L.A., fellow name of Peter Cassidy. A few of us from upstate took the train down, including Burney Sanders. He'd just started handling fighters, and he went down with Dewey, who showed him the ropes. Armstrong liked Dew. Wanted him in the corner, just in case. Liked the way he dealt with a cut—"

"Sugar, that's his secret," Ike interjected. "You slap some sugar in there." Moe slugged him quiet.

"Anyway," I continued, "there's no love lost between Burney and the Angelenos. Sanders sizes up the new guy, this Cassidy, as strictly a know-nothing. Ritchie had to be doing somebody a favor. Burney's not one to let that go by. He pulls Cassidy aside and says to him, with deep sincerity: 'My advice is not to let them use the Swansy Hollow punch in this fight. Both these guys have had a lot of bouts this year. It'd be a shame if something happened here. You ought to take a stand, let everybody know you care about these men, as fighters.'

"Cassidy nods seriously, as if he understands, and thanks Burney for his concern. Burney, of course, grabs me outside and says I've got to get myself into Garcia's dressing room when Cassidy goes in. Sure enough, Cassidy's going over the rules while Garcia's getting his hands taped, and at the end of the standard spiel, Cassidy says, 'And in addition, I decree that neither fighter shall employ the Swansy Hollow punch in tonight's match, under penalty of disqualification. There is simply too much risk of injury.'

"Everybody looks at each other like *Who is this guy?* But no one says a word. I follow Cassidy over to Armstrong's dressing room. He does the same thing: 'I forbid the use of the Swansy Hollow punch.' Well, Armstrong sees all of us trying not to laugh, and he tells Cassidy: 'Don't you worry, sir. In the heat of battle I have been known to rely on every punch known to man—but only someone less than human would be so gutless as to deliver the Swansy Hollow punch to an opponent. As long as I am privileged to fight in the state of California, you will never have to worry about me throwing the Swansy Hollow punch.' "

Big laughs all around. I didn't even have to add Cassidy's absurd declaration of gratitude to Armstrong. No need. I counted empties: two to a man, at least. Even lousy stories would soon float.

"Gar-Kon!" Ike Thurston shouted to the publican. "We could use another round over here!"

"Tell 'em about the English character covering that fight," Johnny Smith prompted. "The writer—you remember."

I dove right in: "I'd hit it off with this British gent, reporter for one of those high-toned sheets over there. It was his first trip to the States for a big fight—"

"You ever try to read one of those English rags?" somebody interrupted. "They're all jammed up like the goddamn want ads."

"—but this poor limey gets stewed. I mean *ruined*."

"Six sheets to the wind," Johnny said.

"Hammered and nailed," Ike embellished.

"Plus, I know he's on deadline for a prefight filing. He thought he'd down a few, drink himself back sober, and write his story. But he didn't factor in the time zones. He's so plowed I have to carry him up to his room. I dump him on the bed, and as I'm leaving it dawns on me about the time difference. So what do I do?"

"Being the great humanitarian that you are—" Johnny, with the assist.

"I write his story for him," I crowed. "Right there in the room, on his own typewriter, with his byline."

"And who'd you have this limey pick?"

"I copped out—called it a draw. So, of course, he ended up looking better than me."

Raspberries and huzzahs around the table. Armstrong and Garcia had fought ten dead heats that night, to no decision.

"Oh, you made that boy into a genius," cried Moe. "Who'd you like?"

"Armstrong."

"How do you *not* pick Armstrong," sputtered Johnny Smith. "Greatest fighter, pound for pound, in the world. No question." All it took to ignite the debate.

"Get serious. It's Louis. Not even close."

"I'll put my money on Robinson. By the time he's through—more titles than Armstrong."

The next round came and bills flipped and floated onto the wet cork of the waitress's tray as she dispensed the drinks.

"Right here, doll. Old-fashioned."

"So, Billy," proposed "Hutch" Hutchinson, "tell us who you pick in this state title bout—Escalante or Burnett?"

Before I could unwind my personal tale of the tape, Ike Thurston cut in. He was sucking bourbon off the finger he'd used in lieu of a swizzle stick.

"Scratch Escalante," he said. "He'll never go through with it now."

"How's that?" I prodded.

"Lost his wife last night. You didn't hear?"

My insides churned. The whole world abruptly bottomed out. I was surrounded by strangers. Couldn't move my tongue.

"Jesus, what a shame," somebody said. "You never know."

"Hell of a thing. Had a bunch of kids, didn't they?"

Ike: "Didn't you guys know? I heard it from my cousin, drives an ambulance outta Children's. They brought her in late last night, but wasn't nothing they could do."

"How'd it happen, did he mention?"

"Lotta blood, was all he said. Jesus, Billy. I figured you must've . . . I'da said something, but I thought, you know, why spoil a good time—"

I hurtled up from the table, spilling half a dozen drinks. No parting *bon mots*. No glances back. I made it through the door, hit the street, turned down Polk, and unsteadily navigated to Market.

This time, no matter which way I looked, the city came up short on solace. It would never quite seem the same to me again.

26

Ida tried to sneak a spoon-load of purėed vegetables into the kid's mouth. He squirmed and smacked his gums and runny carrots dribbled from the corners of his lips. Baby fists banged the high-chair tray.

"Open up. Nummy-nums," Ida coaxed. "C'mon."

A slap caught the edge of the plate. Food shot all over.

"Goddamn it!" Ida slammed down the tiny spoon and shot me a look hot as ready coals. "Can't you help—*please!* I'd like to be able to eat some of my food while it's warm."

I took another swallow of whiskey and vacantly pondered the untouched dinner in front of me.

"You listen now," her harangue went on. "We've got a deal. You act like a father. I'll act like a wife. If you want to spend all your time with those lowlife characters, fine—go right ahead. But so long as we're living in this house, then this boy needs a father he can count on. Once in a while it wouldn't hurt you to take some responsibility. Would it kill you to help feed him? Is that too much to ask?"

I moved food around with a steak knife.

"Do you believe in God?" I asked. Six stiff fingers of sour mash had done nothing to pry the boot heel from my heart.

"What kind of question is that? What on earth is wrong with you?"

"It's a simple kind of question. Do you believe in God?"

"I am not going to have this conversation. It's disgraceful."

The serrated edge of the knife pushed peas and potatoes into a mound.

"Is that where the punishment comes from?" I mused. "Do you think we all get punished by God, or do we do it to ourselves, then hang the blame on Him?"

"You're talking like a madman. Stop it."

My grip on the knife tightened. One quick jab, straight to the heart. Or a swipe across the throat. That'd finish it. Her or me.

Not the kid. The little bastard didn't deserve it, not yet at least. He was innocent, so far as I knew.

The phone rang.

Ida leapt up to answer it. I gazed at the flailing kid. The knife went back to the table, traded for whiskey. I'd been right at the edge, only the thinnest shreds of my conscience holding me in check. Whoever that was on the phone, Ida might have owed them more than she'd ever know.

"It's for you," she seethed, settling back in to resume the feeding effort. "Somebody named Francis O'Connor."

"Something I can do for you, Francis?" He got an earful of weary agitation.

"Tell me why your phone number was found in Claire Escalante's purse."

"How's that?" I was backpedaling, which he surely knew.

"She's dead, in case you aren't aware," O'Connor elaborated when I offered only empty air. "But of course you would have heard. The grapevine. Nonetheless, you and she *talked*, didn't you?"

"My number was in her purse. Why's that news? I told you she phoned me that time. About the story in the paper. Was there something else you needed?"

"I'd say so. Are you near a front window?"

I babbled a bit, but I'd already toted the phone to the curtained foyer window.

"Look outside," O'Connor instructed across the wire.

An SFPD black-and-white was angled in the driveway, idling.

"Inform your wife you need to have a conversation with your old pal and number-one fan, Francis O'Connor. Then you'd be advised to get in that car in a peaceable and timely fashion—or in two minutes that roller has orders to light up your nice quiet neighborhood like the Fourth of July."

27

They didn't head downtown. We went west, cutting into the fog, toward the high-numbered avenues.

The two patrolmen, Jansen and Lust, acted as if they were escorting a celebrity. They wanted assurance that their man, Jack Dempsey, *in his prime, of course, in his prime,* would have beaten Joe Louis. Jack Johnson would have kicked both their asses, I informed them. The remainder of the ride passed in silence.

The door to the Escalante house was open. No light inside. Lust knocked on the jamb and called out. O'Connor materialized from the black recesses. In the blue gloom of the foyer, his figure was a dark mass.

"Thank you, boys," he said, dismissing the uniforms. "Step in, Billy."

I went over the threshold into the void.

A lamp snapped on, harshly illuminating the homicide detective. It chiseled shadowy clefts in his blocky face. Unshaven, he was drawn and haggard. The pool of lamplight fell just far enough across the room: at the foot of the stairway was a horrifying stain. So big it nearly made me gag. I looked away, where the stairs ascended into darkness.

"Where are the kids?" I heard myself ask.

"With a neighbor. And we brought in one of the sisters from St. Ignatius."

"Jesus Christ," I croaked. My eyes refused to detour around the wide patch of blood.

"What about Hack?"

"He's getting an escort up from San Diego. Be here in the morning. The feds offered a plane, I heard, but he wouldn't fly."

O'Connor lifted a manila envelope from an end table and handed it to me: "There are some photographs here I would like you to examine. I'm sure you'll find them interesting."

I blanched. "Not pictures of this?" I nodded at the sickening pond. The distress in my voice was genuine.

O'Connor didn't care: "You need to look at them," he insisted.

I unwound the twine and slipped out the prints.

The bloody boot heel ground in deeper. My shaking hands gripped harsh flash photos: Claire splayed at the bottom of the stairs. The blue and white polka-dot interview dress, bunched above her thighs, soaking in the widespread circle of gore. Four, five, six views. The camera moving ghoulishly closer with each exposure.

Her green eyes were shut, her lips slightly parted. All the fight was gone.

She was finished. *Dead.*

I stuffed it all back in the envelope and shoved the package at O'Connor.

"Why did you feel I needed to see that?" My throat was raw, my head swam. It was a good thing I hadn't eaten.

But there was a trace of a smirk on the cop's face, I'd swear to it. He figure-eighted the twine on the envelope and set it aside. Nodded toward the bloodstain, in case I'd overlooked it.

"The children were staying with the neighbor," O'Connor reported, ignoring my question. "The woman frequently acted as a sitter when the children's mother went to work. Only Mom didn't come to get them last evening."

He pointed his cane at the thick four-square windowpanes in the front door.

"When the sitter looked in, she observed Mrs. Escalante—here. Fortunately, the children could see nothing."

"What was the cause of death?" I somehow inquired.

"The coroner said that all this blood appears to have come from her vagina. Leading to speculation that this may be the result of a botched scrape. Alternatively, it could be some kind of sicko murder—dressed up to look like an abortion gone bad. . . . We'll have to see. There's no weapon. No blood trail."

I edged into the living room. Had to get away from the stain. I stood on the spot where Hack had tried to explain to his son why a turtle wasn't a stupid pet. Hack might've been on to something. That kid would understand now.

"How well did you *really* know this woman?"

"We've been over this. I told you. I wrote a lot about the husband. The wife and I had lunch once."

"Except that you featured a story about her in the paper."

"A result of the lunch. Happens sometimes in my dodge. You bank a piece for a slow news day. Are you getting to a point?"

I glanced between the curtains. A couple out for a stroll had stopped to gawk at the neighborhood death house.

"That lunch was quite a while ago now. Your number was still in her purse. No address book in there. No other numbers. Only yours. Why would you rate that singular honor, do you suppose? Any idea?"

I turned away from the windows and back toward O'Connor. He was crowding the bloodstain, leaning on the cane. For several heartbeats, the house was deathly still. Time had stopped. Claire took her final breath right on that spot, the location O'Connor now policed.

She was gone. I was left with O'Connor.

Then he was coming at me, rumbling unsteadily on that gimpy leg.

"No ideas? I'll give you one—one of *mine*. You can critique it, one writer to another."

I braced for a crack of the cane. It didn't arrive. But he shoved his ruddy mug right in my face. Not a whiff of Scotch. He was sober as a judge.

"You know Hack Escalante murdered Gig Liardi, you know that goddamned well. And you played that kid, you blackmailed him. But he hadn't any money—assuming you wanted money. I think you extracted payments in a currency you liked better—the fighter's wife!

"While this pathetic pug is stationed at a Navy outpost, you're accepting regular installments off the wife. I'm right, aren't I? Goddamn it—I am *right*!"

My mind raced faster than my heart. He was on track, locked in so tightly that for a few perilous seconds he had me doubting myself. His script played, sure enough. The pieces fit. But it was a replica, a ghost image of the truth; motives didn't mesh. Not with what *I* believed to be the facts.

"Then you made your mistake," O'Connor railed on. "You got her pregnant. She might have tried to scare you off by threatening to tell your wife. Maybe that's why you needed her out of the way. Could be she wanted to hide the evidence by getting a fast and dirty scrape.

"One way or another—you killed her."

I wanted to explode, erupt, fight back. Bludgeon O'Connor's flimsy bullshit with the real story. But I couldn't. His road map was all ass-backward. That didn't matter. Everything arrived at the same point: I *had* killed her, in some way.

"I had lunch with the woman, was all," I reiterated weakly.

"Don't continue to insult my fucking intelligence! The manager's deposited in a shallow grave, the fighter takes a powder. Next thing we know, you and the fighter's wife are chummy as can be—then she's knocked up. Currently she's a stiff in the morgue. You're standing here, supposedly an innocent bystander, in the middle of it all. Don't expect me to believe it's one astounding coincidence.

"And let's not forget that devilish little goose chase you set me up for—making a decedent your source for that item about Liardi. That was clever, I'll admit. But what did you once tell me about 'clever'? As it applied to Mr. Liardi's fistic career?"

"Fuck you, Francis. Fuck you if you think you can steam-roll innocent people with half-baked *True Detective* theories. In the newspaper business, we don't go to press with an allegation unless we've got the goods to back it up. If you're going to feature this Wild Bull routine, back it up with something real. Proof. Evidence. Aren't those what makes a case? Or do you intend to just rubber-hose everybody who knew the victim?"

"You, my well-spoken friend, are square in the middle of this crime. I can see that clearly."

"Save the blarney, *friend*."

I stomped past him, headed for the door. Jansen and Lust hovered on the stoop, drawn back by the shouting.

"Jansen," O'Connor said. "Have you the item we retrieved from the car?"

The cop stepped into the light. He held a bulky object wrapped in a lightweight blanket. "Right here."

He folded back the green cloth to reveal a compact shovel.

"Run across that tool before?" O'Connor asked over my shoulder.

"No. Why?"

"It was taken from the Escalantes' Buick. In the trunk. Beneath some blankets. I suspect it may have excavated Mr. Liardi's temporary resting place. Sure you don't recognize it?"

I gave a little chuckle. Tried to stir in an element of disdain. "Follow me," I told him.

O'Connor, and the other two, trailed me through the dining room, into the kitchen. We banged our way through the swinging door. There was barely moon enough to navigate. The last cop through knocked something off a hook on the back of the door and it clattered to the floor. I didn't bother to look. I couldn't afford to have my little show interrupted. Beside the back door I found the light switch.

The backyard bloomed with colors, like some cheerful Grandma Moses painting.

"Hack's wife was a gardener," I said. "That much I know. So she owned a shovel. Big surprise."

I turned and headed out. I didn't want to spend a second more in the kitchen; it was the last place I'd held Claire in my arms. In the corner, right by the door. Hanging from a hook on the door was an empty briefcase, soft and tired. The cop had rehung it by the strap. It hadn't been there the last time I was in here. And if it had been anywhere else in the house, I'd never have noticed it. I passed through the door again, trying to remember . . .

O'Connor stalked me, the cane assaulting floorboards: "She was a gardener. That doesn't change, or prove, a thing."

"There's a shovel in her car—that doesn't prove anything, either."

I strode for the open front door. I'd seen that briefcase someplace before, I was positive.

"Where are you going?" O'Connor challenged.

"Home. Or am I under arrest?"

He hobbled around me, the limp more pronounced, stiffer. Off the end table, he snatched up the envelope that held the crime scene shots of Claire.

"Know why I showed you these?"

"Because you're a sick bastard?"

"Guess again. Fingerprints. Pop out perfectly on photographs. I got a nice, clean set."

"Talk about clever. You could have called up the *Inquirer*, they've got my prints on file. If I was a serious suspect, you'd have paraded me into headquarters to get those prints. You're flailing, Francis. It's not pretty."

O'Connor smiled, as if he relished all this. "You should check my record before you get too cocky. When I swing, I don't miss. And if I find prints around here—or on her body—that match these . . ." He fanned himself with the envelope. "I'll be going for the knockout."

WOMAN FOUND DEAD IN HOME

Claire Escalante, wife of local boxer Hack Escalante, was found dead in their Sunset District home Thursday evening. Her body was discovered by a neighbor, who had been minding the woman's three children during the day.

Police have not disclosed a cause of death.

This is the second tragedy to befall the popular heavyweight boxer this year. His manager, Gig Liardi, himself a local boxer of renown in the early thirties, was last month found murdered in Golden Gate Park.

Investigators declined to comment on any possible connection between the two deaths.

"We're looking at the situation closely," said a Police Department spokesman, "but we are not yet prepared to say that Mrs. Escalante was a victim of foul play."

28

The taxi pulled up across from the Escalante house. The avenue was block after block of stucco bunkers pitched in a stoic stand against the infinite mass of the Pacific. There was no hint of life in the air, save the faint rhythm of the surf and the wheeling, squawking gulls. Drapes in the house were drawn against the cool gray light. Hack had returned to town via a hardship discharge. The few times I'd summoned the stones to call with my condolences, the phone went unanswered.

It was a week since Claire's death notice ran, plugging a one-column margin alongside the appliance ads on page six. More filler for the flagship. If O'Connor had his way, Claire might yet make page one. And so would I, frozen in a *Chronicle* photographer's flash, cuffed, en route to the Gray Bar Hotel.

"Keep it running," I told the driver. "I'll only be a minute."

"No sweat, Mr. Nichols."

I drew my overcoat tighter and crossed the street, scanning the curbside autos. The house didn't appear to be under surveillance. At the top of the driveway I peered through the garage windows: no car.

An SFPD no trespassing notice was tacked to the front door and the place was locked tight. No chance of getting in for another look at that briefcase, to confirm if there was a VW etched into the leather flap. I'd convinced myself that's where I'd seen it before, clutched to the chest of Burney Sanders's secretary. I may have been nuts, but I'd have sworn that in the darkness I'd seen the vague outline of that monogram. I'd found a Virginia Wagner in the phone directory, living on Pine Street, but those calls too went unanswered.

I unlatched the side gate and took the narrow path to the backyard. The garden prospered without Claire, flowering robustly. It would endure for a while. Then all that pampered grace would fall victim to the weeds. I almost heard the back door slam, and expected to see her stride down the steps, spade in hand, still full of life.

Nests of terra-cotta pots were stacked against the side of the garage. I took one to a terraced spot near the center of the garden. Professionally planted, with room to accommodate its growth, was the azalea Claire had accepted from me. I'd seen it the instant I flipped on the lights for O'Connor and his pet bulls. Some of its pastel blooms had shriveled, but it had grown, not just alive, but healthy.

I knelt and started digging a trench around it with my fingers.

Here's where we all end up. My father and mother, below ground and moldering. Gig—who knows what the cops did with his discarded carcass. Now Claire, with all her possibilities, all her potential. Planted in the earth. The ultimate reward.

Fuck off, Father Petri.

A car swerved into the driveway, the engine cutting out. I expected to hear the tattoo of flatfeet. I lurched up and dusted my hands on my mohair overcoat.

Peeking over the gate, I watched Hack open a rear door of the Buick. His brood slid off the backseat, down to the drive. The littlest one, William, could barely walk. His sister held on to him, helped him out.

"Tony, where's your sweater?" Hack asked his older son.

"I packed it," the boy replied.

Hack shut the car door and sighed. The uniform: work pants, blue denim shirt, Eisenhower-style leather jacket. His curly hair was a tangle, his face drained and sagging. The kids scrambled up the drive, toward me. I had to step out.

They pulled up short with alarmed looks when they saw me. Hack was startled too, for a moment.

"It's all right," he announced with hardly a pause. "He's a friend."

The kids trooped into the backyard while I held open the gate. Hack followed. He had a slight limp; the accident Conte had mentioned.

"I thought I'd missed you," I said, shaking hands. I hoped he wouldn't register the residue of dirt on mine. Hack's brutal grip had slackened a bit.

"You did miss us," Hack said. "We took off fifteen minutes ago. Came back 'cause we forgot the turtle." He moved past me into the yard.

The two older kids shambled around the oval pathway, pushing aside plants and flowers, peering into the shrubs. The smallest one tottered, fists clenched at his sides. When he started bawling, no one paid any mind. Hack and I stood shoulder to shoulder, facing the garden.

"The turtle," I said. "I remember him."

"Yeah, you were here the day I brought him home." Hack nearly smiled, but wasn't quite ready for that. Every memory had to hurt right then.

"I tried to call," I said. "I could never get you."

"I'm not much for talking now. Listening either. But I got the card. Thanks."

"Sorry I didn't make the service. Fight in San Jose. Couldn't get out of it."

"Don't worry. I know you got your job to do."

"Has O'Connor talked to you yet? Or is he giving you a grace period?"

He squinted sidewise at me. There wasn't much to read in his narrowed eyes.

"Grace isn't his long suit," he murmured. "What comes after the third degree?"

"We're in a tough spot," I whispered. "He wants you for Gig's . . . murder."

Hack swiveled toward me: "It wasn't a murder, you know that."

"They're calling it that now, though. That's what they're saying."

Gig was strangled, I wanted to say. Put it out there. But I couldn't chance my boy turning on me. Not yet. Hushed, I quickly added: "There's no way to cop to manslaughter. Not after burying the body."

Hack studied his children and drew several deep, shuddering breaths into his thick, powerful frame.

"That's not all O'Connor thinks," he finally said. "He puts you right in there, too. I don't even want to tell you, I won't repeat what he tried to convince me you'd done."

"I know already. He hammered me with all that, too."

"Made me want to kill him. Dreaming up a thing like . . . that."

"He's desperate. He might not be right in the head, for all I know."

I leaned against the fence, hands buried in my coat pockets. Hack surveyed me, a spark in his squint now: "You figure he's swingin' wild, huh?"

I straightened up and redirected: "Mostly. But how could

you not have ditched the shovel? He loved that. Practically gave me a heart attack when he pulled that out."

"He ain't got the shovel," Hack scoffed with a shake of tousled hair. "That one he's got was Claire's."

"Holy Christ." By reflex, I turned away from the kids, talking into the empty space behind Hack. "How'd it get stashed in the trunk? O'Connor made it seem like Exhibit A."

A faint chuckle, of the mirthless variety, narrowly escaped Hack's lips. He waved a huge mitt at the abundant horticultural display.

"You think we could afford all this? All these plants? All the stones and dirt, even? It's expensive when you got three kids—*and* you got to make like you're Bucks Deluxe for the neighbors."

"How's that?"

"She kept a shovel in the car. If she saw a nice plant someplace, she'd dig it up and bring it home. That's the way she was—if she saw something she liked . . ."

The turtle remained resolutely AWOL. Maybe he knew he'd be eighty-sixed from paradise. Meanwhile the smallest kid had fallen flat on his keister and was now crawling around. He produced a steady cry, but his tank was running low.

"Shit," Hack said, pointing to the trench I'd made. "Something's already starting to dig up the place. Goddamn it. She'll be pissed."

"What did you do with the real shovel?"

"Sawed up the handle. Burned it. Got rid of the blade down at the old Sutro ruins. Flung it down in the rocks."

I squinted over at him. "You know Virginia Wagner?"

He looked perplexed. "Who's that?"

"I guess that's what I'm asking."

"What's her name again?"

"Virginia Wagner. Maybe she was a friend of Claire's?"

He rolled it around but shook it off. "I don't know. Why do you think that cop said there was something with you and Claire?"

"She mailed you the article, didn't she?"

"Yeah, she did. That was really . . ." It just trailed off.

"We had lunch one day, and talked. So I could get the grist for that piece. After that—I guess O'Connor's imagination took over. That can happen."

He pointed to his daughter. "Marie said you were here one night. Late."

"Late for a kid, I guess. What—am *I* a suspect?"

"It's tough for me now. Tough to believe in anything, to believe what anybody tells me. How would you feel? Having everything taken away from you."

He stepped closer. For the first time, I felt his raw physical threat. He could bring it, any time he wanted.

"I was having dinner with Johnny Vidal," I suddenly said. "He lives over on Thirty-eighth. You know Johnny."

"Johnny Carnation."

"The same. I stopped by after, to see how Claire and the kids were doing. If there was anything they needed."

He cross-haired me with a glare I'd only seen at center-ring—the cold eye of intimidation, reserved for men he intended to beat senseless. No way I could reciprocate. I focused on the kids instead. Tony plowed through the garden now, trampling the smaller plants and flowers Claire had nurtured.

From the corner of my eye I saw Hack dip into his jacket and withdraw a small envelope. It had a feminine floral border. He held it like he was assaying gold.

"I found this when I was cleaning stuff out," he said, presenting it. "In the refrigerator."

There was Claire's script, across the front: *Billy Nichols—URGENT.*

"I don't know what this is all about," Hack said, his voice a mix of confusion, grief, and brewing anger. The latter was in there, unmistakably, at low boil.

Another goddamn letter. I was a magnet for last-ditch correspondence. My hands stayed stuffed in my pockets; I subtly tried to rub them clean against the lining.

Hack tapped the envelope on my chest, like he was auditioning for O'Connor's role: "Go on, open it," he said. "I'm curious."

If I was marked for punishment, I reasoned, better it come from the bereaved than from behind a badge.

I grabbed the envelope, ripped off the end, and blew it open. Full exposure of the grime under my nails—but Hack was too preoccupied to make a connection.

A dainty piece of stationery, folded.

Hack crowded me: "What's it say?"

Three words, in Claire's hurried hand:

Dempsey vs. Firpo

I showed it to him, massively relieved. Underneath, I was perplexed. The widower was clearly clueless.

"I don't get it," he said. "What's it about? Why'd she hide it in the icebox?"

"No idea." I shrugged. I couldn't conjure up a convenient fib—or the need for one.

"Hey, Tony," Hack called out. "Ease up. You're wrecking the plants."

Tony dropped to his knees, disappearing into the greenery. The baby climbed up and staggered our way. Hack scooped him up and hoisted him onto his hip. A huge paw smoothed the kid's hair.

After a few seconds, Hack's face contorted. It twisted like it did the night he stood over Gig. Before we buried him. Before everything.

"They're not gonna let me keep my kids," he said.

"How's that?"

"These people, lawyers and whoever, say I can't take care of them with Claire gone. That's what this state outfit is putting out, anyway. They claim my kids are better off in the orphanage, at St. Joseph's. Until I figure out what I'm gonna do."

"What *are* you gonna do?"

"First, I'm gonna hafta unload this place. Without her, I'm in way over my head. We always were."

"How about the kids?"

"I'll get 'em back, once I get straightened out."

His eyes were going glassy. He rapidly shook it off, like he walked through jabs in the ring. He kissed his baby and held it tight for several long moments.

"You mean Ginny?" he asked, looking up.

"Yeah, right. Ginny Wagner. That's her."

"Yeah, she and Claire are friends. They used to work together when Claire had a job at this law firm downtown, five or six years ago. She'd come over every once in a while. They'd go out. Not so much lately. Now you mention her, I'm kinda surprised I didn't see her at the service. How'd you know her?"

"I only met her a few weeks ago. She, you know, mentioned the connection."

"C'mon, Myrtle, c'mout, c'mout, wherever you are," came Hack's daughter's plaintive call. Her tiny feet tamped down the foliage.

"She's wrecking that," I murmured.

"It's pachysandra," he replied. "It's tough."

He called to the kids: "I'm gonna get a box for when you find him." He held little William to his shoulder and raised the garage door. I followed him inside. A potting table stood against the back wall, and gardening tools shared space with several dozen cardboard boxes stacked around the perimeter. Storing stuff that overflowed from the house. The car wouldn't fit inside the garage.

I couldn't let my feelings interfere. Hack had never been straight with me, he'd never revealed the truth about that night at Gig's. No telling if I'd get another chance at him. I felt like a shitheel, but the timing would never be better to press him for details: especially as he was holding the baby.

"What made you hit Gig that night, anyway?"

"An accident," he mumbled. He used the free hand to rummage among the boxes in search of an empty.

"Understood. But something set you off. You remember?"

"I don't want to talk about that. Why go over it again, for God's sake?" He shoved and shook boxes, to see how filled up they were.

"You were there when Gig called me that night, weren't you?"

"I don't recall too good."

"He wanted to talk about something. Any idea what it was? It sure seemed important to him at the time. You remember being there when he made the call, right?"

"I told you—I don't remember much. I had more to think about that night, the way it turned out."

"Only you and Gig were there? Nobody else?"

He set the kid down.

The boy stiff-legged over a grease spot on the cement floor, covered with scattered sawdust. Hack didn't turn around.

"What are you talking about?" Both hands free, he roughly shook boxes and brusquely shifted and restacked them, heaving exasperated grunts. "Of course we were alone."

"So what did he say that made you hit him? You *did* hit him, right?"

He shoved a box against the wall and turned on his heels. It wasn't something you'd want to see coming out of the opposite corner at the bell.

"What the fuck are you doing? You act like that cop!" He quickly brought his voice back down, barely under control. "Yeah, I hit him—Christ, you were there!"

He stalked to the far side of the garage and hunkered down, tugging a canvas tarp off other boxes and bundles. He absently pawed through the goods.

"No, I wasn't there," I reminded him. "I showed up after. I didn't actually see what happened. You told me. But you also told me that Gig said something. You guys were talking about some dream he'd had, about you winning the championship—"

"You got some fucking memory."

I picked up Hack's son—Claire's flesh and blood—and held him. The kid wrapped his arms around my neck, like I was family. As if I could be trusted.

"Gig said something about Claire, didn't he?"

Hack clutched a cardboard box and yanked it from between other piled detritus. The junk clattered together but didn't fall. He twisted the box over, spilling dozens of magazines onto the floor.

"Is that why you did it?" I pressed. "'Cause he got out of line about Claire? What'd he say?"

Hack wheeled around and saw me holding his boy. He was surprised. So was I: Hack's eyes were brimming with tears.

"He called her a whore. What would you have done?"

He slammed past me, back into the garden.

They finally found the turtle. Hack ended up crawling on the ground with his kids, but it was the little guy who discovered it, lumbering onto the cement pathway from under the back stairs. The kids shrieked and clapped and Hack herded them back into the Buick. Myrtle was whisked into the box Hack took from the garage. The kids were happy. Small consolation. Even the turtle was getting a raw deal.

Hack climbed in behind the wheel.

"You going through with the Burnett fight?" I asked.

"What else am I supposed to do? Seeing as U.S. Steel's already got a chairman."

"Maybe Burney can get it postponed. If I talk to him and—"

"You done enough. I need the dough *now*," Hack said. Then he added what was really bothering him: "This cop—if he had something, he'd have made his move already, right?"

"That's my take. He's squeezing because he's got nothing."

"I'm gonna make it through this somehow. All you can do, when it really gets bad, is gut it out. That's what I learned from Claire. She taught me."

He cranked over the ignition and the car trembled and shook to life. It jerked when he shifted into reverse.

"She knew how Gig died, didn't she? All along."

He glanced up, his lips tight. Answer enough.

"Yeah," I sighed. "It'd be hard to keep a secret from her."

He stuck his left hand out the window and I gripped it.

"I'd like to get a few more copies of that article you wrote, if I could." He sounded like he was swallowing a hard ball of pain. "She sent me a bunch, but I gave 'em all away."

"Yeah, sure. I'll pull a few."

After they'd driven off, I went back through the gate and finished exhuming the azalea. It was a stupid act, I realized. But some kind of ritual was required. I set the azalea in a pot and packed dirt around it.

In the hole that was left, I dropped my mother's rosary. I kicked earth over the black beads and cross and pounded the dirt with my palms. I stared at my fingerprints in the soil. I beat the ground down with my fists.

I wiped off my face and hands with my display handkerchief and went back to the waiting taxi. There'd be some stiff tariff on the meter for me and my plant.

SECTION S TUESDAY, AUGUST 24, 1948 CCCC*

MONARCH OF THE DAILIES

AN AMERICAN PAPER FOR THE AMERICAN PEOPLE

San Francisco Inquirer Sports

REG US PAT OFF

Through THE ROPES

By BILLY NICHOLS

Amazing as it seems, considering all he's been through in recent weeks, Hack Escalante will be climbing into the ring this Saturday at the Civic to challenge California Champion Purvis Burnett for state heavyweight laurels.

In all our years covering the local fistic fraternity, we've never seen a fighter absorb this much punishment *outside* a ring. First, Escalante's longtime manager and mentor, Gig Liardi, turns up dead after having gone missing for two months.

Then, while Hack's down South doing his bit for the Navy, his lovely wife Claire suffers a severe hemorrhage. She passed away August 15, leaving three young children.

Yet, remarkably, Hack insists on going ahead with the bout, despite hardships that would crush lesser men.

"I told him that I'd postpone the fight for as long as he needed to get himself together," said promoter Burney Sanders. "But he said he wanted to go ahead and fight. Personally, I've never seen courage like this. He's a gallant guy and my heart goes out to him and his children—and his wife, who I'm sure is looking down proudly on her man."

29

Cops were in motion everywhere.

It was a teeming army in blue wool, no tarnish on the chrome badges, menacing leather holsters riding high on every hip. Ambling boldly into the station house—Cop Central—no longer seemed like such a bright idea, once I pushed through the heavy doors and faced a herd of uniformed police.

The night shift was shaping up for patrol. Unfocused power coalescing, marshaling into a brutal force. Lions stretching and scratching, preparing to leave the den and prowl into the Colosseum.

Ordinarily, I got on famously with John Law. To date, anyway.

"I'm here to see Frank Bennett," I told the lifer anchoring the desk. It looked like he was hiding a medicine ball under his uniform shirt. His days pounding a beat were ancient history.

He checked the book: "This an official matter?"

"Tell him Billy Nichols needs a minute."

The bloated flatfoot lit up, stuck a thick mitt across the rail. "Sure, sure you are—can't believe I didn't ID you right off." He worked my hand like one of us was running for mayor. "Remember when you wrote about the Corbett-Fields fight at old Rec Park? You talked about the kids who climbed trees to watch the action from up over the top of the arena? That was one of my boys, sure enough. Still got the clip. How do you like that?"

"He saw a good one. Bennett's here, is he?"

Bennett was paged on the Irish intercom: "Officer Frank Bennett!" the desk sarge bellowed.

Bennett, suited up for duty, popped out of a rear office and came over. I kept a smile in place during his overly effusive greeting, while idly edging away from the desk, beyond eavesdropping range.

"I wonder if you can do me a favor, Frank."

"Name it."

"I'm looking for somebody's rap sheet—if there is one."

Bennett stiffened, the grin fading. I knew this would be a stretch, so I'd come prepared: "I'll make it worth your while, Officer."

I fished out my wallet and palmed a pair of comps to the upcoming State Title show.

"Third row," I noted, flashing them.

"What's this all about?" Bennett ignored the ducats. I scanned him for an open pocket, but he was buttoned tight.

"Little research for a friend," I told him. "He's engaged, date set and all, but there's a rumor circulating that the bride-to-be might have a bit more experience than advertised. That's all. I'd like to put his mind at ease before the ceremony."

A thin smile cracked Bennett's by-the-book veneer. He plucked the tickets from me smartly: "What's this naughty girl's name?"

"Claire McKenna."

I was banking on the maiden name ringing no bells, no connection with the recently deceased Mrs. Escalante. The lives of single women had a way of vanishing down a rabbit hole after they got married—unless they had crossed the line at some point and earned an entry in the city's crime diary.

It was a long shot, but so was everything I did anymore.

Frank consulted his watch, glanced at his mustering colleagues, and quick-stepped toward the precinct's archives.

I sank onto a bench near the door and took on an unobtrusive pose. The desk jockey was miffed that I wasn't cooling my heels within his gabbing range. Nobody else seemed to pay any mind.

Ten minutes crawled by. Paranoia surged each time a bull swaggered past. One of them would know O'Connor, I feared. One of them would have heard the homicide dick's suspicions. Any second now I'd be muscled into an interrogation room.

Bennett finally reemerged, a slim file in his hand.

"Easy does it," he advised. "Civilians aren't authorized to see this stuff."

I took the folder, as discreetly as I could, and flipped it open.

"Who you calling a civilian, Frank? I'm a newspaperman."

"Is that our blushing bride?" he snickered.

The mug shots were a jolt; I couldn't get past them at first. Her hair was tousled, her skin glistened with perspiration, a small trickle of blood leaked from one side of her mouth. Claire offered a defiant glare to all her accusers. It was a mask I'd seen employed plenty of times, in publicity photos of young fighters: summoning up fiery eyes and a granite pose for the flak's camera. The hard sell of hostility and fearlessness.

Claire sold it as convincingly as any pug.

Her demeanor in those wedding portraits flashed into my mind. The radiance and joy evident in those snaps now seemed deeper, more well founded. She'd escaped a dismal fate. Found protection and stability and a second chance. She'd shaken off the past, or so she thought.

The "McKenna, Claire" jacket contained a pair of reports, both dated 1937. Two collars for prostitution, both pinches made in North Beach. She'd lived there in the thirties, I remembered, in a small efficiency apartment.

I got by, she had told me over lunch. *Doing whatever.*

"Looks like your love-struck lad is in for a big letdown," Frank commented. He motioned for me to give back the file. "I gotta get going, Billy."

Claire's second roust featured additional charges: resisting arrest and assaulting an officer. Two police officers, in fact. I skip-read the condensed account. Claire wouldn't get in the wagon, not without a fight. She slammed one cop's hand in a door, fracturing three fingers, socked his backup in the eye. Then the mouth.

They probably deserved their lumps.

"C'mon, Bill," Frank implored. "I gotta hit the street. I'm late already."

I riffled the last few sheets. Routine processing documents. I was about to shut the folder, still unclear as to how this intelligence influenced my predicament. Then an entry popped from the tangle of typescript.

As I yanked the file back from Frank, my eyes filtered out the surrounding text; I was zeroed in only on the name.

"What's this page here?" I asked, separating a document near the bottom of the stack.

"The release form," Bennett said. "What sprung her."

"And this?" I pointed to irregular carboned characters.

"That's who paid her bail."

I ran my finger across the signature, for some absurd reason. Making sure it wouldn't disappear or rub off, I guess. That it was legit.

The broad, burly scrawl held fast to the copy paper. Burnell Theopolous's autograph was eleven years dry.

Burnell Theopolous, soon to be known as Burney Sanders. Seems my old pal started as a promoter and matchmaker in a different kind of sport.

Bennett took the jacket from me, pausing to look again at where my finger had been.

"Burnell Theopolous," he read aloud, then laughed. "Quite the handle for a pimp."

30

A shadow danced across the chilly concrete walls, arcing, bobbing, bursting into rapid streaks: jab, jab, cross, hook to the body, hook to the head. Hack stalked the shadow. Working to bring up a sweat, he hurled flurry upon flurry at the retreating silhouette. At himself.

In a quarter-hour he'd be out under the lights, battling Purvis Burnett for the California crown. Six thousand ticket holders thronged the Civic Center, shelling out a goodly portion of their paychecks to witness what the local kid could summon from the bowels of despair. I hear they drew pretty good at Calvary, too.

I'd done my bit, as I'd promised Burney Sanders: weeks of setup stories, communiqués from the camps filled with dark allusions to the underdog's gallant campaign in the face of grievous odds. Jimmy Ryan made Hack a 3–1 short-ender. No rush of sentimental wagers tipped that line. Burnett was undefeated, 20–0 with 14 kayos. Hack's 48–14–3 record qualified him as a legit contender for state laurels. Burnett's crew liked Hack as the ideal stepping-stone: solid quality, on the downward slide. An attention-getting test for a rising star. Victory would seat Burnett squarely at the IBC trough, in position to forage for a payday against Chester Carter.

Nobody knew what Hack would offer in the pit. The unknown quantity, of course, only pumped up the promotion.

For Burney Sanders, the evening was a success by the curtain-raising four-rounder. Turnstiles spun steadily, and each fan who passed through got a flyer touting the grand opening of the new National Hall—along with an eyeful of the underdressed jailbait hired to hawk the leaflets.

After the prelims I'd adjourned from ringside to give the main-eventers a once-over in the dressing rooms. I'd seen Sid Conte out on the floor, glad-handing, unspooling the usual pitch. Here was his main chance, perhaps his only shot at a toehold within shouting distance of the big time, and he still managed to pimp a few Pontiacs.

Hack was in the dank cinderblock dressing room, alone. The air was fetid with the residue of linament and anxiety. "Shut the door," he grunted, as he shadow-boxed.

"Where is everybody?" I asked, parking half my ass on the rubdown table.

"Gave 'em the bum's rush. You can stay. But I got nothing to say."

He moved side to side in a weaving crouch, taped hands hovering around his temples. The shadow thrown by the dangling overhead light dogged his every move. Shuffling soles and huffing breaths were the only sounds, save the distant and expectant buzz of six thousand souls. The shadow swooped up one wall, darted across the corner. Hack hunted it relentlessly, boring in, until his forehead pressed against the stone. Stark light gleamed off his hunched shoulders, where sweat was now seeping. Muscles pistoned as he threw body shots at his shadow-twin, only a breath between his flashing fists and the wall.

Banging at the door. I reached for the knob.

"Lock it," Hack snuffed.

The pounding got louder. "Coming in!" Conte.

"Stay out!" his fighter yelled.

The door opened partway. Sid peeked in, a befuddled

expression above the ubiquitous vanilla suit. Hack, gliding on the balls of his feet, sidestepped smoothly across the room and thrust a hip against the door, slamming it shut. He flipped the latch, locking us in, his manager out.

"Open up!" Conte pleaded, his voice muffled. "I gotta get changed!"

A fresh pair of white trousers and a garish Hawaiian shirt hung on the wall: Sid's ring regalia.

Hack war-danced around the cell, plenty of bounce in his legs. He'd suddenly stop, set, and unleash a volley of lefts and rights. He moved lightly, and his punches snapped. The essential combo. He shook out his neck, loosening it. Then threw his head back and howled.

It felt like I was trapped in a cage with a wild animal. A surge of adrenaline coursed through me. I could only imagine what was pumping through Hack.

I opened the door to find Conte, slack-jawed. A small group had gathered in the hall: some of Sid's pals, a few beat writers, local and L.A., the functionary from the commission, holding the gloves.

"What gives?" Conte said, elbowing past me. The entourage funneled in. Almost lost in the shuffle was diminutive Jockey John, Hack's cornerman, who'd lace and tape the gloves.

Hack slipped into his blood-red robe. "Bet on me tonight," he advised the group, without bothering to glance at them. "For once, I'm a sure thing."

Hack blew by me, hopped up on the rubdown table. "I've never seen you like this," I told him.

"What's the worst that can happen?" he breathed. "He kills me? So what?" His gaze shifted to the commission rep, approaching with the gloves.

"Let's go," Hack said. "Let's get on with it."

Nothing left to lose, he had no fear in him.

In the corridor leading to the arena floor, Burney Sanders peeled greenbacks from a thick roll, paying off Rodie Hodge, who'd furnished the pulchritudinous posse of bally-girls. Burney had the glow: he'd turned the tip and was flush with the promise of more and better paydays ahead. A hot main event tonight, as advertised, and he'd be in the catbird seat, poised to dominate the local action.

"Hell of a turnout, Burney," I said, squaring up to him. He dismissed Hodge and fanned the cash roll before repocketing it. It wasn't Philly-style; it was well stocked with Franklins and Grants.

"Even better'n I expected," Burney said. "A lot of broads, did you notice? The dead-wife angle really pulled. Lotta new faces, lotta swells. Our boys brought their better halves—musta read 'em your stories."

"You knew her, didn't you, Burney?"

"Knew who?"

"Claire. Weren't you tight with her, back in the days?"

Sanders started evasive maneuvers, like my words didn't even register. Something stalled him. He stood silent and still, a pose I'd rarely seen over the years.

I'd known Burney since we were boys. Once he stopped growing, I finished worrying about what a prick he was. A hot-tempered kid, he'd been. Father Petri had to drag him off meek Jimmy Wheatstraw in the after-school boxing class. He chased down and beat bloody a little kid who'd lifted a paper from his stack. He pounded the shit out of that "Spanish faggot" Fernando, a forlorn, gawky neighbor who liked to draw chalk pictures on the sidewalk in front of his house. He tortured the artistic wanna-be, at least until Fernando filled out. Burney Theopolous stayed five-foot-four.

The bantam shook his head and turned, taking his hands from his pockets. He'd never learned to hide his hackles; right now, they were up and bristling.

"Claire, she knew a lot of guys," he said.

"That I gathered."

"And where'd you gather that?"

"How'd you know her, Burney? I mean, what was the connection? Personal, or strictly business?"

It passed quickly, the feeling that Burney and I would never again be friends. Quickly indeed—instantly replaced by the realization that he never *was* my friend. I was only part of his hustle. Same as Claire.

Sanders affected an edgy smile. "She knew a lot of guys, a long time ago." The smile turned nasty as he added: "Then there are the guys—or should we say *guy*—she knew not so long ago. You read me?"

He *knew*. Burney had the goods on me and Claire. But how? Here I thought I was pinning him in a corner.

"Listen," Sanders said, nudging me back against the wall. A light fixture knocked my hat off and it tumbled to the dirty floor.

"Don't go digging into old shit," he said. A low growl, but with the icy calm of a guy comfortable issuing threats. "You just stick to your job—be a booster. You don't hear me going around talking about how *Mr. Boxing* wanted this Payne character given the bum's rush outta town. And without so much as a thank you. No—I know how to keep my mouth shut. You read me?"

★

Back at ringside, I paid scant attention to the frantic prefight bustle. It unfurled around me, but without me in it. I banged out unknown words to test the action of the Royal, blindly scanned scoresheets of earlier bouts, impolitely ignored the stream of banter and backslaps from front-row regulars.

How had Burney found out about me and Claire?

The obvious answer rose in me like bile: *she told him*.

More than a decade removed from their hardscrabble Depression years—when headstrong hustler Burnell Theopolous first tried his hand at "managing," with a small stable of earners that included a knockout redhead named Claire McKenna—and something still connected the two of them.

Was that what cost Gig Liardi his life? And Claire, as well? Or was *Mr. Boxing* only flailing wildly, hoping for a miracle punch that might save his ass before the final bell?

SECTION S SUNDAY, AUGUST 28, 1948 CCCC*

MONARCH OF THE DAILIES

AN AMERICAN PAPER FOR THE AMERICAN PEOPLE

San Francisco Inquirer Sports

REG US PAT OFF

BURNETT KO'D IN 8TH

Hack Pulverizes Purvis, Wins Cal State Crown

By BILLY NICHOLS

Fight fans at the Civic Auditorium last night witnessed more than a boxing match. They saw a resurrection. Hack Escalante resuscitated his career with a devastating eighth-round knockout, taking the State Heavyweight Championship from highly touted Purvis Burnett, the ebon-hued Angeleno. It is the first title of any kind for Escalante, the veteran San Francisco ring campaigner.

The tousle-haired Italian overcame more than the 3 to 1 odds, as local ring-watchers know. The recent death of the fighter's wife led many to question his desire. Burnett's people had even suggested that the widower would "no longer have the heart" for battle.

But Escalante stunned the younger Burnett with his aggression. He was completely dominant. He bulled his way inside with quick, powerful jabs, fired hooks and crosses in rapid combinations, and seemed to possess depthless stamina. Burnett was off balance all night, and never really in the fight.

The victor, who concluded the proceedings with a thunderous left hook to Purvis's polished dome, offered one of the best displays of ring work seen in a local venue in years. "All our hard work paid off tonight," said the new champ's ebullient pilot, Sid Conte. "The state belt is only the first step. We're ready for all comers."

Escalante agreed with this observer that it was his finest showing ever. Asked to explain it, however, the state champ only said, "I belonged in there tonight. The people wanted a fight—and I gave 'em what they wanted."

Nothing deterred Escalante. Not even the thumb that Burnett, accidentally or otherwise, poked in his eye in the seventh round. It seemed to add fuel to Escalante's fire. He retaliated with

There was a thud on the floor. I dropped the paper to my lap.

The baby had tumbled off the sofa. Christ, his head missed the coffee table by inches. That'd make a nice item:

INFANT DIES IN FALL

> *San Francisco*—Two-month-old William Vincent Nichols died yesterday from traumatic head injuries sustained while his "father," renowned boxing scribe Billy Nichols, read a newspaper nearby. The child's mother, Ida Nichols, is under sedation at St. Luke's Hospital.

The baby's face contorted and he cut loose a shriek.

"Hey, come on, that didn't hurt," I said, rubbing his head. "Shake it off, don't get your mom excited. She'll be all upset. Calm down, it's okay."

Ida hurried into the room. "What happened?"

"Nothing. He bumped his head."

She ran to her son, clutching him to her. "Oh, poor baby, are you all right?" She inspected his head, searching through the downy blond fuzz.

"It isn't serious. Don't worry."

"What happened? How did he hit his head? You've got to be careful of the soft spot, oh, my God!"

"He just slipped off the couch here. He's all right."

"For Christ's sake—weren't you watching him?"

"Course. It's not a big deal. He slid down there. He's okay now."

I raised the paper again, finished reading my story. It was the first time in a long while I'd read my stuff with any eagerness. Hack's performance had juiced me up. He was a whirlwind in the ring, blowing away the pall of guilt and dread that threatened to swallow me up.

Even Hack's taciturn self-assessment was right on target—he'd given the people what they wanted: a fierce symbol. Molten proof that the worst odds can be beaten. I'd filed my copy that night on a wave of enthusiasm—defying the looming specters of Sanders and O'Connor.

Ida punched my leg. I jerked reflexively. She glared at me.

"Be a daddy," she said.

The telephone rang, and I moved quickly from the couch, skirting Ida and the boy.

"Hello?"

"It's Hack."

"Congratulations, champ. Jesus, you were great the other night. I've been calling people, telling them."

"Thanks for that write-up. I know you don't hand out stuff like that."

"You earned every bit of it."

"Anyway, sorry, I hate to bother you about something like this—but I know I can trust you."

"Tell me what you need."

"I think I ought to see an eye doctor."

"Oh, shit. The thumb in the seventh? Is that it?"

"I don't know. Could be. It's still a little fuzzy. I got to get it checked, but without a fuss, you know? Might be nothing, right? Why start rumors and whatnot. Right?"

"You got a problem with your eyesight, the commission needs to know about it. And Sid."

Hack sighed. "I finally won something. For once, I got a chance to get some respect. You understand? I can't have that fall apart now. That's why I'm calling *you*."

"Sid can't fix you up on the QT?"

"I can't trust Sid. But you've always done right by me."

"Yeah, yeah . . . I know an eye doctor, he's my guy. He'll keep it quiet. Dr. Matthews, down on Larkin. Got a pencil? GArfield five, nine-five-nine-three. I'll call him first, let him know what's up."

"I owe you for this. I appreciate all you done for me."

31

I wouldn't call the Hotel Atlas squalid, but it was definitely slouching toward Skid Row. Once it had hummed, hailing wayward wanderers with a vertical neon sign you could see all the way up Taylor—even from the crest of Nob Hill. The neon was extinct, replaced by flat plastic that had little to do with drawing customers. From street-side, its windows showed the telltale signs of a residence hotel: lonesome potted plants and bottles, plus all kinds of oddball objects set on inner sills, the yellowed parchment of mildewy shades yanked down behind, keeping the prenoon sun from slashing into rooms heavy with hangovers.

This was where Hack went to ground, incognito, on the mend after the eye surgery. Claire wouldn't have set foot in the place. Not the Claire I knew. She'd climbed beyond this rung of the ladder, years ago.

It was even money that the lush-hound lounging in the corner of the lobby would glom on to me before the ancient elevator arrived. Some things you can count on. He was one of them. Thickheaded, with dirty strands glued over a dent in his cranium. Clutching the day's introductory short dog in its soggy walker. Eleven-thirty A.M. and he was good and gassed.

"I know you, friend," he happily slurred on his weaving approach.

"Don't think so, pal." Palms out, I looked eagerly for the lift.

"No, no, no . . . I seen you." He reeled back, head cocked to the big picture.

The brass arrow slowly descended above the elevator cage. The rummy looked me up and down.

"Don't tell me. You're around," he hectored. "You're all over the place. A big shot." That was enough ID for him. He shoved his hooch into my arm. "Here—have one on me."

The elevator arrived at last, and I yanked open the grate. "Little early for me," I said. "Thanks just the same."

"Hell with you then. Thinking you're better'n me. Fuck Mr. Bigshot. Fuck him. I better not be here when you get back, that's all I got to say."

His legs did a wobbly box-step as the elevator rose.

The door opened partway, a chain drew taut. This dive was riskier than I figured, if the California State Heavyweight Champion had to double-lock the door.

Hack's face appeared—sort of. His right eye was masked by an occlusor: a piece of shaped metal, perforated with tiny holes and held in place by several feet of white tape.

"Jesus Christ," I said.

"No, just me," he replied. "It ain't pretty, I know."

The room was spartan, tidy, dim. A shade on the lone window was drawn. On the bed was a duffel bag, Navy issue, half-stuffed with clean laundry. He'd been folding and stowing it in a rickety dresser. A hot plate, on a small table by the window, glowed beneath a kettle. The orange coil was the brightest thing in the room. Dismally faded green walls were barren, unless you counted the water stains. The dresser-top, however, was crowded with framed family photos, including a hand-tinted glamour shot of Claire. Someone must have splurged at the ritzy portrait places on Post Street.

My first query came out by reflex:

"Where's the belt?" I asked. "I figured you'd have that out where you could see it."

"Sid's got it. In a safe at the lot."

"Make sure he doesn't hock the thing."

"You want tea? I'm not a coffee man, so I can't—"

"No, that's great. Tea is good."

He pulled a straight-back chair over, but gestured me into the spavined easy chair. It was like sinking your ass into a pot of oatmeal.

"I wanna thank you again for the loan," he said, sitting. "I had no idea it was gonna be that expensive."

"Matthews was topping off the bill," I said. "Skimming a little extra to keep his trap shut."

"I'm gonna pay you back. You can count on it."

I waved that off: "Did it work? Did he fix you up?"

"We'll see."

He chuckled, a private joke, I guess. I rubbed my hands together and glanced at him: too much for that little chair. Yet his whole existence had contracted to this shabby room. Everything stripped away; even the lump of cast bronze he'd earned in battle. Out of his hands, horded by his keeper. He was reduced to making tea and folding clothes. That might be all he'd do too, until the next time he climbed through the ropes.

Hack looked up, touching the eye bandage, worrying a loose tape-end: "That was kind of funny, huh?"

"How's that?"

" *'We'll see.'* Funny choice of words. Maybe not."

I nodded, finally picking up on his joke. He flushed, embarrassed, and lurched up to tend the tea.

"You plan to keep Sid in the dark on this whole thing?" I asked.

"He's in Tahoe for a week with a diamond dealer he sold a coupe to. High roller staying in a lodge up the lake. Sid might even stay a second week, fishing. By then I'll have this off. The doc said you won't be able to tell I had anything done."

"What if it doesn't do the trick?"

"Then I fight with one eye."

"Not a good idea."

"Only one I got," he offered, along with a resigned shrug.

He could have gone back in the Navy. But maybe he felt that wasn't sufficient punishment for all his failures. I didn't ask. I let the champ finish fixing the tea. It was no easy feat. Something as simple as dropping a tea bag in a cup was tricky without any depth perception. He passed me a steaming cup and sat back down. He put his cup on the floor to steep.

"You ever figure out that note Claire wrote?"

I'd studied on that, plenty. I'd decided Claire had never finished it, that *Dempsey vs. Firpo* was a kicker, a subhead for a note she never got to write. As for it being in the fridge—maybe one of the kids stuck it in there. What difference did all that make now?

"Nah, I never made head nor tails of it," I told the widower.

More pressing questions—about Sanders, about Conte, about Ginny Wagner and her briefcase, and their possible connections to Claire and Gig—hammered in my chest, but I couldn't negotiate a tactful transition.

"How are you getting along?" I said. Then added, softly: "You must miss her."

He picked up his tea and slurped some, even though it was too hot. Had to have something to do.

"That's all right," he said, clearing his throat. Man talk.

"Yeah, it's good," I agreed, although I hadn't taken a sip. I drew some in, scalding my tongue. We both looked at the rug.

"One night I came home and . . . It was after the Whitten fight, the second one, remember?"

"Brutal."

"I was beat to hell—you saw it. It didn't even matter that I won, I hurt so bad. That was new. And when I got home everything was dark. This was the new house that we'd moved to, out the avenues. Claire didn't wait up no longer when I'd fight. After all, it was only paying the bills, you know? Not any different if I was a truck driver or a stevedore. I climbed into bed with her and I hurt bad, I'm telling you. All over. And I lay there wondering, you know, if it was all a big mistake. Making up these terrible things . . ."

He paused to take another sip of tea, then shook his head like a mosquito was in his ear: "Aw hell, you don't need to hear this stuff."

"Maybe I do. What was it you were thinking? What 'terrible things'?"

"I think my brain was half scrambled. I was picturing all kinds of sick stuff. Wishing there was some way out. It came to me that I could finish it all—burn down the house, with Claire and me and the kids inside, and everything. Or just run away, keep running, then live by myself in the hills, like a dog. I thought worse things. Worse than that even."

"Everybody has nights like that," I said. Dreams of torching my Mediterranean Moderne manse had interrupted many a night's slumber.

"I'm hopped up with all this horrible stuff when I hear a kid crying down the hall. I go to their room. They slept together, Tony and Marie. Tony, he's standing over at the window staring out, bawling like crazy. My little girl's sitting up in bed, staring at Tony, too scared to make a sound. I couldn't see nothing outside. It's dark. I can't figure what he was crying about.

"Two minutes earlier I'm plotting how to kill everybody in the place. Then I got my arms around my son and I'm telling him it was all right, 'cause Daddy was there and everything would be fine. I knew exactly what that poor kid was going through, you know? That was me, when I was his age. Afraid, all of a sudden, for no reason. Nobody could ever know how bad it was."

I made some sort of sympathetic sound in my throat. Raised the eyebrows.

"Then Claire comes in behind me. Before I can tell her no, she switches on the lights to see what's wrong. Tony looks up, he sees me, he starts screaming again. You was at that fight, you remember. My face was all fucked up. Split lip, one eye like a boiled sausage, six stitches on top of the other one. Tony'd never seen me looking like that. The more I hugged him and said it was all right, the more upset he got.

"I was pissed at Claire for turning on the lights. But then she did the damnedest thing. She walks over and takes Tony and says, 'Your daddy got hurt, but we love him even when he's ugly.' And then she starts kissing me, all over my beat-to-shit face, right in front of the kids. Pretty soon they're laughing and telling her *where* to kiss me—thought it was the funniest thing they'd ever seen."

The last stray wisps of steam rose off the tea. "I should have known better," I murmured. "She should have told me."

Hack leaned toward me. "What? What'd you say?"

"She should have told me," I repeated, watching his bandaged face contort. He belonged to her. I never belonged in the picture.

From my inside breast pocket I pulled three trimmed clips of the piece I'd filed about Claire Escalante and her boxing husband. I handed them to Hack.

"She should have told me that story. For the article. Here are the copies you wanted. If she'd told me the story you just did, I'd have put it in there." Hell, it would have been the lead.

He held the flimsy tear sheets in his huge hands, perusing them.

"Shoulda had a picture of my girl," he whispered, then set the clips gently on the floor.

She didn't want her picture taken, I almost said, but Hack spoke first:

"Did she say how rough she had it growing up? Way rougher than me. She taught me how to get through things, you know, deal with the shit that happens all the time, over and over. Know what she said?"

"No. Tell me."

"'Keep your clothes clean. Put one foot in front of the other.'"

"Simple enough. Does it work?"

"As long as you don't quit, you ain't hit bottom. You run into Pete on your way up, by any chance?" He pantomimed guzzling a pint.

"His clothes weren't too clean. The feet didn't work too good, either."

"That is something I will never be."

"Claire didn't want her picture taken," I finally said, pointing to the clippings. "For the story."

"To go along with your article? Get outta here." His eyes drifted over to the movie-star pose in its frame. "She loved to have her picture took."

I fought my way up from the dead springs of the easy chair and carried my tea to the dresser. My opening had appeared; my advance had to have finesse. Gig had no tact when it came to Claire, and according to Hack, he got dealt swift and definitive retaliation. I had no urge to follow in his footsteps.

I delicately separated Claire's portrait from the others: Tony and Marie screaming bug-eyed on a ride at Playland-at-the-Beach; baby pictures of all the kids; Claire surrounded by her brood on the back steps of the house; the same wedding photo that dropped out of Gig's scrapbook.

"Could Claire have been afraid of somebody seeing her in the paper?" I suggested.

I studied her eyes, even greener in the tinted print. Hack shuffled in his seat.

"Afraid of who? I don't get you."

"She said no way she'd have her picture in the paper—like she was worried about it being in there. I'm wondering if there wasn't some reason behind that."

"You must be dreaming. No offense. Claire would have jumped at a chance to have her kisser in the paper. She used to say she was better-looking than the girls in the Magnin's ads. It was true, too."

"So she didn't seem . . . nervous or scared about anything?"

"Claire was never scared of anything."

I returned the portrait to Hack's collection; couldn't look at it anymore. I imagined those eyes staring up at the ceiling as the blood left her. Was she scared then?

Next to the dresser several boxes were stacked in the corner. Sitting on top of them was a big book with a pebbled brown leather cover, bound with a rawhide cord. I flipped through it. It was an exact match for the one O'Connor had found in Gig's apartment: same precise layout, same cribbed lettering in the margins. Except all these photos and clippings—mostly written by me—featured a promising heavyweight named Hack Escalante.

When I turned, the heavyweight was huddled on the small chair, elbows poised on his knees, rocking slightly, looking for all the world like he was waiting on the bell.

"This your scrapbook?"

He gave a little phantom nod, as if that's all the question merited.

"Funny, it looks exactly like one Gig showed me once. Of his career." I didn't know exactly where I'd gotten this new set of balls, but I wasn't about to give them back. I stood there, slowly flipping the pages, perusing the rise, peak, and plateau of Hack's career. The only sound in the room was his breathing, and the regular flipping of the thick pages. From 1935 to 1948 neither of us said a word. The win over Purvis Burnett, his biggest fight ever, wasn't in there yet.

"It was Gig's," he finally said.

I set the book on the bed next to the clothes. "It's a nice piece of work. He give it to you?"

"I took it."

"How come?"

He gave a big heavy sigh, like he was drawing gas for the last round. "Near the end there, I gotta tell you . . . Gig was losing his marbles. It wasn't easy to be around him."

"How so?"

"He was angry all the time. And mean. To me. When he didn't have no right to be. It was all about him, how he did everything for me and I never appreciated it. He'd bitch that nobody respected him enough. He'd pull out that scrapbook and go through it page by page, pointing out some little thing that nobody knew about each and every fight, telling me that that's what made the difference in my winning or losing. He'd go on and on, until you'd have thought that it was him in there taking the beating. I'm telling you, he was off the deep end."

"Why'd you take the book?"

Hack lurched to his feet and came at me. He nudged me aside and snatched up the scrapbook. "'Cause that's me in there. *Me.* Not him." He went back to the chair and flopped down, clutching the damn thing like it was some sacred tome. "He didn't deserve it," he finally said. The words hung there, heavily.

"How well did you guys know Burney Sanders? Did you or Gig have any dealings with Burney beyond him promoting the occasional fight?" I ventured.

Hack's befuddlement seemed genuine. But then so had his tearful tale of giving Gig a little nudge on the chin. Much as I hated to admit it, I was having trouble gauging the truth. Could be I'd grown so accustomed to crafting my own version, I couldn't recognize the real thing.

"I don't catch your meaning," Hack said. "I only know Burney to talk to, when he's paying out my purse. Gig may have known him more, but I didn't figure them for pals. Not at all."

"How about Claire? She acquainted with Sanders? Ever?"

"Not that I know of. How come? What's Sanders got to do with the price of rice?"

"I don't know," I sighed, and sat heavily on the edge of the bed. "I'm just fishing." The loose ends seemed miles apart. Hack was either ignorant of any incriminating links, or I was too deep in—or too afraid—to press him farther.

"Did you ever get the final word on what happened to Claire?" I found myself asking. "You know, the cause?"

"Some kind of hemorrhage, I don't know. The cops say she might have had a bad abortion, but they're crazy. Desperate, like you called it."

I rescued a stack of laundered T-shirts as they slipped off the bed.

"There should be something you can do," I breathed. "It's only that . . . I don't know."

"Such as what? You mean like sue somebody? I'm no slick article like you. I don't know what to do. They'd make a fool out of me. And even if, what's money gonna do, anyway? It can't ever bring her back. She dies in a hospital, she dies in a wreck, she dies at home—what's the difference? She's dead the same, any which way."

If I ever filed such blunt philosophy, I'd get fired first, strung up later.

Hack crossed his burly arms and looked away, to the window. He stood abruptly and jerked up the shade, flooding the room with daylight, then stalked back to the chair.

"She's still around," he said flatly. "Every so often, she comes around."

I hoisted myself off the kip and stepped back to the ratty easy chair. Hack's unbandaged eye tracked me, watched me ease myself back into the crusty chair.

"How's that?" I asked.

"She had her way. Like magic. I never could have got through the Gig thing without her. She taught me how to stand up to the cops. I don't know where she got it from. It *was* like magic. She could convince me in a second, build me up. Like you, a little, if you take my meaning. Making things happen, easing it over. That don't go away. She put it in me. I still hear her. I can still see her."

He leaned closer and I could see movement behind his one good eye, and something coursing under his skin.

"She's watching me now, I can feel it. Waiting to see if I can come up with something. On my own."

"What would that be?"

"A real fight, maybe. Or a way to prove, once and for good, that I'm not some chump."

"Nobody thinks that. Take my word on it."

"My kids could, pretty soon. That's all that matters to me anymore. I need them to be proud of me. Anybody can pump gas or lay bricks or tar a roof. Not everyone can climb in a ring. That's something *I* can do."

He popped up and paced, so far as he could. It felt like we were back in the dressing room at the Civic.

"I'll tell you what," he said, heating up. "Help me get a real fight. Get me Carter. I swear I'll give you something to really write about. I'll give you a big-time story. Then my kids will *really* have something to paste in that book. Something they can be proud of."

I looked away from him, to the write-ups of his wife strewn on the floor, my name tagged on them.

"Hack, I'm no miracle worker."

His left eye gleamed with determination or delirium. I couldn't tell which. The right offered no clue beneath the occlusor.

"I don't believe you," he scoffed. "You got the same kind of magic Claire did. She made things happen. You can make this happen."

32

I left Hack in the Atlas, with his clean clothes, bloodied cornea, and desperate hopes. Fresh air was what I needed, in the worst way. Plastered Pete was curled fetal on the lobby couch, baking in a patch of sun. Hack's shreds of redemption weren't that far removed from the absurd heroics in a drunk's loopy daydreams. What was there that separated Hack and this snoozing souse? Weren't they both destined to be as sadly destitute? Time would stalk Hack, inexorably, methodically, wearing down his muscular defenses and burning out his will, until he succumbed at last.

No taxis idling on Taylor. I drifted downhill, figuring to hail one at an intersection. But jumbled thoughts kept me on the hoof.

In a way, I desired and even envied Hack's naïveté. There had to be some measure of comfort in his blind belief that there was a way out of this mess. To him it was simple, primitive: he only needed the right person to hit.

Get me Carter.

Tough colored fighter out of Jacksonville, a character he didn't know from Adam—that was who represented salvation for him. Besides me, of course. *Mr. Boxing.* The magic man. The white knight who once wished him dead, so I could have his wife to myself.

Hack's faith in me remained unwavering, even in the face of O'Connor's sinister suppositions. Was he really that simple? Or like any bullheaded boxer, was he merely sticking to his fight plan, trusting that what had worked for him so far would be what carried him the distance?

At Bush Street I spotted a Yellow cab a block away. Squinting into the sun, I could barely make out the illuminated on-duty sign on its roof. I scanned farther up Bush, scouting for a free hack in the flow of traffic. That's when I registered the sign for the Temple Hotel, and felt the full gush of guilt I'd labored mightily to mask while sitting face-to-face with Hack.

It was there, in a rented room, that I'd fallen in love with his wife. I wasn't sure what she was up to, but that didn't really matter. I fell. Even though I'd seen the suspicious bruise, even though I suspected our lovemaking might be some type of negotiation, I fell. I'd seen her face, her eyes, as I spun out my stories—and realized she was the audience I'd always wanted. Sometimes I could still feel the weight of her, lying on me, as I regaled her with fables from my youth.

The Dempsey versus Firpo fight—we were in the Temple when I told her that story.

I hadn't even seen the taxi pull up beside me. I was well into the crosswalk, asking to get crippled.

"You flag me, mister?"

I climbed in the back, rethought the note Claire had written. What an idiot I was. When Hack had turned the message over to me, my great fear—and desire—was that Claire had left behind a testament of her true feelings for me. I read *Dempsey vs. Firpo* only as a reference to the story I'd told her, my engrossing yarn. I'd pathetically inferred a validation of my gifts as a raconteur—proof that I had moved her in some way. My ego had me construing her words as an aborted attempt to pen an appropriate response.

Where in the *hell* did I get off?

The cabbie had driven two blocks before he was able to catch my eye in the rearview: "Where to, bud?"

But what if Claire wasn't *reacting* to my story at all? What if she was *using* it? To communicate something else entirely. In a code only I would understand.

I'd wanted a love letter. But now I realized that I might be looking at instructions, from the other side. I was spooked as hell.

"Temple Hotel," I told the driver, who flashed exasperation at the short fare.

A double-meter tip helped smooth his feathers. I hustled from the hard glare of the street into the cool vault of the Temple lobby. Before I pinned a tag on Leo Most, he'd already pegged me—and bent over to look for something in a closet off the front desk.

He straightened up holding a strongbox.

"I was expecting you'd come by," he drawled, setting the box on the counter and sliding it across, as if it belonged to me.

I played along, gripping it as if I'd gotten a package at the post office, addressed to me. This one had a pair of heavy latches, and built-in combination locks.

"What's the setup?" I grunted at Leo, my best O'Connor impression.

"A lady left it, couple of weeks ago now. Told me I was to give it to you—nobody else—and only if you came in looking for it." Leo looked suddenly sheepish. "You did come looking for it, right?" Claire had remembered the story I'd tossed off about Leo Most, how I figured his debt to me would keep his lip zipped when we'd punched in on the hot-sheet clock.

I kept up the flatfoot facade, acting like Leo was supposed to be delivering dope I already knew, as if I was testing *him.*

"This woman have a name?"

"No, sir, Mr. Nichols."

"Redhead, right?" I straightened up my shoulders. "Built?"

Leo looked suddenly skeptical. "No, sir. She was blond. Kind of . . . slender."

Blond? What the hell was this now?

"What did she look like?" I quizzed him.

Here was a Negro who'd negotiated his way through prison. No easy feat. But when he had to describe a white woman to a white man, he couldn't seem to come up with the words. Finally, he said, "She looked kinda like a movie actress I seen, only I can't remember her name."

"You'd never seen this woman before? Here?"

"No, sir."

I took the measure of the strongbox. The combination locks were daunting—for about five seconds. Then I tuned right into Claire's wavelength, amazed at how she'd broadcast a terse report for one listener only.

Dempsey vs. Firpo.

My fingertips rotated the numbered rings next to the latches: 091 on the left tumblers, 423 on the right. In sequence, 09/14/23. The date Dempsey defended his title against the Wild Bull of the Pampas. The date William Nicholovich decided to become a writer. The genesis of a character known as Billy Nichols. A story I'd told Claire right here, in room 412.

The latches popped open. I dug a Jackson and a Lincoln from my wallet.

"Gimme a room," I snapped, worried that Leo could hear my heartbeat echoing in the vaulted lobby.

"One key?" he asked.

"Just one," I said, pushing the bills across the desk. He politely acted like the greenery didn't add up.

"Keep it," I told him. Leo palmed the cash. One glance in his unblinking eyes, and I knew he'd stand up, down the line.

I grabbed the key. The box under my arm, I hurried to the open elevator.

After a couple of hours in that gloomy hotel room, sifting through the contents of the strongbox, the stray pieces started falling into place. I was able to skip past the dead-ends and the missed turnoffs and began to see my way to the truth.

It was always a kick to be the man with the answers. It was a kick in the teeth to find that there was an alternate agenda, humming beneath the very world where I imagined myself to be King Shit.

By four o'clock I'd navigated all the angles, gotten a handle on how things could fit together. I thought I understood not only what had happened but how I might fight my way off the ropes. For that matter, why not score a huge upset? I'd been handed the core of it, the ugly facts, the gritty evidence. Now I had to work it, polish it, craft it into the best story I'd ever written.

I owed Claire that. She'd risked everything to stock this strongbox—and she knew that she wouldn't be alive if it was opened.

Back in the lobby, I queried Leo again.

"This blond you talked to—she was pretty, right? Pointy features. Had a high voice, kind of girlish but all business, right?"

He considered the assessment, then nodded. I asked him for a phone book.

There was no answer at the Pine Street listing for Wagner, Virginia.

SECTION S SATURDAY, SEPT 8, 1948 CCCC*

MONARCH OF THE DAILIES

AN AMERICAN PAPER FOR THE AMERICAN PEOPLE

San Francisco Inquirer Sports

REG US PAT OFF

Through THE ROPES

By BILLY NICHOLS

Strolled with several old-timers through the Mission the other day. As usual when we crossed 16th Street, talk promptly turned to the glory days of National Hall, where these guys earned nickels, dimes, and cauliflower ears slinging leather in their prime.

"Where'd it go?" Joe Roche suddenly hollered. He spun every which way looking for the old ramshackle structure with the small marquee jutting out over the sidewalk. "Don't tell me they tore it down!"

"It's gone," wailed Vic Grupico. "They got some palace in its place!"

Relax, fellas. The "palace" on the site of the old Bucket of Blood is the spanking *new* National Hall, a glittering jewel of a fight club that will simultaneously replace and revive the glorious bandbox. It's the culmination of a dream for promoter Burney Sanders, who after years of effort, will finally reopen the hall next month.

"This is going to be the finest boxing club on the West Coast," Sanders crowed. "Maybe the best in the whole country."

The wily Sanders has a silent partner in the enterprise, and judging from the expensive and lavish remodel job, he must be a man who loves to gamble . . .

33

Gazing through the panoramic plate-glass office window, Eddie Ryan surveyed his kingdom, Golden State Racetrack. From this base, the horse-race impresario oversaw an empire, which encompassed courses and betting windows throughout the West. He swirled the ice in his drink, smoothed down his hair, and assessed the amateurs below as they silently swayed and surged with excitement. Around the far turn, a pack of horses stampeded from the afternoon sun, galloping madly for the wire. The track announcer's captivating call crackled from a speaker in the wall, but it wasn't as riveting without the background of bellowing bettors and thundering hooves.

Ryan turned from the finish, lips liquor-wet, eyes equally moist. "Goddamn, the beauty of this timeless pageant," he said. "It's enough to make you weep."

Discounting a penchant for verbosity, Eddie had plenty in common with his estranged brother, Jimmy. With their fair skin, lofty foreheads, lacquered blond locks, and crooked, shiny smiles, they might have passed for twins. Eddie had a dozen years on Jimmy, but even so, they shared plenty of the same friends and associates. At the top of that extensive roster you could pencil in ruthless influence peddler Artie Samish, the most powerful unelected "official" in the state, the Secret Boss of California.

The Brothers Ryan weren't fraternal, however. Eddie had sanded down suggestions of the sinister, while Jimmy chose to cultivate them. Where Jimmy sported top-shelf threads, Eddie cloaked himself in folksy, rust-hued tweeds. Jimmy hired bountifully endowed ingenues to front his club. In Eddie's operation, you got to look at buttoned-up librarians and bookkeeping grannies.

I'd been ushered into Ryan's discreetly opulent office by a prim, well-tailored secretary who could have fielded calls at a Montgomery Street law firm. The cast of characters who'd enlivened Eddie's prewar ascension, fringe dwellers like Duck In and Duck Out, Dirty Shirt Sullivan, Lying Tom O'Farrell, the Sheik, and English Jack Bates, had been issued their walking papers. Too much colorful history, potential tarnish on Eddie's freshly minted respectability.

Ryan stepped back from the floor-to-ceiling glass. "Eddie, are you crying?" I teased, grinning. I glanced down at tiny pockets of jubilant winners, swamped by an ocean of ticket-tearing chumps. "You just made a small fortune. Again."

He shambled to his desk, after a detour to the liquor cart for another dose of single malt. I waved off a drink; Eddie took up my slack. He fingered some papers, but he was miles away.

"Makes me sad, Billy," he mused, dropping onto his throne. "Sad because I'm moving out of here. Setting up an office downtown. I'll miss all this."

Perched across from him, I occupied a boxy chair upholstered with creaky red leather.

"Covering your tracks?—so to say?" My tone was bland.

The remark earned the first straight look since I'd entered: "Meaning?"

"Meaning you're ready for Samish to deliver the goods. A slot on the Board of Equalization, maybe, deep inside the machine, where the money lives. A politico can't be running racetracks. A legitimate address is only the first step in a new direction, am I right?"

"Here I thought we were just renewing acquaintances. When did you start covering politics instead of sports?"

Ryan figured I was working him. Too direct, too early. I backtracked: "You remember when we first ran across each other, Eddie?"

"Can't say that I do. Seems like you've always been around —as long as anybody."

"It was back in the days. I got an invite to that big bash you hosted. Roberts-at-the-Beach, after Blackie swam across the Bay. How much did you drop on that caper, anyway? Or was it all a stunt?"

Ryan chuckled to himself, eyes glistening.

Blackie was a harness-racer, owned by Shorty Roberts and his brother, Wilford. Shorty would have Blackie do the horse-paddle in the Bay as part of his training. He bet Ryan the horse could swim across the Golden Gate. Eddie said no way. The sturdy old nag—with Shorty hanging on to his tail—made it in just over twenty minutes, not far off the human record. Ryan cheered Blackie on at the finish, tears streaming down his cheeks. Next day he threw an all-stops-out party to honor the swimming steed. Blackie held court in the middle of the dance floor, munching on a bale of hay.

That story said a mouthful about what a sentimental sport Eddie Ryan was. But it didn't tell it all.

"Those were great days." Eddie nodded, like he'd been reading my mind. "Gambling was fun then. Shit, everything was fun."

"Not anymore?"

"Not in the same way. Not since the war. Those stuffed-shirt clowns in Sacramento, they never wanted me in this state. They certainly relished taking their pound of flesh. Did you know this was the only track the government allowed to operate on the Coast, during the war? The ward-heelers jammed their greedy hands all the way into my coffers—Army Emergency Relief, Western Defense Command, War Effort and Welfare Funds, all the VA hospitals, not to mention your man Hearst's War Wounded Fund—I financed them all. I was proud to do my patriotic duty. But half of what that money was supposed to fund never got built. Been to any of the veterans hospitals? They're a disgrace. A sinful shame. I curse these lethargic and larcenous legislators. They, of all people, have the gall to mandate that I keep my nose out of politics? Because of my *disreputable* livelihood? Can you appreciate the hypocrisy of it?"

"Does that mean you want to knock heads with them?"

"I can do a better job than any of those pork-barrel parasites."

"But first you have to—with Samish's help, I guess—clean up the gambling connection. Plus you'll need to keep Jimmy under wraps."

Ryan glowered. He tilted his glass, drained the Scotch, inhaled an ice cube, and cracked it between his teeth—another sibling-shared habit. Funny how Jimmy, the villain, was the abstainer.

"Eddie, can I suggest something?" I placed the envelope I'd brought along on his desk. "Take a break from the booze. Ceremonial ribbon-cutters have to be able to see straight."

He planted the empty tumbler on the leather blotter. "Remind me again why you invited yourself here," he slurred stonily.

"Research. Concerning the reopening of National Hall. Relating to the possible return to the glory days of boxing in this town."

"I've heard that song. Why talk to me? Memory serves, last time you were in this office, I turned down a chance to underwrite that enterprise."

"Memory serves all right, Eddie—it was over a year ago, and I was helping out Burney Sanders. He always dreamed of owning the old Bucket of Blood. He twisted my arm, asked me to appeal to your sentimental side."

"You did a decent job, as I recall."

The Bucket of Blood was *San Francisco*, I'd enthused, laying down ground cover for little Burney, my boyhood chum. *National Hall was the rugged heart of the Irish Mission District, fertile territory for guys who took no shit but would give their last quarter to a beggar on the street. If the Bucket went under, down with it would crumble all the memories of the local scrappers who built this city side-by-side, day after day, and mixed it up after dark. Every true born-and-bred was either a fighter or a fan, blah blah blah.*

My grandstanding came up empty. "You were a tougher sell by then," I informed Eddie. "That pitiful nostalgia didn't grab you anymore."

"Like I told you, the war changed everything. We're older now. No wiser, but a lot less reckless than we used to be." I had to wince at that, considering what was in my envelope. Play one card at a time, I reminded myself.

"All that aside, Eddie, they're saying it's your money Burney's parlaying to bring back the Bucket of Blood. Any truth to that?"

Ryan shook his head. His gaze drifted to his aide-de-camp, the crystal decanter. "How do these ridiculous rumors get started?"

"People like me start 'em. This one's not out the gate yet, but it's rarin' to go."

Eddie's Scotch was forgotten: "What are you pulling?" His eyes were wide.

"Looks to me that Sanders is getting his bankroll from you."

"But I'm telling you that's not so—you were right here when I nixed that. I've got no connection to that futile scheme of his."

"I wish that were true, Eddie. Truth is, you are connected —even if you don't know it."

I leaned forward and slid the envelope farther across the desk: "Here's your connection."

Ryan didn't know where I was headed. Otherwise, he'd have reacted like his brother, with an icy stare that warned you not to play him short. He seemed tired and perplexed as he fumbled with the clasp. I couldn't tell if it was nerves or hooch making his fingers tremble.

He shook out the contents and I watched his face plunge five stories.

Without a second's hesitation, he tore up the photos. The pictures showed him, sans his formal evening wear, in a clammy horizontal clinch with a beautiful naked woman, who was also a wife, mother, lover, and actress: Claire Escalante.

Eddie deposited the jagged pieces in a waste can beside the desk, his jaw muscles working. He torched the envelope, igniting it with a big onyx lighter, then dropped the burning oaktag into the basket, atop the photo fragments. Flames licked the sides of the bin.

Edward P. Ryan lived in the wealthy, woodsy enclave of Hillsborough, not too far from Bing Crosby. Mrs. Ryan, Vivian, was well-situated in the finer circles and surfaced regularly in the society pages, stumping for women's volunteer groups. Eddie had a pair of pretty daughters. One was a sophomore at Stanford. If he could shed the horse-racing stigma, he'd have the perfect image for politics: assuming he steered clear of scandal.

Ryan stood unsteadily, lurched to the liquor cart, claiming the decanter and a seltzer bottle. He gave the waste-can flames a quick spritz of seltzer, and dispensed himself a longer draught of Scotch. It didn't matter that he burned the pictures; I'd had an assistant in the pre-press shop print dupes. The production apprentice knew nothing about Edward Ryan; it was nameless mail-order smut to him.

"I know how you feel," I told Eddie. "I wish burning them would make it all go away, too. But those are just prints. It's the negatives that carry weight."

Ryan stared me down, speechless. I hated his expression, disgust and disappointment clouding his eyes, dragging at the corners of his mouth.

"It's not me that's shaking you down, Eddie. I don't have anything to do with it. It's Sanders. He's the one blackmailing you."

Ryan's chest rose and fell, heaving under the tweeds. I'd heard somewhere that he had a heart problem. I hoped I wouldn't be the last one to see him alive. I gave him a couple of minutes to regroup, to move the puzzle pieces back and forth.

Through the speakers came the nasal blare of the track announcer, identifying runners in the next race as they headed paddock to post.

"It's not Sanders," Eddie finally croaked. "It has to be Jimmy. He's out to get me."

"Wrong, Eddie. It's Burney. Bet your life on it."

"Where do you fit in? How'd you get the pictures?"

"My source was the woman."

Ryan was close to apoplexy: "You can't . . . how would you . . . how do you know that, that—*whore*?"

I ought to have defended her reputation, explained that she was as much a victim as Eddie. But I was tired of spinning long, sad stories. I cut straight to the finale:

"She's dead."

"Because of this mess?"

"That's the way I see it. And she's not the only one."

"Sanders *killed* her?" He was stunned. There was genuine concern in Ryan's voice. I wanted to believe it was over the death of something other than his political aspirations.

"I'm not certain that he did it," I had to admit. "There's no solid evidence to that effect. But he's behind it."

"Who's the woman? You never answered me that."

The old Eddie would have known. Back when, he lived in the circuit, had advice for all the local fighters, trinkets for all their wives. The new model Eddie had strayed in more ways than one; he'd betrayed more than his wife.

The blackmail photos explained, of course, why Claire wouldn't allow a picture to accompany my article. Ryan surely would have recognized her.

"It doesn't matter," I said curtly. "She's somebody Burney had on his string, from a long time ago. He used her—blackmailed *her*, actually—into setting you up. How'd you meet her?"

"It was about a year ago. She latched on to me at the Village, at a fund-raiser for Pat Brown's campaign. She was beautiful and bright—and very flattering. And, as I should have seen—very professional. I . . . made a mistake."

"Kind of error any one of us could make," I said. One I'd have made repeatedly, and gladly.

"Save it. What's *your* play?" Ryan snarled, not buying that

I was on his side. "There's a reason you got those pictures. What do you want for them?"

"I don't want to see you taking it in the shorts. That's why I'm here. I'm guessing you didn't get the negatives when you shelled out the hush money?"

"No. I'm still getting strung along."

"He can go on bleeding you forever."

"No kidding."

"Which is why you're sucking down Scotch like it's going out of style. That approach won't win friends, much less influence people."

He shoved the stopper back into the decanter: "I'm not calling the cops, if that's what you're about to propose. If this gets in the record, it goes in the papers. I can't humiliate my family like that. The newspapers would love to bring me down. The only thing they like more than a rich philanthropist is a philanthropist with his pants around his ankles."

"Skip the cops. You won't need 'em. I've got the negatives now."

Eddie made a steeple of his hands and waited for my pitch. Ryan hadn't gotten where he was through faith, hope, or charity. He wasn't expecting any of those from me.

"A heavyweight title fight," I declared. "That's what I want. Even trade for the negatives. Staged right here, in the city. You bankroll it, I'll set it up. We bring Chester Carter out. You underwrite it, you get the negatives."

The announcer blared the start of the day's featured exacta. We heard the distant sound of wailing bells and gates slamming open. Ryan stood and sauntered to the built-in speaker, switching off the rat-a-tat race call. Whichever jockey and mount finished first, Eddie was in the money. That counted for nothing now. He'd been five or six sheets to the wind. My sobering news folded a few of those and tucked them away.

"You promote it like you're blackmailing me into a beneficial deal," Eddie said.

"That's exactly right. We'll make it a charity show. Contribute part of the gate to a war memorial or some such. If we're not careful, they'll make you mayor."

"You've already got this lined up," he said, propping himself wearily on the edge of the desk.

"Not completely. But I do have one requirement. You'll be the copromoter. Sanders gets equal billing."

Ryan's face went angry with reddening blotches: "What in Christ's name? First you say he's blackmailing me, then you want me to go partners with him?"

"Freeze him out of a show this big and he'll be gunning twice as hard for you. Instead, we give him what he's always wanted. Put him on top of the world. Make him the big wheel he's dreamed of being since he was a kid."

"Want to tell me why?"

"He'll drop his guard. That's what happens when you get full of your own juice. Trust me on this one. When you start believing your own PR, that's when you're ripe for the picking."

I got situated in a phone booth at the Turf Club. It was half past five in the evening in Jacksonville, Florida. That's where the heavyweight championship belt resided. Mining my broke-back contact book, I dug up Carter's management team, Jake Elster and Don Dillon. The operator made the connection.

Those seconds waiting for an answer, the muted ringing in my ear, they were as close as I'd come to what Hack must have felt, stalking toward those hot ring lights. Everything on the line.

"Don Dillon. Manager of the heavyweight champion of the world."

"Don. Billy Nichols, the *Inquirer*, out in San Francisco." I didn't wait for him to acknowledge me, offered no standard palaver. "Got a solid proposal for you," I opened right up. "A sure thing, gift-wrapped."

Once I stopped jawing, they bought right in. I could hardly believe how fast. Dillon and Elster saw it clearly: road-showing Carter, against some outclassed journeyman in the opponent's backyard, would draw a sellout crowd and major money—before the champ had to risk the crown in a rematch against leading contenders Jersey Joe Walcott and Ezzard Charles, or, perhaps, an unretired Joe Louis.

Eddie Ryan had verbally approved a combined purse of twenty-five large. Dillon wanted twenty-three of those for his boy. I countered with twenty as top-end. Elster broke in to inquire who the fuck I was, to be brokering a title fight. I didn't rise to it. They couldn't draw flies back East against Lesnevich; a change of scenery might be indicated. Twenty was a very reasonable offer, I maintained. They talked expenses, over and above. I said, Why quibble?

The challenger was an afterthought. They took the name, but didn't seem to need the record or the reputation. Figured it didn't matter, I guess. What did the Coast have that could stand up to the Jacksonville Jewel—or Jim Norris's IBC combination?

34

"American Boxing Club, Burnell Sanders, Chief Executive" was freshly lettered in gilt-edged enamel on the pebbled glass of the half-open office door. The ABC chief, as advertised, was inside, going over the books. He totaled his blood money with a belligerent, obsessive scrutiny. I figured there was a code for the regular cash infusions covertly squeezed from Eddie Ryan. The chiseler probably didn't even toss Claire a token gratuity for enticing Ryan into his cage. He threatened her instead, saying he'd tell Hack the truth about his wife's former "career."

Claire's fear of Hack's reaction—*that* was valid. You could ask Liardi. Sometime after he'd called my office on May 12, but before I arrived at his flat, Gig made the mistake of calling Claire a whore to her husband's face. It was the last insult he'd ever issue.

As for what Gig wanted to tell me that night, I had no idea. I liked to think that he'd somehow tipped to Burney's extortion scheme, and was going to spill it to me, just to get even with Sanders for years of grief. But for all I knew he could have been asking me over to help pick out new wallpaper. Liardi may have had no connection at all to Burney Sanders. But by walking into Gig's apartment that night, my life had taken a whole new course—one that led inexorably to this moment.

I quietly nudged open the door. The scratch of my match jerked Sanders's snout out of his ledgers. He gave me a startled flash of unclassified hostility.

"You nearly gave me a fucking heart attack," Burney said.

A quick once-over of Sanders's new digs revealed a scaled-down version of Ryan's regal appointments. Burney was determined to rise in the pecking order, no matter what it took. Success had come to me early and easily. I didn't really grasp the desperation of characters like Burnell Theopolous, their need to separate themselves from the rabble, to prove that they belonged in the black, with the untouchables. Even if it required a federal offense. Why not? Guys risk their life in the ring for a shot at big money—what's a little extortion among friends?

I noticed a safe that Burney had installed in the wall. It was off to the right, and open. I wondered if that's where he'd kept the evidence, and which of the two ballsy dames had lifted it.

"Where's Virginia?" I cracked. "I thought she handled the paperwork."

That earned a suspicious gaze. "She's gone," he said. An ominous choice of words. I'd called her number dozens of times without getting an answer.

"Shitcanned, huh? Like you said."

"That's right. Do a favor for people and what do you get? Stabbed in the back."

I smiled as I drew a draught of the Macanudo. "Yeah, I know what you mean. She knew Claire Escalante, you know. They used to work together at a law firm downtown. I'll bet you didn't know that."

"Whatd'ya want?" Burney said, fixing me with his top-of-the-line glower. It was amusing to watch him play it tough, now that I held the hole cards that once were his. I looked for the fear in his eyes, some clue that he suspected that his blackmail fodder had been delivered into my hands through the efforts of Ginny Wagner and Claire Escalante.

"Relax, Burney," I said, moving toward the desk. "I'm not shaking you down. I just wanted to tell you that Carter will come West to fight Hack. As soon as you can set it up. The money side's already handled. Eddie Ryan'll bankroll it. You'll copromote with him. Given at least a month's lead time, we should sell out the Cow Palace. That's a giant step past National Hall—but I figure you're man enough for it."

The look on Sanders's face, utter stupefaction, would have to tide me over for the moment. If I were Hack, and knew what I knew, I'd have pounded Sanders's face into ground chuck. Prior to heaving him out those new frosted louvered windows. On balance, though, I was meaner than Hack. I wasn't going to let Sanders off that easy. First I'd let him take a juicy bite out of his dream and inhale some of the rare air at the top of the heap. Then I'd drop him, the full distance, past rock bottom.

"You pulling some kind of fast one?" Burney asked, his mask back in place.

I scrawled the number for Carter's people on his desk blotter: "Call 'em. I greased the skids. Elster and Dillon. Trust me, they're champing at the bit."

"You talked to Ryan, too?"

"Oh, absolutely."

"He'll guarantee the purse—plus expenses?"

"Sure. Not to mention, he wants you as his copromoter, Burney. Thinks you're aces, a genuine operator. You could even end up in Eddie's shoes one of these days."

Sanders paced the room, a banty rooster pecking at fresh scratch. I let my cigar fight off the smell of new paint. After watching Burney's brain pan-broil for a minute, I picked up the phone and held it out to him.

"Call Sid. Let him know you landed the big one. He's on vacation, at the lodge. I've got the number."

"You rock-solid on this?"

"Stake my career on it."

Burney should have known better. Each of us, always, ought to know better. But when everything you want stands in front of you, waving you closer, how can you resist?

As he dialed the number, I sauntered over to the safe. Inside I could make out several bundles of cash and some bound cardboard wallets. Missing, of course, was an envelope full of prints and negatives. I recalled the look Virginia Wagner had given me that day I stopped by here, and the extra little squeeze of her hand. She and Claire had conspired to swipe Burney's blackmail fodder. I was certain of it, even if I couldn't nail down the particulars. And I might never know them if Burney'd already gotten even—with both of them. I hoped Ginny Wagner was someplace safe, and that she wouldn't turn up in the obits one of these days.

"You shouldn't leave this thing unlocked," I said over my shoulder. I swiveled the well-greased door of the built-in safe. When I turned, suspicion was congealing on Burney's face.

Then his call went through.

"Sid! Burney Sanders. How the hell are you? . . . Well, I been fishing, too. And I hooked you a fight. A good-sized one . . . Carter . . . That's right. I'm not shitting . . . Step up, my friend. This is for real. Carter, out here, for the title."

There was a long pause. Sanders rubbed his chin and waited.

"Sid's speechless," he said, cupping his hand over the mouthpiece. He couldn't contain a smile, a big ear-to-ear shit-eater.

"Stop the presses." I grinned, flipping closed the door to the safe.

Emerging into the night on Sixteenth Street, I pivoted to scope out the facade of the new National Hall. Here were the dimensions of a man's desire: the rehabilitated marquee, the scrubbed bricks and ornate filigree, the small but sparkling box office. Gig Liardi and Claire Escalante died, the way I saw it, that National Hall might live again. Snuffed out so Burney could fabricate a tawdry monument to his cheap ambitions. A hard pill to swallow, if you didn't read the paper every day. Maybe you missed all the never-ending squibs about guys shot in the back trying to lift a twenty from the till. Brief items featuring wives slitting their husbands' throats after ten years of beefing about her runny eggs.

Walking toward Mission, I grew conscious of the lightness in my body. My feet barely touched the pavement. I floated to a phone booth at the corner and dropped coins. Was this what flooded Hack's veins in the dressing room at the Civic? The weightlessness that came with *kill or be killed*?

The operator put me through. A woman answered, the merest trace of a Yokohama accent.

"Grace, I need to speak to Francis. It's Billy Nichols on the line."

O'Connor was there in an eager instant, but played it smooth: "Mr. Nichols—what might your good nature generously deliver to me?"

His fingers and toes must have been crossed, praying for a breakdown, confession, or betrayal. Expecting that I'd do his goddamn job for him.

"Our man Escalante, he'll be fighting for the heavyweight championship of the world," I informed O'Connor.

"That a fact? Isn't that th—"

"Consequently, if you're ever going to make a move on that Liardi matter, do it now—or drop it. This is Hack's single shot at the big time, and he doesn't need your complications lousing him up. The story breaks tomorrow. Once there's a head of steam, it'd be ugly if you try to ruin the local hero with a batch of flimsy circumstantial evidence. You'd look like a fool. Maybe even louse up a promotion. We in agreement?"

"Who in the fuck do you think you are?" I'd grown accustomed to such words; they didn't slow me down at all.

"A newspaperman," I told him. "On deadline." I hung up as he prepared to launch a volley of his patented, preheated verbiage.

Next day, I broke the title fight story, front page box above the fold, jump to Sports. That started the machinery cranking, selling this as the biggest boxing match ever in the city of San Francisco. As the two-star hit the streets, the phone began ringing, and a five-week promo push had been roughed out.

I'd even given Eddie his play, alleging that the profits from the bout would underwrite a nondenominational chapel honoring the valiant veterans of WWII. As if Jim Norris and his racket boys would turn any of that money loose. The books on this one would be deep-sixed down with Davey Jones.

As expected, Jimmy Ryan checked in with an opening line, installing Carter as an 8–1 favorite.

For several nights I thought my position over, staring at the ceiling while Ida and her baby slept. It wasn't tough to talk myself into the next logical step.

At midday I walked up to the Bank of Italy on Market, addressing a sweet-faced teller who had beautiful, slender hands.

"I'd like a balance on my savings account, please."

She consulted the files, then returned and wrote the total on a scrap of paper, in delicate script. She slid it across the marble counter.

I'd already made my act of contrition, per Father Petri's request. Now how'd you like to see an act of faith, Father?

I'll show you an act of faith.

Jimmy Ryan was toiling in his element, squirreled away in his wagering warren beneath the Loew's. Midget carnation pinned to his vest, monogrammed cuff links, hair slick and shiny, the picture of a prosperous bookmaker, amid the chalkboards and racing wires. He strutted out of his office to greet me.

"Billy! Whatd'ya know?"

"Jimmy. How's tricks?"

"I hear you had a big hand in bringing the Carter fight here. My compliments."

"Tell your brother—he's the guy." Jimmy froze his end of the banter. I picked it up: "Any change in the numbers?" Vamping, trying to get my pulse steady.

"Eight-to-one still. I'll keep it there as long as I can. Pull in the suckers. The yokels will bet it down over the next few weeks, especially if you start building Hack up. Once it shortens to around three-to-one, we'll have gotten everything out of it."

"Do me a favor."

I handed him the scrap of paper from the bank.

"Handle this for me, would you? All of it, Hack to win."

Jimmy blanched. What little color he had drained into his starched collar.

"This isn't my idea of a gag, Bill."

"It's not. It's on the level."

"You don't bet, Bill. You never bet." Aberrations made Jimmy jittery.

"Have to do everything once, the man says."

He grabbed my arm and hauled me into his office.

"You got inside dope, goddamn you. Give it up."

"Jimmy, this time around I'm an amateur like everybody else."

"You've never fucked me. If there's a fix in, I have to know. I gotta be able to lay off. Who the hell out here has the juice to work something with Norris? Did Carter fuck with somebody? Are they making him throw this one?"

"Jimmy, listen to me. I think Hack's gonna win this fight, straight up. He's in great shape, he's got nothing to lose, and he'll have the whole town behind him. He's used to fighting guys bigger than him. Carter is like a middleweight in comparison. Hack'll hurt him. Especially to the body. Carter's people, they don't know how Hack hits to the body."

"And you're going to tout all this in your buildup?"

"I'm legit here. And I'm asking you again—get me down for this."

The bookie's face said that I was ready for a soft room somewhere.

35

"Biggest hands I ever seen," intoned Jockey John, using ten yards of surgical tape to mummify the tools of Hack's trade. He said it before each of Hack's fights, a whispered invocation.

Sid Conte anxiously watched Jockey John work, peering over the shoulders of a pair of spies dispatched by the State Athletic Commission. The stiffs were making sure everything was on the up-and-up. Conte was resplendent in a wild silk aloha shirt and billowy biscuit-colored trousers. The outfit would be easy to spot between cantos, even for pewholders near the rafters.

I'd come over from Chester Carter's dressing room, elbowing across the teeming corridor, through Conte's entourage.

"How's the house?" Conte asked me, looking up from the cuticle he was gnawing.

"A mob scene. Unbelievable."

Conte whirled on his fighter and trainer: "You guys are too fucking calm," he groused. Maybe he meant it to be funny. It wasn't.

Jockey John smoothed out the final strip on Hack's left hand. Gauze, surgical tape, heavy adhesive—three layers formed a snug wrap. "How's it feel?" the tiny trainer asked.

Hack punched his palms a few times to work suppleness into the bandages. He dropped his chin in approval.

"You need rubbing? How's the arms?"

"I'm good," Hack mumbled.

Conte barked, looking to impress his minions: "Okay,

okay—now box a little, get the sweat going." Sid was exuding enough for everybody.

Hack slid off the rubdown table. Besides the hand wraps, all he had on was a jock and thick white cotton socks. Jockey John braced him as he stepped into the heavy leather cup. Over that he slipped on white satin trunks, with red waistband and piping. Hack heaved a few deep breaths and started shadow boxing. His dark curls danced rhythmically.

The cacophony outside grew louder. Rows of fired-up fans stomping their feet.

"You're the only one that picked me," Hack grunted, winging body punches in my direction.

"'Cause you're gonna do it, Hack. I haven't been wrong since Sharkey beat Schmeling."

"Hear that?" yelped Conte, clutching Hack's shoulders. "He ain't missed the call on a title fight in . . ."

"Seventeen years," supplied Jockey John.

"Seventeen fucking years! See that, Hack? This is it!"

Conte was about to give someone a heart attack—himself, with any luck. Jockey John piped up, to stifle Sid: "Billy, you seen Carter? How'd he look?"

"Relaxed. He was reading the paper."

He'd also been surrounded by hulking Jim Norris and the entire IBC braintrust, a medley of muscle and money that suggested losing was not an acceptable finale for the champ's evening.

"Fuck Chester Carter," Conte said. "Hack'll make sure he's good and relaxed. He probably thinks this is walkover." Sid thrust a finger at Hack, who kept on huffing and jabbing. "We're gonna give him a beating, so as to set his ass straight."

"All of you out," Hack said. "Gimme ten minutes alone."

"That ain't right, Hack," Sid said. "We're here to help you."

"Everybody leaves—or I don't fight."

"Go get 'im," I said, heading for the door.

"Thanks for—everything," he said. Hack's huge paw enveloped my hand in a brutal grip. At first I thought he'd let me hang behind, like that night at the Civic. But the moment passed, and the whole crew shuffled out into the smoke-choked corridor, leaving the challenger alone with his shadow.

In the main arena of the Cow Palace, the crowd swarmed over a cement floor slick with chipped ice, stale popcorn, and spilled beer. Gliding here and there amid the throng were provocatively gowned young women, hired by the Saints and Sinners to solicit donations for the Children's Milk Fund.

Nudging through the swirl, I drew glances of recognition and picked up fragments of the accompanying buzz: *You believe he picked Hack?* handily beat out *Good call—our boy's gonna do it.*

At ringside my spool waited in the Royal. This would be the first heavyweight championship coverage I'd ever filed with a hometown dateline. Emmett Brown, who'd reffed an undercard bout between local lightheavies, leaned over the ropes and hollered down: "Billy! This the biggest turnout you ever seen in this town?"

I pushed up my specs and squinted into the far reaches of the cavernous hall. Fistic parishioners, cheek by jowl, all the way to the roof.

"Is this fantastic, or what?" came a familiar scratchy

voice. Burney Sanders pushed in beside me, so wound up he nearly vibrated. "I said all along we'd draw sixteen," he crowed, raking back his loose pompadour and scanning the restless masses. "But shit, we're gonna do better'n eighteen. You oughta see it outside, they're rocking the fucking ticket booths."

"Not bad for your first big one," I said. "Everybody's here."

"Except the fucking fire marshal—let's hope." Burney showed crossed fingers. I took that to mean he oversold the show.

I roughed out a scoring sheet, marking off the fifteen-round distance.

"You know, Burney, you had a serious problem with some seats here in front," I mentioned over my shoulder.

"What're you talking about?"

"Could be there were double-printed tickets."

Burney whispered in my ear: "Eddie might have been greasing some big honcho pals. You know the drill. Don't make it a federal case. You got a seat, right? Everybody's happy."

"And what's with these characters?" I said, indicating a scaffold dangling above the ring, weighed down with photographers and movie cameramen. Television cameras had aced out many of the longtime press lensmen for prime positions. Another way Norris was changing everything. Burney endorsed all of it, brown-nosing the boxing boss like a terrier sniffing up a Great Dane.

"What happens when one of them has to take a piss during the fight?"

"You got a hat," Sanders laughed. He clapped me on the back, scurried off.

Enjoy it while you can, Burney. I'll make sure you get a good clip to show off in the joint.

Mayor Elmer Robinson was escorted to his seat, where he rubbed shoulders with Governor Earl Warren. The governor had been there for most of the prelims, his wavy white hair a target for peanut marksmen in the gallery. A row back, hale and hearty and glowing as if the whole spectacle was a benefit for him—Artie Samish. Down a few seats, a discreet distance from Boss Samish, Edward P. Ryan presided. He and the missus modestly acknowledged the bows and scrapes of city and state officials, union chiefs, miscellaneous high-rollers. Ryan's rictus was fixed, his eyes glassy with success, or Scotch. His big charity donation had him posturing like prime politico material.

A solid knock across my shoulder: the polished brass tip and burnished rosewood of Francis O'Connor's cane. I sloughed it off and went on blocking out the scoresheet.

"Stand up a moment," O'Connor said. "I don't want to have to lean in there."

"Better take your seat, Francis. We're ready to jump off here."

"Went out on a limb with the local lad, I note." He was overloud, stoked with several Scotches, no doubt. Nearby ringsiders glanced toward us, including famed radio announcer Don Dunphy, warming up behind his big pill-shaped mike, a few seats over.

"I don't imagine that should come as a surprise," O'Connor went on, "seeing as you've compromised yourself entirely for this kid."

I stood, turned, and squared up to him. "I'm working, chief," I said, low and hard. "You had the chance to make your play. Now cop a seat."

He bodied up, pressing his blocky frame against me, dropping his voice: "Listen to me, you self-important son of a bitch. How'd you like it if I hauled you and your dimwit contender downtown tomorrow and sweated you both like a pair of petty crooks?"

"You've got zilch, Francis. And you know it."

"I've got your fingerprints, you'll recall. In Liardi's flat and at the dead woman's house. They were everywhere."

"My prints are all over San Francisco. You could tie me in with a whole shitload of cases, I guess. Want to run me in now?"

"You've become an arrogant bastard, and way out of your depth, to boot."

"Pipe down, Francis. You're embarrassing yourself."

"I'm not the one who's due to be embarrassed, you cocky fuck. You and the husky stand to lose more than this fight." He tugged on a lapel of my suit for emphasis. "I can write, too, you know. Been doing it all my life. Think you're the only artist who can weave the facts into a tight, convincing story? I'll manufacture a witness if I'm forced to. It's as easy as making a man disappear. Except I'll win. I won't fuck it up."

I gazed into his flushed face, letting the words sink in. O'Connor'd gone around the bend. He wanted to win too badly. Much as I feared him, I had grudgingly respected his cunning and good sense. But he'd lost those now—just as I had, laying down that bet with Jimmy.

We'd all gone screwy. Something had to give.

"Show up at Jimmy Ryan's club after the fight," I said, brushing his fingers off my jacket. "I've got new dope—and you'll be able to wrap up the whole thing. Liardi and Claire Escalante."

O'Connor summoned every last glint of intimidation into his eyes, but he backed off. The surge of ticket-holders soon swallowed him.

Scotty Butterworth, the venerable voice of Monday nights at National Hall, began the ritual introduction of celebrities. Boos rained on the politicians, as was traditional. Huge cheers for Jack Dempsey, equaled only by the ovation for Joe Louis, there courtesy of the IBC. The poor, broke Bomber doffed a beige fedora and sauntered to center-ring, faintly recalling recent days when he ruled the canvas kingdom.

Last introduced was Eddie Ryan, cautiously navigating the ropes. He proudly proclaimed the night's gate would clear forty thousand bucks for the veterans' charity. "Every one of you has helped deliver a beautiful gift to our valiant fighting boys," he said with a candidate's cadence. I'm sure Norris was moved to tears.

Houselights dimmed. Darkness spread over the arena, bringing forth a tumultuous roar.

The challenger, at the center of his tight pack of handlers, was ushered from the catacombs of the Cow Palace. Spectators pushed and shoved for a glimpse of the local gladiator. Referee Jack Overstreet had to wedge his way into the ring by pressing closely to Hack's back. The entourage climbed onto the apron and Hack, swathed in a scarlet robe, a white towel draped over his head, clambered through the ropes.

The humid air throbbed with a heavy thundercloud of noise. Hack's face glistened with sweat in the spotlight's glare. He raised one wrapped fist to the crowd, then shuffled in a patch of resin, scowling.

Wild cheers turned to boos and catcalls as Chester Carter bounded into the ring. In an immaculate white terry-cloth robe, he shadow boxed gracefully in his corner. He was implacable, immune to the baiting of the hostile locals. Jake Elster was the opposite: small, hyperactive, more owl-faced than ever in new horn-rims. Elster patrolled the outskirts of the canvas, kicking it with a worn wing tip. He'd griped all week that the square was too soft, too small, a disadvantage for his rangy, mobile fighter.

The portly, tuxedoed Butterworth stepped into a stationary spotlight, savoring his big moment: "Ladies and gentlemen! Introducing your contestants for tonight's main event! In the black corner, weighing in at 182 pounds, from Jacksonville, Florida . . . The heavyweight champion of the world . . . Chester Carter!"

Respectful applause lost out to louder hoots and hollers.

"And in the white corner, the challenger, weighing in at 205 pounds, the California state heavyweight champion . . ."

The roar swelled.

". . . from *San Francisco* . . ."

Steady thunder.

". . . Hack Escalante!"

Deafening.

"Fifteen rounds of boxing for the heavyweight championship of the world," boomed Butterworth.

Fans kept the din fever-pitched as cornermen tugged the burgundy gloves over the taped hands of each boxer. The laces were tightly cinched, then wrapped with more tape. The combatants pawed their resin-dusted corners, then moved to center-ring for ceremonial instructions. Back in the corners, robes came off. Hack was sweating well, his dark curls dripping. Carter shook out his sinewy arms, ebony flesh gleaming in the lights.

The mob's howl rolled through the smoke haze. Highwatt spots in the rafters cut like lightning through the clouds, flitting across the elevated canvas square.

"Yeah, you did all right for your first big show," I said to myself, taking off my glasses and pretending to wipe something out of my eyes. "God Almighty couldn't have staged this any better."

In the Royal was my lead, batted out during one of the prelims:

> They sent the hometown kid into the pit tonight. A shy but stalwart San Francisco boy went in quest of boxing's golden bauble

36

"And here we go—Carter and Escalante come straight out at the bell and lock up at center-ring. They're trading short body punches. Neither man is hesitating or holding back. Both seem determined to take command. It's a fast start to this Heavyweight Championship bout."

Radio announcer Don Dunphy chattered away to my left. His voice seeped from millions of radios: in Los Angeles bungalows, Kansas City rib joints, New Orleans nightclubs, San Francisco orphanages, where kids lay awake, listening.

Instead of sharpshooting off his jab, Carter's usual strategy, he opened up toe-to-toe, to see what the challenger had to offer. Escalante dug a right into Carter's midsection. The champ delivered a stiff jab that stood Hack up, but only for a moment.

Escalante rushed Carter, backed him up with sweeping punches from both hands. Carter backpedaled to the ropes, fending off the flurry. He uncorked a fierce right cross—it skimmed the side of Escalante's face, just grazing his nose. Hack kept the pressure on. Carter threw another loaded right. It missed. He reset quickly and followed with a brisk uppercut. That caught Escalante on the forehead, snapping back his head, shaking that mop of curls.

Carter was quickly on him with another right. Hack kept coming, hunched in a crouch. Carter set himself, saw an opening—but Escalante got inside, banging a hard right to the champion's ribs. Carter backed up, warding off the attack with snapping jabs. A couple landed. Escalante still tried to press, looking for the body.

Carter skipped away, wary of that big right hand. There it was again—this time to the head—Carter leaned back and it sailed by, just wide of the mark. You could hear the crowd whoop at the force of the swing. It left Hack off-balance. Carter side-stepped, looking for an angle, the right spot to set and throw hard.

The bell ended a furious opening round.

I hammered the keys of the Royal, making fast, crooked notes:

> chet fast wants to stay away and box
> hack too anxious hard rights to body.

Hack was the aggressor, but Carter took the round. I scrawled a 6 on my scoresheet for Carter, a 5 for Hack.

One minute, and the timekeeper clanged open the next stanza.

Escalante continued to bore in, with that crouching style. Carter backed up, matador to the onrushing bull. Carter moved easily around the ring, watchful, choosing his spots. Hack gamely tried to cut off the ring and draw the champ in front of him, where he could do some damage. Carter starting peppering Escalante with jabs, but not snapping them. He laid the left out there a lot, pushing it against his opponent's forehead. Measuring, fending. Carter hooked suddenly behind the jab, and scored with it. Hack just kept boring in. The champ was scoring, but didn't seem to be hurting Escalante. Carter pumped out two more jabs—

Now. The opening was there, in the way Carter turned from a body punch, even as he was jabbing. It was right there, I could see it clearly.

Hack saw it, too.

He slammed a vicious right under Carter's heart. Everybody in the first few rows winced. That had to hurt like hell. Hack was trying to get a good look at Carter's eyes, but the champ jumped on his bike. Hack lunged ahead, throwing another right that Carter took on the arm. Their bodies collided. Carter went hard into the ropes. A short step back and Hack threw a flurry of body punches, like he was slugging the heavy bag.

In the distance, beyond the grunts and tattooing of leather on flesh, a roar came from the crowd. Carter pulled away. Hack hustled up with a left hook, caught the jaw. Suddenly the place exploded. Photographers fired their flashes from the scaffolds overhead.

Carter was right in front of Escalante, his dark sinews vivid in the ring lights. The champ was listing to one side, bouncing on his left leg. Hack attacked, swinging a wide right meant to pitch Carter in the opposite direction. But the champ's head wasn't there anymore and the punch sailed past. There's a push against Hack's shoulder, and they scuffled along the ropes just above me. Hack's soles scraped heavily across the canvas. His legs were getting heavy already.

Hack turned to steady himself. A jab banged his ear. Dropping down, he sent a left into Carter's torso. Not hard or clean, but there was some give to the champ's body. Again Hack sprang forward, trying to land a right to the head before Carter's gloves could come up.

Hack followed with a surging series of lefts and rights to the head. Carter couldn't dance away. He could only plow forward through the blows, gloves beside his temples, arms tightly tucked.

A solid left slipped in, tagging the upper part of Carter's jaw. The champ's mouthpiece gleamed out from his grimace, then disappeared into Hack's wet curls as they jostled into a clinch. Overstreet let the infighting go even after Carter had tied Hack up—either he was letting them both take a blow, or he was letting the local kid have a couple of free ones inside. Hack tried to force the top of his head onto Carter's chest, to leverage him back and get punching room, but Carter's long arms wrapped around him, desperately tying him up. Carter shot a look to the ref. He was looking for help—a show of concern, maybe worry.

Ref Overstreet's voice came out hollow and thin: "Break! Break!"

Carter brusquely shoved the challenger's shoulders and Hack reeled off balance, just a fraction of a second. A right cross whooshed past his chin. Carter was willing to risk hitting off the break—a sure sign he'd underestimated his opponent. Hack thundered forward, his stamping charge shaking the ring. He buried a volley of rights to the body.

There was some rubber now in the champ's legs. Hack threw a high left hook as Carter bounced against the ropes, but Carter bent quickly—instinct—and the punch flew over his head.

Before Hack could get off the following uppercut, the bell ended the round.

The clamor was ear-splitting now, the smoke an inferno. Hack moved back to his corner, oblivious to the chaos he was generating. Jockey John yelled at him to sit down. Conte was behind them, hollering and slapping his hands together.

"Uppercut," I heard Hack grunt, spitting out his mouthpiece. "Thought I had him."

Tarantino and Conte yelled at once in response, but

Hack wasn't hearing any of it. He was staring across the ring. In Carter's corner, Jake Elster was going off, screaming at his fighter. I made out only two words clearly: "fucking bum."

My heart pounded as I banged the keys:

```
big round for hack. right to body turned
it. chet rocked by left hook holding on
legs buckled fury body combos bell might
have saved him
```

I scratched down a 6 for Hack. It could have been his best round ever. I wanted to give Carter a 3, but I awarded a 3-point swing only if there was a knockdown. Carter weathered it—that counts: 6 to 4, Escalante.

Screw it, 6 to 3½.

"Pretty big spread," came the critique in my ear. A hand rested on my shoulder. It was the young AP guy.

"He hurt him, hurt him bad," I explained, a little too keyed up.

"Just taking the bait," advised the wire service stringer, his smile broadening. "Carter is leading him in."

"We'll see."

"Real talent knows how to set you up," the franchise hack said, shaking his head. He was patronizing me, the asshole. "It's usually a trap," the tinhorn went on, scribbling his own notes. "You should expect that from Carter by now."

"You saying I don't know what I'm looking at?"

"Hometown boy. I understand."

"Fuck you." Wit deserted me.

The critic sketched a laugh and turned away.

★

Hack charged out at the bell, on the attack. He unloaded another hard right to the body and Carter circled away, now clearly wary of the right. Carter scored with a pair of quick slashing jabs—and followed with a big right hand that missed. Hack just got under it.

Hack came right back: a looping right cross that snapped Carter's head to the side. The champ fumbled out of there, flat-footed, not on his toes like he was earlier.

Hack doggedly pursued. Carter planted himself at center-ring and fired a blistering fusillade. In his half-crouch, Hack tried to avoid the shots. Then he came back slugging—retaking the offensive. The two went toe-to-toe, trading a furious barrage.

The entire arena leapt up as one screaming mass. Each man gave as good as he got in the most savage exchange so far. Hack kept pounding Carter with the right to the body. It forced the champ to retreat outside. Hack pressed—and Carter nailed him with a sweeping left hook.

It looked like a trickle was coming from Hack's nose. He didn't seem fazed. Definitely blood, smeared above his upper lip, starting to come freely.

Hack pivoted and drove another blow to the body. Carter answered with a left, too low, close to a foul. Hack ignored it and just kept coming. He tossed a countering left, more like a swat really—it knocked Carter off-balance onto the ropes.

Hack swarmed over him. Another right to the mid-section—and Carter was covering, pinned on the ropes. Hack hurled punch after punch—it was hard to tell how many landed cleanly. Carter wanted to shuffle away, but Hack bulled him back against the hemp.

Carter showed a lot of mouthpiece as he tried to weather the storm. Hack connected to the head, a glancing left. He followed with a thundering right—out went Carter's mouthpiece, skittering across the canvas. He was trapped against the ropes.

Then the bell.

> a fast pace. too much for big men. how long can they go this way? 3rd canto never to be forgot. First one rocked then other. Chet open for short left hook inside. Big right hand.

I scored it 6–5, Escalante.

Hack slumped heavily on the corner stool. Jockey John squeezed out the sponge over his palpitating body. Hack spit the mouthpiece into the trainer's hand and sucked air.

"You knocked his piece out," Jockey John reported. Conte hollered, "You nailed him! Knock his fucking teeth out this time! You're the one, Hack! It's you!"

Jockey John asked Hack how he felt while Conte continued to rave behind them.

Hack gasped. "My legs . . . I don't know . . ."

Round four.

The two fighters clashed near center-ring. Again Hack led with a big right to the body. Carter missed with a short, sharp jab. Carter's middle had taken a pounding. He retreated, trying to stay on his toes, moving side to side. He needed to score from longer range.

Hack's body attack was dictating the fight.

Hack crept in, crouching—and Carter rattled a pair of quick left hooks off his chin. Solid blows. But Hack stayed right there, delivering another body shot. No matter what Carter served, Hack came right back to hammer the middle.

Carter was up, keeping his distance, avoiding the furious infighting. Hack stalked, curls dripping with sweat, bobbing after the champion. Moving toward Carter's corner. Both seemed fatigued after the exchanges of the last ro—

A flash right nailed Hack, and his knees buckled. He tumbled in and reached out for Carter, trying to clinch. The champion tried to twist his way out, to slip free and slug. The sudden jolt was Carter's boldest shot of the fight.

Carter shook loose and got punching room. Hack stayed right on him, like his shadow. Carter backed to his right. Hack caught him with a looping left hook. Out of nowhere. He followed with a hard right—

Carter was shaken, looking to buy time and clinch.

An uppercut undermined Hack's chin.

He bulled Carter back against the ropes. Muscled him over, like he weighed nothing. He trapped Carter in his own corner and came strong with both hands. Carter tried to drop into a crouch, but Escalante forced him back with his open left glove. A big right hand slammed into Carter's shoulder. Another to the ribs. Carter had nowhere to go. Hack was giving it everything he had—using the left to measure and the right to punish.

"And there's the bell," Dunphy keened into the mike. "Carter has managed to endure another big round by the challenger! Ladies and gentlemen, we could be looking at a huge upset here tonight!"

Hack didn't move. Elster banged against him. "Fuck is this? Move it!" he screamed. The ref grabbed Hack's arm and pulled him away.

Carter shook his head and scowled. He didn't have to

search for his corner. His pins didn't seem wobbly. He was still far from queer street.

Hack stiff-legged it to his corner. Ten feet that seemed like a death march. Conte looked numb. "You're doing it! You're doing it!" he kept chanting over and over.

To Sid it didn't register how heavily Hack dropped onto the stool, or how feverishly Jockey John worked on his thighs. The fighters hadn't even gone halfway.

Conte wriggled his hand past Jockey John and gripped Hack's shoulder, absorbing a bit of his intensity, feeling that white hot spotlight turning toward him.

The spectators were sweating it out, too. They didn't hoot or whistle now between rounds. They sensed something more than a diversion. The blood was up, and their hearts had moved into their throats.

Five.

Both led with big rights, both barely missed. Ringsiders wheezed at the closeness of the punches.

The gladiators wanted it to end, right then.

Thousands wailed in the dark, voices going hoarse. Carter stepped to the side, then quickly in, crowding. His eyes were keen. Wolf eyes. A short hook to Hack's head. Not much behind it. A feint, really.

Hack flinched, like he was trying to dodge something he couldn't see clearly.

A fraction of a second, and Carter had fired another punch—a right—quick, hard. Traveled maybe six inches.

"He's down! Escalante is down! A sharp right cross has put the challenger down. The ref is waving Carter to a neutral corner . . . Escalante is on his back . . . He's turning over, trying to get to his feet . . ."

The crowd went silent. For a moment Carter hovered imperiously, right fist still cocked. He lowered it slowly.

Down on the canvas, Hack searched for his legs.

Carter didn't see the referee directing him to the corner. He knew it was time. He'd been here before.

Overstreet barely glanced at the timekeeper, whose white-gloved hand was ticking off the seconds. He picked up the count at three. His timing was automatic; he'd been here before.

The ref peered into the eyes, trying to gauge whether Hack would be able to continue if he beat the count.

I could see it coming, the short right over the left feint. Hack couldn't. He must have bit on the feint because of the bad right eye. Carter figured it out, set him up perfectly. I wanted to yell *Duck*, but what can you do?

Hack's heart couldn't talk his legs into it.

Ten.

Jake Elster charged his stoic fighter. He wagged a finger under Carter's nose and crowed, "What did I tell you! You did it! You did it!" Carter had the mien of a man who'd spent a full day in white hot sun, making big rocks small with a sledge. While a burly guy played his ribs like a xylophone.

The house, so recently wild, fell silent. The fifth round lasted eighteen seconds, ten of which Hack spent on his back.

Jack Overstreet bent above the fallen contender, resting a hand on his shoulder, waiting for his people to tend to him. Hack wasn't hurt too badly. Still, his legs were gone. He needed help.

Nobody came through the swelling group in the ring, so Overstreet hoisted Hack, lifting under his arms, helping him stand. He maneuvered the wobbly challenger back to his corner. Conte was a statue, stunned. Jockey John's face shone with tears.

San Franciscans filed out, sated. No amateur postscript fisticuffs among the beery patrons, no anger left unreleased. The mob had been humbled and convinced by the decisiveness of the finish. All questions answered, with professional dispatch.

The breakdown crew got ready to dismantle the ring. I was still ringside, hunched over the Royal. I chewed an unlit cigar while threads of sweat trickled from under the band of my hat. About an hour remained to file copy, to make the first A.M. street edition.

In more than twenty years, I'd never missed a deadline. Not once. Now all those years, rolled into one, were a lengthy Sunday stroll. Tonight was the test.

My money, my fabulous rep, the flawless prediction streak—I'd blown them all. Had I really convinced myself that Hack had a legitimate chance in this fight? Or did I place that bet just so I could feel myself wade into the deep water with him? Maybe I thought that I needed to risk something, even if it was only money, in order to make restitution. Well, I was right there with Hack now, barely treading water, facing the hard truth: the day always comes when everything you've got isn't nearly enough.

A depressing notion, perhaps—but liberating, too. Spare me the hope, the gaudy ritual, the incantations, the railing against unfair odds, and the desperate summoning of faith. Our time in the ring is about survival, no more, no less. It's about cruelty and glory, about having a job to do and getting it done.

It's about putting one foot in front of the other, until they find a way to stop you.

The shiny black keys of the Royal stared up at me. They were used to being hammered, as I banged out words that would become column inches cast in hot metal. Write the story. Let all the rest slip into the void. What matters is the work at hand. Bring it back, spare and vivid, the noise and sweat and desire. Make them see it, make them smell it. The loyal readers want testimony, something that will stand. A tribal memory.

I punched keys. The carriage jerked and shuddered.

> They sent the hometown kid into the pit tonight. A shy but stalwart San Francisco boy went in quest of boxing's golden bauble, and 18,432 frenzied fans saw him fall victim to the slashing fists of reigning champion Chester Carter, in a short, savage, and unforgettable heavyweight contest that shook every earthquake meter within a hundred miles of the raucous Cow Palace.

"Mr. Nichols?"

The kid was barely a teenager, beanpole body wrapped in dungarees and a droopy canvas coat. Round specs and a poorboy cap. I'd be lying if I said I didn't instantly identify the sharp eyes and the eager mouth. I remembered this kid, all right. I'd had cause to think of him a lot lately.

"Is there any way that I could be your runner?" he asked, breathless. "Take your copy to the paper for you?"

He wore his cap backward, too, like that nervy Nicholovich lad.

"How you plan to do that, kid? You got a phony license?"

"My dad'll drive me," he answered, motioning behind him.

Tony Bernal, typesetter, nodded and smiled. He'd chauffeured me enough over the years.

"He's a big fan," Tony called over, keeping his distance, not shilling too hard for his son. "Wants to be a writer when he grows up."

"All right, but don't look over my shoulder," I warned the boy, turning back to the keys. I didn't grouse, though, when I felt him right behind me, peering at the emerging words, driven letter by hard-earned letter, onto the page.

The kid kept close but quiet for almost thirty minutes, as I steadily pounded prose. Only twice did I refer to my notes. When I'd nailed "30" to it, I tore the long sheet out of the spool and thrust it at the boy. Nearby, Tony abided in a first-row seat, smoking, a crossed leg dangling.

My new runner was all puddled up and shaky. Moses couldn't have looked more stunned when he got hit with two arm-loads of stone. "It's a great story," Tony's boy said quietly, taking the sheet.

"File the top copy with Fuzzy in Sports," I told the kid, even though his father knew the drill. "Keep the bottom one yourself. Someplace safe."

His eyes spread wide, like eggs cracked into a skillet.

"Go," I growled, shooing him away. "You got a job to do, for chrissakes. We don't have all night."

37

It wasn't tough to locate Burney Sanders, even in the delirium of the Daily Double. He was tucked in beneath towering Jim Norris, who couldn't be missed. Big Jim had changed into his postfight finery, resembling a Kentucky colonel who'd taken a wrong turn on the way out of the Derby. Little Burney was incandescent, a small man living large, set smack at the center of the action, finally. He was the undisputed winner on the night the local hero fell.

Sanders cackled and clapped hands when he saw me approach.

"New gate record for California," he bellowed. "You gotta lead with that in your story, Billy! There's the angle—the city's back in the big time!"

His sandpaper voice was ratcheted up to get over the blare of the jump band. High-rolling boys and girls, riding the surge of adrenaline turned loose by the bout, caroused with abandon.

"I already filed it, Burney," I told him, stepping close. "But it's all in there. Not to worry."

I gave a nod to Jimmy Ryan, who soaked in the scene while lazily holding up a pillar. Ryan was presiding in elegant white evening jacket with blue gardenia boutonniere. My life savings currently lined his pockets, but that didn't show. He was measured and cool in victory, Chester Carter recast in ivory.

Sanders's raspy prattle was back: "Billy, meet my new best friend—Mr. James Norris."

My hand got swallowed in the fleshy grip of boxing's latest puppeteer.

"Escalante damn near had you looking like a genius," Norris japed.

"Won't earn either of us a bonus," I deadpanned.

Norris's minions bustled around, very East Coast in seersucker suits, high-buttoned collars boosting the blood pressure in their smug, self-satisfied faces. Sanders panted among them, the horny terrier looking for a place to stick his shiny prehistoric dick.

"Seen Sid?" he barked at me. "Jim's got a hell of an offer for him. Could make Hack a nice piece of change."

I gave Norris the brow-lift.

"We're bringing back Louis," the big man announced portentously, furrowing his beetle brow. "We feel Escalante can make a good showing in Joe's return bout. Hack certainly deserves it after the effort he displayed tonight."

In one heartbeat you could trace the geometry of that setup. Norris needed to appease the television people with a major coast-to-coast attraction. Only Louis versus Carter filled that bill. They'd use Hack to build Louis back up. Escalante'd earn a decent payday. But not to win. That wasn't on the program.

"We know Hack needs the money," I said, noting the hub-hub at the entrance of the club. If Norris could have seen my face, he'd have been treated to an honest reaction to the shit-stink of corruption that wafted off each of them.

A wedge came barrel-assing through the throng, headed our way: O'Connor, finally. Backed by a pair of bulls, one uniformed, one plain.

Where was Scotty Butterworth when *I* needed him?

"Chin up, Billy," Jimmy Ryan said, sidling over and offering a pat on the back. "Can't pick 'em all. Have a drink on me. Celebrate. Tonight we went big time."

"I'll pass. Still working."

O'Connor loomed, body drained of patience. His cohorts looked ready, willing, and able to spoil a man's good time.

Come strong, I coached myself. Otherwise, you may as well stay in the gym.

"Mr. Norris," I boomed. "Like you to meet Detective Francis O'Connor, most tireless, vigilant, irascible homicide investigator in the city and county of San Francisco. Francis, may I present Jim Norris—he runs boxing."

They shook, O'Connor's ego not allowing him to comment on my blustery charade.

"And this, Detective—this is Burney Sanders, promoter of tonight's epic contest."

"Great fight," O'Connor conceded gruffly.

"We did all right," Burney said. Modesty fit him like a cheap suit.

"Francis," I said, "you'll be wanting to talk to Burney, specifically about the late Claire Escalante."

Fair to say I'd never seen the shade of red that blazed out from Burney's collar and ate up his face. "What the fuck is this?"

Norris sensed the sudden change in the weather and started barking drink orders to his cronies. I looked to Jimmy, who I definitely didn't want to witness what was coming out of my sleeve next. "We could use some privacy," I said.

Ryan, the implacable host, gave me a sharp look and stepped to the center of the play: "Gents—follow me."

I shook Norris's damp paw on the way past. "Good to meet you," I said with half a smile.

★

Jimmy ushered the simmering troop through the kitchen: me, O'Connor, and his two stony flatfeet escorting wild-eyed Burney. Ryan pointed out the exit, and the lawmen, true to form, blew through hard. We spilled into a narrow alley, choked with cans of trash and crates of empties.

Burney gaped at Jimmy, as if he expected better accommodations. Ryan pulled shut the door, leaving his clientele to sort things out. Sanders started spewing and sputtering like a starving man who'd had his smorgasbord upended.

Now let's see how you can grovel for scraps, Burney.

O'Connor made a rapid move to reassert his rank: "You had better not be wasting my ti—"

"I've got some photos I'd like *you* to look at," I said, cutting him off. I pulled the creased envelope from my breast pocket and slapped it against the gun flap of the detective's mackinaw.

In the circle of light from the caged bulb above the exit, O'Connor squinted at copies of the Eddie Ryan blackmail pictures. I could tell he ID'ed both grapplers.

"What significance is this supposed to have for me?" the Irishman said gravely. More blarney. He was holding the first real evidence in a murky case; he knew it—you could hear it beneath the usual palaver.

I waded in with a terse accounting:

"Sanders employed Claire Escalante to set up Eddie Ryan. He blackmailed Ryan with these photos, then used the proceeds to bankroll the reopening of National Hall."

Burney spat curses and threats and ignored O'Connor's warning to shut up. "This is all trumped-up bullshit. You guys don't have a fucking clue what's going on here. No idea! I'm getting railroaded."

O'Connor nodded to the plainclothes bull, and one

backhand to Burney's throat quickly overruled his defense motions.

"Burney used to pimp around North Beach," I went on. "Claire was in his stable, before she met her future husband. Lots of water under that bridge, but Burney tricked her out again for his big score. Either she went along, or he'd make sure Hack got a detailed history lesson."

"This is strictly bullshit," Burney wheezed. "I got my dough free and clear. From investments. I'm a legitimate businessman."

"Claire got scared when Burney got greedy," I said, pressing on. "The Ryan scam worked so well he pictured more setups and shakedowns. She threatened to blow the lid if he didn't let her off the hook. So he found a way to get rid of her."

"Cock*sucker*!" Sanders screamed. "You're cooking all this up!" He wheeled on O'Connor. "You see what he's doing—trying to pull a fast one. He was banging that slut himself. If Hack ever found out, he'd kill him. Now he's running this crazy cock-and-bull story to cover his tracks. He's looking to bury me, to save his own ass!"

That scored a point with O'Connor, I could tell. But Burney was flailing, undisciplined, too eager to throw a telling blow. It was my time now, my chance to feint and deal. Like Carter had done earlier. Lead him, turn him . . .

"Sure, Burney, that makes perfect sense," I chided, laying it out there like a lazy, pawing jab, daring him to come in under it. "Me and the fighter's wife? *Wake up.* Who in their right mind would believe that? Not in a million years. Why would I be that stupid?"

"You were dicking her all right—I got the proof and you know it, you fucker."

That was my opening. "Proof?" I asked, faking surprise. "Like what? More pictures?"

Burney knew he had dropped his guard, like a scared, outboxed simon-pure. He tried to retreat from his gaffe: "I saw 'em . . . I don't know who took the pictures, but I saw 'em, saw 'em with my own eyes. This one and the broad, going at it in a hotel room."

This notion clearly intrigued O'Connor—and let him see Sanders for the seedy, extortionary hothead that he was.

"You can produce these photos?" O'Connor asked, poking his cane at Sanders's belly. "I'd be most interested in them. They might go a long way toward explaining a great many things."

O'Connor waited for a response. Sanders stalled. The cop rapped his cane on the concrete, itching to hit something. His body swelled with a deep exasperated breath.

"If you can't deliver those pictures," he sighed, deflating, "then it will be your story against his—" The cane swung toward me, slapping against my thigh. "That, I'd venture to say, would leave you—Mr. Burnell Theopolous—effectively unarmed in this battle of wits."

O'Connor had popped out Burney's right name. The detective had done legwork; he'd traced Claire back, he'd read her arrest jacket.

"Do you possess these photographs, Mr. Theopolous? Or have access to them?"

Burney was squeezed, and he knew it. If he had the pictures, he'd have a hell of a time explaining how he got them. Without the pictures, he couldn't pull me into the frame. His flailing defense had given O'Connor a fresh trail to sniff, just as I'd planned. He'd now come strong at Burney, the way he had at me, to see if anything rattled loose.

"Cuff this moron," O'Connor told his associates. Pure

grandstanding. He had little more than a good story to work off. "Let's take Mr. Theopolous in on suspicion of murder."

"No!" Burney cried, flying to pieces. He waved wildly at the photos in O'Connor's hand. "How'd Nichols get *those* pictures? He was in on it with the wife. Him and that whore, they were the ones running the scam! This is a frame. I didn't kill her. Word of honor, swear to Christ, I didn't do it! Yeah, I went to talk to her, 'cause I thought she had some papers that were stolen from my office. We argued about it. It got out of hand."

He was trying to build an alibi, rearranging bits and pieces of the truth, painting himself as the wronged innocent. I was familiar with the formula.

"You gotta see, she was trying to work me," Burney babbled. "*I* was the one that was getting screwed."

Hideous pictures burned through my mind. Claire's last moments, as she struggled to protect herself. Unable to keep Sanders and his goon at bay. No one there to protect her. I had to fight off the urge to smash Burney's skull.

"She kept mouthing off, so he hit her, just once, to set her straight. Like this fuck just hit me. It was only a body shot. She doubles up and starts twisting around. Then she starts bleeding all over the place. From nothing we did! It couldn't have been. Something was already wrong with her! I'm not going down for a murder rap! This is bullshit—you guys are trying to frame me."

"Keep your mouth shut until you talk to a lawyer," O'Connor advised him. "Put this idiot in the car," he told his deputies. For the first time, they appeared content.

Sanders continued pitching his fit as they dragged him into the side street beside the club. From around the corner, Burney's shouts faded.

All these years later, in another dirty alley, I'd scored a TKO without lifting a finger. The outcome, of course, still hung on the judge's scoring.

O'Connor limped toward the side street, then turned and cross-haired me down the barrel of his cane.

"All very intriguing and colorful as hell," he said. "You realize, however, it doesn't solve *my* case. I heard nothing in all that stage-show hullabaloo about Gig Liardi. You have a storyline to help me pin that one on Sanders, too?"

"No. Claire Escalante killed Gig." The answer made O'Connor wince.

"What in Christ's name are you selling *now*?"

O'Connor fell in step as I turned the corner and headed toward the gathering at the end of the block, where Burney was being rudely stuffed in a squad car.

I made my last play, giving O'Connor another letter from my coat pocket.

"Here's her confession," I said. "She left it in a lockbox. She knew Burney would come after her. This explains everything."

"How'd you come by it?"

"It seems that people trust me. To do the right thing."

He squinted at the handwritten page in the dimness, then asked for a condensed version: "What does it claim, in so many words?"

"It says Gig found out about Burney's extortion scheme. He was about to blow the whistle. Remember the cut-up picture in Liardi's scrapbook? He was going to send it to Eddie Ryan. Expose her. Queer Burney's deal, and screw things up between Claire and Hack."

"The better to work his own angle, maybe?"

"Could be."

"Blows to the head notwithstanding, you think the husband knew nothing of his wife's sordid affairs?"

"Not a bit. Claire went to Gig's and begged him not to say anything to Hack about the photos, her connection to Sanders, her stint as a hooker. They got into a helluva fight. She tried to strangle him and he fell, just like you figured it. Hack showed up and helped her cover the whole mess—the two individuals your witness saw."

"That makes the kid an accomplice," O'Connor cut in.

"You'd do the same, Francis. For Grace. You said as much."

O'Connor sighed and looked away, like Carter had looked briefly for the ref. I was wearing him out.

"You're asking me to believe this dame would square off with a former fighter?" O'Connor was looking at Sanders in the backseat of the squad car.

"You read her jacket. Along with those solicitations you must have seen the bout with the two cops. Broken hand, black eye, loose teeth. Not hers, mind you. You saw Theopolous in there, too—but it meant nothing to you. Until tonight. That's a detail only I'd have known."

"How'd you have the opportunity to examine that file?"

"I'm a reporter, Francis. I protect my sources."

The clamor grew louder as we approached the mouth of the narrow street, heading for the white glare and rubber-necking traffic on Polk Street.

"It's a neat and tidy story," O'Connor said. "How do I know you didn't write it yourself?"

"You want to see me in there, don't you? Maybe some-day, Francis, I'll take you up on that offer of a drink. Maybe you can explain why you wanted so badly to see me as a suspect."

"Ah, but you are in it, most assuredly," he whispered. He

flapped the letter, distractedly considering it. "You're finding ways to write yourself out—any way you can."

"Francis, in fifteen minutes you'll be down at headquarters, with full bragging rights. You've cracked the Liardi murder and broken up a blackmail ring to boot. If you want to scotch a promotion to Chief of Detectives, knock yourself out. Keep rooting around for stuff that's not there. Time was, you wanted my help with the Liardi case—well, you got that, and plenty more in the bargain. With my compliments."

The sidewalk in front of the Daily Double was packed with gawkers, partiers, and passersby. The floor show was a guy getting rousted beneath sizzling blue gaslight, while the band kept on swinging. The neon script bounced off the dark windows of the black-and-white rumbling in the loading zone. Burney Sanders, né Theopolous, was hunched in back, cuffed wrists behind him.

"You're a dead man," he mouthed, for my benefit.

O'Connor moved toward the roller's front door, then hop-stepped the few paces back to me. "Even if this story holds up," he said, "I'm not all that likely to forget that you tried to show me up."

"Fair enough. I won't forget you tried to make me out a murderer."

"Say your prayers that the photos he mentioned don't turn up."

"They won't."

O'Connor jockeyed his bulk into the front seat and slammed the door. Like true showmen, the cops capped off the festive atmosphere by firing up the squad car's siren. Its wail drowned the be-bop streaming from the Daily Double, and its scarlet strobe washed the whole block of Polk.

I turned to find Jimmy Ryan observing the action, whirling multicolored lights splashing over his bright jacket and smile.

"Will we be reading all about that in your column?" he asked. People streamed across the street toward the club, pulled by the commotion. Jimmy was carefree as ever; no matter what went down, he wound up on top.

"It's after presstime. All you'll read from me is how 'They sent the hometown kid into the pit tonight. A shy but stalwart San Francisco boy went in quest of boxing's golden bauble . . .'"

"But came up just short," he said, shaking his head and draping an arm across my shoulders.

Sid Conte emerged from the club, drawn by the siren. He'd swapped sweat-soaked ring wear for a fresh custard suit. He radiated, tanned and laughing, a turned-out babe on each arm, gold jewelry gleaming. You'd have thought he was wearing the title belt as a cummerbund.

"What the hell is he so happy about?" I asked.

"He bet on Carter," Jimmy whispered in my ear. "Our boy is finally square."

Jimmy snickered when he felt me tense, and held me back when I made a move for Conte. Sid looked over and waved—he'd probably already inked that bullshit deal with Norris, laid his future percentage down with Jimmy on some new, irresistible longshot.

"Speaking of bets . . ." Ryan crooned, turning me around. "Sorry I never got around to booking yours." He pulled from the welt pocket of his vest the folded slip of paper I'd gotten from the bank teller. He tucked it into my shirt pocket and secured it with a single firm tap.

"I knew something was up," he said. "With the fight, or

else with you. Known you a long time, Bill. You're a good guy in a rough racket, and you're not a liar. That bought you a break. I figured you needed one. If you'd been thinking straight, you'd never have picked Hack. Not in this lifetime."

Part of me soared, way up, over this stretch of Polk, above the whole goddamn city. I peered into Jimmy's eyes, straining to isolate his largesse from his larceny.

"What if Hack had won?" I asked.

"Hack wasn't going to win," Jimmy scoffed, like he might patronize a child. "C'mon—Hack? Heavyweight champion of the world? Are you serious?"

Part of me floated over my hometown, lording it over the scrappy but juiceless citizens. Another part slithered down, dead weight on a muddy slope. Once more, something bitter rose in my throat.

"I guess that means I owe you one, doesn't it?"

The bookmaker gave me his best Cheshire grin, crooked and charming. His greed and generosity were an alloy, inseparable. Staring at those bloodless lips and those guilt-free eyes, I saw that Eddie Ryan was right: his brother could have orchestrated the whole blackmail scam—sleek, corrupt, and untouchable, vindictive for the pure sport of it.

"Bill, you got a kid to look after now, don't you?" Jimmy said. "Get over your fever, boy. Get back on the beam. Show up for work tomorrow and quit screwing around, will you? Billy Nichols is a big part of the mix around here, brother. I don't want anything to happen to him. I need him."

38

I walked down to Market, waving away several offers of a ride. The Orpheum's marquee had been extinguished. Twin rows of glowing amber street lamps, stretching from the waterfront, were the only lights still burning.

Waiting on a streetcar, I hungrily inhaled cool, misty air. In less than an hour trucks would roll from the *Inquirer* bays. The first edition would hit the street. I figured they'd go with at least a four-column photo across page one, most likely Hack dropping to the canvas. My piece alongside, two-column width, first graf in bold.

Folks would pluck it off the front stoop, or scoop it from the rack, *ooh* and *ahh* over breakfast or riding the rails on the morning commute. Jazzed by a shiver of high drama. Not hearing a note of the deeper story.

Hack, if he was lucky, would sleep through the day. Maybe he'd be fortunate enough to catch some sun through a window, easing the aches, remorse, and emptiness. Eventually, Sid would corner him, crowing about the great deal he'd concocted to face Louis. Hack would pick up the phone and seek my advice. Sell your soul to those bastards for every last dime, I'd tell him, if it means you can retire flush, and get your kids back. And if my scheme for O'Connor was going to work, I'd have to convince Hack of something tougher—letting his late wife take the murder rap for him.

The headlamp of a streetcar crawled toward me. In the background were some of the links that forged the chain of my life: the roof of the Hearst Building, the place where I lost my teeth against the curb, the overhead wires that guided my father and me home every night to Butchertown. Closer was the spot where Claire had gunned her car at the light, afraid we were being followed. While she'd been sweating bullets, I nattered on about crafty Jimmy Ryan and his big-shot brother.

That was back a ways. When I thought I knew it all. Before I knew better.

In the dimness of my study, I exhumed the strongbox from the rolltop and unlocked it. Ida and young Vincent were asleep down the hall.

I'd given Eddie Ryan his incriminating negatives, as soon as he'd signed on to bankroll the fight. Now I dug out Sanders's additional blackmail fodder, stuff he never got the chance to use: the prints and negatives shot from the fire escape outside room 412 of the Temple Hotel.

Trapped in the exposures you could see pain and guilt in Claire's eyes. At least I could. As for the face of the guy with her, he held few secrets at that moment. Despite the mustache, he looked like some eager kid—which maybe isn't such a bad thing to be.

I picked up my leather-wrapped lighter, which was shaped like a boxing glove. I flicked up a flame, held it to the corner of a print, and dropped it in the waste can. I fed the pictures, one by one, and the negatives, into the fire. The images were mine alone now. Nothing but memories.

I'd stared at those photos on a few tortured occasions since claiming the strongbox, but the letter—that I'd read over and over, dozens of times. And not just to learn the handwriting well enough to forge the phony confession I gave O'Connor.

Dear Billy,

You'll be shocked when you see the pictures. I want to believe you will forgive me.

If you have the juice and the guts I suspect you do, you'll figure out a way to make Burney pay. He's the guy responsible for all our troubles. But I don't want Hack to know the truth. I want him to believe he married the woman you wrote about in the paper. The woman I wish I was.

Sanders is using these pictures to blackmail Edward Ryan. And Ryan isn't the only one. Burney and I have a history. I hoped you wouldn't find that out, but knowing you, you did.

The first time at your house was my idea. You were right, I wanted leverage on you. I couldn't figure why you covered for Hack, what angle you were playing. I didn't trust you. I'd say "sorry" for my suspicious nature, but it's well earned.

It wasn't cops following us that day. It was Burney's guys. He thought I was going to spill the setup to you. They banged me around pretty good. Then he got the idea of setting you up the same way we'd done Ryan. So he'd have Mr. Boxing in his pocket.

Of course, something else happened in that hotel room. It always does in the kinds of stories you tell. I don't know if I fell in love exactly. You did, I know. You helped me find some things I'd lost along the way. You have this way of talking about the world that made me want to be part of it again. Like there was some good reason to keep at it. All your magic stories. I loved that. I couldn't let a bastard like Burney tear down what you'd managed to build up.

So I stole this stuff from him. Right out of the office. He couldn't figure a girl having the guts to go against him.

Guess again, Burney. I'm going to stash this stuff with your man at the Temple. You'll figure out my little code. Smart guy.

But if you are reading this—it probably means the worst has happened. Don't blame yourself, like you did with your father. It's just a shame how things can turn so bad. That's how it is for some people. I thought I'd left all that behind, but life just wouldn't leave me alone.

Promise me you'll look after Hack. He has a good heart. He didn't mean to kill Gig. He just wouldn't let anybody talk about me like that. He thinks I'm some saint. Not to mention, he thinks you're the greatest guy in the world.

I wish things could have been different. Wish I didn't have to make the trip to that awful clinic. Between you and me, that kid would have been something.

You and your stories. You've got a gift. You can make people think about who they are, and what they could have been. Your old man would be proud of you, believe me.

Love,
One more fan

It was her final testimony, written for me alone. It humbled anything I'd ever read or write. The most painful part, of course, is that all her fear and guilt were probably unnecessary. Hack would have forgiven her as easily as I did. But she couldn't forgive herself. We never do.

The dwindling flames licked the sides of the waste can. She'd spelled out my downfall and redemption in a single handwritten page. You can't burn a thing so perfect. The fire receded to flickering wisps, until there was nothing but a gummy mound of ash.

"Honey, is everything all right? I smelled smoke. Scared me to death."

Ida stood in the doorway, clutching the robe around her.

"Everything's fine. I'm coming to bed now."

I tucked Claire's letter inside my *Ring Record Book*, 1948 Edition, and flipped it shut.

Ida walked over to me, her face edging into the lamplight. She stood looking at the messy desk, and the potted azaela amid all the jumbled paper. Her squint showed bewilderment. I slipped the record book back among other volumes on the desktop.

She reached for the azaela: "You should put something under that. You'll ruin the desktop if you—"

"Don't worry about it," I said. The words came out forcefully enough to back her out of the light.

"How'd the local boy do?" she asked sheepishly.

I clicked off the light and moved, half-blind, toward her dark shape.

"The local boy did his best," I said. "I guess that's all you can hope for."

—30—

AUTHOR COMMENTARY

When *The Distance* was awarded the "Shamus" for Best First Novel by the Private Eye Writers of America, I had to laugh. Literally. I gave the judges five minutes to rethink their decision.

"There's no private eye," I cracked. Maybe there'd been a mistake. Maybe I'd have to relinquish the prize plaque.

I didn't mean to be irreverent or disrespectful. I was just amused by such an unexpected capper to this novel's long, strange history.

The Distance was not conceived as a crime novel. Or as a mystery, whodunit, thriller, or noir. Certainly not as a private eye story. The goal, originally, was to recreate, and explore, a world I *sort of* grew up in.

From the 1930s through the 1970s, my father, who passed on to me his (adopted) name as well as a knack for facile wordsmithing, was one of the most respected boxing writers in the world. For decades he contributed a daily column to the Sports section of the San Francisco *Examiner*, "Shadow Boxing." Today, if there *were* any daily boxing writers still in existence, they'd get about as much respect as the anonymous writers toiling on obit duty.

That alone should explain my desire—hell, my *obligation*—to write this book. As a boy I witnessed the steady erosion of everything that defined my father's life. I felt compelled to recapture his world, to bear witness to it, before it disappeared into nothing but faded newsprint, scratchy film reels, and faulty memories.

Original drafts of *The Distance*, sketched as far back as 1983, told an entirely different story. Certain locales, themes, characters and anecdotes were always in place, if begging refinement. But the storyline? Well, there were two. One followed a renowned sportswriter, the other his pugilistic alter ego, a tongue-tied heavyweight. The narrative encompassed both their lifetimes. Plenty of prose was spent on the protagonists' twilight years, reflecting on various triumphs and losses. Interwoven flashbacks contrasted the lives of fistfighter and storyteller, in a quest for profound analogies. The scope was vast and kaleidoscopic, charting changes in San Francisco from the dawn of the 20th century through the early 1980s. It was dense, character-rich, hugely ambitious.

Not to mention unreadable.

This writer had not yet learned the essential rule of effective storytelling: what you leave out is as important as what you put in.

The epiphany came through writing a book called *Dark City: The Lost World of Film Noir,* which plumbed my fascination with shadowy crime dramas of the mid-century past. Repetitive viewing of 87-minute clockwork constructions proved revelatory. A motto emerged: Better to be accessible than definitive.

The unwieldy manuscript was resurrected; a pair of noir-inspired changes immediately enacted: The sprawling, epic-length, dual-protagonist, third-person saga was pared into a compact first-person narrative. To kick-start things, one character—who survived to the bitter end of every previous draft—was cold-cocked into a corpse on Page One.

Just like that, my gallant stab at a mainstream literary opus became a work of genre fiction. Suddenly, the world I'd striven to recreate was trapped in "formula."

Only instead of being cornered, I was liberated. Characters sharpened themselves to a keen edge when introduced in relation to a single, galvanizing event—the mysterious demise of boxing manager Gig Liardi. Scenes assumed urgency, the story found legs, self-revelatory dialogue now made intrinsic sense. Billy Nichols, freed from heavyweight aspirations, started moving like a spry, flashy welterweight.

Soon enough, however, I found myself fighting—sometimes brawling outright—with the constraints of writing a "mystery." I was concerned that ravenous crime fiction readers might feel they'd traveled this terrain before, and dismiss the look and language of Billy's world as hardboiled clichés. As a result, every step of the rewriting process required jabbing, feinting, setting up and knocking down certain "genre" expectations. Not only the "mystery" elements—those gimmicky trapdoors this type of story demands—but the structure, focus, characterizations, and most critically, the conclusion.

My biggest complaint with most mystery fiction is the tyranny of the tidy ending, in which order must be restored. From the moment it was decided that Gig would take the count, *The Distance* was destined to have an ambiguous ending, reflecting this writer's belief that under serious scrutiny, any "solution," be it in literature or in life, only leads to more questions, more interpretations, more possibilities, more *stories*.

For me, the point was never "whodunit?" The point was how Billy Nichols deals with never knowing the truth about a crime in which he becomes an accomplice. Call it noir, if you like—the ambiguity, the dread, the lingering suspicion. I'm comfortable with order never being restored, because I don't believe it's there in the first place.

It wasn't until my father died, in 1982, that I was really accepted into the boxing fraternity, at least on an honorary basis. I wrote a eulogy that I delivered—over Monsignor McKay's protestations—to a church filled with a lifetime's worth of Mr. Boxing's friends, associates, and acolytes. I said what was required, without fear or regret, trying to strike a balance with the pious homilies. That testimonial ushered me into what was left of the fight crowd. I was one of the few young people who'd always make time to listen to their stories (sometimes repeatedly). These tales formed a circuit of cruelty and nobility that helped forge my perspective on the world.

Not long after that, I started work on *The Distance*. From inception, one of its core elements was the notion of "the circuit." It refers not only to the familiar itinerary of newsrooms, gyms, restaurants, arenas, and nightclubs, but to the vital, sometimes lethal, energy that flows through those places and connects otherwise isolated people.

The Introduction to this edition represents, for me, the fusing of a personal circuit.

One evening in 1969 my dad brought home from the office a copy of a book called *Fat City*. It had been sent to him by the publisher with the hope it would, in Mr. Boxing parlance, "rate a tumble" in his column. My father never cracked its spine, although he vaguely recognized the lean young author on the jacket as a "kid" from Stockton who'd regularly shown up in the circuit, quietly asking lots of questions.

I read *Fat City*. Although too callow to really appreciate the adult complexities, or the relentless, melancholic undertow, I realized something crucial lurked in its pages, waiting for me to catch up.

I revisited the book when I was about twenty. It changed my life. In its pages were the men who figured so vividly, but so inarticulately, in my own life. They were rendered with a gravity and a depth and a sensitivity that made sense of what I'd seen, but didn't know how to express. The adrenaline rush some guys got from boxing, I got from Leonard Gardner's words—which transformed lives I recognized into Art.

Fat City is, in some ways, what allowed me to offer that eulogy to my old man. It also convinced me that my life would be incomplete unless I crafted a novel of my own. I re-read *Fat City* regularly. It remains the book against which I measure myself. *The Distance* is a far cry from the spare splendor of that masterpiece. That Leonard Gardner found value in my effort, enough to merit his writing the Introduction to this edition, is my proudest accomplishment as a writer.

Eddie Muller
San Francisco, 2004

DELETED SCENES

Billy Nichols' recollections of his early newspaper days made up a major portion of the novel's earliest drafts. Many of those tales survived in later first-person revisions. Here's one of the last to be cut.

Working as an office boy, I became the Sports department mascot. I had to pull my poorboy's cap down, comically low, to keep copy editors from yanking my ears, which stuck out like a couple of coffee cup handles. That's how they'd grab my attention. Not that I minded, shameless go-getter that I was. My antics even caught the eye of Edmund D. Coblenz, the paper's executive editor, one of the biggest pillars in the Hearst empire.

"Cobbie," like me, was a great fight fan. He was paid regular visits by a guy named Eddie Graney, who ran a thriving billiard parlor at 5th and Market, just up the street. In his younger days, Graney, resplendent in black tie and tails, refereed most of the city's championship fights. You can still find him counting out beaten boxers on barber shop walls all over town.

During one of Graney's visits, Coblentz summoned me. Half a dozen men, none of whom I recognized, were crammed in his office. Cobbie was always immaculately dressed, smelling of fine cologne. Small and neat and fresh, like the white carnations that lived in his buttonhole. He introduced me, a thirteen year-old kid, like *I* was Hearst's right hand.

Graney handed me a stopwatch.

"Don't take your eyes off this," he commanded. "Start it when I say so."

He posed as if standing over a fallen fighter.

"Now!" he shouted. His index finger counted out a steady toll of ten, his voice calling the seconds like he was in the middle of old Coffroth's Arena.

Everyone looked at me for confirmation.

'Ten seconds—exactly!" I blurted.

Graney repeated the feat three more times, his cherubic face flushing a deeper pink with each repetition. Laughter erupted proudly from him every time I confirmed his precision. Applause filled the office.

As he ushered me out, Coblentz dropped two bits in my hand.

This became a ritual. Cobbie always called me to handle the watch. The cast of looming men, however, was always changing: plainclothes cops, Chamber of Commerce types, politicians, lawyers over from the Hall of Justice. The routine, I came to realize, was nothing more than an ice-breaker, a prelude to whatever serious business needed to be negotiated.

I got sick of Graney's florid face and smug chortle. I eagerly looked forward to the day he'd miss a beat. It came about ten months later. When I looked up from the stopwatch, Coblentz was drilling me with his eyes.

"Ten seconds—exactly!" I marveled. I tossed in an amazed shake of the head for good measure. Earned me six bits on the way out.

"I may not always know what's going on," I told my father later. "But I know what people want to hear."

Sometimes I wonder if that hasn't been the secret of my success.

Another excised scene from Billy's early days showed his precocious rise through the reporters' ranks, a young turk competing with the Inquirer*'s regular boxing writer, Jack Lewis. It also explained how he became an expert on boxing lore that happened well before his time.*

Young Stuhley stood in the middle of the crowded dressing room, naked except for his jock, leather cup, and soggy hand-wraps. His manager, notorious barrel-chested, baby-faced ex-pug Spider Kelly, sliced off the wraps while a gaggle of reporters threw Stuhley questions. It was his first big win as a main eventer at National Hall. The room was so small the stink of sweat and liniment stung every nostril.

"When'd you know you could drop him with the hook?" Jack Lewis asked.

"Not 'til he went down," laughed Stuhley.

"Not likely," I said, just loud enough to be heard. I was pressed in with the pack of reporters. When I noticed Stuhley glance at me, I said: "You got that left hook from the Spider. Textbook, just like he used to throw it."

Lewis lowered his notebook, turned, and stuck his pencil into my chest, drawing a streak down my brand new tie.

'When the hell did you ever see Spider Kelly fight? Why don't you keep your mouth shut once in a while and let people do their job."

I stared at the streak of lead on my tie. A shadow crossed over me, and for a second I thought Lewis was going to make a move, maybe knock me to the floor. When I looked up, Spider Kelly was toe-to-toe with the pissed-off reporter.

"I taught Stuhley to throw the hook, true enough," he said. He crowded Lewis, close enough to count the sweat beads popping out on his forehead. "The way me pal McGrath worked it out with Sharkey. This lad's on the square. And I don't want to see no mention of it in your column tomorrow, seeing as *you* didn't make the connection."

Lewis stepped back, stumbling when the pack parted. "What the hell is this?" he stammered. He looked around for support, but didn't find it on any face.

"Lewis, how come you never give the local lads a boost?" Kelly demanded. He tossed the spent handwraps at the reporter's feet. "Maybe it's 'cause you're an Eastern boy at heart, huh?"

"This is bullshit," Lewis said.

"So's picking on a kid."

Kelly moved back to his fighter and grandly gestured for more questions. His boyish face glowed brightly beneath slickly-parted and plastered-down black hair. Lewis had vanished in the pack.

As everyone filed out, somebody kicked me in the ass. I turned to find Kelly winking at me. "Seen you 'round," he said. "How old are you?"

"Sixteen."

"Old enough. Come by the place sometime, it's—"

"On Fillmore. I know where."

"McGrath and me, we'll set you straight. You like boxing, we'll tell you how it was when there was real fighters: Jeffries, Sharkey, Ketchell—Tim and me, we'll fill it all in for you, lad."

The character who went from major to minor over the course of many revisions was Gig Liardi. He was Hack's bête noire throughout, always a tortured, unlikable guy. In the final draft, the relationship between Gig and Billy was distilled into a letter Francis O'Connor finds in Gig's apartment. The New York excursion described in that letter was once a 24-page chapter in the lengthier third-person narrative. This was its core:

A blond sectetary with little round glasses leaned into the anteroom. "Mr. Jacobs will see you now," she said.

Billy led the way, Gig and Hack following. A short bald guy, almost bursting from his three-piece suit, was still in the doorway, talking a mile a minute.

"See you later, Sol," said a nattily-dressed young toady, ushering the guy out. "Gentlemen?"

"Billy Nichols. This is Gig Liardi. Hack Escalante."

"You're the writer," the slick kid stated.

"That's right," said Billy. Parker must have given him a big build-up.

"You won't be able to sit in on the meeting."

Billy started to explain about his "in" with Dan Parker, but was cut off.

"Those are Mr. Jabos' rules. He can't discuss business with a writer he doesn't know personally. You're welcome to wait. Perhaps he can see you later."

"Nah, it's okay. I'll just . . . Gig, I'll meet you later. I got other guys to see. I'm at the Rex. Call there. I'm not in, I'll leave you a message where I am. I'll catch you later."

Billy backed away as the toady took overcoats from Gig and Hack. The fighter looked like he'd just had his tongue cut out, which wasn't far from the truth. Billy smiled at the secretary, gave a little wave as he exited. He rushed down the dim hallway to the elevators, clutching his hat like a soggy bag of sandwiches, and threw a short left at the brass button marked DOWN.

Mike Jacobs had hard beady eyes and his dome was covered with a thin burr of soft white hair. *Julius fucking Caesar*, thought Liardi. *That's who this yid thinks he is.*

The promoter wore a white shirt with a droopy collar, the top button snugly fastened. Had a black sweater over it, a checkered sports coat over that. Like he was afraid of catching cold.

Everybody shook.

"Big hands, huh?" said Liardi, nodding at his fighter. Jacobs' thin lips curled inward in what appeared to be a smile. He took another appraising glance at his visitors, then gestured to a pair of deep leather seats in front of his desk. Gig and Hank sank in. Jacobs stepped over to the blinds and stared out between the slats. *Jesus Christ, that's not a nose*, Liardi thought. *It's a goddamn beak.*

"Mind if I tell you guys a story?" Jacobs asked. "Before we talk any business?"

"Yeah, sure." Liardi smoothed his pants leg.

"I used to put on all kinds of shows when I was younger, even younger than the kid here. Sold steamboat rides, hawked theater tickets, had the refrshment concession for just about every social event in Tammany Hall. You guys know Tammany Hall?"

They both nodded. Neither knew Tammany Hall.

"Small stuff, really. And you get tired of hustling, of having to try so damn hard. I wanted people to come to me for a change, see? So I took all my dough and leased a place called Dreamland Pier on Coney Island. All kinds of arcades, the whole bit. I was making all my contracts, but just before the season opened, the pier burned down. Somebody called me and told me and I went down there the next morning. I just stood there, wondering what I was gonna do, you know? Those burned piles and twisted up girders, half in and out of the water, they was all I owned in the world. So I'm just standing there feeling sorry for myself when this Dutchman comes over. He's got a fishing pole over his shoulder and one of them wicker baskets in his hand.

"You have anything to do with this place?" he asks.

"I almost gotta laugh at that point. I say, 'Yeah—I own it.'

"He says: 'I'd very much like to go out there and fish.'

"So I say: "Go right ahead.' I'm almost laughing, I swear.

"So he goes to the end of the burned-out pier and he starts to fish, like nothing. Pretty soon a couple of other guys come along and join him. So I wait awhile, just sitting there, and pretty soon there's maybe fifty guys fishing off that pier. The next day I hire some guys to put a big cyclone fence around the entrance. Then I put a turnstile and a ticket booth in, and hung a sign saying: FISHING OFF THIS PIER—50 CENTS. SATURDAY, SUNDAY, HOLIDAY—ONE DOLLAR.

"No overhead. In one year I made more money off those fisherman than I'd have made if the pier hadn't burned down. And you know what? They coulda fished from the beach for nothing. What d'ya think of that?"

"Shrewd," said Liardi.

It was an off-hour at Dempsey's place on Broadway and 49th. As New Yorkers hustled through the slate gray day, Billy's head started to fuzz from three bourbons and no lunch. He sat at the bar, looking up at the wall-sized mural of a leather-skinned Dempsey beating the shit out of Jess Willard under a cobalt blue Toledo sky.

The Champ wouldn't be in till later, Billy'd been told. He knew Dempsey a little, through their mutual friend Joe Benjamin, "The Shiek of San Joaquin." He'd taught Dempsey some style when the Manassa Mauler came through San Francisco in 1914. Nichols wanted to greet Dempsey like a brother, pump his hand in front of a bunch of gawking strangers, cut up touches about their pal Joe and the California boys. Get back a little pride.

Liardi blew in, hands plunged in his overcoat pockets. He made straight for the bar, didn't even see Billy on the stool nearby.

"How'd it go, Gig?"

Liardi slid along the rail up next to Nichols.

"I told him to get fucked."

Billy pushed away his empty glass. "What happened?"

"Guy's an asshole. Thinks he runs the whole sport. Makes us sit there like a couple of school kids while he tells us all about the business. Then outta the blue he pulls out all these notes and starts rattling off this shit about Hack, says it's from his 'West Coast sources": no defense, gets hit a lot, cuts too easy. He's just jewing me, you know, trying to knock our price down.

"Finally I says to him, 'Look—the kid can fight. Give him a shot on an undercard at the Garden and he'll sit your hotshots on their ass."

"You said that?"

"Yeah! He smiles. Got that thin nasty little smile, right? Supposed to scare you. He says maybe Hack should fight at the Oval or St. Nick's or someplace first, see if he got the stuff. Then he says, get this—'Garden crowds got no use for pugs.' I remember that distinc'ly. With Hack sitting right there. I'm pissed, but I keep telling myself he's only jewing me, it must be his way. So I go back at him, you know? I build Hack way up. I mean, up *here*. Got him knocking guys out, breaking their ribs, making 'em cry."

"What's Hack doing all this time?"

"Playing dumb. Which, as you know, he's fucking perfected. Me and Jacobs go around like this a while more, then he starts laughing. Claps me on the shoulder and shakes his head, you know, like I passed some test, like I made his club. Then he pulls out a bunch of papers and says, 'You wanna read it, you can. But I'll save you time. What it says, on every page, is that I am The Boss. You come into this town and you wanna fight at the Garden, you are gonna sign these papers. You do good, you get to be part of the Twentieth Century Boxing Club.'

"I say, 'What's in it for me?'

"He goes, 'You wanna fight in New York, you sign.' I ain't stupid, I know the drill: Hack shows the stuff—they take over, put in the picture whoever they want. But Hack losses *one* fight—and I'm stuck with a broken down kid who knows he'll never make it big. So I say 'I'd like to see something that guarantees my percentage.'

"He says, 'Ain't you heard? No guarantees in this life.'

"I shoulda punched him right in the fucking beak, is what I shoulda done."

Liardi short-stopped a pantomimed right cross. He angrily pushed away from the bar, throwing up his hands. "They got it all sewn tight."

'You could have figured that going in, Gig."

"I told him where to put his papers."

"So you didn't sign, huh?"

"Kiss my ring and we'll let you play our game. That's all he was saying to me, not negotiating man-to-man. Well, I'm the one taught the kid how to fight. I'm the one did all the work. I ain't handing him over just like that. Be lucky if they gave me a goddamn train ticket home."

"How'd you leave it?"

"Told him to kiss my guinea ass."

"You said that?"

"I think I said, 'We don't need your contracts and we don't need you.' Maybe it was simpler than that: 'Fuck you.'"

"And that was that, I take it."

"I might have said we'd think about it. I don't remember."

In early versions, the story focused as much on Hack Escalante as on Billy Nichols. The following depiction of the fighter's domestic life made it into every revision, in one form or another. In the final manuscript, it became a story Hack tells Billy—with modifications—after Claire's death. This is the original draft.

It was half past one when Hack got home, pushing his way in through the back porch door, blocked by still-sealed paint cans and wrapped-up rolls of wallpaper. The last of the furniture had been delivered that afternoon. It was piled chock-a-block throughout the house. Chairs upside down, sofa on its side, dresser drawers stacked empty. More pals of Gig's. Hack's wounded muscles groaned at the prospect of arranging all this stuff in the morning.

He walked upstairs, past the room where the kids were sleeping, his eyes slowly adjusting to the dark. Claire had managed some order in their bedroom. She'd set up the bed and made it, gotten the nightstands in place, put the lamps on them, then probably passed out face-first on the cool sheets, exhausted. The baby was in its crib in the corner. For a moment he just stood there, watching the two of them breathing.

She stirred, but didn't open her eyes when Hack set himself down on the edge of the bed.

"You win?" she mouthed into the pillow.

"Don't turn on the light," he replied.

She'd laid out his striped pajamas. He slowly undressed his aching body, gingerly put on the pajamas, and stretched out next to his wife. For fifteen minutes he stared up into the gloom, seeing flashing gloves and blurring lights. Faces at the edge of the ring. He could hear the yelling, like a hum inside his head.

"Gig's going crazy," he told the ceiling fixture.

Claire made a muffled sound, but didn't wake up.

"We're going in circles. Fighting the same guys over and over. He's afraid of something, like if I get too good he's gonna lose me. He gets crazy ideas all the time, has these nutty dreams how we're gonna make all this money and fight for the title. 'But it'll be *our* way,' he keeps saying. I got no idea what he's talking about. When a good fight comes up, against a guy where we can make out, he finds a reason to call it off. I don't know what to do. I don't think I can stay with him no more."

Claire's breathing got deeper. Hack sighed and turned away from her, onto the side where his ribs didn't hurt as much. He shut his eyes. The shouts of the crowd got louder. Behind a pawing jab, Whitten's eyes tracked him.

"You gotta do something," she said softly.

"You heard what I was saying?"

"But it's more than that."

"What d'ya mean?"

"I don't want you going to war."

"Well, I don't wanna. Fuck."

"You won't have a choice. You're twenty-four. They've got a uniform picked out."

"It may not happen."

"It will."

"So what am I supposed to do?"

"Join the Coast Guard."

"What the hell you talking about?"

"You'll be doing your duty by enlisting, and they'll stick you someplace you'll never get shot at. And you'll make a steady paycheck. Which will help."

A scream came from down the hall. Hack was through the doorway before Claire had reached for the lamp.

Marie was kneeling in the bed, eyes wide above the blanket clutched around her. Tony was standing before the uncurtained window, a tiny figure in the blue moonlight. His little gasps left white circles on the cold glass. Hack knelt and took his son in his arms.

"What's the matter, you all right?"

Tony's sobs rattled Hack's chest. Claire entered, fumbling for the wall switch.

"Claire, don't turn o—

Light filled the room. Tony looked into the face looming over him. His dread turned to horror. A monster was clutching him. Battered purple lips moved beneath nostrils caked with blood: "C'mon, it's okay. Be a big boy." Grease smeared a cheek swollen up like a boiled sausage. A line of spikey black stitches jutted out above his father's eyebrow.

"I'm still Daddy," Hack said.

The boy pushed away. His fingers, as if on their own,

reached for the stitches. They poked his tender fingers like wire. He tried to scrape them off. Instinctively, Hack clutched the tiny hand in his massive fist and jerked it away. Tears spilled, from both father and son.

"What the hell are you doing?" Claire rushed up behind them.

"He's scared of my face," Hack said, turning to her. She couldn't stifle a startled gasp. Hack stood up and handed over his son.

"You lose?" she softly asked.

"Won. Barely." No trace of pride. He went to the light switch and dropped the room back into darkness. Leaning against the wall, Hack stared out into the garden.

"What am I gonna do, Claire?" Why couldn't I ever learn to do somerthing else? They'll think all their Dad can do is fight. What can I *do*? Why is *this* the only thing?"

He threw a punch at the wall. It went half an inch deep.

Tony burst out crying again. Marie joined in.

"That's great," Claire muttered, bundling her boy into her robe. "Asshole."

Hack stepped close. His huge hand reached for his son's face.

"Hey, champ—I'm sorry. I didn't mean to scare you. Were you having a nightmare before? What was the matter?"

Tony's face pressed into his mother's breasts, refusing to look up.

"C'mon, what was it?" Hack implored. "Can I make it better?"

Tony's tiny voice asked: "Is the turtle gone?"

Hack had told the kids the turtle should live outside. Once it had crawled into the bushes, they all started crying, figuring it was lost forever.

"No, he's out there," Hack said. "He's sleeping. Like you should be doing."

"I don't want him to go away. Can't he stay in the house?"

"He's happier outside, hon," Claire said. "Things oughta be where they're happy."

The boy started in again with the tears.

"I'm gonna take him in with us," Claire said. "He'll never go to sleep otherwise."

"You'll have to take Marie then, too."

Claire hoisted Tony to one shoulder and scooped Marie up in her other arm. Hack watched her go down the hallway, watched her hips beneath the robe. The sight used to get him hard, when he'd watch her stride down the aisle of the streetcar, before he even knew her. She closed the door to the bedroom with her foot. Miraculously, the baby hadn't woken up.

Hack waited a couple of moments for the spinning to settle down, then he went downstairs and turned the sofa upright. He wanted to throw it all in the street.

"Tony. Hey, Tony. Wake up." Hack's voice.

Claire's eyes popped open. She'd left the lamp on. Her son was curled against her, finally asleep. Hack was on the edge of the bed. In the lamplight, his battered face looked like a wax mask beneath the tousled curls. She noticed his hair was damp, and his pajamas were smeared with dirt.

Hack reached across Marie and shook his son's narrow shoulder.

'Tony, c'mon—wake up."

The turtle was on the sheets between the children, cautiously inspecting its new surroundings.

The following scene took place near the end of the original draft. It's the mid-1970s. Most of the people named are real, although they'd probably never have appeared together, same place, same night. Ray Caits isn't the name *of a real boxer.*

Sammy Stein basked in the spotlight, clutching the dangling microphone. He was wearing the powder blue tux tonight, the spangled lapels glittering. He'd gotten it years ago, from Blackie down on Fifth Street, half off when Sammy came through with a dozen first row ducats. He turned to all corners of the auditorium as he spoke:

"Before we get to our main event, ladies and gentlemen, we'd like to take a few moments to introduce to you some of the pugilistic luminaries in our presence here tonight, all part of San Francisco's glorious fistic legacy."

Billy Nichols scanned the "crowd." Barely seven hundred, tops. Nobody came to the Civic anymore. The Bay Area had grown so much, spread so far into outlying areas, there was no central action anymore. It was all on television now, not in clubs and arenas. The streets around the Civic were empty after dark, except for transients and beggars, camped out in the plaza directly across from City Hall.

After expenses, this show would be lucky to scrape a grand, Nichols figured. When attendence dropped, they started pricing the best seats too high, to compensate. That only dispersed the audience, kept them from being a crowd: clusters of slumming stockbrokers sitting in the "Dress Circle," hooting at the card girls; beefy laborers wobbling back to the twentieth row with a beer in each fist; furtive Mexicans perched in the cheap seats, sneaking hits off a passed-around joint. Lots of space in-between.

"A popular favorite who fought many great bouts in

this very building, and challenged for the Middleweight Championship of the World . . . Let's have a big hand for—Jimmy Lester! Jimmy Lester!"

Lester bounded through the ropes, red knit bell-bottoms flapping as he danced around the canvas, waving. These days Jimmy was a security guard at a warehouse near the airport.

Sammy gave big intros to some oldtimers who still religiously attended every card: Esau Ferdinand, Johnny Gonsalves, Vic Grupico, Georgie Duke. They were treated to only a smattering of applause, most of the fans too young to have seen them in their prime. But they accepted it with broad smiles, and gracious salutes, and each of them went to both corners to touch the gloves of the main event fighters. Waiting on the bell, Reyes Cruz and Terrence Willeford seemed a million miles away as the retired boxers toured the ring.

Show them some respect, Nichols thought. But then he caught himself: *Hell, they're just trying to stay calm. Don't get sentimental. Just watch the fight.* He roughed out a scoring sheet with his Ken 722. They didn't make that pencil anymore, and he was almost halfway through his last case.

Across the ring from Billy, Cruz's cornermen pointed toward ringside, trying to get anybody's attention. An old guy in grimy cap and jacket, frayed pants and broken-down brogans, was climbing the stairs to the apron. "Hey, hey—somebody get this guy!"

It took a few seconds, since his eyesight wasn't what it used to be, but Billy jumped right up and stretched across press row. His body creaked when he leaned forward. Slapping the canvas shot pain from his liver-spotted hand up to his shoulder. But he kept smacking the apron, at least a dozen times. Finally, Sammy Stein looked over. Billy pointed to the old guy shoving away Cruz's cornermen, folding himself through the ropes. A security guard was coming down the aisle.

"Ray Caits," Billy shouted. Light Heavyweight contender. Early Thirties."

The guard started up the ring steps.

"Ray Caits, ladies and gentlemen!" Sammy Stein shouted. "A great light heavyweight contender of yesteryear!"

Caits yanked the soiled tam-o-shanter from his head and waved it high, straightening as tall as he could.

"The Excelsior Assassin," Billy called to Sammy. He looked from Caits to the corners: Cruz and Willeford were looking away, one at the canvas, the other into the rafters.

"Known in his day as The Excelsior Assassin," Stein blared into the mic. "Let's hear it for Ray Caits!"

Billy scanned the sparse crowd: standing, pointing, laughing—and clapping. One hand sarcastic, the other sympathetic. The applause grew louder.

Caits swung his cap wildly, almost losing his balance. He staggered, but got his legs under him. As the applause faded, he found a neutral corner and disappeared.

ACKNOWLEDGEMENTS

Since the publication of this novel's first edition I have lost my right hand, my bullshit detector, my prose polisher, my drinking buddy, and my best friend. Erik S. McMahon was all of those things and more, and his contribution to this book cannot be overestimated. We all miss you, partner.

Many thanks to Tom Fassbender & Jim Pascoe, UglyTown kingpins, for maintaining a sense of adventure and commitment to quality in a publishing arena of spirit-sapping mediocrity. UglyTown is founded on their vision and enthusiasm, not forecasts and spreadsheets. Tom and Jim deserve success, and if Billy Nichols, in some small measure, helps them achieve it—that's what I'll find most gratifying about this edition.

The old man would dig it, too.